Windknocker

The Last GaspeRs
WiN iN The End —
I hope You Enjoy This
STORY —

Bud Malley

Windknocker

A Novel of Friendship, Summer Sausage,
and Last Gaspers

By
Bud Malby

Edited by Andy Malby

E-BookTime, LLC
Montgomery, Alabama

Windknocker
A Novel of Friendship, Summer Sausage, and Last Gaspers

Library of Congress Control Number: 2010940682

ISBN: 978-1-60862-232-0

First Edition
Published November 2010
E-BookTime, LLC
6598 Pumpkin Road
Montgomery, AL 36108
www.e-booktime.com

FOR MY FRIEND JEFF SPACKMAN

Who taught me that friendships like the one described in this book are possible.

Chapter One

I was raised in a small town. It was the kind of place where they roll up the streets at night, or at least that's how my mother described it. Main Street sported two bars, called pool halls in the local vernacular, and a Red and White grocery store. That's Red and White as in a company name. Peeling yellow paint on a clapboard building describes its actual home.

I was born in a house on the "good" side of the tracks, at the base of a hill opposite St. Bartholomew's Catholic Church. That was December 7, 1916. My Aunt Bertha, who was in love with the number seven, prophesied my life would be enriched because of it. She didn't foresee that a quarter-century later my birthday would be associated with infamy.

My father tried to name me Dakota after a character in a book he'd read, but the priest at St. Bart's insisted on a saint's name for my baptism. "Mr. Moosington, remember, I have to translate it into Latin," he chided.

"Latin?" My dad exclaimed, startling those gathered. "The Dakota I learned about was a saintly man."

Father McFeedle gave him a blank stare.

"Well, I admit, he had his faults, and maybe was a little too fond of strong whiskey," dad added.

Seeing the man of God's neck start to glow above his stiffly starched collar, dad tried to extricate himself.

"No, he wasn't a Catholic, but close. His wife was an Episcopologist."

That earned him a jab in the ribs from my mother, both for his impertinence and the deliberate mispronunciation of a church's name.

Undeterred, Dad tried again. "Can't you just make up a Latin name, something like, *Et come too Dakoti?*"

Somberly, the priest shook his head, and that's how I got tagged with the name Bartholomew. Bartholomew Moosington. No middle name because my mother thought that was mouthful enough. As monikers go it looks good on paper, but to my everlasting chagrin, rather than being called Bart, or at least Moose, I would be known as *Mew*! I would keep that fact secret from my peers, religiously so, in later life. But to those closest to me, I would always be just plain *Mew*. I place the blame for that squarely on the shoulders of my best friend, about whom you'll learn shortly.

My father wasn't Catholic and he wasn't religious, but he's *"full of grace,"* the aforementioned aunt always said. Regrettably, it would take me another sixty-plus years to learn what she meant. I thought she dismissively pulled out the phrase to cover my father's bent toward irreverence.

In my early days he still went to church with us. My dad, being a fidgety person, could no more keep from squirming during a Solemn High Mass than could an adolescent boy being lectured about the consequences of an erection. Worse, my father would interrupt during a boring sermon, thinking, I guess, that someone must rescue the trapped listeners. His observations were colorful, perceptive at times, and often a contest to see who got the last word.

On one such occasion, Father McFeedle was expounding on the narrative of when Jesus confronted the woman caught in adultery. You're right to assume this was long before I mastered big words like that. I was still a babe in arms at the time. My recollection is taken from a page of our family lore.

Father McFeedle made a giant mistake. Jesus had turned away from his questioners that day and wrote something in the dirt. "And what," Father McFeedle thundered from the pulpit, wagging his finger straight at my dad, "do you suppose Jesus wrote?"

My dad never sidestepped a question, especially one so directly put.

"I think he wrote, *'stupid nincompoops!'*" he blurted.

Dad also never said anything quietly, and a ripple of gasps swept the congregation as Father McFeedle's face turned beet red.

"It stands to reason," my dad went on, oblivious to the stir he'd caused, "that Jesus was fed up with that crowd and their stupid questions."

Before he could really get on his soapbox, or add a few animated gestures to his exhortation, my mother intervened and shut him up with an elbow to the ribs. Father McFeedle finally found his composure and muddled through the rest of his lecture. Most of his sermons didn't ask pointed questions after that.

My mother, on the other hand, was the model Catholic. Steeped in the ritual and mystery of her religion, she worked tirelessly to imbue me with those same qualities. Occasionally, her indoctrinations and behavior lessons would provoke a scowl from my dad, but he didn't interfere. I didn't stray from what she instilled in me as the one true faith, but I did give her reason to think so.

Sam, my dad, did shape my religious upbringing. Considered a heretic by most Catholics I knew, Sam Moosington's common sense would be the safety net that kept me rooted in reality. As a youngster, however, he kept me confused.

"Your mother is a real sober Sally," he told me one day. "Why, if Jesus had been that serious about God, he would have died of a stroke long before that Roman bastard had him nailed to a cross. And then where would we be?"

Answering his own question, he continued: "You and your mother wouldn't have Holy Communion to partake of on Sunday, and me, I wouldn't have the *'bread of life'* to rely on seven days a week."

He then returned to what he was doing, chuckling as I tried to figure out what he meant.

I grew up an only child, and in luxury compared to the boys I came to know. I met the first of those just before I turned three; on a day my dad took me to the train depot to pick up some freight for his hardware store. He was a youngster my age and his name, for a boy, was nearly as strange as the one placed on me. We called him Leezie.

Chapter Two

A massive black steam locomotive sat on the railroad tracks, breathing wisps and gasps of steam. My two-year-old brain was overwhelmed, and couldn't translate the image of this fire-breathing giant with what I'd only seen from a distance before.

I glanced at Leezie, who stood with a fat little thumb in his mouth, gazing up at a man framed by the window of the engine. Leezie, I noticed, wore the same kind of grey-striped cap as the man who hollered, "Who's your friend, boy?"

Leezie hunched his shoulders and looked over to my dad, who said, "Tell him it's Bar-tholo-mew!"

He tried, but the only thing recognizable was a very loud, "Mew!"

"Well howdy there, little Mew," the engineer shouted over a belch of steam. Leaning out the cab, he said, "Here, catch!" Two wrapped horehound candies landed on the depot platform.

I jumped back, bumping into my dad, but Leezie pounced upon them like a baby bird on an overdue worm. When I opened my eyes a candy jiggled in his outstretched palm. I took it. Leezie hesitated, probably to make sure I knew what to do with it, before he popped the other in his mouth.

"Stand back!" The same voice from the monster yelled. I jumped six inches when a cloud of steam whooshed from the front of the engine, and had no sooner hit the ground when the big drive wheels jerked. My eyes grew to the size of milk bottle bottoms as the wheels lurched and spun against the steel rail, making a huge racket.

The wheels caught, shaking the ground, and with one last shudder, the engine began to move. "Hiss-poos, hiss-poos," the black giant said. It scared the peewaddin out of me, and I ran terrified to my dad. The only good thing about the experience is I was too young to be embarrassed by the sobs that my dad chuckled over. Console me he did, and I buried my head on his shoulder, watching apprehensively as the train backed its way to the water tower seventy-five yards away.

My gaze caught a man standing upright on the monster, reaching up as the engineer slowed alongside a wooden building with a round metal tank on top. A hand grasped a rope, and the man pulled a twelve-foot spout downward until it connected with a bigger pipe sticking up from the engine. Water sprayed, hissing and steaming, before he got it positioned.

I looked down at Leezie's pointing finger and he explained it to me. "Rinking," he said.

A last tear trickled off my nose when Leezie asked, "See my 'ruck?"

Leezie had a strange way of talking, undecided like the locomotive standing in one place before its wheels moved, but once in motion everything was fine. I had to admit he spoke much better than me, but as I was to discover, he had an older sister to encourage him.

My dad set me down and said, "Now, Little Mew, if that's what people are going to call you, it's time you had one of Mrs. Smith's molasses cookies."

Leezie's dad, John, led the way to the depot. I nudged my dad, gesturing at John's empty shirtsleeve.

"He lost an arm in the war," he whispered.

I frowned.

"I'll explain later," he said.

I took note of the train station for the first time, a two-story affair with rounded eaves that overhung half of the upper level. Nailed on the end, between the bottom and top stories, was a big sign naming the station, in this case, our town. Since this was before I learned my letters, I can't tell you what it said.

We passed through the most interesting room I'd ever seen, and mounted a staircase to the upper level. This is where Leezie lived, in an apartment above the station agent's office. It was a bright and homey place, but tiny compared to our big house, which my dad boasted had three times the square footage.

Two glasses of buttermilk appeared from a bottle that Mrs. Smith took from the icebox. My mother's name was Mary, which I liked, and I frowned when I learned Mrs. Smith was called Hildred.

Leezie downed his buttermilk and two cookies before I got the glass to my lips. Molasses was my favorite cookie and I intended to savor it, but gobbled quickly when Leezie jumped down. He ran off and pulled a box out from under his bed. He returned and presented me with his toy truck.

It was magnificent! Homemade, I'm sure, by his dad. It consisted of three boards, each shorter than the other, butted together on one end and then nailed one on top of the other. To my untrained eye it looked like a realistic truck bed and cab. Jar lids were tacked on for wheels, and a smaller flat lid, attached where you'd expect to find the dashboard, served as a steering wheel.

All of my toys were shiny, brightly painted store-bought types, but this was a real truck. I jumped down and drove it around the floor, while Leezie made engine and honking noises. Then I discovered there was a trailer that went with it.

It seemed like we played all afternoon, which turned out to be less than half an hour. A toot from the train's whistle startled me, and Leezie jumped up and scampered to the big double window that overlooked the train tracks. I followed.

We leaned over the back of the davenport and craned our necks to the left. I saw the monster coming, black smoke pouring from its stack. Had I paid attention I would have heard Hildred's dishes rattling in the cupboard, but my eyes were glued to a big number 79 on the front of the engine, growing bigger and bigger.

The top of the locomotive passed us at eye level, and I could practically look into the innards of the beast. I saw Leezie make a pulling motion with his arm. Simultaneously, the engineer reached up and gave two jerks on the steam whistle. We were waving and laughing frantically at the keeper of the horehound candies, and he rewarded us with one last Whoooooo.

Just when I thought I'd seen everything, the end of the train approached.

"See! See!" I screeched at my dad. The train was pulling its own little house behind. Emblazoned on what I later learned was the caboose was a big Union Pacific emblem.

We left the way we'd come and weren't half way across the intriguing room I'd noticed before when a clicking sound got my attention.

"Watch this," my dad said as John Smith hurried over to his desk by the window. He took a hat off a peg. Well, kind of a hat, because his only had the bill of a cap that fit on his head with a strap. It was a funny color, like a dark green.

Mr. Smith sat down and I watched as his hand started clicking, at least it seemed that way to me.

"He's talking to a man fifty miles away," my dad told me.

The clicking grew louder and faster. Mr. Smith had a very heavy hand that pounded the key like my dad's fingers beating the table when he listened to an exciting boxing match.

"John is the fastest telegrapher on the line," my dad said.

It all escaped me. A simple term like fifty miles was beyond my comprehension, not to mention talking that sounded like flying grasshoppers.

"Come on, Little Mew," my dad chuckled, taking my hand to help me across the tracks. "Say goodbye." I turned and waved feebly to Leezie and his dad. Leezie's fat little thumb was in his mouth and his bright, inquisitive eyes watched me intently, but he didn't wave.

I was so tired that I fell asleep during supper. I dreamt the night away with pleasant visions of toy trucks, black giants and horehound candies. Those images were interspersed, of course, with pictures of a boy who could eat a cookie faster than I could say the word.

Chapter Three

Father McFeedle retired in the fall of 1921, not long after Petey Gorman moved to town. Being almost five at the time, by my reckoning I was almost grown up. What I remember about Petey, eighteen months my junior, was his ability to jinx any sermon Father McFeedle tried to deliver. He was a sickly child and seemed to protest his condition most stridently when the priest mounted the pulpit.

"It's no wonder Reverend Feedlededom retired," my dad said one morning. "How would you like it if a wailing banshee interrupted your sermon twenty-two times in the first hour?"

My dad had never forgiven Father McFeedle for refusing to let him name me Dakota. Plus he hated long sermons. My mom took a deep breath. She smiled and said, "I grant you he doesn't give the best talk."

"Do you mean Petey or Feedlededum?" dad asked.

Mom grimaced and dad quickly changed the subject to Father McFeedle's replacement. "Gustav Goldsworthy? That's not a name that exactly rolls off your tongue," he said. "Is he young or old?"

Somewhere in between, mom replied.

"Don't matter," dad said. "As long as he's not long-winded. I'll give a listen to him and Petey on Sunday."

The following Sabbath, the new priest introduced himself, saying, "I am Father Goosestave Gold-swarthy."

My dad always paid attention to the slightest anomaly in the pronunciation of proper names. I could feel laughter shake his innards, which he didn't suppress well, releasing a stifled guffaw when Petey sounded off. An elbow to the ribs by mom distracted him, and we sat straight-laced, listening.

Petey drowned out the next several sentences, giving Dad the chance to whisper in my ear.

None too quietly he said, "Gustav was bad enough. His Irish mother must have been gargling potato water to make it sound like *Goosestave*."

That earned him another jab aimed at the ribs. But he was still bent over, and instead of hitting him in the midsection it caught him on the ear.

"Ouch!" he exclaimed. That startled Mrs. Melody, who was half asleep in front of us. Her flowery hat went flying when she bounced a good two inches off the pew. She didn't exactly shout, just grunted loudly. Dad massaged his ear and smiled amiably when she turned to investigate. He picked up her hat that had landed in his lap and politely handed it back, murmuring, "I think you dropped this." In the meantime, Father Goldsworthy, save for a menacing scowl, carried on unperturbed.

That glower would become his trademark. With it, Father could quiet an unruly child, or most adults, and do it faster than you could say *Hail Mary*.

There were two exceptions to this intimidation, and one, as you may have supposed, was my father, Sam Moosington. Dad either ignored the priest's glares or scowled back just as threateningly. He also disregarded, according to my mom, too much of what the priest said. Ironically, they became real friends.

Dad also refused the Catholic obsession of calling him *Father*. "That's for hair-brained Catholics that think priests can't tread water and have to walk on it," he told me, admonishing at the same time: "don't tell your mother I said that."

The only time I remember Dad relenting on the issue of titles, he botched it. That occurred when he introduced Father Goldsworthy to a gathering of our Catholic relatives, saying, "This is our minister." Mom turned Santa suit red with embarrassment, and Dad quickly corrected his gaffe, changing *minister* to priest.

I don't know if Father Goldsworthy had a troubled past. On top of some real personality quirks, he was authoritarian – demanding, short-tempered, unbending, unfeeling. And he ruled Saint Bart's with an iron hand. Thankfully, that list did not include a depraved fondness for boys. In spite of the priest's negatives, some experienced his softer side. Regrettably, I never did.

He was not Irish at all, as I soon discovered. In fact, he had been born in Africa to Belgian parents. Mystified, my dad responded to the revelation with, "I always wondered what Irishman would name a kid Gustav."

His aloof demeanor didn't fool everyone, for there was another not the least intimidated by him. I first noticed this the same morning when we left church.

My best friend, Leezie, was waiting for me. He had with him his pet bird, a goldfinch he had named Arthur. Arthur was only part of Leezie's menagerie, which also included a turtle, two pollywogs in a tin can and a giant garden-variety spider named Mike. Arthur, who couldn't fly because of a broken wing, was Leezie's favorite and the only pet that traveled about town with him.

Petey Gorman was petting Arthur's head when I walked up. Leezie grinned when he saw me, and said, "Gee Whiz, Mew, me an' Arfur got tired a waiting." I mumbled something about a long sermon.

"Want to go climb the big tree?" he asked.

The biggest tree in town was the one in the churchyard, one that Father McFeedle had chased us out of countless times. I shook my head, unable to keep the panicked look off my face. Father McFeedle always let us off with a mild scolding, but the new priest might consider tree climbing a serious sin. I suggested something that wouldn't bring the wrath of God down on us, but Leezie objected.

"We played marbles and looked at your picture book yesterday," he reminded me.

Minutes later I discovered the church crowd had gone. We had just settled on the day's entertainment when Father Goldsworthy came out. I noticed Leezie studying him intently, and before I could stop him, he moved closer. Father was trying to kick the doorstop loose and wasn't paying attention. He jerked at the sound of Leezie's, "Mister?"

My dad had explained to me Leezie's speech problem, saying, "He stutters." It's one, among many, reasons my mother didn't want me to play with him.

Now that Leezie had Father Goldsworthy's eye he pointed at his head, saying, "Wh-wh-wh-what's that funny hat?"

Father Goldsworthy gave him a withering stare that would have melted glass. Leezie just smiled and asked the same question again, demonstrating by touching his own cap. By this time I was interested too, because our recently retired priest had not worn a hat.

That didn't make me any braver, and I hid, not too successfully, behind the wing of an angel statue. I honestly thought Leezie would get turned into the pillar of salt from one of my mom's favorite Bible stories.

Instead, I heard Father Goldsworthy say, less gruffly, "It's called a biretta."

"Let you see mine if I kin see yours," Leezie said, holding out his grimy engineer's hat. I nearly died on the spot, but to my surprise, Father Goldsworthy removed his odd-shaped black biretta. It was square, with each side forming a peak in the middle, and was topped with a furry ball. Leezie examined it from all sides, and bending down on one knee, cocked his head at an odd angle to inspect the underside. He giggled when he squeezed the little pom-pom on top. By the time Father Goldsworthy put it back on, Leezie had fired off at least three more questions.

I thought the interview was over, for the priest turned abruptly, only to turn back just as suddenly.

"What's that in your hand, child?" he asked.

"Arfur," Leezie said, opening his fingers to reveal the bird.

Had my vantage point allowed, I would have seen the lines around Father Goldsworthy's eyes soften momentarily. I did witness one of his hesitant fingers reach out and stroke Arthur's feathers. He acted for a second that he might pick it up, but suddenly jerked his hand back.

"Off with you, urchin," he said, and disappeared, his passage marked by a rustle of robes and the slamming of the door.

Arthur was only the beginning of a long line of pets Leezie would own. Among those was a legendary dog that would try Father Goldsworthy's patience unlike any human.

Chapter Four

My second-best friend was a girl. She was Leezie's sister, Betsy. I saw her running up the street about the same time Father Goldsworthy disappeared.

"Leezie," she panted to a stop. "Mom wants you."

"Wh-wh-wh-what for?" he said.

"Your stupid spider got loose and is up in the cupboard, that's why," she said.

Betsy was nine years old. She had beautiful black hair, rosy cheeks and cute dimples when she smiled. I was sure her eyes sparkled even when she was asleep. Since Leezie and I had become inseparable from the age of two, she helped raise both of us. We watched her brother race for home with his patented fluid gait. Although chubby, he was a natural-born runner.

"Ick! I hate spiders," she said.

I scoffed at her girlish timidity, but stopped short of calling her a 'fraidy cat. She reached over and messed up my hair.

"Ick," she said again, trying to wipe her hand. "What did your mother use to grease that rat's nest?"

"Vaseline," I said proudly.

She laughed and tousled my hair again.

"Catch me if you can," she shouted, and took off running.

I gave chase for appearance's sake, but Betsy could outrun any boy her age. A block later I stopped. She turned when she reached the railroad tracks, and waved. I put two fingers in my mouth and gave her a piercing whistle. Dad taught it to me and called it his *wolf whistle*.

Months later the word spider gave Leezie the inspiration that solved the first dilemma that complicated our young lives. My mother had decided I would be too young to start school in 1922, which meant I would end up being a first grader when Leezie was already in second grade. That was unacceptable!

One night the following spring, Betsy was studying for a spelling contest. Her mother had promised her a new ribbon if she could spell ten words in a row correctly. The last one happened to be *spider*, which she got right, adding an "ick" to the end.

"Betsy could larn you your ABC's" Leezie announced the next day. "An' mebbe larn you to read words." He went on to explain how jump-starting my learning might change my mother's mind. "Betsy already larned me A and B," he said.

Our study started in May and continued for most of the summer. Betsy was patient and had a knack for teaching. She was also demanding, which didn't work well with Leezie. I, on the other hand, was eager, had a good memory, and slowly but surely learned my letters. Stringing them into words, however, required all of Betsy's talent.

I suppose Betsy's personality had more to do with it than skill; plus, I loved her like the sister I never had. No matter what we did, she worked it into her lesson plan. For example, she would say, "What's that, Mew?"

"A dog."

"How do you spell *dog*?"

"I dunno."

And the spelling lesson would begin. To break the monotony if I tired of her regimen, she would challenge us to a contest. It might be a race, which she always won, or a two-against-one tug-of-war.

In August I told my dad about my secret study program and the theory behind it. When I recited my ABC's, it was one of the few times I'd ever found him without words. Finally, he said, "Betsy taught you all this?"

"I can read a couple of words too," I answered.

Being a staunch believer in *"Strike while the iron is hot,"* he hustled me home to repeat my story.

Skeptically, my mom sat me down, saying, "I don't blame you for trying, Mew, but Betsy is only in the fourth grade – hardly teacher material."

I started my ABC's, and before I reached H, her mouth was agape. I stumbled between Q and R, but corrected myself and finished with a flourish. "AND Z," I said triumphantly.

"I do declare, I do declare," she said, so astonished that she couldn't finish her sentence.

"There's more, Mary," Dad said. "He says he can read a little too."

I ran off to my room and came back with a book I'd gotten for my last birthday, one she had yet to read to me. Opening it, I stumbled over the first lines of a story about a boy and a beanstalk.

"Betsy could have just read that to him," mom said suspiciously. "He probably just memorized it." She took the book out of my hands and riffled the pages. "Here, try this one," she said, pointing to several lines.

I got butterflies in my stomach at the unfamiliar words. Mom didn't like the Smith family, particularly Leezie, and her suggestion that Betsy was devious unsettled me. Dad intervened.

"Blast it all anyway, Mary," he said. "The boy's not applying for your precious Notre Dame."

He grabbed the book. "You get one hint, Mew," he said, putting his finger to the page. "This word is *Puppy*."

Getting the biggest word out of the way helped, but not much. I took a deep breath, and tried to remember what Betsy taught me.

"Well?" mom said.

"My puppy has," I shouted when it came to me. The rest was easy. "Big ears," I said.

"I declare, I declare," mom repeated her surprise.

Dad took a pencil from his pocket and handed it to me.

"Write your name," he said.

Mom gasped when I wrote very crudely, on a piece of paper, *Mew*.

I had scraped by, barely, but the issue was settled and I started first grade that fall. Betsy was so proud of me that she detoured each morning, with Leezie in tow, to walk me to school.

After our second report cards came out, she devoted more time to tutoring her brother. He was hard to motivate, and had real struggles with arithmetic. Each afternoon, after the last bell rang, she would be waiting for us.

"Let me see it," she'd say to Leezie, and he would hand over whatever paper the teacher had given him. She was encouraging, but kept after him to do better.

"You have to pass, Leezie, or else Mew will go on to second grade without you."

"Are you going to be a teacher when you grow up?" I asked her one day.

"She's going to be one of them mishneries," Leezie answered for her. "She told me so when we was three."

"He means missionary," Betsy said, and made him repeat the word until he said it right.

"I'm going to go with her," Leezie said, "to scare away them pygmies."

"Not if you don't learn to count, and how to tell time," Betsy chided.

I wasn't sure what a missionary did. By the sparkle that danced in her eyes when they talked about it, I thought it might be something I should consider.

My mom defined *missionary* for me.

"You mean far-off countries?" I asked. She nodded.

"To help people and make them good Catholics?" She nodded again.

I wasn't sure how Betsy would accomplish converting the heathens into good Catholics, but I was sure she'd find a way. She had, after all, shepherded Leezie through first grade. Just getting by that hurdle seemed to build his confidence.

Winter, an out-of-the-ordinary winter, arrived early that year, and Betsy started missing school. She had the mumps first, and then a bad cold. Just when we thought she was all right, the three-day measles made an appearance in town. She recovered again and almost returned to her old self, although she couldn't run as fast.

I learned to worry, picking up my cues from the adults. One night I eavesdropped when Sam said to mom, "The doctor thinks Betsy might have rheumatic fever."

I didn't know what that meant, but the way my dad said it scared me. Fortunately, it turned out to be false, and Betsy bounced back again. But it wasn't until nearly Thanksgiving that some color returned to her cheeks.

Leezie and I carried her books to and from school each day, thinking that would help. It did, and slowly she regained her old vigor and feistiness. As seven-year-olds we didn't comprehend much about grave health consequences. Betsy was too close to me to entertain such thoughts anyway.

The Christmas season arrived and the weather got even worse. The day before classes were let out for the holiday, Betsy gave me a homemade Christmas card that simply said, *"Merry Christmas to my best friend."* I still have it.

School was dismissed an hour early the next day, but she didn't meet us at the front door.

"Where's Betsy?" I asked.

A momentary cloud crossed Leezie's face. "She don't feel good again," he said.

Chapter Five

Betsy died just before New Year's 1923, on probably the darkest day of a long, hard winter. She had come down with bad case of Scarlet Fever the day before Christmas and her short life of eleven years came to an end five days later.

Information travels fast in a small town, faster than the smell of smoke from a neighbor's chimney on a frosty morn. I heard the awful news before my dad could break it to me.

Harry Capphammer had stopped at the grocery store before coming to the ice skating pond at the edge of town, and had overheard people talking.

"Hey," he said to me, stuffing his mouth with what remained of his hoard of holiday fudge. "'esy," slurp, "'mif 'ied."

"What?" I said, watching him wipe a dribble from his chin and swallow.

"Leezie Smith's sister died. I heard Gravedigger Bill say it at the store," he said, as if he didn't know whether to cry or have another piece of fudge.

I ran all the way home, falling down twice because I hadn't bothered to take my skates off. Arriving at the door, sobbing and disheveled, I heard my mother shout, "Mew, don't you dare wear those skates in the house."

Noticing something was drastically wrong, she rushed to where I sat in a heap on the kitchen floor, struggling to get the blades unstrapped from my shoes.

"What is it?" she cried, alarmed. I told her.

That night I found a perch in a corner of the parlor, listening to the adults talk. I had grown wise, knowing that if I remained perfectly still they wouldn't notice me eavesdropping and chase me off to read a book or something. As my eyes followed each speaker, I couldn't help saying, over and over: *"Poor Betsy." I* repeated it in my head, thinking each time of her, Leezie, John and Hildred.

It had been a harsh winter and the town was practically snowbound. Our only lifelines to the outside world were the daily passenger trains.

"The doctor came on the train yesterday afternoon," I heard one of the men say. "But by that time it was too late for Betsy."

"Strawberry Fever," another remarked, shaking his head mournfully. "There's no cure once it gets a grip on you."

I knew what he was talking about because I'd had a moderate case of Scarlet Fever two years before.

My tongue had turned bright red; I know because my mother let me look at it in a mirror.

"It looks like a strawberry," I had said. My mom smiled, giving me a rub down with olive oil for the nasty rash I had on my face. It was far worse behind my ears and under my armpits, not to mention places that aren't to be talked about in public. My dad brought home some Carbolized Vaseline, which helped but didn't stop the terrible itch.

I wasn't allowed meat because depriving the victim of protein was thought to help. I didn't care because my throat was too sore to swallow anyway. I had to gargle with salt water, which burned my tongue so bad I could barely stand it.

There were two times when my rocketing fever kept my mom by my bedside all night. When I'd thrash myself awake, she'd calm me. The clacking of her rosary beads would then lull me back to sleep; no doubt the reason the sound still comforts me. At the end of several weeks I recovered, and *my* case wasn't severe. I couldn't imagine what poor Betsy must have suffered.

"How are John and Hildred doing?" I heard the deep, raspy voice of the town butcher, Blinky, ask.

"Busy right now," my dad answered. "They're burning everything Betsy came in contact with and dousing the place with alcohol so they can get the quarantine lifted."

The Smiths hadn't been the only ones placed under quarantine by the county sheriff that winter. I'd seen the big official notices nailed to the doors of Billy Archer's and Suzie Gallagher's houses, too. No one, under dire penalty, was allowed in or out during the illness.

"What about the funeral?" Mr. Peachtree, the school principal, asked.

"Friday at the Lutheran Church," my dad answered.

The next afternoon my dad rushed home with the news that the quarantine had been lifted and took me to visit Leezie. Leezie was in a serious mood and we talked in a corner while my dad consoled John. Hildred's eyes were red but she bustled about and brought us a plate of cookies. She gave me a big hug, and I hugged her back.

After a while, my dad dropped me at the house and went back to work. Before I got one foot in the door my mom grabbed me, complaining up a storm about making such an important person wait. She helped me off with my coat and brushed my clothes. Standing back, she inspected my appearance, only to quickly wash my face and comb my hair. Not satisfied, she bent down and brushed my shoes.

"That's better," she said, and pointing toward the parlor, whispered, "in there."

Father Goldsworthy sat in my dad's big chair, waiting for me. I found it strange, and thought, *he only comes for Sunday dinner.* At least that's the only time I remember him visiting.

"Sit down, son," he said. "Pay attention to what I say."

Father Goldsworthy was a kind enough man providing you could get around his gruffness. He said he was sorry about Betsy and tried to explain something that was much too complicated for me to take in. He ended by reiterating his dictum.

"Since Betsy's funeral is going to be in a Protestant church, Mew, I can't allow you to go. I'm sorry," he said.

I noticed he'd eaten onions for lunch when he excused a slight belch. He mumbled something else about creating a scandal and got up abruptly.

"You belong to the one true church, Mew, and you should be proud of that." He patted my head, saying, "Run along now, while I speak to your mother."

"What does he mean?" I asked my mother after he left. She explained as best she could why Catholics couldn't attend other churches. "But it's for Betsy's funeral," I wailed. "I have to go, Mom; Betsy was my friend."

She shook her head sternly, saying, "Now, Mew, you know we have to do what Father says."

The day they laid Betsy to rest was foggy, and eerily quiet. It was cold too, the coldest since 1901, they said. My mother stoked the fire in the parlor stove and read to me from a book she'd given me for Christmas. It was the story about a saint. Usually, I liked stories of that genre, but this one, about Isaac Jogues, a Jesuit Missionary killed by the Mohawk Indians, was too gruesome. Ironically, the same Indians had captured Saint Isaac twice. The first time a group of Dutch Protestants had bargained for and secured his release. This irony was completely lost on my mother that day. I had to feign attention but the story failed to interest me. Maybe it was just the day.

My dad came home and I watched his clothes steam as he stood by the stove. Finally, he stopped shivering and settled back in his chair.

"Sam, did you remember to wear your long johns?" my mom asked.

"Of course I did, Mary," he answered, pulling up the cuff of his pants. "But they don't help much in the cold out there today."

"*Poor Betsy*," I thought again. The experience traumatized me. I couldn't assimilate the feelings of hurt and betrayal. The anger driven into my unconscious that day would surface much later – about forty years, in fact.

My dad tried to console me, but didn't interfere. Theirs was a mixed marriage. In their pre-marriage counseling he had signed a paper consenting that any children would be raised Catholic. Even though it strained their relationship at times, my dad was a man of his word, even in a hard case like Betsy's funeral.

The next evening after an early supper, my dad said, "Come on, Mew, get your coat, and I'll take you to see Leezie."

I was afraid to go and hesitated, not understanding how I would explain my absence from Betsy's funeral.

"Come on," he repeated, sterner this time.

I wouldn't describe the atmosphere as festive, but there was a marked difference from my last visit. Leezie greeted me with a slap on the back, wanting to know if I'd like to see his Christmas present. It was a sled with wooden runners that were perfectly curved on the ends. John Smith, with the help of the school's shop teacher, had built it.

"See," Leezie said, holding a wax chunk that Hildred had melted down from old candles. "You wax the runners with this."

"Hello Mew," I heard Hildred say behind me.

I turned and for some inexplicable reason, to me at least, ran sobbing into her arms. "I'm sorry, I'm sorry, Mom Smith. I'm sorry I couldn't come," I blubbered.

She held me tight for a long moment. "It's alright, Mew," she whispered. "You're just a wee boy. It's not your fault."

Chapter Six

Spring-like weather arrived.

"Thank God," my mother said on a morning that brought a warm wind filled with the twittering of birds.

The town seemed to throw off the shackles of winter, although a few days yet remained on February's calendar page.

We would have to wait, of course, for the official equinox, but this harbinger was reason enough to send me on a frantic search for my baseball bat. It was my duty, as the owner of the only privately owned such utensil, to have it ready when the time came. This year I was determined to have it in hand before Leezie asked, "Did you find it yet?"

There were plenty of local reproductions, some cruder than others, but mine was a genuine *Louisville Slugger* with Ty Cobb's name on it. He wasn't my favorite player; Babe Ruth was.

Leezie loved the bat, and would say on his way up to the plate, "Gimme Ole Cobber, Mew, and I'll show you how to smack the ball." He chided me about Babe Ruth too, saying I favored him because, "He's a Catholic, like you." I'd deny it, of course, but secretly it made me proud to know that about The Babe.

One day, when we were on our way home from baseball, we stopped at the blacksmith shop. Leezie had the bright idea to heat a nail in the forge, which he used to burn my name into the bottom of the bat.

"Give me the knob end and hold on tight," he said. "I wants to make sure I gits it nice and deep." My name, *Mew*, was still there, long after I lost track of Old Cobber.

I interrupted my search and made a trip to the outhouse. On my way back out the door, I reached up to the ledge where my mother kept her secret stash of cigarettes. They were gone. *Oh-Oh!* I thought, jerking my hand away.

My mom smoked Chesterfields, secretly, in the outhouse. She was so tricky about it that I only discovered it by accident. My dad had rigged a device that triggered a spring when the fold-down seat was dropped to make a person's stay more comfortable. That, in turn, caused a little sign to pop up outside the door. Neatly lettered, it read. *"The stinker has a thinker."* I'm sure we were the only ones in town with such a luxury.

As I stood waiting one frosty morning, hopping from one foot to the other, I noticed smoke coming out of the half-moon vent. Intrigued, I hid behind the woodpile and waited. I watched as my mom come out and tossed a spent cigarette aside. On a later visit I explored the outhouse and discovered her Chesterfield cache.

On this day, finding that her cigarettes were gone posed two problems.

First, Leezie and I wouldn't have a place to filch our furtive smokes. We snitched them from my mother's supply – discreetly, of course, so she wouldn't miss them. On average, that occurred once or twice a month. It was more during the summer, when the town's gardens had an ample supply of green onions that we nibbled to mask our breath.

The second difficulty was that my mother always gave up cigarettes for Lent. Father Goldsworthy used a big word, *"penitential,"* to describe this forty-day season leading up to Easter. Leezie could never stutter his way around *"penitential,"* so he invented, *"quit-official"* to replace it. Since Lent was a period of mortification, which Catholics did by giving something up, I liked his description.

My mother would admonish me: "You have to do something serious, Mew, to make yourself worthy for Easter."

I remember the first time I consulted Leezie about it. His eyes got big like a hoot owl's, and he said, "Gee whiz, Mew, what are you going to do?" We explored several ideas before he finally suggested, "Why don't you give up cigarettes like your mom?"

That became my secret concession, but I added something trivial like gum drops just so I could tell Father Goldsworthy.

Giving up my twice-monthly cigarette habit, of course, didn't have the same ramifications for me as it did for my mom. During Lent she became terribly irritable. Well, maybe that's too mild a word to describe what came over her.

My dad would run out of patience by the end of the first week and say, "Mary, you're getting meaner than Uncle Bob's three-legged bull during mating season."

"Sam Moosington!" she'd snap back. "Don't you dare compare me to that awful creature."

That's the way it went all during Lent, as they snipped their way through the season. My mom's idea of "getting worthy" came to an abrupt end on Easter morning.

"There she is," my dad said when mom appeared at the bottom of the stairs, decked out in her latest finery, a radiant smile on her face.

"Good morning, Sam," she greeted him with a loving kiss on the cheek. Then sweetly to me: "Let's go, Mew; it's time for church."

Mom could scarcely contain herself during the service, knowing Lent was officially over when Father Goldsworthy pronounced the final prayer.

The aura of bubbling happiness lasted all day. Easter dinner was never served on time, however, because mom's preparations were constantly interrupted as she made up for lost time with frequent trips to the outhouse.

"I just hope that Jesus doesn't smoke," my dad would quip, watching mom skip down the path. "If he does, it would be just my luck to die during Lent."

The first time he said it, I just frowned.

"That would mean Jesus would quit smoking during Lent too," he explained.

"Huh?" I said.

"Putting up with your mother during Lent is one thing, but I sure don't want to run into Jesus having a nicotine fit at the pearly gates."

Since I didn't know about nicotine fits, or the pearly gates for that matter, I still didn't get it, but dad thought it was pretty funny.

I found my bat that afternoon, right where I'd left it, in a closet on the back porch. Five minutes later Leezie appeared and said, "Did you find it yet?" I nodded, giving him a put-out look for suggesting I'd forget.

"Let's get going then," he said. "Harry, and Billy are waiting."

"Hold up a minute," I said. "Look at this," revealing a brand new baseball I'd kept secret from the horde of presents I'd gotten for Christmas.

"Holy catfish, Mew!" he exclaimed with reverence that wasn't exaggerated. "It's a Reach!"

A.J. Reach supplied baseballs for the big leagues. "It's the same one they use in the majors," I said proudly.

Leezie held it up to his ear then tossed it in the air a couple of times. "I'll bet I can hit this a country mile. Come on," he shouted, racing across the front yard. "And bring Old Cobber with you."

We played an ingenious game we called *Workup*, perfect for a small town with never enough players to field teams. The first arrivals got the cherished positions, which is why Leezie was in a hurry. The earliest four became the batters, while the others took up positions in the field. It happened on the first day that Leezie started at second base and I nabbed shortstop, just ahead of Billy Archer.

The first batter that day was one of the girls, Lucy Pong, who hit a fly ball to Leezie. They traded places. Leezie hit a grounder and was thrown out. He started over in left field and the rest of us rotated. The next hitter struck out and we switched again. This time I played first base.

Leezie, incidentally, was a terrible hitter until he got his first pair of glasses. That didn't happen until he was in the eighth grade, when

John Smith traded the doctor his grandfather's pocket watch for them. Leezie was, however, a terror on the base paths if he ever got on. His chubby legs, churning a cloud of dust, reminded me of my mom's wind-filled bloomers flapping spasmodically on the clothesline.

Our playing field was a rough diamond marked off next to a farmer's pasture. The bat and ball comprised our only equipment, save a worn-out glove the blacksmith had given us, which we stuffed with rags for a catcher's mitt.

Gravedigger Bill, when he wasn't otherwise engaged, was a fixture as umpire, and imitated the theatrics of the best major leaguers. Leezie could perfectly mimic his *"Steee-rike-tha-ree!"*

The game never ended; it started again the next day in the same positions where we left off. Scoring didn't matter; how long you remained a batter is what earned you bragging rights.

On this afternoon, Harry Capphammer threw the first pitch of the new season and we played until almost dark. Famished, and dreaming of meatballs and gravy, I was surprised when I arrived home to find three carpenters hammering in the back yard. Instead of supper, I was horrified to find the kitchen table littered with drawings.

Joe Krautamiller looked up, started gathering his papers. My mom bounced from her chair, saying, "Mr. Krautamiller is going to build us an indoor privy."

I mouthed the words back at her.

"Yes," she beamed. "Isn't that grand?"

Sidney Bakefield, the banker, owned the only other house in town with such a modern apparatus. I'd never been in it but Leezie had. He delivered papers once, substituting for an older boy, and feigned an emergency when he came to Bakefield's place. Ruthie, the housekeeper, let him in, saying, "And mind you, young man, be sure you put the lid down."

Ruthie must have been listening at the door because she chased him out after she heard the toilet flush a fourth time.

Construction on our new *"facility,"* as my mom called it, lasted into the summer.

"We should have a grand opening," my dad joked on the day Joe Krautamiller and his crew packed up their tools. "What do you think, Mary?"

She wrinkled her nose. "It's just a privy, Sam."

It was more than that, though. It had a place for her wringer washer and a swing-out window to let the smoke from her Chesterfields escape. More importantly for my mom, it had a big white bathtub. That ended the ordeal of Saturday night baths in a portable metal tub on the kitchen floor. It also began the unheard of ritual of taking a bath on Wednesdays too.

"Gee Whiz, Mew," Leezie said. "Now you can wash your elbows on Wednesday and save up your toe jam for Saturdays."

Chapter Seven

I was getting old. My tenth birthday followed Leezie's by three weeks. He got a new slingshot that his dad made using red rubber from the worn-out inner tube of a Model T. We took it out one afternoon and were stalking crows when Abner Pong happened along.

"Lemme see that slinger," Abner said, trying to grab it out of Leezie's hand.

"Beat it, Abner," Leezie said. "You wouldn't know what to do with it anyway."

"Come on Smith, gimme it. I just want to shoot a rock through that Yid's window." He hooked a thumb toward a small house occupied by a family that had moved to town the week before.

"Scram, Abner," Leezie said.

I made a face at him and he lunged, imitating a cat with a hissy fit. I jerked back and Leezie stepped between us.

"Whatsamatta, Mew-Mew?" Abner taunted. "I scare you?"

Leezie gave him a shove and Abner pushed back. They stood nose-to-nose for a moment before Abner backed down.

"Stupid Yid ain't worth it," he mumbled. Turning abruptly, he swaggered down the street.

"Big bunghole!" I shouted after him, getting in the last word. I looked toward Leezie, who stood snapping his slingshot, staring at the Yid's house.

"What's a Yid?" he asked. I hadn't thought about it, and shrugged my shoulders.

"Abner said it like Yid is a naughty word," he said.

I still didn't say anything, but my mind was working on it.

"There's a language," I said, suddenly remembering a story my mother had read me. "It's called Yid-a-nese or something. Maybe it's what Yids speak when no one is listening."

"I bet Father Goldsworthy knows about Yids," he said.

"Why?"

"He talks Latin, don't he?"

It wasn't unusual for Leezie to consult Father Goldsworthy about any matter. Pestered is more what he did, with an endless list of questions. Leezie wasn't intimidated by Father's gruff manner, and they had what might be best described as a father-poor waif relationship.

I wanted to rush home to wash my face and comb my hair first, but Leezie would have none of it and barged in without knocking. I was mortified.

"Yes, yes, what is it?" Father Goldsworthy said, appearing suddenly from the room where I attended catechism class. "Oh, it's you," he said, acknowledging Leezie and giving me a long look down his nose. "What is it this time?"

"What's a Yid?" Leezie asked.

Father Goldsworthy answered out the side of his mouth. "It's a Jew."

Leezie turned to me. His look told me we'd come to the right place, because Father had said the name much like Abner had.

"Are they bad?" Leezie followed.

"Cursed are the Jews because they killed the Christ." He said it with a jerk of his head that caused him to reach up and catch the funny hat he wore.

Leezie blinked twice and stifled a snicker. I tugged on his coat sleeve, hoping for a quick retreat. Instead he asked, "What's that mean?"

Father Goldsworthy sighed and motioned toward the catechism room.

He told us the story of how the Jewish people had rebelled and killed the Christ, bringing upon their race a curse and the contempt of all right-thinking Christians. He actually said, "All right-thinking Cath- er- Christians."

"But are they bad?" Leezie asked again.

Father Goldsworthy thought for a moment. "No, not if you mean do they go around doing naughty things. I've known a few Jews," he said, using the same way of saying the word, "and many of them are quite good citizens."

"How can they be bad and good at the same time?" Leezie asked. I was squirming in my chair, wishing he'd shut up.

"I didn't say they were bad," Father said. Bad, came out like a backfire from Gravedigger Bill's old Ford. "I said they were cursed."

From past experience Leezie knew the conversation was ended and got up. Father Goldsworthy frowned, more at me, I'm sure, and led us to the door.

"Wow!" Leezie said, "Now we know what a Yid is."

"Do you believe him?" I ventured.

"Maybe," he answered, "but there's something inside that don't want to."

I did more investigating, thinking about it mainly, and decided that, like Father Goldsworthy, I didn't care for Yids either. Had the matter stayed there my immediate future would have been much more pleasant.

Two weeks later my dad came home from work and announced at supper that he'd hired Mr. Frank to help out at the hardware. Without thinking I blurted, trying to imitate Abner's way, "Why did you hire that Yid?"

"Oh-Oh!" I thought as I watched the smoke pour out his ears and singe the hair on the top of his head.

"What did you say?" he asked.

Timidly, I repeated it.

"That's what I thought."

Gently he put his knife and fork down and got up. He took me by the short hairs on the back of my neck and I came off my chair like I was propelled by Leezie's slingshot. Dad had a firm grip, and goose-marched me out the back door to the woodshed. There, he tanned my rear end with a paddle.

Finished, he said, "Mr. Frank is a son of Abraham, Mew, one of God's chosen people. Don't you ever talk about a Jew that way again!"

He left me there, crying my eyes out, barely knowing what I'd done. Later, I crept into the house where my mom was waiting. Thinking I could manipulate her to take my side, I told her an abbreviated version of what Father Goldsworthy had said to us.

"Sit down, Mew," she said, "and listen while I tell you a story."

The tale began some two hundred years before, and was about a man in a far-off country called Russia. The man had been drafted into the army and became a war hero, his uniform carrying the weight of many medals.

"He returned to his village, married and started a family," my mom went on. It was my favorite kind of story and she had my full attention.

"They were poor," she continued, "and the other villagers perse-cuted them."

I started to object, but she continued. "One day the army swept through the village and killed the family, all of them, except one son who hid in a manure pile."

"But-but-but," I protested, "he was a war hero."

"Yes," she said, a small tear rolling down her cheek. "But he was a Jew, and they slew them for no other reason save they were Jews."

"It makes me mad," I said.

She went on, not hearing. "The man's name was Ezekiel, Mew, and he's your grandfather, several times removed."

At first I didn't make the connection. "You mean like Grampa John?"

"Sort of," mom said, "if you keep counting your grandpas back-wards you'll eventually come to Ezekiel."

I bowed my head, contrite and proud at the same time. "Wow!" I said.

"Let's go find Abner and beat him up," Leezie said when I told him the next day what had happened. He didn't spare Father Goldsworthy either, saying, "I knowed he was wrong about Yids."

Chapter Eight

Catholic boys went to church summer school. It lasted for two weeks and was taught by a stern nun imported from the Catholic boarding school in the county seat. Sister Evangelica, from the order of Exalted Virgins of Mary Immaculate, was short, and the big metal cross she wore was too long for her squat frame. To keep it from clunking against our desks, she carried it in one hand, using it like a director's baton to emphasize whatever she said.

I was nine going on ten, and Sister Evangelina chose that year to educate us in the evils of sin. She waved her cross in one hand and THE BALTIMORE CATECHISM in the other, making us memorize the relevant parts. For instance, she would shout, "*Besides depriving the sinner of sanctifying grace, what else does mortal sin do to the soul?*"

All in one breath, we would recite this answer back to her: "*Mortal sin makes the soul an enemy of God, takes away the merit of all its good actions, deprives it of the right to everlasting happiness in heaven, and makes it deserving of everlasting punishment in hell.*"

Then she would say, letting the words roll off her tongue like it was God Almighty himself working her voice box, "And do you want to be the enemy of God by eating meat on Friday?"

Eating meat on Friday was her favorite mortal sin, and to Sister Evangelica it was on a par with murder. She scared the daylights out of us, and we yelled back "No! Never!"

If we weren't noisy enough, she would bang her cross on the nearest desk, usually Petey Gorman's, and say, "Louder, children! God can't hear you."

With that lesson in high moral theology in mind, you'll be equipped to understand what happened to me later in the summer. I never blamed him, but I'm sure it was Leezie's fondness of food that caused one of the greatest traumas of my young years.

I committed the ultimate mortal sin, and you can easily guess which one, since it happened one Friday afternoon when Leezie said, "I'm hungry."

We were standing in front of the meat market – not a normal hangout for boys, but a place that served several of our needs. The butcher was friendly, and if not busy could be counted on to sharpen our pocketknives. Today, however, Leezie was after bigger game, and quickly engaged Blinky – our private nickname for the butcher – in conversation about his selection of luncheon meats.

It was comical to watch.

"What's that one?" Leezie stuttered.

"Salami," Blinky answered, his right eye fluttering like the slats of a venetian blind in a stiff breeze (hence the nickname).

"Th-th-th-THAT one?" Leezie asked, tapping the glass face of the cooler.

"Summer sausage," the butcher answered.

Leezie screwed up his face, obviously confused, then said, "It aren't summer yet."

Blinkly chuckled, only to be confronted with, "Looks awful salty."

The banter continued, with Leezie angling for a sample and the butcher feigning umbrage at my friend's insinuations of poor quality. Their conversation aggravated Leezie's stuttering, or more likely he used it to confuse Blinky. It did appear to, for his eye-blinks per minute picked up considerably.

Suddenly, Leezie went back to the summer sausage. "How much for that salty one?" He whistled through his teeth at the price, giving at the same time a crestfallen look to the butcher. "I couldn't tell if I liked it without a taste first."

"Well why didn't you say so in the first place?" Blinky said, hiding a smile behind his hand. "Woulda saved me five minutes alistenin' to your jabber." He took the roll of summer sausage out of the case, cut two generous samples and served them on butcher's paper.

Leezie's disappeared in an instant. I suppose it was the look of pure bliss on his face that made me ignore the lessons that Sister Evangelica had taught me. I grabbed my piece of the summer sausage, and devoured it, savoring every morsel.

"Well?" Blinky asked.

"It's the best summer sausage I ever et," Leezie said.

"Be sure to tell your Ma that," Blinky said. "Now be off with ye. Go pester some other poor soul."

We ran to the end of the block – not fast mind you, because we were slowed by Leezie's snickers, which were uncontrollable when he was especially pleased with himself.

The enormity of my transgression started to dawn on me later, just before six o'clock, when the smells of my mother's Friday night salmon loaf wafted under the door or my room.

"You look a little green around the gills, Mew," my dad said during supper. "You've hardly touched your salmon."

I put on a good front and dug in with false gusto; the last thing I needed was for my mother to sense something amiss and start prying.

The night was miserable. The taste of the summer sausage lay like a glob of rancid butter on my tongue. It was a mortal sin; there was no doubt. "I'm an enemy of God," the lesson from the Baltimore Catechism came back to me. "I'm deserving of everlasting punishment in Hell," I sobbed.

I crept off to the new privy in the middle of the night and bent over the toilet, stuffing my finger down my throat. *"If I can vomit out the sausage maybe that will make it right,"* I thought.

Somehow I made it through breakfast without my mother taking note of my condition. *"She can't see into the blackness of my soul,"* I comforted myself, only to be reminded, *"but God can, and he hates me."*

Leezie knew the catechism better than I did. He helped coach me to get the answers right in my exams for altar boy. As a result he retained many of the fine points better than me. Put another way, I knew the answers, but often didn't know why the questions were asked.

I hurriedly ate a second bowl of oatmeal to appease my mother and went out to find Leezie.

"Gee whiz, Mew!" He said after I told him what troubled me.

We were scrunched in our secret hideaway underneath the train depot platform. Leezie brushed some of the spider webs away from a floor joist and found the key to our treasure box. The box, a foot long by five inches deep and eight inches wide, was a discard from the hardware store, originally used to ship auto parts. The railroad padlock had fallen into our hands thanks to a brakeman, who dropped it in the weeds one day and was too impatient to make a thorough search for it.

The treasure box contained an odd assortment. Among other things were two broken pencils, a deck of cards missing one suit, a fifth-place ribbon we'd won in a three-legged race, and our extra fish hook and line. Most important was my spare copy of The Baltimore Catechism. It might seem strange – me being a Catholic and Leezie not – to find such a volume here, but not if you remember that Leezie had a special interest in spiritual things. Plus, there was the fact that I had no one else my age to confide such matters to.

Leezie worked the key in the lock and it snapped open. He took out the catechism and quickly found the right section.

After several moments he gave me a somber look, saying sadly, "Sister Evangello were right, Mew."

I had hoped an expert opinion might let me off the hook, but my worst fears were realized.

"What can I do?" I mumbled.

Leezie did some more research, concluding, "Says here you have to go to confession."

"No!" I exclaimed. "Father Goldsworthy would tell my mom."

Leezie shook his head. "He can't."

"You sure?"

He nodded.

"I don't care," I said. "I won't."

Then a strange thought struck me. "If I go to hell, I won't ever see Leezie again." I started to cry.

"Don't cry, Mew," Leezie said. "That won't do no good. Father Goldsworthy won't no more than bawl you out."

"You sure?" I said between sniffles.

"God probly don't even care anyhow," he said.

"Yes he does," I said indignantly, bumping my head against a rafter when I tried to stand up to stamp my foot.

"Don't neither," Leezie argued.

"Do too," I shot back.

Our argument went on for several more *do not's* and *do too's*, until I resolved to show him. I'd go to confession.

That didn't prevent me from putting it off until the last moment. I ignored the Saturday night opportunity when most of the parish went to confession. Instead, I waited until Sunday morning, thinking Father Goldsworthy would be in a hurry and let me off easy, possibly even chide me for bothering him with something so trivial. That meant another night of pain and suffering and nightmares of a fiery under-world presided over by the devil.

"Oh God, please let me live until morning," I prayed. "I promise I'll go to confession and never eat meat on Friday again."

It must have worked, for I woke up to bright sunshine with a burning desire to rid myself of what troubled me. I thought perhaps the hardest part was behind me, but it didn't turn out that way.

"Bless me, Father, for I have sinned," I said after entering the confessional. Next followed several contrived minor infractions to camouflage what was coming. "Also, I ate meat on Friday," I said.

"What?" Father Goldsworthy barked in a voice sure to be heard by those assembling for Mass.

I repeated my confession in a shaky voice. That at least caused him to drop his tone and he gave me a long lecture in a whisper. It was a loud whisper to be sure, and I still feared inquisitive ears would hear him.

"For your penance," he concluded, "say two decades of the rosary. AND," he practically spit in my ear, "see me after Mass."

Fortunately the rear of the church, where the confessional was located, was dark and no one could see my red face. The embarrassment was partly caused by catching my pocket on the doorknob. When it released, the door sprang back from the elasticity of my wool pants and slammed against the casing like a gunshot.

"Confession is good for the soul," Sister Evangelica had also drummed into us. I raced through my penance, and afterward felt relieved. By the time I had dressed into my altar boy's suit, I was on cloud nine. Even Father Goldsworthy's stern lecture after Mass, equating eating meat on Friday with divorce, bank robbery, and blaspheming the Pope, failed to dim the joy of being rid of my sin. I was no longer God's enemy.

Chaper Nine

In later years, Leezie would call the event, which led off a sequence of semi-disasters, *"the dung-ho flop."* It happened in the spring after we turned ten, and was a failed attempt to tip over the town marshal's outdoor toilet.

In our tiny village it was a time-honored prank, but one, we learned the hard way, that was best reserved for older, huskier boys. It wasn't that we were totally ignorant, because we did recruit Harry Capphammer and Billy Archer to help. Both of them were exceptionally stout for age ten.

On the night of the great escapade we each took our positions. Leezie could do a perfect imitation of a hoot owl, so he would be the lookout, and *hoot* if the marshal, who should have been asleep, appeared. That there were no hoot owls where we lived never entered our minds. Leezie took up his station near the back door, and I admonished him, "Hoot like crazy if you hear anything."

Everything went according to plan until Harry tripped and fell against a pile of boards that were stacked upright against a wood shed. They toppled over and hit the chicken coop on the way down. The startled chickens woke the neighborhood with their frantic clucking, arousing several dogs from slumber.

The marshal, clad in his long underwear, bolted out the rear door only to stumble over Leezie, who was parked on the step. He got distracted because the back flap of his long johns was caught on an eyehook on Leezie's boot. He finally ripped it free, saying, "Quit that hootin', you little whippersnapper, and tell me what you're doin' here!"

Leezie let out a long litany of frightened stutters. About the only thing that didn't disappear in his jumble of stuttering were the words, "the shit house."

It was still too garbled and confused the marshal.

"Say it again, and quit that goldarned stutterin', he said.

This time it came out a little clearer, and the marshal exploded, "My privy? You was tryin' to tip over my beautiful two-holed terlit?"

Leezie nodded and our goose was cooked.

Although we had struggled mightily, we came nowhere near tipping it over. That counted for little. The next day, the three of us watched, each holding a shovel, as Marshal Bitterfoot had the toilet moved off its hole. When it sat leaning slightly on a set of rollers, he said, "Now, you little buggers start digging."

That was our punishment, the disgusting job of loading the contents of the gaping hole onto an old truck. Leezie escaped the marshal's wrath, but not that of his mother. She scrubbed his mouth with soap for saying the "S" word. That didn't prevent him watching us from a safe distance, however, with a gleeful glint in his eye, wearing, for emphasis, his dad's World War I gas mask.

My mom blamed Leezie and took pity on Harry and Billy. After we finished, she insisted they take advantage of our new bathtub. Harry was shy, but his mother wouldn't let him back in their house until he got rid of the smell.

"Gosh, Mew," he said, coming out of our bathroom. "I ain't never had a bath in clean water before."

Leezie may have gotten out of the punishment, but it didn't mean the marshal forgot about him. The second small catastrophe took place after, but was caused by the Fourth of July celebrations.

I still had some wands left over. Leezie called them *sizzle sticks*. Slender and almost two feet long, they were loaded with slow-burning gunpowder that when lit, burned bright red for almost a minute. The forerunner of *sparklers*, my dad ordered them from San Francisco and Leezie loved them.

He drooled over the display each year at the Hardware, but never had two dimes in his pocket at the same time to buy one. So, one Saturday morning after my dad told me to fill the wood box, I spotted Leezie coming up the street.

"I'll give you one of my sizzle sticks if you help me," I told him.

"One?" He howled.

I upped the ante, offering in addition two gumballs and a used yo-yo string.

"I don't got no yo-yo to put a string on anyhow," he complained.

"Nope, it'll cost you two sizzlers."

About that time my dad came out the back door, casting an eye in my direction. I quickly whispered, "Okay, two of the sizzlers, but you can't tell nobody I give 'em to you."

He had the opportunity to tattle, as it turned out, but didn't.

That night, Leezie lit them off in a plowed field on the edge of town by the railroad tracks. The location was good, but his timing was awful. He insisted on having them both going at the same time, and became so engrossed in what he was doing that he forgot about the nightly passenger train.

He did put on quite a show, standing in the middle of the tracks doing crisscross motions and spraying red sparks with reckless abandon. He jumped three feet when the train engineer sounded the whistle for the crossing. Suddenly, I'm sure when the trainman noticed the red danger signal in front of him, he set the emergency brakes.

The train made a terrible racket of screeching metal and blowing steam, and with a final clatter came to a stop, hissing and crackling, a hundred yards from Leezie. He stood bug-eyed, still twirling his burnt-out sizzle sticks.

It wasn't until Leezie noticed men climbing down from the locomotive that he took off like a scared jackrabbit. I thought he would seek refuge in our hideaway under the depot's platform, but instead he ran straight for Beelzebub's doghouse, next to the back door of their upstairs apartment.

Naturally, the trainman and the town marshal came looking for him. If it weren't for the fact that his dog, Beelzebub, took a bite out of the trainman's backside, Leezie would have gotten away with a reprimand. The marshal, however, the memory of his beautiful two-holed *terlit* still quite fresh, grabbed Leezie by the collar, saying, "Caught you again, you little whippersnapper, and you cain't stutter your way out of this one."

The marshal had to stop and catch his breath after the night's exertion.

"What do you think we should do with him, Joe?" he panted to the trainman.

Leezie was shaking like an earwig caught in a spider's web by this time, and watched the marshal stop and light a cigarette. He blew a puff of smoke at Beelzebub, who sneezed and retreated part way into his doghouse.

"I'm believin' a month's worth of cleaning spittoons at the pool hall should learn this little rascal a lesson."

The trainman, a Catholic, happened to be a friend of Father Goldsworthy's. He took Marshal Bitterfoot aside and talked him into a different punishment. Instead of cleaning spittoons it was decided that Leezie would work for Father Goldsworthy, and mow the church lawn for a month.

"A slap on the wrist," my mother said when she heard of it.

Beelzebub had been Leezie's constant companion since Betsy died. John Smith had named him that because he came home one day to find the puppy had scattered a new box of stick matches all over the floor. We called those *"Lucifers"* growing up, which is how John coined the name. Leezie and I called him Bub for short.

Bub was a cross between a Newfoundland and a Labrador. He loved our swimming hole under the railroad trestle south of town, and in winter could be found chasing ice skaters. He could fill in for missing baseball players and was as adept at catching ground balls as our best shortstop.

The dog was the cause of the third small calamity that befell us that summer. These were cumulative, and none of them sitting alone would have been long remembered. Bearing that in mind, store in your memory that the punishment meted out by the marshal put Leezie in close proximity to Father Goldsworthy. It follows, then, that the dog was part of the package.

Father Goldsworthy had a great dislike for dogs, and was always shooing Beelzebub off church property. Bub, of course, didn't limit his visits solely to when Leezie was mowing the grass. Twice the priest stumbled over him sleeping on the back step, and once caught him napping on a davenport in a sitting room. Bub developed a great affection for Father Goldsworthy. Alas, the fondness wasn't mutual.

One Sunday morning in late summer, he set the congregation a-twitter when in the middle of services; Bub wandered into church and parked himself at the corner of the altar. Father Goldsworthy was a humorless person, and when he spotted Bub, he nearly swooned. He waved off help offered by the parishioners and attempted to run the intruder out of the church. That only caused Beelzebub to think he was finally paying him some attention.

It ended up a circus. Father Goldsworthy chased Bub around the altar until the dog knocked over one of the tall candles, setting fire to the fringes of Father's long vestments. A quick-thinking altar boy (I was home in bed with a cold that day) came running with some holy water and doused the fire, but Beelzebub wasn't finished yet.

Father Goldsworthy looked up only to see Bub munching the consecrated communion hosts that had been spilled during the fracas. Father Goldsworthy fainted and spent a few days confined to his room. After a visit from the local bishop, it was decided the priest needed a long vacation.

My dad heard the story from Gravedigger Bill and repeated it for years. Sam Moosington was the best storyteller I know of, especially if it had humorous side, which this one did. My mother corrected him if he exaggerated, but even she couldn't suppress a smile this time, despite the sacrilegious nature of the event. Catholics took sacrilege seriously, but in this case, most parishioners overlooked the blasphemy in light of the involvement of an innocent dog.

After the excitement of the past months our lives settled into more normal routines. The Bishop rotated priests to serve in our vacationing pastor's place. One of them, whom Leezie quickly dubbed "*His Watchership*," spent time trying to observe Bub to see, I suppose, if he exhibited any special quirks after eating the holy bread.

"He reminds me of a caterpillar," Leezie said on one occasion, as we watched the priest from the bushes.

The priest was a pompous, tiny fellow who spent most of his time observing the dog and reading Latin prayers aloud from a book. His falsetto voice matched his body language, which indeed did resemble that of a caterpillar in a great hurry. He only stayed two weeks before being replaced.

The next big event of the year occurred with the arrival of the annual tent revival meeting.

"The holy rollers is back!" Abner Pong announced breathlessly one afternoon just before the start of school.

Neither Leezie nor I knew what the term meant, but that didn't dampen our excitement. It also set off our yearly bickering over Leezie's suggestion, "We oughtta go."

An idea like that gave me the shivers, which I thought I hid well, and I refused to give in to a litany of, "Youse just a big fat chicken."

I shot back an equal number of "am not's," until he gave up. I never admitted that the threat of Abner's ridicule was a bigger obstacle than the fact that Catholic boys didn't go to Protestant tent meetings. Curiosity, however, fueled by catching glimpses of the two-night performance from our concealed vantage point, made me wonder what I'd do if Leezie really dared me.

Religious scruples didn't work in reverse, and after the revivalists left town, Leezie took up a familiar refrain. This would eventually lead to *real* disaster. It began when Leezie said, "Why can't I be a altar boy like you?"

Chapter Ten

My life would have turned out much differently if I had never had the idea in the first place. I didn't tell him, but I had actually thought about Leezie's question, *"Why can't I be a altar boy like you?"* during the weekend of the tent meeting.

Once the notion took hold there was no stopping it. Gravedigger Bill added fuel when he announced one day that Father Goldsworthy would return in two weeks. Meanwhile, his last replacement was due to arrive the next Sunday.

I mulled this over then called a secret meeting of the other altar boys, Forrest Knocker and Petey Gorman. Petey was epileptic and didn't see much service, especially since the time he had a fit during catechism class. It was horrible, but fortunately his older brother was there and prevented him from swallowing his tongue. I still had nightmares about it and got stomach cramps if I was left alone with Petey.

Leezie on the other hand befriended him and had his brother teach him what to do if Petey suddenly swooned. I was the senior altar boy and took charge of the meeting, and yes, I made sure Leezie attended, just in case.

"Ba-ba-ba-BUT," Leezie complained after I mapped out the plan, now fixed in my mind. "I wanna be a server just like you guys."

That meant he wanted to be full-fledged altar boy, but it didn't take long for us to decide otherwise. Leezie was too excitable and we'd never be able to teach him the Latin responses before Father Goldsworthy got back.

"But Leezie ain't Catlick," Petey interjected.

I smiled and said, "But the new priest coming this week won't know that."

Petey and Forrest laughed together, and we agreed the Benediction service on Sunday evening would be perfect. Benediction started in the back of the church and went up the aisle to the front. Thus, the congregation would only see Leezie from the rear. When it was over, the priest and altar boy exited in opposite directions, so we doubted anyone would notice our switch.

The best thing about it was my mother was having a tea party that evening and wouldn't be there. The service was always sparsely attended and never lively, and would be even less so this Sunday, the last day of fishing season.

We spent the rest of the week coaching Leezie.

"What about his bibbed overalls?" Forrest asked on the day we snuck into the church so Leezie could try on the altar boy's cassock and white surplice.

"And dem boots," Petey said, pointing to the scuffed pair with a hole in one toe.

"I got new ones for school," Leezie announced. That took care of one problem. The bibs would just have to do.

Sunday arrived and I confess I was more nervous than Leezie. The new priest was late, which solved our worry about any kind of close inspection. We had guessed right – no one took notice when our neophyte altar boy made his debut. Rote and rigid ritual worked to our advantage. Father and altar boy made their procession from the back to the front of church and not an inquiring head was raised.

Everything went smoothly until the priest stepped behind the altar and greeted those assembled with the Latin phrase, "*Dominus Vobiscum*" (*The Lord be with you*). Leezie was supposed to respond with something akin to, "*Et cum spitituo*" (*and with your spirit*), but what came out was, "And how do you do."

That caused a few snickers from the middle pews. Were it not for that, it's doubtful the priest would have noticed, as altar boys generally mumbled their responses. Father Luther Martin peered down at Leezie and made the mistake of starting over.

"Dominus Vobiscum," he repeated.

Leezie was getting edgy and grabbed his white prompter card, looking for a response that would satisfy Father Martin. He found the reply, "*Gloria in excelsis Deo*" (*Glory to God in the highest*), and although he did an excellent job garbling the words, it still came out like, "Do you like Jello?"

Father Martin scowled but went on unperturbed. The two of them struggled through the fifteen-minute service and what Leezie lacked in eloquence he made up for with his ability to be angelic. The climax came when Leezie had to load the brass thurifer with coals to burn the incense. We had worked on this procedure until Leezie had it down pat, we thought.

The clumsy contraption has a lid that slides upward on chains to expose a cavity where the altar boy is supposed to place the lighted coals. Next, he adroitly hands it to the priest, who spoons in the incense.

Adroit Leezie was not, and he dropped the hot coal on Father Martin's foot. Father was wearing sandals and grunted when the coal sat sizzling, caught in the webbing of his footwear. He grabbed the tong out of Leezie's hand and when he bent over to snatch away the glowing ember, knocked his head on the bottom of the thurifer, bending his glasses at a cockeyed angle.

Leezie started to giggle, causing ripples of the same in the pews behind him. Finally, Father got the coals placed in the thurifer, slid the lid down with a clang, and swung the smoking apparatus several times as he hopped gingerly on his burned foot.

After they limped off the altar at the conclusion, Father Martin had a long whispered conference with Leezie. We weren't privy to the contents of his admonitions, for all we observed were Leezie's rapid headshakes.

"What did he say?" I asked Leezie.

"That I needs a haircut and my elbows washed, and wanted to know if my boots were too big for me."

I breathed a sigh of relief, figuring we had just carried off our biggest caper ever. That is, until I came home from school the following Thursday, only to be met at the door by my mother. How she found out I don't know. It only took a moment for me to sense something had gone terribly wrong, for there was a livid frost covering her eyes. She didn't tiptoe around what put it there, either.

"I've never been this humiliated in my life," she blurted. "How dare you scandalize this holy parish with your sacrilege."

I didn't dare ask what she meant or feign innocence. I had never seen her so angry. She didn't become coherent until almost bedtime, and then only long enough to outline my future. That contained one major pronouncement: I was going away after eighth grade to a Catholic high school.

"And there," she said, starting to shake again, "maybe they can teach you respect for holy things."

I breathed a sigh of relief when she left, since that was four years off. By then she would surely forget, I hoped. My biggest fear had been that she would tell Father Goldsworthy. He, incidentally, never did find out.

Ironically, Leezie's one experience was enough, and he never again pestered me about being an altar boy. He had a strong inclination toward spiritual matters, but going to the same church I did wasn't going to provide the answers he sought.

After a month my mom settled down, and I started to breathe easier. I had been on my best behavior. The first week of November I brought home one of Father Goldsworthy's prizes for best catechism memorization. The holy card, picturing Pope Pius XI, brought a smile to her face, and she hugged me, saying, "I'm very proud of you," followed by, "no more foolishness."

Thankfully, the last memorable event of the year didn't fit the category of misdeeds. I was still ten years old, though, as this happened the day before my birthday.

It was bitterly cold out, a precursor to another long winter. I could barely understand what Leezie was saying through his chattering teeth. We were headed back up the hill to make another run with our ice dolly.

"Pu-pu-PUSH!" He said, straining against the front of our contrivance, specially suited for the conditions. Bub, who loved the snow, added a growl to emphasize the need for greater effort.

The ice dolly was a heavy handcart my dad used for moving equally heavy things around the hardware store. The hill, sheathed in ice and covered by snow, was a service road that ran to the back of the school. Due to its weight, the dolly, with her big iron wheels locked with a stick, would slide on the ice and attain remarkable speeds before she hit the huge snow bank at the bottom. It was tricky, but so far the three of us had managed to bail off the speeding monster just ahead of the crash. Bub would land feet first and then start barking for another ride. Getting the ice dolly back up the hill, however, was another problem.

"Push," Leezie said louder. "We is just about there."

I grunted, slipped, and grunted again. Just as we gave one final heave, Leezie's feet went out from under him. He cracked his chin on the front support and let out a wail that attracted attention from the janitor burning trash behind the gym.

"Leezie! Are you okay?" I shouted, bending down to see if he was hurt. He moaned and pulled a bloody hand away from his face. I felt suddenly queasy, close to what I imagined Petey Gorman must have felt just before he threw one of his fits.

"I bit my lip," he said. "An' it hurts."

"Whaddayamean?" I shouted back.

He got to his knees and spit out a huge mouthful of blood. I didn't know what to do or what to say. It was the first time anything bad had ever happened to one of us.

"Don't cry, don't cry," I stammered, panicked by the red puddle in the snow, not knowing it was me doing the crying.

He looked up, and I could see more blood running down his chin. Bub had a grip on my pant leg, growling in a furious effort to get me to do something.

Luckily, the alert janitor arrived, and after several remarks about stupid kids, got Leezie to his feet. I helped the man, who had to have the biggest beer belly in town, walk Leezie to the school.

"Hurry," the janitor kept gasping. "And quit your goldarned blubbering."

Leezie remained stoic, but my mother later excused my behavior on the grounds that he was in a state of shock. Our itinerant doctor was in town on his twice-monthly visit and stitched the nasty gash just below Leezie's lip.

"You're a lucky young man," Doc Able remarked. "Lucky you didn't break your jaw."

As it were, Leezie had bitten completely through the soft tissue below his lip, imprinting perfect impressions of two upper teeth in the flesh. The scar would be permanent, and he would wear it all his life as a proud reminder of our childhood.

He was too sore to attend my eleventh birthday party the next afternoon. In addition, the doctor's regimen of rinsing his mouth with salt water every hour kept him confined.

When Leezie whined about it, Doc Able chided him. "Do you want to get blood poisoning?"

That summer Leezie had carved several willow whistles, a talent I could never master. His dad brought me one, with a note from Leezie, which read: "*Happie Burthday frum L.S.*"

I didn't know it at the time, of course, but our childhood, which started with a molasses cookie and ended with one last ride on the ice dolly, was over. Before I knew it we had survived the next two years of school. In sixth grade we had Miss Fanny for a teacher, with her constant admonitions to Leezie that there was no such word as *thunk*.

Chapter Eleven

Miss Fanny was a carbon copy of Sister Evangelica in temperament, but the opposite in stature. Tall and gaunt, she ruled the classroom with a long wooden ruler. She started off the year trying to call Leezie by his real name, Eleazor, but the snickers it aroused were more than she could snuff out with a smack on the back of a hand.

That didn't endear Leezie to her, and he spent a lot of time writing on the blackboard. I'm sure he baited her with his mispronunciation of "*think*," and we lost count of the number of times he had to respond when she said, "You get right up here, Leezie Smith, and write on the blackboard, *it's think, not thunk*."

She had a sick spell toward the end of that year, and Leezie was too quick to forgive, I thought. He chopped wood for her and ran errands. In retrospect, it probably had more to do with him passing and being promoted to seventh grade. His grades were borderline, and she could have held him back, but didn't.

My mother's threat continued to hang over me, but seemed to ride the waves of my religious seriousness. I lived in mortal fear that I would do something to displease Father Goldsworthy and she would learn of it. I worked hard to earn her trust after the altar boy deception, and as the end of the year approached I was more confident she would change her mind about sending me away to school. Alas, for all my efforts, it was an innocent game of marbles that spelled my doom.

Marbles required finesse and a strong thumb, neither of which I had. Leezie was good, but Abner Pong possessed all of the above, plus a killer instinct to win. We seldom let him play, but one day in the spring of our eighth-grade year, he talked us into it, saying, "I'll shoot left-handed."

We forgot that Abner was a switch hitter in baseball, batting equally well from either side of the plate. He didn't like team sports, especially football and basketball. My guess is he didn't like to fail. He was a runner, and track is the sport he excelled in, and did so beyond belief.

The playing field for marbles was a crude circle scratched in the dirt, six feet in diameter. Each of us, five in all, dropped our marbles randomly inside the circle. Believe me when I say that with the scarcity of money, each boy remembered which marbles were his.

We drew straws and play commenced. Each of us had a shooter marble. It could be a special one, even slightly larger, but for most of us, we simply used our favorite. If you knocked an opponent's marble out of the circle, you got to keep it.

I went first that day. I lodged my shooter between the thumb and first finger, squinted at a likely target, let go, and didn't hit a thing. Leezie did much better and in two quick shots added three marbles to his collection, getting two with one shot.

Abner sneered and hunched down, a picture of perfect concentration. Twenty shots later he finally missed. Petey Gorman managed to hit one out before it was Leezie's turn again, and he got two. On his last try his shooter hit a pebble and spun off to the far end of the circle.

Abner smirked, saying, "Youse guys play like babies."

Nonchalantly he shot the rest of the marbles out. He started to pick up his winnings only to be interrupted by Petey, jabbering and hopping from one foot to the other. Finally, the rest of us caught on to what he was saying.

"Abner's shooter still in de circle!"

Sure enough, it was, resting just inside the line. That was a possible disaster for Abner. It had been caused no doubt by his showing off and forgetting to put the right spin on his shooter, so it too left the circle.

Leezie's shooter was still in the ring, meaning he had another play. The rules of the game stated that if he could knock Abner's shooter out, Abner would have to forfeit all his winnings, with the loot going to Leezie.

"It's the rule, Pong," Leezie said when Abner attempted to brazen his way out of his mistake.

He blustered, but knowing he couldn't intimidate Leezie, tried another tactic. He challenged him to a bet.

"Ca-mon Smith, sweet the pot for ole Ponger," he whined.

Leezie shook his head and pushed him aside.

"How much you want to bet," I spoke up?

He reached into his pocket and hauled out a nickel.

"This much, Mew-Mew," he snarled. "You got the guts to risk that much of yer rich pappy's money? Or is you Catlickers 'fraid to?"

"Dewit, Mew," Petey chanted, "dewit, dewit." I swallowed hard, revving up my courage, and decided I would.

Leezie bent down, looking at an impossible shot. He was a good six feet away. The dirt surface was rough and littered with tiny ridges and stones.

"No brushing the ground," Abner reminded him.

Petey – I was shocked by his bravery – admonished Abner, insisting he put his winnings in a pile to be guarded by the rest of us until the matter was settled.

"Babies," Abner grumbled. But he complied.

The shot Leezie took was remarkable. We watched his thumb tighten and his eye line up with his target. We were all tense.

Leezie made a perfect arching shot. Leezie's shooter, his pride and joy, was cobalt blue and sparkled in the sunshine as it rose above the ground a good six inches. We held our breath as it began its descent. *Plink!* It hit Abner's a glancing blow. But it was enough to propel it outside the ring.

Abner was furious, but didn't have a choice but to forfeit the marbles he'd won. He started to walk away but I grabbed his shoulder.

"Don't forget my nickel, Pong," I said.

"Stupid Catlickers," he said, but forked it over. I winked at Petey and scowled at Abner, almighty proud of myself.

My conquest was short-lived when Abner wheeled and slugged me hard in the stomach.

"Oomph!" I gasped as all the air left my lungs.

Leezie was on him in a second, and before I got my breath back, had wrestled him to the ground. Not, however, before Abner clipped him with a right that put a bruise on his cheek.

"Say it, Frog Face!" Leezie shouted. "Say it!"

Clamped tight, Abner squirmed.

"It's time to say *uncle*," Leezie sang. "Come on mister Turkey Breath, say it."

Abner didn't have much choice. Leezie outweighed him by forty pounds and had him pinned with both knees sunk deep in his armpits. "Uncle!" Abner screeched. Leezie let him go and we watched him sulk off.

I never said a word about my wager, but someone told my mother the whole story. Mom had a phobia about gambling. Her dad had squandered the family's livelihood betting on the horses, finally ending up in jail for trying to fix a race. I won't go into her half-hour lecture on the evils of betting, only the conclusion.

"And now I catch you gambling!" she said with a shocked grimace. "I just don't know what I'm going to do with you."

What she did was carry out her threat. Early that summer, long enough after our eighth-grade graduation so as to not raise too many eyebrows, she put me on the train. I went to live in the city with my Aunt Bertha.

She let me have a whispered goodbye with Leezie that morning at the depot.

"Here," he said reaching into his pocket. "Something to remember our good times with."

He handed me his cobalt blue shooter. I took it and must have looked like I was going to cry because Leezie said, "Don't cry, Mew; I can't stand it when you do's that. You'd a-thunk you was never coming back."

In turn I gave him the gift I'd smuggled out without my mother seeing. I bent down and rubbed Bub's ear, thinking he had such a sad expression. He stuck out his paw and I shook it. Turning to leave, I suddenly remembered something.

I hollered over my shoulder, "And it's think, not *thunk*, just like Miss Fanny tried to teach you."

"I just wanted to rattle your pea brain," he shouted after me.

Leezie just stood there as the train jerked several times and then started to move, a bewildered look on his face. He raised a hand, feebly it seemed to me, and waved goodbye.

The quiet after the train's departure settled on the platform, but Leezie continued to stand there. He blinked when it appeared to fall off the face of the earth where the railroad tracks dropped into a deep gorge north of town, but saw the black smoke pouring from old Number 87's stack as she came out the other side. The smoke soon vanished on the morning breeze. Several minutes passed before his gaze wavered and he noticed his dad watching from the shade of the depot.

"See what Mew give me, Pop?" Leezie said, tossing him a baseball. "His brand new A. J. Reach."

John Smith caught it. "I hope you plan to use it," he said.

Leezie shrugged his shoulders, saying, "Why'd she have to do it, Pop?"

His dad started to speak, but Leezie went on: "Mew will be like a orphan up there in that place," he said, sweeping a hand in the direction he's last seen the smoke. "An' you knows Mew ain't one to make friends easy. Who's to stick up for him? He aren't worth a hoot in a wrasslin' match. I tried to learn him how to box but he can't think and fight at the same time. Why'd she have to go an' do that?"

"Catch!" his dad said, tossing the ball back. "Who knows what notion got into Mary's bonnet, but Mew will be alright. I can promise you that."

"You sure, Pop?"

"As sure as I think I smell breakfast cookin' upstairs."

Chapter Twelve

Leezie felt like he'd been kicked in the gut. He sank into a deep depression. Outwardly, few noticed. The exceptions were his mom and dad, Sam Moosington and Petey Gorman. John Smith watched him spend hours leaning against the corner of the depot, tossing the baseball Mew had left him from one hand to the other. When he tired of that, he'd kneel down and pet Bub, who never strayed far from his side.

"He worries me some, Hillie," John confided to his wife.

"He's so heartsick, I know," she replied. "It's almost like we had a death in the family."

That wasn't entirely true. Leezie spent as much time worrying over his friend as he did nursing the hurt inside. The pain was deep; he knew that. Ironically, Sam Moosington would be the one who found a way to alleviate some of it, and get him back on an even keel. That was later, though. In the meantime, almost a week passed before Leezie did something on his own.

One afternoon he got up the courage to visit their secret hideaway. He found the key to the treasure box, hesitated a moment and then worked it in the lock. He took out the Baltimore Catechism, laying it aside. In its place he put the A. J. Reach baseball.

"It don't feel right to play without him, Bub," he said, giving the dog a pat on the head. "I'll just leave it here." He took the baseball out again, rubbed it down and made several imaginary throws. Bub growled, probably prompted by the far-off look in Leezie's eyes.

He put it back and locked the lid, thought a moment, and decided to keep the key. Taking a piece of paper, he wrote down the exact measurements of the box. He put that in the same pocket with the key.

"I'll give this back to Father Goldsworthy," he told Bub as he picked up the catechism. Riffling the pages, he said, "This here is a whole book of tellin's, Bub. Tellin' you this an' tellin' you that. It don't even talk about mutts like you."

He smiled. Bub's tail thumped and he stuck out his paw. Leezie shook it.

"Lots of tellin's," he went on. "An' lots of nays..." His voice trailed off, but picked up again.

"You ever wunner about the teller behind this here book, Bub? I don't guess you would," he grinned. "You's just a dog. But I wunners about it lots. I think I likes you better than this here, Mr. Teller person." He patted Bub's nose with the catechism. "He talks too much, and ain't too nice in the stuff he says."

That was lofty thinking for a boy his age. It was typical, though, and not much different than conversations he'd had with Mew. Stuffing the catechism in a back pocket, he put the box back in its place.

"Can you loan me some scraps?" he said the next morning to Thor Johnson. Thor ran a handyman's shop and dabbled in cabinet making.

"What for?"

"Wanna make me a box," Leezie answered. "Kin you help me?"

"Guess so," Thor said. "But you have to help me load Cleo Todd's cupboard that I built."

Thor wasn't busy that day and they set to work. Johnson didn't pry into the purpose, but noticed Leezie was being unusually particular about how it went together. As he cut the boards, Leezie hammered them together.

"They has to fit tight, Mr. Johnson," Leezie said, "I can't get this one right."

Thor took his plane, scraped off some rough edges and handed it back with a laconic, "Try this."

When they finished, Thor made him leave the box in the shop. "It's my way of makin' sure you show up an' help me load the cabinet," he said.

As it turned out, Leezie had to wait two more days to get back to the hideaway. A railroad inspector was in town doing his monthly snooping. Finally, he was able to retrieve the treasure box. He took the baseball out, hesitated a moment, but put it back. He reached into his pocket and took out a note he'd written, and placed it in the box.

He had struggled composing what it said, and took great pains to print it neatly. It read: *"You has to keep watch over this until I comes back for it."* He put the treasure box inside the one Thor had helped him build and nailed the lid on tight.

It took him another three days to paint on a thick coat of tar, waiting between each application for it to set well. When he was satisfied his waterproofing would withstand the next biblical flood, he wrapped the tarred box in a gunnysack.

He knew of only one place in the world that could be counted on to remain undisturbed. That's how the sealed treasure box came to its resting place for the next half-century, buried next to Betsy's headstone at the cemetery.

"I feels better now, Bub," he told his dog. "In case he don't come back, me and Mew's box will be safe here."

Sam Moosington later said it was spur-of-the-moment inspiration. He too had watched Leezie wrestle with the loss of his best friend.

"It's funny he doesn't mope more about it," he told the one-armed depot agent. "I suppose he does, though, on the inside, and that pesters me."

That kind of worry was on Sam's mind on a morning he looked up and was surprised to see Leezie walk into the hardware store.

"You've got that serious look about you, Leezie," he said, ambling over to where Leezie was examining a stack of Big Chief pencil tablets.

"Why would you need a tablet? School's out for the summer," he chuckled. "Or didn't you hear that?"

"Ain't school I was thinking of," Leezie said, returning Sam's grin.

"It was right there," Sam later confided to John Smith. "That providence hit me with a two-ton idea."

Sam had broached it to Leezie this way. "I saw those eighth-grade races the last day of school. How come you let Abner beat you like that?"

"Let him?" Leezie snorted, "Abner's faster than a double streak of lightning, that's why."

"And you're not?" Sam said.

"I juss can't never catch him." Then Leezie smiled, saying, "Mew always telled me it's cuz I'm too fat."

Sam reached out and pinched the roll around Leezie's tummy. Pudgy maybe, but I wouldn't say you're fat.

"Plump, I calls it," Leezie said, patting his belly.

"What would happen if Abner were the one chasing you," Sam said, "instead of the other way around?" Leezie gave him questioning look. "Come on over here, I want you to look at something."

Leezie followed and appeared even more puzzled when they stopped where various shoes were displayed. "Heft this," Sam said, picking one from a box.

"It's heavy," Leezie said. "What are it?"

"Runners use those to practice in," Sam told him. "It has lead shot sewn in the lining. The extra weight builds up your muscles. I saw them at a market in Seattle last year, and bought a pair."

"You would a thought a big searchlight suddenly came on in the store," Sam later told John.

"He got the idea, did he?"

"More than that," Sam said. "He made it his own."

John frowned.

"I could hear those little wheels turning in his head, and they made quite a clatter, I can tell you that," Sam added.

"I don't got the money to buy even a plain set of shoes," Leezie had complained.

"Try them on anyway," Sam told him.

Leezie hesitated, but then a gleam came into his eye and he sat quickly on a bench, unlacing his boots.

"It's a perfect fit," Sam said a moment later, running a professional hand over the arch and toes.

"My legs always give out at the end of the hundred," Leezie told him. He was so excited that Sam had to have him repeat what he said next. "That's when Abner leaves me in the dust."

Five minutes passed and they struck a deal.

"Two weeks' work, three hours a day," Sam said. "Are we straight on that?"

Leezie gave him a quick yes.

"And you don't get paid until the work is done."

Another yes, this time faster.

"An' you'll throw in one of them double Big Chiefs?" Leezie said.

Sam nodded, smiling inwardly at the boy's ingenuity to wrangle something else in the bargain.

The hardware was a diverse business. Leezie cleaned windows and hauled trash. The hardest was turning the grinding wheel while the blacksmith sharpened plowshares. Counting nails into bags of fifty was easy by comparison.

"I never knowed you had so many nails," he told Sam one morning. "It makes my head swim doin' all this numberin.'"

At the end of two weeks, he walked away with his shoes and an extra thick version of a Big Chief pencil tablet.

"Here," Sam said. "Don't forget this," handing him a pencil embossed with the hardware's name and address.

That evening Leezie started his quest to beat Abner Pong in the hundred-yard dash. He didn't have a coach but had an innate sense of what he should do. He measured out a hundred-yard course in a pasture on the edge of town. Every day for two hours he ran mock races, chanting aloud the sequence of, *"ready, set, go."* Somehow he knew that was important. He tried to gage the rhythm and would then launch himself from the starter's position, eating up every yard as fast as he could go.

Once each week, Sam Moosington would appear. "Just checking up on you," he'd say. Then a small memo book would come out of his shirt pocket. Sam would turn to a tally page at the back, saying, "Think you can beat last week's time?"

"Maybe, if you don't flub the ready, set, go," Leezie snorted with fake indignation. The first time Sam had gotten it wrong, shortening the sequence to, "*ready, go.*"

Petey Gorman was Leezie's only confidant in this endeavor. On each visit, Sam stationed him at the finish line to raise an arm when Leezie broke the imaginary tape. Sam then noted the sweep hand of his watch and marked down his time. It would be nearly a year before they could honestly say he had improved, since his watch only measured in full seconds.

Each week Sam left thinking the same thing: "*I've never seen a boy so earnest about anything.*" He missed his own son terribly, even though they visited him and Aunt Bertha often. This was different, though. Working with Leezie filled him with pride and good feeling.

The training regimen didn't end at the hundred-yard course. Each night, shortly after supper, Leezie put on his boots. With Bub setting the pace, he would run to the cemetery and try to sprint to the top of Meadowlark Ridge.

After his long run, he would write in the Big Chief Tablet. He wrote letters to his friend, Mew. He never mailed them or even tore them from the tablet. His first attempts were stilted and self-conscious. Homespun therapy they were at the beginning, but he quickly learned to express himself through the written word. His first, composed in the summer of 1929, is still quite juvenile.

Deer Mew!!!
How are you? I am good, so is Bub. I miss you. So duz Bub. I been running. Old Abner better watch out.
Yor buddy... L. S.

He did write Mew real letters, often copying excerpts from those in the Big Chief Tablet. This tablet and several future companions were reserved for a special purpose. They would chronicle nearly fifty-five years of a friendship that few are privileged to know.

Chapter Thirteen

I got the wishbone from are Christmus goose today an' wished you was home. I'd let you practice with my new telegraph key. Pop is learning me to send code. (dash dash) (dot) (dot dash dash) That's how to spell Mew. I thunk I wazan't sad no more 'til Christmus come. Member last year when we ice skated all day an' Bub stole the lunch yor mom fixed???? Duz you ever feel sad??? I brung in wood for old Missus Melody an' she give me a penny an' a cookie. The next day she died of a bellyache. I give Bub half the cookie but we didn't git sick. Yor buddie, (dot dash dot) Smith.

If you leave out the dot-dashes, Mary Moosington would probably have echoed Leezie's melancholy that Christmas night. She and Sam were spending the holiday with her sister, Mew's Aunt Bertha. The news of Abigail Melody's death came two days before Christmas, and rattled her.

She looked across the room in Mew's direction, marveling at how he'd grown the past six months. *"He's not had an unhappy moment since he got here,"* she thought. *"Just look at him, he's so self-satisfied."*

She really meant that Mew was growing conceited. It alarmed her because she knew the cause was the pampering and money Aunt Bertha had lavished on him. Childless, Bertha and her husband, Horace, were fabulously wealthy. They had insisted the boy attend not just any Catholic boarding school, but an exclusive one. It was part of the agreement when Mew went to live with them.

Sam was the first to notice the difference, saying, "If I didn't know better, I'd say Mew is taking on snooty airs."

"*It doesn't matter,*" Mary consoled herself. "*The die is cast and Mew is getting the Catholic education he needs.*"

Sam had sold the hardware store in October. While in the city they planned to find a place to live until Mew graduated. The move wouldn't be permanent until Sam's commitment to the store's new owner was over, possibly in a year, maybe more.

Mary tended to be future-focused and sat back, thinking about what kind of bonnet to buy for Easter. Then she recalled the sudden passing of Mrs. Melody. "*I must remember to pray often for a peaceful death,*" she thought, echoing her Catholic obsession with dying.

"I never once thought about that," she confessed to Sam later in the spring.

Mary almost died in the middle of March. Had it not been for Leezie, she probably would have. Sam was away on a buying trip and by the time he arrived home, the emergency had passed.

It took several weeks for Mary to recuperate. Pneumonia was the culprit. Half the town was either down with it or some other sickness brought on by a cold and damp spring.

Leezie's mother, Hildred, nursed Mary for five days, through one escalating crisis after the other. It was the bitterest of pills for Mary to swallow. She had always stopped short of saying she hated Hildred because John was a Mason, but made her dislike known.

"I must have been in a delirium," she said, "because all I remember is her sweet voice singing to me."

Sam would look up from his paper each time she retold this tale, smiling, nodding for her to go on. Mary could never make it through the next part without crying.

"If I live to be a hundred, Sam," she'd say, "I will never be able to make amends for the way I treated her. She is the kindest, most Christian woman I know. And to be reminded that I ever thought otherwise – it's just too abhorrent for me to think about."

"Don't forget Leezie," Sam would remind her.

Neither of them fully understood Leezie's role, nor would he ever tell them. It began with an ominous feeling Leezie had that morning when he first got out of bed. It continued to nag him at school. He tried to concentrate on his work, but putting the heaviness out of his mind simply didn't work. He skipped baseball practice and went home to get his dog. Then he started making the rounds of acquaintances."

I wunner what it is," he said to Bub, "this feeling I gots."

Petey Gorman wasn't in school so he checked on him first. He was okay, recovering from a bad seizure. Next, he looked in on two old women he ran errands for. He checked on Blinky's mother-in-law, who had a bad heart, but nothing was amiss with any of them. Then he went to see Abner Pong, who was supposed to be sick. Abner made him listen to a new dirty joke he'd heard.

"He must be alright, Bub," Leezie said, "at least he don't seem no different."

The bad feeling grew with each place he went. "Maybe that's it Bub," he said, when a sudden thought hit him. He rushed across town to see the old man who had taught him how to make willow whistles. Pete Peterson, however, was fine, sitting in a chair playing his violin.

Dejected and puzzled, he decided to go home. Bub grabbed a stick and they wandered, guided more by where that landed than by following a beaten path. Normally, Leezie didn't take the route past Mew's house anymore, but he soon found himself in front of St. Bart's Church. He gave the stick another heave and it landed on the lawn of Sam and Mary's place across the street. Bub got distracted, and Leezie went to get him. He reached the sidewalk and suddenly stopped. The feeling hit him again. His heart raced and what breath he could take came in little short gasps. He looked up. Shivering, he thought, *"there's no smoke coming out the chimney."*

He found Mary semi-conscious and incoherent on the floor of the sitting room. The inside of the house was freezing, but when he touched her he jerked his hand back. She was burning with fever. Panicky, he shouted, "Bub, go fetch Mom!"

Bub pranced on his front feet but didn't move.

"Bub!" Leezie said sternly. "Go git mom!"

The dog skittered across the kitchen floor and disappeared out the door.

"Yes," Mary said to Sam, dabbing at several tears. "Doc Able said I was probably on the verge of going into convulsions. I thought Leezie was an angel that had come to rescue me and I'm not so sure he wasn't!"

"I tried to pay Leezie something for all the work he did around the place," Sam later told John. "But he wouldn't take a penny."

John just smiled.

"In fact, he gave me the most put-upon look I ever saw."

For his part, Leezie tried several different ways to explore the experience in his Big Chief tablet.

Father Goldzworthy come bye and give Mary the extra munction. (Leezie'a rendition of "Extreme Unction," the Church's sacrament for the dying.) *I knowed she weren't dying, cuz sumbody warned me to go find her. Why would Mr. Teller go to all that trouble if he didn't mean Mary to keep alive????? Father Goldzworthy said she were dying, and the extra munction sacrermunt was to git her into heaven.*

Spring did arrive shortly after this incident, bringing with it another peculiarity. Leezie quit the baseball team.

"I'm starting to worry about him, John," Hildred revealed to her husband. "He's changed so much in the last year."

"Most of it for the better," John replied.

"But he doesn't have any friends, save Petey Gorman."

John was thinking of several old widows that Leezie did chores for, and the way he continued to look after Mary when Sam was out of town.

"He's happy, Hilly, you have to admit that."

Hildred nodded and then laughed, recalling Leezie's smile from the night before. Cantankerous old Mrs. Lollyford had put it there with her constant chirping about all the racket he made chopping wood in her backyard.

"I just told her, Mom, I couldn't help it if I forgot to bring my rubber axe."

"I wish he would grow some," Hildred went on. "Mary told me that Mew has shot up five inches."

John started to interrupt only to hear, "All he does is run, run, run. Why, that alone should make him a little less plump."

It was John's turn to laugh, and he said, "I think that has more to do with his mother's cooking."

Changing the subject, she asked, "Is Mew coming home this summer?"

"Not according to Sam," John answered.

"You're not going to tell him, are you?"

"I already did," John answered.

The news upset Leezie more than either of them knew. At the same moment he was on Meadowlark Ridge watching the sunset. Glum, he said, "Why can't Mew come home, Mr. Teller?" *Mr. Teller* was part of his vocabulary now. He used it in place of *God*, ever since the day under the depot platform when he'd discussed the Baltimore Catechism with Bub, asking the dog, *"You ever wunner about the teller behind this here book, Bub?"*

Leezie repeated his question. "Why can't he, Mr. Teller?"

Unexpected, a thought flashed across his mind. *"Don't believe everything you hear."*

"Di-di-di-did you hear that, Bub?" he stuttered, jumping to his feet. "Mr. Teller says Mew might be coming home anyways."

Mr. Teller was part of his makeshift therapy, but had suddenly thrown him a curve. Quickly, he changed his mind.

"I takes that back, Bub," he said. "He really didn't say nuthin'. I juss thunk he did."

Still, throughout the coming months he remembered. Each time he heard news of Mew, hope would collide with the certainty of what couldn't be.

On the first day of September Leezie was sitting atop the water tank, watching for the smoke of old number 87. School wouldn't start for another week, and he was trying to remember where the summer had gone.

He turned philosophical, thinking, *"Gee whiz, I'll be fourteen this year. By then it'll be a year and a half since I seen Mew."* He started making plans, which included asking Coach LeRoy about being manager of the basketball team. Slowly, after several nods, he fell asleep.

"Leezie! Leezie!" He heard his dad shouting. He thought he was dreaming. It came again. "Leezie! Leezie!" This time he jerked awake and looking up to see John Smith running down the tracks toward him. He was waving something in his hand.

Quickly, he climbed the ladder to the ground and raced toward his dad, sure that something dire had happened.

"Leezie!" John panted when they met at the pump house. "Mew's on his way home!"

Leezie was too startled to take it in, and John shoved a telegram into his hand, saying, "Here, read this."

It read: *"Mom and Dad. I have to come home. The boilers at school broke down."* It was signed, *"Mew."*

"When, Pop? When?" Leezie asked, his heart racing.

"He'll be on the next train," John answered. "Didn't you see her smoke from up there?"

Chapter Fourteen

The echoes from the great financial crash of 1929 reached the ears of all, but one note – the lonely wail of the train whistle – continued to offer a measure of normalcy. When Engine 87 blew for the crossing north of town, people checked their watches, noting the time – eight minutes past eleven. A fifth passenger car had been added the day she brought Mew home.

An hour after Mew had stepped off the train, an expedited freight rumbled though town without stopping. John Smith's telegraph key rattled, alerting the next three stations down the line. More trains meant more work, but as he had confided to Sam Moosington, "I'd give my other arm just to keep this job."

Late that same afternoon, a local freight train stopped at the depot. Several large crates were unloaded from a flat car. John secured them under a tarp. They remained there overnight.

The next morning, Leezie watched from his upstairs perch as a dilapidated truck backed up to the platform. Three men got out. Two were workers, and the other obviously a preacher of some sort.

"It has to be him," Leezie thought. "I seen him last year."

The workmen shifted the containers to the ancient Ford's flat bed. *Careful*! Leezie read the parson's lips before a final grunt hoisted the last crate aboard. They all got back in the cab. Leezie smiled, knowing full well their destination.

"Jiminy crickets, Bub!" he exclaimed, giving the dog several excited pats. "The holy rollers is back in town!"

Mew didn't react when Leezie told him the news. He was still getting over the culture shock of being home.

"We oughtta go listen to them holy rollers at that revival meetin,'" Leezie said. He got no response.

Instead, he heard Mew say, "Uncle Horace lets me drive his Stutz Bearcat."

Leezie didn't seem impressed, so he added, "She's a hundred fifty-five horsepower supercharged straight eight."

For a boy who used foot power for transportation, the Stutz was beyond comprehension. *"He sure acts different,"* Leezie thought. *"Looks funny too."*

Leezie remembered watching Mew get off the train the day before. *"Swaggers,"* he thought, *"and look at them britches!"*

Aunt Bertha had picked the bell-bottomed pants out for Mew, and would have been offended at Leezie's description. *"Mew looks like he's walkin' around in two flour sacks."* Mew thought the blue-grey flannel matched his carefully slicked-back hair. Smiling, he had looked down, sure that he could see that oily reflection in his shiny black shoes.

"A Stutz," Leezie said, trying to act informed. "Honest?"

Mew wagged his head even though that experience had been the one time Uncle Horace let him help steer from the passenger seat. "She's a real beaut, Leezie," he said.

From his arrival in the city, Mew had never been homesick and never suffered from the separation the way Leezie had. His days were filled with too many exciting and expensive things to do. He was popular in school, not realizing that being the nephew of a rich philanthropist like Horace Weathersome would demand his acceptance.

The broken boiler at school, however, turned out to be a rude awakening that he didn't always get his own way with his Uncle.

"I can just stay here at the mansion," he'd informed Uncle Horace.

His aunt and uncle were leaving on a long-planned trip to Europe, and renovators would start a major remodel the day after.

Sadly, Horace had shaken his head, decreeing, "You must go home, little nephew."

Mew protested, but Uncle Horace put his foot down.

"Aunt Bertha and I agree. It would be less bothersome, or should I say, less worrisome?"

Mew pouted and Horace patted him on the back, saying, "It's for the best."

Leezie interrupted his thoughts, saying, "Abner is workin' on Mr. Barkum's hog farm."

"Huh?" Mew responded.

"The revival meetin,'" Leezie reminded him.

"I ain't scared of Abner," Mew shot back, lapsing into the local vernacular that the Jesuits had pounded out of him.

"You ain't chicken no more?"

Memories of yesteryear flooded Mew's mind. *"I wonder what I'd do if he really dared me,"* he thought.

"I ain't," he said.

"Ain't what?"

"Ain't chicken."

"Are too," Leezie insisted.

Finally, the age-old chicken argument made them laugh. But Mew was backed into a corner and he knew it. The façade of his audacious demeanor and the fashion show he'd purposely contrived for his arrival were wearing thin.

"Alright," he said boldly. "But just to shut you up so you never ask me again."

"What have I done?" Mew thought, and blamed Uncle Horace once more for making him come home. Yesterday he had been completely unprepared for the shock he experienced getting off the train.

First was his mom's friendliness with Mrs. Smith.

"Oh Hildred, just look at him," Mary gushed. "See, I told you he had grown."

Mary had put her arm around Hildred and hugged her proudly.

"You stay away from those Smiths," he remembered her words almost exactly. *"They're trash and black against Catholics."*

Aunt Bertha had shielded him and hadn't revealed just how sick his mother had been. As a result, Mew had no idea what happened to make his mom's worst enemy her best friend.

Next he heard a dog barking and looked up to see Bub racing toward him. Instinctively, he dropped to one knee and braced himself. Bub nearly bowled him over, and seconds later found Mew's arms around the dog. Bub's tongue found his face, but Mew didn't care. He held his old friend tight, noticing only that the lump in his throat was growing.

Last, after he stood up, he spotted Leezie.

"You've just grown up, and he hasn't," he recalled Uncle Horace's counsel when he'd shown him one of Leezie's letters. "You can't help it, Mew, if he only speaks about juvenile things."

"Sophisticated" is another word Horace used to point out what he termed *"your different stations in life."*

Leezie's smile, wide enough to cross a creek on, caught him off guard. The scar on his lip that Mew remembered so well melted any stuffiness that remained, and Uncle Horace's wisdom vanished. They hugged each other, as you would have supposed.

"Why did my mom kiss you on the cheek at the depot?" Mew asked, coming out of his brief reverie.

"I dunno," Leezie answered. "I guess she likes me."

Try as he might, that was all Mew could pry out of him.

The rest of the week passed in a blur. Old Cobber came out of retirement, and the sounds of all-day baseball games echoed off the diamond at the edge of town. Mew reverted to being Leezie's self-appointed track coach, and they spent hours running mock races. The desire to beat Abner in the hundred-yard dash had always been mutual. Mew adopted the training regimen and idea like it had been his own.

In the beginning, however, he balked at the heavy running shoes.

"They already made me faster," Leezie told him.

Mew wrinkled his brow in a professional frown.

"Don't believe me, do you?" Leezie said with a big grin. "Just you watch then."

The first time Leezie exploded from the starting line, Mew lost his skepticism.

"Wow!" he exclaimed to Bub. "I ain't never seen him run like that."

He was so excited he could barely contain himself. The rest of the week he kept up a constant chatter of encouragement.

"You can beat him, Leezie," and, "work harder, work harder." After one intense session where Leezie ran twenty dashes in a row, Mew said, "Quit carping about it. You need to lose some of that blubber anyhow."

Leezie laughed. "I already has," he said, clutching the roll around his belly. "You just can't see it yet."

Mew walked part of the way, but always joined Leezie at Meadowlark Ridge to watch the sunset. "Here he comes, Mr. Teller," Leezie would say as Mew panted up the last incline. "Ain't he some sight, Mr. Teller? It's just like it were before he went away."

The revival meeting hadn't come up again. Mew hoped Leezie would either forget about it or be too tired to go. Leezie didn't forget, though. Even after a particularly hard workout Mew put him through on their last day together, Leezie still said to him, "I'll meet you at our old hiding spot and we can sneak into the revival tent."

The revivalists had moved their tent to a field opposite the park. Mew was surprised to find nearly every seat on the rough benches taken, but they were able to find a degree of anonymity in a dark corner near the exit.

Mew was uncomfortable, feeling like a fly at a gathering of swatter salesmen. The preacher was unfamiliar, a last-minute replacement due to a family emergency.

The preacher warmed up the crowd with several lively hymns. Mew marveled that the people sang so happily, not to mention loudly. "*Ain't like chapel service at school*," he thought. Expecting bombast laced with hellfire and damnation, he was surprised at the preacher's gentle manner.

Leezie strained to hear, wishing they had chosen a seat closer to the front. The message was simple and down to earth. Mew found nothing to argue or intellectualize about. Leezie's senses were bombarded, or so it seemed, with words that resonated one moment and confused him the next. His interest flagged until the preacher's voice grew louder, and he held aloft a Bible.

"And who," Leezie heard him say, "And who do you suppose, dear people, is the teller behind the story we read in this book?"

Teller-teller-teller – the familiar words reverberated like rolling thunder in Leezie's soul.

"Is it David, or Mark?" the preacher continued, peering at the crowd to see if anyone would hazard a guess. "Could it be Isaiah or a man even more famous, like John?" Again, no answer came. "It's all of them? Did I hear someone say that?" He paused for effect several moments, scanning the crowd.

"No! dear people," he thundered. No!" His voice faded to a bare whisper. "The teller of this book is none other than God himself."

The words *"God himself"* echoed inside Leezie's head, magnifying each time one eardrum tossed them to the other. Abruptly, the preacher appeared to cut short his sermon. His gaze swept the assembly, making Mew uncomfortable when it stopped an instant in their dark corner. Then, without breaking stride, he offered an invitation for those who wanted to come forward for prayer.

Mew was startled when Leezie jumped to his feet. He stumbled over Bub, who had weaseled his way under a tent flap and parked himself half under the bench. An usher helped steady Leezie and directed him to a short line down a side aisle.

By the time Leezie reached the front several minutes later, the crowd had begun to thin.

"What is it, son?" The preacher asked him. "You don't appear troubled – puzzled maybe?"

"I come to ask about the Mr. Teller you talked about," Leezie told him.

"Now it's my turn to be puzzled," the man said.

Leezie gave him an abbreviated version of the story about his Mr. Teller. He started back where it first began before he buried the treasure box by Betsy's headstone.

"I talks to him sometimes – Mr. Teller, that is," he concluded. When the preacher raised an eyebrow, Leezie elaborated, adding the part when he asked: *"Why can't Mew come home, Mr. Teller?"*

The preacher chuckled. "I thought it might be something like that," he said softly. "It's not often the Holy Ghost stops me in the middle of one of my better sermons. Would you like to meet for real this Mr. Teller of yours?"

"Kin you do that?" Leezie asked, hardly believing his ears.

"No, but I can remind him we're here and ask him to join us."

Leezie nodded, and the preacher laid his hands on his head and prayed quietly.

"Jiminy crickets, his hands are warm," Leezie thought. Bub had wandered unseen to the front and sat motionless beside Leezie, save for an occasional thump of his tail. Leezie didn't notice when the preacher moved quietly to the next person. Something had stirred within him.

The loss of Betsy resurfaced, followed by the past months of misery, loneliness and heartache. The images became stronger. New ones were added, like the ridicule he suffered over his stuttering. *"Your stutters won't save you this time."* Those words, and the scorn on the marshal's face, which he saw again, had hurt more than being punished for stopping the train. Then, like a dying campfire, the images sputtered, flared again, and slowly died out.

Leezie's sudden gulp of air startled Bub. It was a familiar sensation, much like just before a big race, when unprovoked, his nervous system caused a sudden intake of breath. He'd had several experiences of having the wind knocked out of him, but this was the opposite. He finally let the air out, and a deep calm settled over him.

"I was hoping you'd still be here, young man," the preacher said. "I brought you something."

Leezie looked up, not realizing that several minutes had passed.

"What is it?" Leezie asked, reaching out for a slim black book.

"It's the story of your Mr. Teller," he said.

Leezie opened the book and hadn't gone far before stopping. "Gee whiz, I should a already guessed that. Mr. Teller is Jesus, ain't he?"

The preacher sat down. Leezie told him about the great weight that had lifted when the sad memories had disappeared. The preacher explained as best he could what it all meant. They got up, and Leezie looked around, breathing a sigh of relief when he saw Mew waiting, although not too patiently.

The preacher smiled. "Go with Mr. Teller," he said with the warmest smile Leezie had seen since he told Betsy he'd passed first grade.

Leezie snapped a finger, letting Bub know it was time to leave.

"What was that all about?" Mew hissed. "I thought them holy rollers was about to kidnap you."

Leezie laughed, saying, "The preacher said I got borned again."

"Whaddayamean, borned again?" Mew said.

Chapter Fifteen

That night Leezie fought against falling asleep for fear the mood would leave him. He woke up twice, the second time laughing. It reminded him of a time in Miss Fanny's class when he'd started snickering about something and couldn't stop.

Tonight, however, he made no attempt to quell his merriment. He went to sleep, his belly jiggling until deep slumber quieted it.

"Leezie!" he heard his dad say, "Leezie! Are you going to sleep all day?"

His eyes popped open.

"What's so funny," John said.

"Nuttin', just had a funny dream I guess. What time is it?"

"It's almost nine o'clock in the morning," John said. "You'd better hop a jig or two. Mew and Sam will be here before you know it."

It was Sunday. Sam had announced a surprise on Thursday, that today he was taking them to the County Fair. Leezie could count on one hand the number of times he'd been to the county seat, and he had never been to a fair.

Mew was crabby that morning. Not the best day to be ill-prepared for the reemergence of his friend's tomfoolery. Leezie watched Mew make eyes at Mandy Bright. Mandy, once a gangly girl that Mew liked to tease, had grown up.

"Mew!" Leezie whispered.

Mew elbowed him away.

"Psst! Psst!" he tried again.

That got his attention long enough for him to whisper louder, "Mew! You oughta button your pants!"

It got the usual result; only this time Mew's face turned a deeper shade of red. Two seconds later he knew he'd been suckered and the chase, which was not really a chase all, began. Leezie's feet were glued to the ground by his loud snickers, and he had no option but to endure a good-natured pummeling.

For a boy practically born on the railroad tracks, Leezie had seldom ridden the trains that were so much a part of him. Mew got tired of admonishing, "Quit your gawkin'" each time his friend tried to squeeze him out of his window seat. "Them cows will be there on the way home. You can count them then, and multiply by two for all I care. That's if you still remember how."

"You mean like two times two, and four times four?"

Mew nodded, saying, "What's two times twelve?"

Leezie did some quick counting on his fingers, and answered, "Forty-eight."

"See," Mew said. "You don't remember, because it's twenty-four."

"Nope, it ain't," Leezie said. We was talkin' about cows, and cows got four legs. So two cows times twelve cows is forty-eight legs."

The argument that ensued lasted about five minutes, and finally ended when Leezie got in the last, "Does too."

Sam Moosington was taking in the banter. "*I guess I don't need to worry about their friendship,*" he thought. "*Somehow they will find a way to keep it together.*" He smiled, watching Leezie make another try for the window seat. This wasn't the fretful and serious boy he'd known the past months.

Forty minutes later, Sam got up when he heard the train whistle. "There it is boys," he said pointing out the window. The fairgrounds were on the edge of town, and from their vantage point they got a panoramic view of what to expect.

"A Ferris wheel," Leezie exclaimed. "Look at that, Mew!"

The County Fair was small, but the biggest that Leezie could imagine. They jumped off the train before the final screech signaled a stop. Sam didn't try to stop them. He smiled again, watching Leezie run ahead only to turn and admonish Mew for being so slow. This time Leezie took Mew's hand, making him keep up, which was easy, as their laughing and giggling made it hard to run.

"Meet me on the midway at noon," Sam hollered after them.

"I didn't know there was that many kind of rabbits in the world," Leezie said, leaving one of the exhibit barns. A lot full of shiny new Fords captured their attention next, followed by a building full of ducks and geese. The morning went by on fast-forward. They happened upon a baseball game between rivals from neighboring towns, and decided to take a rest.

"It's too bad these guys don't have a bat like Old Cobber," Leezie said after watching two pop flies and four strikeouts.

"Old Cobber?" Mew said. "That's just for us."

They watched, interspersing their chatter with memories from their own exploits on the diamond. Talk about the city and what Mew did there had been avoided by both of them. Leezie decided to bring it up.

"You play baseball at that school of yours?"

"Softball," Mew answered. "We call ourselves The Crusaders. I'm learnin' how to pitch."

"Softball?" Leezie said, incredulous. "Sounds like a sissy game."

"The ball ain't soft, just bigger, and you pitch it underhand."

"Show me how it works," Leezie said, picking up a baseball. When Mew frowned, Leezie said, "Just pitch me some of them underhanded sissy throws."

Mew smiled. He paced off the right distance and after taking off his coat, floated a lob to Leezie.

"Petey Gorman could hit that one faster than Bub treein' a cat," Leezie shouted. "Come on fire one in here."

This time Mew gave him the full windmill motion and the ball hit Leezie's hand with a smack.

"Better," he admitted, licking his stinging fingers. "Now play like you wants to strike out Abner."

It would have been called a *ball* but not by much.

"Youch!" Leezie wailed when Mew put all he had behind it.

Mew watched his friend dance, trying to shake off the pain. "That weren't no sissy toss," he said finally.

Sam Moosington met them at the food stand on the carnival's midway. "You hungry, Leezie?" he asked.

"Naw," he answered. "But I might be able to sample one of them hot doggies."

"Hot dogs were invented by a man at Coney Island," Sam said. "Did you know that, Leezie?" he asked, watching him bury a sausage under a blanket of mustard and onions.

"Mumf-ey-mumf-mumf-ogs?" Leezie answered with half the hot dog in his mouth. A big swallow brought a clarification. "Then how come we don't call them Coney Dogs?"

Mew matched him dog-for-dog until Sam said, "Save room for cotton candy."

"Wow!" Leezie exclaimed. "That beats a whole ton of Milky Way bars." He savored his first experience of the carnival delicacy and asked Sam if he could have another.

Mew winked at his dad.

"I win our bet," he whispered in his ear. Sam frowned. "Remember, dad? I bet you that Leezie never had cotton candy before."

Sam smiled and handed over their wager, a shiny new quarter.

Sam left them with an admonition to be on time for Mew's train. They hadn't gone twenty feet when Mew's stomach lurched at a voice behind them.

"Well if it ain't Mew-Mew," came the familiar snarl. "And his sidekick Fat Lousy. What brings you two homos out in pubic?"

Mew turned and gave Abner Pong a shove. Abner pushed back, and, laughing, said to Leezie, "Heard about you practicing up for the hundred. Won't do you no good. Old Ponger will whip your lard butt anyways."

"Wanna bet?" Mew said.

"On what?" Abner said, breaking into rollicking laughter. "That I finds some nooky afore you does?"

"No, sewer mouth," Mew shot back. "That Leezie beats you in the hundred."

"How much?"

Mew reached in his pocket and brought out a half dollar. Abner's eyes widened. "You know I don't got that kind of money."

They settled on a dime.

"Just remember, No-Chance-Fat-Lousy, to bring a snot rag to wipe your blubbers with."

He did an about-face and started to walk away. Suddenly he turned and shouted over his shoulder to Mew. "An' don't forget to bring this ole poontang getter his dime."

With that he swaggered toward the exit.

"What's poontang?" Leezie asked.

Mew turned red in face, but answered, "Something like nooky, I think."

"They larn you that in school?" Leezie asked.

"No!" He said, stamping his foot. "Doesn't Abner make you mad?"

"Not today," Leezie answered. "Come on, let's go find that freak show."

They did, and soon forgot Abner existed as the sights and sounds of the carnival captured their attention. Leezie had never seen a midget before, or the likes of Tattoo Man, who sported more of them than skin. A small Ferris wheel anchored the carnival's attractions, and they rode it three times. A balky gasoline engine that reminded them both of Gravedigger Bill's old Ford powered it.

The day passed as perfectly as any two boys could have hoped for. Finally, it was time to head for the exit. They walked along with an arm over each other's shoulder, talking excitedly about what they'd seen. Abruptly, Mew stopped.

"Look there," he pointed.

An old man sat on a stool, half asleep, holding a sign that read, "Pictures while you wait 75¢." Mew dug in his pocket and counted out the money he had left, and came up short. He looked to Leezie, who took out his handkerchief and after untying the knot, found four pennies.

"We've only got sixty-eight cents," Mew told the photographer. He grunted and laboriously counted out what Mew dumped in his hand.

"Business is slow," he said. "But I can only give you one picture for that much." They nodded and he said, "Sit down on that bench and don't squirm or move a muscle."

The process seemed to take forever and Mew was starting to fret about his northbound train. Leezie and Sam would board the one for home an hour later. The old man stood behind his ancient camera with a big hood over his head, fiddling and making endless adjustments. Finally, he said, "Smile." They heard a long ca-click.

Next, he worked at a table, this time with a larger hood over everything. They heard clinking and sloshing sounds, and waited and waited. About to give up, they heard him say, "Here you are boys, and not a bad likeness."

They looked at the amazingly clear and only slightly grainy reproduction.

"That's you, Mew," Leezie said. "There ain't no guess to it."

"Do you want a onvelup for it?" The photographer asked. Leezie hesitated and took out his jackknife. Before Mew could stop him, he sliced the picture into two pieces. He took his half and wrote, "*To Mew from your best buddy Leezie – County Fare 1930.*"

"Write on your half," he said, proffering it to Mew. Mew hastily duplicated the sentiment on the back of his picture.

"Kin we have two of them onvelups?" Leezie said, looking up at the old man.

A grumbled about dumb kids not knowing the cost of things, but handed over two wrinkled and badly soiled envelopes. Hurriedly, they stuffed the pictures inside and after exchanging envelopes, raced for the exit.

They barely made it in time for Mew's train. Just before boarding, Mew turned for a last word.

"Leezie, what did you mean last night at the tent meeting?"

"I doesn't know."

That brought an impatient frown to Mew's face.

"All I knows is I feels like Arthur. You remembers Arthur, don't you?"

The train jerked, and Mew's frown grew.

"My pet bird," Leezie said.

Mew smiled and nodded.

"When Arthur's wing healed up and we let him fly away, you is the one that said, *'he's free!'*"

Mew didn't get it.

"Tha-tha-that's hu-hu-how I feels," Leezie stammered.

The train started to move. Mew jumped on the first step and tried to make himself heard above the noise.

He shouted: "Whaddayamean, borned again?"

Leezie shrugged.

Mew would one day joke that it took much longer than expected for him to get a satisfactory answer.

Chapter Sixteen

Leezie and I drifted apart after that. Of course, it didn't help that on Christmas of that same year, my dad, Sam Moosington, announced, "We're moving to Seattle!"

It happened so fast I had no time to think about it. Protest was out of the question, since despite the Great Depression, Dad had landed a plum of a job. He was to be the head of the purchasing department for a new passenger plane that the Boeing Aircraft Company planned to build.

For years, my recollection of Leezie was the one etched by that one perfect day at the county fair. The half of the picture that Leezie had given me gathered dust on a shelf before getting mislaid. After a while it became harder for my mind to bring up the face of a chubby kid, dressed in his best pair of bibbed overalls. Probably because it always disarmed me, I could still see his broad smile. A pittance, when you stop to think about it, but these images were all I had left as reminders of happy times.

I recall little of the actual train ride to Seattle except the giant mountain ranges that barred our way. By the time we arrived, the familiar I'd known for fifteen years, including Leezie, seemed to be a million miles away. It took weeks for me to adjust, and until I did, I felt like a chicken without a hen house.

The Great Depression was not something I noticed or felt, until my dad changed that, and I grew up overnight. My mom made sure I was sheltered from "*those people*" and pampered me almost as bad as Aunt Bertha.

The University of Washington was near where we lived and I became a freshman there in 1934. I didn't adjust well to becoming a small fish in a big pond and it wasn't long before Sam Moosington grew tired of my constant pouting.

The day my life changed started innocently enough. I remember it well. It was a rainy weekend in November. Dad said to me, "I want you to come with me tomorrow."

"But Sam," my mom weakly protested. "Mew will miss church."

"No he won't," dad snapped, adding in a softer tone: "Don't fret, Mary; it's time he saw the gospel instead of just hearing about it."

I looked to my mom, but it was obvious this argument between them had already been settled. Her face had a familiar resolute expression and reminded me of that day long ago when I first learned of my Hebrew ancestry.

The next morning I put on my college blazer and beanie, my best shoes and a starched shirt. Since I was going through a rebellious stage, I didn't wear a necktie.

Dad took one look at me and said, "Find a pair of old shoes, Mew. Boots would be better if you still have them." I must have looked defiant, for he followed with, "You'll thank me later."

I compromised, settling on some old worn oxfords. After taking a last look in the mirror I thought my attire was still stylish and presentable. I turned quickly at the sound of a familiar honking from the street. Looking out the window I saw the same decrepit bakery van that had appeared at our door every two weeks for months.

"Ho, ho, Sam," the driver said.

He was the biggest Negro I had ever seen, and with an equally huge grin he chuckled, "Who's this young dandy?"

"Meet the Reverend Elijah Poppinjay," Dad said.

"I ain't a real reverend, Sonny," he said.

I saw a worn Bible wedged between the gearshift and his side of the seat.

"I don't got me a paper sayin' I's a reverend is what I means."

My fingers felt like fragile matchsticks in his fierce grip.

"My friends, and they's not many, mind ye, calls me Jay Jay," he added.

How we squeezed in the cab was the first miracle of the day.

"You work that wiper," Jay Jay said, tapping a lever on the dash. "Your pop knows what to do with the other."

I guessed the van to be about a 1927 vintage. An equally cantankerous clutch and an engine that coughed its way through Seattle's downtown streets complemented its mechanical wiper blade system.

"Where are we going?" I finally asked.

"We's goin' to offer are social respects to them Hooverites," Jay Jay answered. "Pay 'tention now to what ye's doin'. "I cain't barely see where we's a goin."

I worked the wiper lever faster, clearing the windshield. "Hooverites?" I questioned.

"Hooverville," my dad spoke up.

We drove on, passing the market on Pike Street, empty of customers this early in the morning, and entered a part of the city I had never ventured into. The streets narrowed and got much rougher, causing a wrestling match between Jay Jay and the steering wheel.

"Faster," he admonished me again, and I cranked the wiper handle to the highest speed I could.

Abruptly, the street ended. *What now?* I wondered.

Jay Jay backed down an alley and came to a jerking halt in a parking lot.

"What do you think, Sam?"

"Rain's supposed to let up this afternoon," my dad said. "We might need a push to get back up the hill, but we can make it."

Jay Jay nodded, and with a grinding of gears he nosed the van onto a muddy track. We slithered from side-to-side for what seemed a great distance. Finally, we stopped again. I looked down a slope to the valley below. Spread out as far as I could see was a great city, not great like in splendid, but enormous. A haze that even the rain couldn't wash away covered the site like a smoke colored carpet.

"What's that?" I stammered.

"Welcome to Hooverville, Sonny," Jay Jay said.

They named these shantytowns after the president blamed for the Great Depression. Every big city had one. I discovered this and much more about them later. I would become an avid reader of the newspaper and discovered Seattle's Hooverville, to my astonishment, had been written about extensively.

The second miracle of the day was that the van and its passengers made it safely down the hill. Jay Jay didn't stop there, but continued on, deep into the squalor, stopping at last beside three shacks. They leaned against each other, using their mutual support to stay upright. It was one building, I soon learned, when Jay Jay said, "We's here."

"Where's here?" I asked.

"My church, Sonny," he said. "Welcome to the Shanty Cathedral."

I was tempted to say I was getting tired of *being welcomed to all of these strange places*, but followed my dad out the door. I immediately sank ankle-deep in the mud, and felt the slop seep inside my shoes. A smell I had never experienced before wrinkled my nose. The air carried the strong stink of an old outhouse filled with wet garbage, laced with an acrid smoke of burning railroad ties and moldy leaves.

I quickly discovered there was work to be done when dad opened the back door of the van. It was filled with small bags of flour and boxes of meat. The meat was unfamiliar to me and my upturned eyebrow must have caught my dad's attention.

"Ham hocks and soup bones," he explained, handing me more boxes.

All of this we carried into the church. By the time we finished, the mud had ruined my fancy clothes.

The food disappeared into the hands of the horde that soon appeared. I fast realized that all the work we'd gone to was not even a drop in the ocean compared with the need. I looked on in anguish as a man with a crippled child in tow arrived just as our meager bounty ran out. The boy, about five, had a club foot. Then I saw something that truly surprised me. Another woman took part of what she'd received and shared it with the latecomer.

"I'm going for a look around," I said to my dad, and left. I didn't catch his uneasy expression or the whisper Jay Jay planted in his ear.

"Doan worry, Sam. Floyd will watch him."

I hadn't gone far before a young man about my age appeared at my side. To break the silence I finally asked, "What's your name?"

"Fff-Fff-Fff-Floyd," he stuttered.

I laughed. In fact, his stuttering seemed to break the tension I'd been experiencing since early morning. Floyd, however, bristled, and threatened to bloody my nose. I explained how he reminded me of my best friend.

"He stutters like you," I said.

Floyd took back his threat. "Is your friend stupid too?" He asked.

"What!" I said.

"People that stutters is dumb, ain't they?"

"No! Who told you that anyway?"

Floyd answered with a shrug.

"My friend Leezie is pretty smart, and is really good with figures when he sets his mind on it."

That brought a smile to Floyd's face. "I know my arithmetic's too," he said. "But I don't tell nobody."

He wasn't kidding. I posed several math questions to him and he answered them all correctly. Then I tried to stump him with a basic algebra problem. He took a roundabout way, but came up with the right solution.

I clapped him on the back, saying, "My dad says that if you know arithmetic you can learn just about anything."

"Sam says that?" he said.

"Yes, and don't ever call yourself stupid again, cause you're not."

We turned down a different path. "Where's this lead to?" I asked.

"Don't you want to see where I live?"

"Sure, where is it?"

"Over yonder," he said. "Come on, follow me."

Floyd's shack was much like the others, but smaller and pieced together from whatever scraps of lumber and tin he could find. It was a gloomy, six-by-eight enclosure that reminded me more of an animal's den than human habitat. But it was neat. Stepping inside, I was surprised to find it had a dirt floor.

"That's yourn," Floyd commanded, pointing to a wobbly wooden box. "Set!"

He started to sit on a bent and rusted bedspring raised off the ground on flat rocks. A holey blanket covered it. Abruptly, he changed his mind.

I watched him rummage first in a tin can, then a sack.

"What's that song you're humming?" I asked.

Floyd grinned. "My momma's git-ready-for-church song," he answered. "She sing it on Sunday mornin's and it just popped into my head."

He sang two lines and I recognized the tune, SHALL WE GATHER AT THE RIVER?

"There it is," Floyd said, and brought a wrinkled piece of paper out of the sack.

"My pappy give me this when I left home, an' I been savin' it," he said.

It was a stick of gum.

Floyd unwrapped it. "Sorry I don't have nuthin' better," he said.

I heard the gum snap when he broke it.

"It ain't much, but it's all I got to offer," he said, pressing half of it into my hand.

Our eyes met. He blinked and so did I.

I shuddered, and not just because of the gum's brittleness. I knew he had shared more than just his prized possession. A sudden heretical thought crossed my mind, one that I quickly buried, but still allowed my mind to recite: *"What if this is what Holy Communion is supposed to be?"*

Savoring the sweet taste of the gum, I took off my prized beanie.

"Here," I said, handing it over. "Something for you to wear."

Floyd's eyes brightened and he favored me with a lopsided grin, when he reached for it.

"The W goes toward the front," I said, and jumped up to set it on his head properly.

His rotten teeth detracted from an otherwise good-looking face, but didn't lessen the sincerity of his smile.

Floyd, it turned out, had no family in Hooverville.

"Rode the rails from Indiana," he told me.

"How old were you?" I asked, confused, knowing he didn't arrive here overnight.

"Leaved home when I was nigh onto fifteen, I reckon."

"By yourself?"

"Yup."

The third miracle of the day was that I still would be at Hooverville had I not had Floyd for a guide. The network of paths and alleys rivaled any labyrinth ever devised. The rain had stopped, bringing the residents from their shanties.

Many times as we wandered through the maze, Floyd introduced me to the denizens of Hooverville, saying simply, "This is Sam's boy." I stopped blushing after the fifth approving nod, but puzzled that so many people knew Sam Moosington.

The autumn sun was getting low on the horizon when we made our way back to the Shanty Cathedral. Suddenly, Floyd stopped, pointing off in the distance. I followed his finger and found Seattle's skyscrapers ringing the ridge above Hooverville. The setting sun and a brilliant rainbow lighted them. The dazzling view took my breath away, and put a lump in my throat.

Floyd put it in his perspective: "I feels like I's in hell and I's lookin' toward the Promised Land."

Chapter Seventeen

I made several trips back to Hooverville but never saw Floyd again.

The smell of the experience lingered a long time. Once I learned there was a world outside the comfortable one I was used to, I made a decision that would frame my life, well, forever.

Seven years later an elaborate ritual took place in the great cathedral in Seattle. No, not the shanty at Hooverville, but an ornate edifice named Saint James. It was late April 1941 when I was ordained a Catholic Priest.

It wasn't an easy choice but I suppose having a seminary practically in my back yard helped. My classmate at St. Edward's Seminary and fellow priesthood inductee that day was Percival Knox. Percy, or Ox, as some called him, was from Athol, Idaho.

Jay Jay came to the formal celebration my mom put on after the ordination and relieved some of the stuffiness Catholics are prone to.

"Where 'bouts you hail from?" he asked Percy.

"Athol, Idaho," Percy answered, "but I'm transferred to this diocese now."

"Where! Where did ye say?" Jay Jay asked.

I could see his deep frown and guessed what put it there. Percy repeated his origins, enunciating perfectly, and spelling it for him.

"Whewie!" Jay Jay exclaimed. "For a second I was thinkin' that must be at the butt end of places." Jay Jay laughed loud enough to twist several heads and turn Percy's face red. Percy was a solemn guy, and one who took his new officialdom status seriously.

So did I. Our ordination placed us on a high pedestal, and rightly so. For the skeptical, I could prove it from the Baltimore Catechism: *"Catholics should show honor and reverence to the priest because he is the representative of Christ Himself and the dispenser of his mysteries."* If that weren't enough I had a quote from a recent Pope committed to memory: *"The priest is indeed another Christ..."*

It couldn't be any plainer, and I believed it. Heady stuff, and for this still wet-behind-the-ears-baby-in-priestly-garb, it fed the ego that often led me to think too highly of myself. Sam Moosington had a word for it: *"haughty."*

"I got this question, Sonny, that be a buzzin' in my head for seven year," Jay Jay whispered in my ear.

I had the foolish thought, which I quickly stifled, to remind him that the proper form of address for a man of my status was *"Father."* I was standing awkwardly in an alcove where he had cornered me.

"What question?"

"That little damsel, Kitty Crotchdale," he said, raising a suspicious eyebrow. "Ye use ta be sweet things together back in them college days."

"It was Couchmall," I corrected.

"What ever happen a-twixt Miss Coochmail and sonny boy?"

My heart fluttered, triggered by memories of first love. Kitty was also the first person I had confided to that I was thinking of becoming a priest. Naïveté is another of my faults.

Instead of explaining it to Jay Jay, I replied, "She jilted me."

"Ah, the ladies," he said with a wistful look. "A little jilt here and a little more over there, an' pretty soon a boy feel like a bean rattlin' in a jar."

He laughed uproariously, and before I could fend him off my backbone and sternum rattled against each other. Jay Jay didn't know his own strength when clapping a person on the back, which he did often.

"You can't be serious," Percy said to me later that night in our room at an apartment for priests. "Surely that crude creature can't be a man of the cloth."

I jumped to the Reverend Poppinjay's defense and tried to explain the world as seen by Jay Jay. But every attempt to counter Percy's disdain was met with a rejoinder.

"Come, come now, my friend," he said. "He's not even a believer in the one true church."

Both of my eyebrows shot up and I'm sure the hairs on my head followed.

"So it matters not a whit what he thinks our good Lord might say to him," Percy pompously added.

After seven years I was used to Percy's black-and-white mentality. He was less rigid about other things, but when it came to what we called *"Mother Church,"* he was threatened, defensive and combative.

I squelched my temper and finally shut down the argument by reminding him, "We have a busy day tomorrow."

It was customary for a new priest to visit the bishop on the morning after ordination to receive his first assignment. We made certain to arrive early. The straight-backed chairs in the anteroom grew increasingly uncomfortable as the noisy clock on the wall ticked off the minutes. An hour passed, and we were both more nervous than two pigs in a smoke house.

Finally, the door to the bishop's office opened and a dapper little man with a pencil-thin mustache stepped out. "Which one of you would be Father Knox?" He asked. Percy stepped forward.

Thinking the spruced up dresser to be one of the bishop's minions, I ventured a question about the delay.

"Don't know about that," he said, rubbing his mustache, I guess to make sure it was still there. "I run Marty's Delicatessen downtown."

Sensing my puzzlement, he explained. "I send over lunch twice a week for his highness."

"Lunch?" I questioned.

"More like a four-course meal." Then the little man rolled his eyes. *"No more caviar unless I lower the price and the au jus is not rich enough*," he complained today. "Just imagine that kind of effrontery, Father, and how it degrades my culinary acumen."

I didn't answer, not knowing what to say.

"Never mind," he went on. "We worked it out. Just took longer than expected."

He was quite a personable gentleman, solicitous too of my own welfare.

"Oh, you're one of the new priests from yesterday," he said, and with that pulled a small case from his pocket. A business card appeared and he wrote something on the back.

"Here," he said, extending it to me. "This will get you a dime off any of our ready-made sandwiches."

I barely had the chance to offer a thank you because he turned and, tipping his hat at the same time, whistled his way toward the door.

Percy came out and his flushed face set off my alarm bells. He smiled and whispered quickly in my ear, "Bothell!"

I gave him a disbelieving look.

"Honest," he said.

Bothell was a small town on the north end of Lake Washington, a mere eight miles from St. Edward's. Percy hadn't gone far but it was a good first assignment.

I heard someone clear his throat and nearly fainted to find it was the bishop standing near the door.

"Now that I have your attention," he said gruffly, "perhaps you can grace my office with your presence."

The bishop's gruff was worse than his bark, and he set me at ease. When I left five minutes later I was walking on air. He shook my hand warmly and said, "Make your appointment for a month from today. By then we should have heard from Rome and we can wrap up the details."

I was going to Rome for advanced theological studies. I could hardly believe it.

Chapter Eighteen

The bakery van was parked at the curb, and Jay Jay stood beside it in his baker's uniform. I acted pleased to see him because in the excitement of the past hours, I'd forgotten his pledge to be my taxi man.

"Where to, Sonny Boy?" he said.

Nonchalantly I answered, "Rome, if you please, my good man."

"Seattle don't gots no Rome I knows about."

I explained, gushing excitement. My enthusiasm was met by a frown that would have caused an angel to tremble.

"What's wrong?" I said.

"I knows about them Nazzies, that why," he said. "Ain't ye heard that Mister Hitler is raisin' a rumpus in them parts."

"Don't fret about me," I said. "Even the Reverend Poppinjay knows the Good Lord takes care of his own."

"Bunny rabbits don't nibble the grass that mister lion be nappin' on," Jay Jay countered.

The banter went on but his concern didn't faze me. Either I was too exited or had been too sheltered from events in Europe. Temporarily, until the Vatican answered, the bishop was sending me to help out at my home parish.

When Jay Jay heard that he set the war raging in Europe aside, saying, "T'will make yo mama happier than a kitty cat in a cream bucket."

A week passed as I did all the things expected of a newly ordained priest. I ran errands for the pastor, tidied the room where the first graders met for catechism and assisted the two associate pastors.

"Sounds like you're a glorified altar boy," my dad said on my first visit home.

Mom bristled but didn't take up the argument. Instead, she asked if I wanted more to eat. I declined but did accept her offer for a second piece of apple pie.

Later, as Dad helped me on with my coat, Mom said, "Wait a minute, Mew. I forgot something."

I watched her rush to the kitchen and rummage through her miscellaneous drawer. She ran back waving a piece of paper in the air.

"Here it is, dear. A letter came for you last week. I wonder what it is."

The postmark was a familiar one, and I'm sure it had aroused her curiosity. I decided to wait to open it.

Father Gregory had given me a sparsely furnished room above the gardener's quarters. I had a bed, a chair, a washbasin, a tiny chest and a wastebasket. The odor of fruit peelings, cigarette butts and soggy paper reminded me I'd forgotten to empty the latter.

The letter was from my long-forgotten hometown. I sat down and tapped it against my knee several times. The handwriting was unfamiliar. I hesitated, wondering if I should first show it to Father Gregory, but decided his permission wasn't necessary.

Inside was a typewritten notice from *"The All-School Reunion Organizers."* A detailed schedule listed several events for the one-day reunion. I sneered at the grammar error in the bold heading: *"YOUR INVITED."* The salutation was handwritten with purple ink: *"We sure hope you can come."*

"How long has it been since I was last there?" I mused. *"Nine years? No, the county fair was in 1930, so it had to be over ten."* I read the school reunion invitation again and Leezie's chubby features intruded. *"I wonder if he got an invite."* I hadn't heard from him for three years, and that quick note had come from Oregon.

He used to write more often, that's if you can put his sloppy penmanship and D+ marks for grammar in the category of written communication. There, if you need it, is another example why my Dad's word – *haughty* – describes my seminary snobbery so well. I did reply to *some* of his mail but my academic pursuits gave me a good excuse for ignoring him. If I had any remorse at the moment it didn't show. I was snug in the consolation that my hard work was being rewarded with a trip to Rome.

I wadded the invitation and tossed it angrily in the trash, thinking, "My success would have never been possible in that small, culturally deprived place."

"*Hicks from the sticks.*" Wasn't that a popular expression I'd heard often since leaving? I vowed to empty the wastebasket on the morrow and be done with it.

I had the dream on Wednesday night. Nightmare doesn't describe it. Maybe eerie.

The location was the apartment at the depot where Leezie lived. The dream images replayed the events exactly as they had when I first met him. Hildred served the molasses cookies and set the milk on the table. After Leezie gobbled his and ran to get his toy truck, the scene changed dramatically.

I spilled my milk when I heard a roar, and ran and hid under Leezie's bed. The train was coming. I peeked out and no one was there, save Betsy. She sat serenely reading a book. The noise of the train grew, shaking the building. Soon, it was like being inside a great thundercloud.

The bed shook, plates fell off the table and at the last minute, the piercing shriek of the steam whistle shattered the glass of the window. All at once it was quiet and I risked another look. Something rolled across the floor toward me. It was my baseball bat, *Old Cobber*. I heard a wailing, only to discover it was my own. I was all alone.

I jerked awake, my pillow wet with sweat and the blankets in a tangle. "Where on earth did that come from?" I wondered. "*I wonder what book Betsy was reading.*" The title had eluded me in the dream and I lay awake pondering. In an hour I was asleep again.

Daylight brought a pounding on my door. It was the gardener, wanting to know where I left his rake. I had borrowed it to clean up some trash – part of my never-ending chores. Cursing myself for not putting it back, I decided I might as well start the new day an hour early.

I sat down, meaning to read from my Breviary. The tome, written in Latin, is a collection of psalms and Bible passages. It was considered a serious sin if a priest did not read the prescribed selections each day. My nose wrinkled, which reminded me of the still un-emptied wastebasket.

I almost dozed off, until these words popped off the page: *"Joseph received the word of God through a dream."* It made me shiver.

"The invitation!" I thought. *"What if my dream was some sort of signal from the Almighty about that?"*

I hadn't reached the plateau that God would send me private messages – yet. Maybe a more mature priest would expect to, but the very idea frightened me.

In spite of that, I knew I would eventually dig the invitation out of the garbage. When I did it smelled and had shrunk into a wet ball. Gingerly, I peeled the layers apart, smoothing it on the floor. Although I half hoped it wouldn't be, the paper was still legible.

Still, I played a mental game of *"Yes I will; no I won't"* for another week. I bought a train ticket finally, wishing again that my mom hadn't remembered to give me the letter. It was too late to notify the reunion committee I was coming but I doubted anyone would notice, or care.

The two-day trip took me south to Oregon before turning eastward. Roosevelt's Lend Lease plan to rescue the embattled British was in full swing, which meant we were stopped often to let fast freights carrying military cargo pass. It made me feel important when people, including old men and women, would gladly give up their seats on the crowded coaches to make a Catholic Priest more comfortable.

"My supply of Old Gold cigarettes will last forever at this rate," I thought each time a passenger asked, "Want a smoke, Father?" Oddly, I was always on the receiving end, and never thought to reciprocate.

Sleep was difficult but I didn't go hungry. Food was plentiful and the passengers were generous, sharing cookies and sandwiches. One gentleman even offered a leg of lamb.

"Want another chop of lamb, Father?" he would ask, never letting me reply, but carving off another huge slice with the biggest jackknife I had ever seen.

The train was behind schedule and I began to wonder if I would ever reach my destination. Oregon's eastern landscape, bleak and barren, seemed to never end. I kept checking the railroad timetable, thinking, I suppose, that would hasten my progress.

At last, I reached the junction where I changed trains. The new conductor reassured me, "Yes, we're running behind, Father, but we should get you there before dark."

I didn't realize my anticipation had been growing until the last fifty miles of familiar scenery awakened old memories. A man sitting next to me remarked, "I sense you're from around these parts, Father."

"Oh?" I questioned.

"When we crossed the river back there, you acted like it was a place where you suddenly remembered you'd lost a gold watch," he said.

I smiled, savoring the recollection that it was one of Sam Moosington's favorite fishing holes.

My seatmate asked me where I was going and I told him.

"The only person I know there is the one-armed depot agent," he said.

"Do you know his boy, Leezie?" I asked. "He's my best friend." I twitched in surprise that the sentence slipped out.

"Nope," he said, making me think he didn't know John Smith that well either.

Finally, sometime between sundown and last light, the train rumbled over a familiar creek. I looked down at our favorite boyhood swimming hole; sure I could hear the sounds of laugher and splashing. That was quickly smothered by three lonesome "whooo-oohs" from the locomotive. I suppose it wasn't any different to my ear than any of the other thousands of train whistles I can recall; but tonight it was, for I knew the engineer was whistling for the crossing at the edge of town. The rays from the twilight sun cast eerie shadows on the first building I recognized, the hardware store.

"*It looks like the little burg is closed down for a long after-supper nap,*" I thought as the train slowed. After a final screech of metal and hiss of steam, it stopped. I was home.

A friendly passenger helped me lift my satchel from the rack above my seat. I nodded my thanks and fiddled with my collar. I waved off the porter's help as he tried to beat me to the door.

"Watch that lass step, Mr. Father," he said. "I dinna get my step-off stool put there."

The harried clerk at *Railroader's Roost*, the town's hotel, gave me the shock of my life.

"A room?" he said, "That's a laugh. We're all booked up for the reunion."

The possibility of being stranded with no place to stay hadn't entered my mind. My crestfallen look must have caused him to give me a better look in the dim light.

"You a priest?" he asked. My nod sent him shuffling through a pile of papers.

"Ah-ha!" he said at last, pulling one from the stack. "I have a reservation for a Father Mew."

"*Moosing–*" I started to correct him but stopped. "Yes, that's me," I said. "But how is it that I have a room reserved?"

"Look, Padre, I just hand out the keys and collect the money. Do you want it or not?"

"Of course, of course," I answered. "But does it say there who rented the room?"

The clerk rattled the paper and held it up to the light, moving it progressively closer to his nose. "Nope."

Fearing he might change his mind, I dropped my satchel and produced a fountain pen, quickly signing the register. Finished, a room key danced in front of my eye, dangling there until I reached for it.

"Must be your lucky day, Padre," he said. "Number fourteen, upstairs and around the corner to the end of the hall."

The ancient stairs each squeaked a different note. At the top railing I looked back, nodding my thanks.

"Dining room's open 'til eight if you're hungry," the clerk said.

Number fourteen's lock refused to budge. I spent several frustrating moments working the key. A bare bulb on a long cord hung from the ceiling.

"At least I can see," I muttered, just as the antique tumblers rewarded me with a reassuring click. The room was neat and inviting. The bed looked especially welcome, and I lay down to test the mattress. Before I knew it I was asleep.

Chapter Nineteen

"*Where am I?*" The nightmarish thought flashed like a blinking light as I tried to rouse myself from sleep. A door slammed down the hall, bringing me back to reality. I sighed and my heart settled down. The room was dark and I stumbled over my satchel. The electric bulb suspended from the ceiling bumped my head and I flailed at it before catching it on one of its gyrations through the air.

I splashed my face with water and just decided I was fully conscious when I heard a faint tapping. Someone was at the door.

The aged lock was just as cantankerous from the inside, and it took me several tries before it budged. I came face-to-face with a man about my age balancing a tray with a towel draped over it. The man, whom I took to be a hotel employee, was slim and slightly taller than my six feet. His weathered face had a rugged handsomeness to it. My eyes fell to the floor, taking note of work boots and worn trousers held up by leather suspenders. A bright red neckerchief topped a blue shirt.

"Yes, what is it?"

His only response was a somber gaze. I repeated the question.

I didn't recognize the voice that finally spoke.

"Better watch out, folks might mistake you for Father Goldsworthy."

"Wha- What?" I stammered.

"He could never remember to fasten his fly either."

I gasped, and losing all of my priestly composure looked down, relieved to find my pants were buttoned. I heard a chuckle, and then the snicker I remembered so well. A tooth-marked scar below his lower lip jolted my senses, but the smile, always a dead giveaway, caused me to go weak in the knees.

"Leezie?" I croaked. "Is that you?"

"Well, I ain't the pope!"

My lips moved but my tongue refused to form any words, at least I didn't think so.

"Boo-da-dit-a-youz?" I said.

He eyed me quizzically.

"What's that supposed to mean?"

The towel came off the tray with a flourish, revealing half a loaf of bread and some still-steaming beef stew in a tin bowl.

"Aren't you going to invite me in? I brought you some supper."

I backed into the room and Leezie followed.

"Sorry I couldn't meet your train," he said, setting the tray down. "Had to work late."

He turned and I found myself buried in a bear hug. His arms were powerful. Stepping back, he eyed me from head to toe.

"I can't hardly believe it's you, Mew – that you're standin' here." He dabbed at a wet spot under one eye. "It's been so long I scarce knew what you'd look like. But your Father Goldsworthy costume gives you away." He snickered again.

I didn't get a chance to say anything because he hugged me again. I had a huge lump in my throat, overwhelmed by how happy he was to see me.

"Didn't recognize me, did you?"

In my defense I said, "You were just a fat little kid the last time I saw you."

"Pudgy," he said. "I weren't never fat."

He insisted I was hungry, which I was. I ate and Leezie talked. Wordy had not been his strong point growing up, but I listened now while he told stories, made jokes (mostly about himself) and filled in the past eleven years of local yore. Suddenly, I dropped my spoon and I just sat staring at him.

"Leezie!" I coughed, wiping away the gravy running down my chin. "You don't stutter anymore!"

Leezie's whole face followed suit when he smiled. My mom once described it, saying, "His smile comes from some happy place inside him."

It appeared to me in this instant that happy spot must have grown.

"I'll tell you all about it, Mew, but tonight is for rememberin' an' catchin' up."

"Most of them is probably up in the cemetery that you knew," Leezie said when I asked about some of the old timers. "Blinky, Gravedigger Bill and Petey Gorman's papa are a few."

He hadn't mentioned Father Goldsworthy, so I did. "Old folks home," he said.

"Where's Petey?"

"Don't nobody knows where he's at right now," he said. "Probably hoppin' freights around the country."

I flashed to Petey and Floyd sharing a boxcar.

"Does he still have those fits?"

Leezie nodded. "An' sometimes he goes wild an' gits himself locked up."

"Jail?" I said. "Petey?"

I was surprised so much could change in so few years. Leezie had grown up and become barely recognizable. Old friends had died. Petey Gorman had gone missing. And Father Goldsworthy was in a home for old people. *Was he senile too?* I wondered. But I was afraid to ask that. *Where have I been?* was all I could think about.

"Remember the marble game, and the way Petey stood up to Abner?" Leezie asked.

At times the recollections would come rapid-fire, first me, then Leezie. More than once he got up to leave only to remember something and sit back down. There was something contagious about him, always had been, and my stomach ached from muscles unaccustomed to so much laughter.

It was past one in the morning when both of us decided to call it a night. I stopped Leezie as he heading for the door.

"How did you know I was coming?" I asked.

"How you mean?"

"I didn't tell anyone is what I mean. So how did you know?"

"If you want the truth, I met every train for the past two days."

"So you were just guessing."

"No guess to it," he said. "I just didn't know when." The way he said it made me think it was true.

"Did you believe I wouldn't?"

"I knew you was fightin' agin' the idea," he said. "At least every time I talked to the Windknocker about it, I got that notion. But then the feelin' went away. Rentin' you a room was my idea; figured you might not count on the hotel bein' full."

"Windknocker? What's that?"

Leezie chuckled. "God, my friend Jesus, name them however you wants. I just calls him the Windknocker."

I nodded sagely like priests are trained to do when they haven't the slightest idea what to say. It made me nervous the familiar way he talked about Our Lord.

"I expect he got your attention and you changed your mind somehow," he said.

Before I could agree, he asked, "What was it?"

"Just a dumb dream," I said, sure my face was getting red.

"Dumb dream! Bet it wasn't at the time."

The feeling of being all alone under Leezie's bed after the train passed was still fresh, and I nodded.

"Well, it don't make a difference. You're here and that's the matter of it." He chuckled again. "Why act so surprised?" You being a priest and all; I'd a thunk you knew all about stuff like that." He gave me an affectionate pat on the back and left.

"The word is thought!" I hurled after him, watching him retreat down the hall. "Not thunk! Surely you remember Miss Fanny telling you that."

"I only said it to rattle the peas in your brain," he hollered over his shoulder.

He disappeared around the corner before I could get the last word.

Chapter Twenty

The same clerk was on duty when I left the hotel for the festivities of reunion day.

"Hey, Padre," he shouted as I was going out the door. "How was the stew?" I gave him a thumb's up.

I stood a moment on the front steps. My eyes took in all the small hamlet had to offer in seconds. I marveled at how little had changed. It seemed as though someone had held back the hands of time only to release them this morning when I stepped onto the porch of Railroader's Roost.

"All this place needs is a boost into the twentieth century," I thought. I would eat a lot of words this day.

My first lesson was to discover the locust trees in the town park had grown up like everyone else. By noon the place was packed. Thankfully, Billy Archer and Harry Capphammer arrived with Leezie. Leezie winked at me, saying, "Billy and Harry bet me that you wouldn't remember them, so tell them you do." Harry, I would have recognized. He had always reminded me of a big dog – big in the sense that the large breeds are usually friendlier. He shook my hand and patted me on the back, and I was glad to see he hadn't changed. He was the same gentle Harry.

Billy, on the other hand, would have fooled me. He had a serious look that he didn't have in his youth. What threw me off the most was his tall, lean frame. Billy came from a family of short, squat people. He was quick to remind me of the one thing from our growing up years that I would have rather forgotten. "Do you remember the night we tried to tip over the marshal's outhouse?"

"No, I don't think so," I said.

"Sure you do, Mew," Harry chuckled.

"The *dung-ho flop*? How could you forget that?" Leezie said.

"Now that you put it so eloquently, it all comes back to me," I said.

The three of us had a good laugh and I noticed Billy's eyes still had the mischievous glint I remembered. He also chose the moment to deliver the first comeuppance I received that day.

With a distinctive playful smile, he said, "I suppose you think we're all a bunch of hicks in these parts, bein' you're from the big city now."

Harry Capphammer came to my rescue. "Mew wouldn't ever think that, Billy. He comes from here, remember."

I should have gotten down on my knees, begging their pardon for ever applying the adage *"hicks from the sticks"* to them, but didn't. Everyone was friendly, solicitous and genuine. They welcomed me home, making me feel like a conquering hero.

My second just deserts came in the form of the ultimate surprise, when the scene shifted that afternoon from the park to a tour of the school building. Compared to St. John's and St. Edward's it lacked just about everything, save the memories I discovered were stored there. Miss Fanny's classroom looked exactly the same.

"Leezie Smith, you get right up here and write it on the blackboard," I remembered her scolding. *"The word is 'think', not 'thunk!'"*

Eventually our wanderings led us to a corridor lined with sports memorabilia and pictures.

"We had a good team that year," Leezie said, directing my eyes toward a large picture of a basketball team.

"Good? That's all?" I scoffed. It seemed Leezie was downplaying what winning a county championship meant. To me it was a big accomplishment.

We were looking at a photo of 1932's titleholders. Leezie was the manager that year, and his face had the biggest smile.

I saw the trophy case at the end of the hall and headed for it. Looking back I saw no one had followed, and noticed Billy Archer with a goofy smile on his face. He was pointing to a different place on the wall.

I should have guessed if Leezie had captured any accolades it would have been where they honored track athletes. My first reaction was astonishment, but I couldn't ignore what was right in front of my face. I stared at a framed newspaper article from 1934, with the dazzling headline, *"Smith shines at state championships, brings home third-place trophy in the 100."*

I gulped when I read that Leezie had come within a whisker of winning it all. The times were so close it must have been a photo finish.

"Lean and conditioned like a Greek Olympian, Leezie Smith bolted from the starting blocks like a scared jackrabbit, leaving the state's best flat-footed at the gate," the writer's down-home prose read. *"Fleet and fluid, with legs pumping like well-oiled pistons, Smith rolled like a tumbleweed driven by a winter's gale for the tape stretched taut 100 yards away. Only a desperate lunge at the finish cost him ultimate victory."*

"Leezie!" I said. "You're a hero. How come you didn't tell me?"

He shrugged, but I knew the answer. Since an early age he had been closed-mouthed and seldom boasted.

"Read some more."

His smile told me I had missed the best part.

"Coming in fifth was the county's undefeated champion, Abner Pong."

I had to read it twice before it sank in.

"Leezie!" I shouted.

I didn't realize it, but Billy told me later how I leapt into the air and danced a jig up and down the hall.

"I never thought priests did them sort of things," he chided me.

"Leezie!" I bellowed louder. "You did it! You beat old Abner!"

His near feat of winning it all meant nothing now. In our small-town league, whipping my old enemy was tantamount to Jesse Owens winning the hundred at the Berlin Olympics.

"Old Abner doesn't look too happy," I said, tapping the picture. "I hope you rubbed his nose in it real good."

"Naw," Leezie said. "He was so sad I felt sorry for him."

I started to protest.

"Besides, Mew, Abner is still the best runner. You knows that too."

I gave him a skeptical look.

"I just beat him at the start and he couldn't catch me," he said.

"All that practice getting the rhythm of ready-set-go right," I said. "Is that what did it?"

He smiled, which was the only answer I got.

It didn't matter to me, but I thought he was being too modest. As we walked away, I was still shaking my head and had an arm around him. I think it was one of the proudest moments in my life.

The official part of the reunion ended with huge platters of the pig that had been roasting all day. A bonfire lit the growing darkness. Starving, I wolfed down the succulent pork, hardly coming up for air.

"You musta forgot," Leezie said, poker-faced. "Today's Friday an' you're eatin' meat faster than Blinky could cut it if he was still around."

I was ready for him this time and rattled off a reply with even more casualness.

"It's not Friday and you know it, my once-fat little friend. But just to make sure, I turned it into fish before I ate it."

The embers left in the fire glowed, illuminating little but the faces of those who remained when the crowd went home. Boisterous to begin with, the talk eventually turned more serious.

Since I had been sheltered from their world, it surprised me when Harry asked, "We going to war? What do you think, Mew?"

"It's them damned Japs that's going to start it," Billy interrupted. "You can bet your Model A's radiator cap on that."

"Hogwash," Harry countered. "That Nazi bugger Hitler already gots most of Europe. And now he wants to whip up on the English. That's hittin' mighty close to home if you ask me."

Out of my depth and not wanting to lecture Harry about geography, I still managed to make a near fool of myself.

"I wouldn't worry about the Nips," I said. "They aren't going to attack anyone. Their navy is second rate and their army is just a bunch of malnourished midgets."

"See Billy, it's just like I tole ya. It's them Nazis," Harry said.

I got into deeper trouble when I tried to expound on a paper I wrote in seminary about the Church's Just War Theory.

"Just war?" Leezie spoke up for the first time. "I thunk people got killed in wars."

"Leezie don't think no war is good for nobody," Harry added.

I noticed there was no censor in his tone; in fact, if anything it held a fraction of respect.

"Tell that to the Nazis," I said.

The debate went on and I felt my temper rising each time Leezie expanded his argument against war. We had been trained that priests proclaimed and no one disputed what they decreed. Obviously, my friend wasn't aware of that.

"What you need is another beer," Leezie said finally, and a bottle magically appeared in my hand.

Soon the mood changed, and we forgot our cares for one more day. Billy's harmonica appeared and the singing started.

"Be our song leader like you used to," Leezie whispered in my ear.

"I don't know the new tunes."

"Don't anyone cares about that."

I told Billy and he played the first lively notes of *"Happy Days are Here Again."*

"Let's hear you sing," I shouted, leading them through the toe-tapping lyrics. Others appeared out of the darkness, attracted by the sound. I was getting hoarse by the time it all ended, fittingly so with the moving words of a ballad from the first war:

"So wait and pray each night for me, Till We Meet Again."

"Amen," Billy said when we finished, "till we meet again."

"I seconds that," Harry said.

"Wait and pray each night for me," Leezie spoke up, "an' I'll do the same for you."

I didn't say anything. Regrettably, I wished I would have.

Chapter Twenty-One

"Would you a married her?" Leezie asked.

We were sitting on Meadowlark Ridge the next morning after leaving the cemetery. A strange feeling had come over me when we visited Betsy's grave.

"Yes!" I whispered, surprised at the intensity that the answer left my lips.

"We was only seven," he said. "How do you know?"

"Destiny, I guess." It was the best reply that came to mind.

"Now you feels like you got cheated?"

"Yes," I shot back.

My vehemence startled Leezie, but not me. I had had this conversation with myself more than once, often imagining marrying Betsy. This morning had just shown me the strength of those feelings.

"It wasn't to be," I sighed. "God had other plans."

"God?" Leezie said. "Betsy died, remember. The scarlet fever took her."

"He could have cured her," I protested.

"And he coulda stopped Mary from sending you off to school," Leezie said. "And he coulda kept Petey from his spasms, and he coulda made Abner a nice guy. And, and, and – but God don't know nuthin' about all them ands. We's the ones that toss all them ands at him, expectin' him to agree."

It was my turn to be startled, but once Leezie began it was hard to interrupt.

"All I knows is you wouldn't know what good is if you hadn't felt right here how bad bad can be," he said, tapping his chest with his fingertips for emphasis.

His homespun wisdom went completely over my head.

"Didn't they teach you that in them schools?" he asked.

Actually, they hadn't. *"The Lord giveth and the Lord taketh away"* was about as close as we ever came to explaining the perplexity of why bad things happen to good people.

"The Windknocker is good," Leezie said. "That's the only thing I knows for sure."

"It seems like if this Windknocker of yours would have spent half the effort taking care of Betsy as he did your stuttering, we'd both be better off," I said, trying to hold back a sneer.

"Maybe he just knows more about the stutters than fevers," Leezie said.

It was a facetious remark, and his smile told me that was the end of the conversation.

On the walk back to town I did manage to pry out of him the silly notion he had of calling God the Windknocker. It made me uncomfortable because to tell it he had to take me back to 1930, and the visit we made to the revivalist's tent.

"The preacher said I got borned again," he said. "But what really happened is I got the wind knocked into me."

"Huh?" I questioned.

"The Holy Ghost came a ridin' on a big wind; you remembers about that, don't you?"

I guessed he was referring to the day of Pentecost. There is a description of a wind that preceded the disciples receiving the spirit.

"A symbolic wind? Is that what you're saying?" I asked.

Leezie chuckled. "No! It were real, Mew. My lungs filled up. I didn't figure it out 'til later when I was readin' the book the preacher give me. Anyhow, that's why I calls him the Windknocker. He knocked the wind into me, and I ain't been the same since."

"And I suppose your stuttering just went riding off on the same breeze."

"Nope. The Windknocker took me out of that hell gradual-like. I probably woulda talked myself outta believin' what he did if it happened all at once."

My mind flashed back to Hooverville. Floyd stuttered and had talked about being in hell too. I smiled.

"You got that chessie cat grin on your face, Mew. What's so funny?"

I told him about Floyd.

"And he had this stick of gum," I explained. "In fact, he had carried it with him all the way from Indiana. It was hard as a nail, but it was the only thing he owned in the world. He broke it and gave me half." I could still taste the brittle offering.

Leezie snickered. "And you Catholics think God only uses bread to make communion betwixt two!"

I flinched because he had practically stolen my own thoughts of the time. Still, I didn't reply.

I had lost the theological high ground and it made me mad. I was already uptight with the familiar way he talked about Our Lord, but having to listen to his supposed born-again experience put my stomach in knots. He was just an impressionable fourteen-year-old at the time.

"*How,*" I thought, "*can an adult continue to put stock in such malarkey?*" I consoled myself with the thought that over time he would probably mellow and come to realize that religion wasn't about experience, but working toward perfection.

He gave me a head-to-toe inspection after I changed into my priestly garb.

"Sorry I won't be able to see you off," he said. "I'm good at stopping trains if you remember."

I grinned.

"And if you ever need a good altar boy, I've got experience," he added with a chuckle.

We both ended up sitting on the bed, happy that it was too late in the morning for our shrieks of laughter to disturb the other tenants.

My side hurt and tears were running down Leezie's cheeks before it subsided.

"Them were good days, Mew," he said. "Even if I flopped being an altar boy. An' those times is still a part of you and me."

I nodded, wanting to say something, but he waved me off.

"No sense tryin' to make out like they didn't happen."

I knew Leezie's little speech was his way of reminding me that our friendship was important.

Possibly, if the world hadn't exploded a few months later, and the bishop hadn't turned my own life upside-down when I got back to Seattle, I would have paid more attention to the vow I'd taken that day – to remember that Leezie was important to me.

Chapter Twenty-Two

Lamentably, the day came when I wondered if I would ever see Leezie again.

The world exploded on my birthday, December 7, 1941, and the trip east for the school reunion was the closest I got to Rome. But the bishop still decided I needed further education. Much to my dismay and chiding from Percy Knox, I was back in school again, studying business at Seattle College.

"After that, you'll be working for me," the bishop told me.

He didn't offer solace for my crestfallen look, just told me to straighten up and be happy doing what I was told, which I did.

Fate intervened, however, when the bishop died in a car crash. A new one was appointed, and after I graduated from business school, he assigned me to a small church north of Seattle. The fact that Father Thomas Midgeon was the pastor brought more than a little ribbing from Percy.

"Tyrannical Tommy!" Ox responded when he heard the news. "You'll be working under him?"

I nodded.

"I don't envy you that assignment; he's a holy terror, I'm told." He laughed at his cleverness, adding, "Good oxymoron, don't you think?"

He offered a few more rumors about my soon-to-be boss. Next, he lectured me with several clucks of the tongue, which only served to remind me what I already knew: priests assigned to obscure places had less chance of promotion.

Father Midgeon, alias Tyrannical Tommy, was not what I expected. He showed vestiges of kindness from a bygone era and did not suck lemons. His dour countenance was genuine, needing no such stimulus. His list of rules was short, consisting of, "Don't screw up and we will get along fine." No doubt he noticed the twitch in my left eye and tempered his edict considerably.

"I can't do what I used to, and am counting on you to run things," he said.

Before I could say I was ready to do that, he repeated, "Don't screw up," and blew a cloud of smoke in my face.

Tommy smoked a pipe, using a tobacco that would have overwhelmed the smell that I still remembered from Hooverville. The pipe bobbed when he talked, acting as a sort of delay to his words, no doubt because they had to travel the length of the stem and through the smoking bowl before being released to the listener. How garbled they were depended on how much spittle was present in the apparatus at any given time.

Lucky for me, by the time of my arrival, Tyrannical Tommy was worn out, in ill health and drank too much. I learned first-hand that his moniker had been justly earned. For the most part I was the acting pastor, unofficially of course, and it was an opportunity any young priest would have envied.

Financially, the parish was in terrible condition. I had sailed through the accounting courses at Seattle College and quickly put those skills to work. I stopped considerable amounts of petty pilfering and siphoned off money that Tommy had set aside in an extravagant plan to build a grotto in honor of the Virgin Mary. He had several fits of near apoplexy over that but came around as our books started to balance. We negotiated a scaled-down version of his pet project and built the monument. He dedicated it to *"Our Lady, Queen of Grace and Purity."*

My work soon caught the attention of the bishop because our parish assessments started arriving on time and over quota. Tommy suffered a stroke a year later and the bishop found he was short-handed. He named me acting pastor.

"Aren't you the lucky one?" Percy peevishly agreed when he heard the news. Had Ox not been so puffed up about his own reassignment to the Cathedral in Seattle, he might have seen that his gain is what caused my good fortune. The bishop had nearly doubled the staff of assistants in his office and at St. James, temporarily draining his pool of priests.

"You won't be getting any help, and if you embarrass me because you're still wet behind the ears, I'll hang you out to dry," the bishop told me with a stare that convinced me he'd been to the same school of withering looks as Father Goldsworthy.

Being wet behind the ears did cause more than one mistake, but none big enough for the bishop to hear about. In any event, I had the priest's secret weapon to fall back on – authority – which I wielded often. Authority is a great equalizer, and no one questioned mine.

Throwing my weight around, however, was no help in dealing with the war raging around the globe. I was inept in my attempts at consoling people when the dreaded news arrived that a loved one had been killed. I began to live in fear of the Western Union messenger. It was his task to carry the notifications from the War Department announcing those deaths. I wanted to hide every time I heard his bicycle rattling down the street, and breathed a sigh of relief if he pedaled on past. Panic gripped my innards if instead he stopped to fetch me because what he carried was for a parishioner.

Tyrannical Tommy, in one of his good moments, had lectured me about loneliness.

"It's a lonely life we lead, Father M," he said. "There's no one to offer you a hand when life gets you down."

I barely listened at the time, but his words struck home when I received the news on a wet, gloomy day in the spring of 1943 that Harry Capphammer had been killed. Gentle Harry had died when General Rommel's Panzers ripped into the ill-prepared Americans at Kasserine Pass in North Africa.

Shortly after I recovered from the shock of Harry's death, more bad news arrived. The USS Helena, survivor of several major engagements, was torpedoed in the South Pacific. Torn in two she sank, carrying my old friend Billy Archer to a watery grave.

"Til we meet again." Billy's words from our last night in the park came back to me. Harry, I remembered, had added a wistful second to the notion. Grief nearly overwhelmed me, but I suffered in silence with no one to talk to or express the numbness I felt. Percy Knox made a half-hearted try but his pious sentiments failed to reach me. My only consolation was that it made me more aware of what others had endured. At least now when I offered sympathy it was genuine. It did little for my own pain, though, and I began to think it would never end. However, just when I thought it couldn't get any worse, it did.

In late July I had received a hastily scribbled V-Letter from Leezie. (A V-Letter was a paper supplied to soldiers that, when folded and licked, became an envelope. No postage was required.)

"Don't tell nobody," it read. *"I'm in Sisalie, and there ain't no way to tell you about the hell of this place."*

Leezie had surprised everyone and joined the army the day after Pearl Harbor. *"Thank God,"* I thought at the time, hoping it was a sign he was throwing off the shackles of his Windknocker nonsense. Still, I couldn't imagine him shooting at someone. His cryptic note was the first I had heard from him and caused a new wave of anxiety for me.

The newspaper stories about the landings on Sicily had captured everyone's attention. I was thankful I didn't know at the time that Leezie was in the thick of it. Now, I read every morsel the papers offered, following the soldiers as they fought their way inland, crossing later into Italy.

And I worried myself sick.

I prayed in the only way I knew how, firing off *Hail Marys* and a constant litany of, *"Jesus, Mary and Joseph, pray for us."*

Once, I remembered something Leezie had said: *"Just tell your frettin's to the Windknocker and let him worry over it."*

I frowned, knowing my apprehension was bigger than such a simple notion.

Nightmares about losing Leezie plagued my sleep. I lost weight and struggled to put up a good front to my parishioners. I stewed about my lack of faith and wondered if others saw that what I preached to them I didn't practice myself.

"*Suffering was a gift from God.*" I had been taught that from the cradle. "*Harry and Billy? Maybe I could let them go that way,*" I mused. "B*ut not Leezie!*"

I got a case of hives right after Thanksgiving and wondered if they were a punishment to correct my wayward thinking.

On a rainy morning two days before Christmas, I was sitting in my cramped little office, grateful that the terrible year of 1943 was nearly over. The mailman arrived and I gathered the usual pile from the floor beneath the mail drop. A post card flipped out of the stack and I caught it in mid-air.

The front had a garish black-and-white picture, emblazoned with the words "*Leavenworth Prison.*" I turned it over, recognizing the familiar scribbles.

"*Dear Mew,*" it read. "*After I got out of the hospital they stuck me here. I can have visitors after 90 days. Your friend, Leezie*"

I sat in stunned silence. Then I started to cry, shedding the tears I should have when Harry and Billy died. My sobs were a mixture of grief for my two dead friends and relief that at least Leezie was safe. I felt like I'd gotten a reprieve from a death sentence, and slowly my tears changed from grief to joy. I didn't recognize it but it was as close as I had ever come to having a spiritual experience.

That changed later, after I learned what Leezie had done to land in a federal prison in Kansas. When I did, I wrote him an angry letter, chastising him for sullying the memories of Harry and Billy. I would end up eating those words when I learned what had actually happened.

I have studied what I have written here about my first assignment as a young, ill-prepared priest. I acknowledge it is on the gloomy, downhearted side, but reflects well my thoughts of the time. The war years, especially 1943, were an awful time for me. There is no good way to gloss over what I and others experienced.

Providentially, on the third day of the New Year, I received an urgent summons from the bishop. My career was about to take a decided turn for the better.

Chapter Twenty-Three

When I answered the bishop's summons he blew so much smoke up my behind that my shorts still have nicotine stains.

Admittedly, the meeting didn't begin that auspiciously. One of the bishop's favorite tricks was to make a subordinate uneasy by subjecting him to a quiz on a quirky point of church law.

"Moosington," he said, "just stand there a minute, and let me pose you a question." He shot me a withering glance and I hoped he couldn't see my knees knocking.

"Suppose, Moosington," he said, "that you're called upon to render a decision put to you by a mother and daughter." He went on to explain that the pair lived on opposite sides of a riverbank. The river, it turned out, was a church matter, because it was also the boundary between the Central and Mountain time zones.

"The daughter, who lives in the Central zone," the bishop said, "wants to attend Sunday Mass at the mother's church. But," he said, waggling a finger, "that's Mountain time, an hour earlier."

I guessed what he was leading up to. Catholics were obliged to fast starting at midnight if they wanted to receive Holy Communion. I was about to get a new wrinkle to an old question. Sure enough, I was right.

"Does the daughter start her fast at midnight her time or should she go by the clock in her mother's kitchen?" the bishop asked.

I'd learned that the bishop put confidence and quickness above correctness. I blurted, "Her time and not the mother's."

My answer brought a crafty smile to the bishop's lips, and he told me to sit down.

"Sometimes, Moosington, it takes the wisdom of Solomon to resolve thorny issues like this," he said, adding with a grave look about him: "We must always have a ready answer for the ignorant layperson."

I didn't think past my conceit in getting the answer right, or I might have seen just how silly our exchange had sounded. It was 1944, however, when quibbling over unimportant minutia was thought to be what saved a person, or sent them to hell.

"I'm proud of you boy," the bishop said, getting to the point of why he had called me. "I knew all along that giving you Midgeon's parish was a good idea."

In spite of the fact he meant no such thing and had only filled a vacancy because he had no one else, I still soaked up the limelight.

"Now I have a tougher task," he announced. "Are you up to it?"

"*Seattle here I come!*" kept flashing through my mind.

I was to be the pastor of a financially troubled parish in west Seattle. Due to an abundance of priests, promotion in the church was worse than a peacetime army. What had just happened to me was like going from private to general with all the steps between eliminated.

I stopped daydreaming about a victory parade when the bishop's fist slammed the desk.

"And by the holy mercies, if your assistants give you any crap because you're still a youngster, just you let me know," he said. I frowned and he added, "I'll put the fear of Jesus in them."

The job turned out to be so stupidly simple I'm still surprised the bishop didn't tumble to it. Donations were never a problem in any church I served, and all I did was use what Seattle College had taught me about business and accounting. Like clockwork, the bills started getting paid on time and a surplus appeared in the parish banking account. The bishop thought I was a miracle worker, and I never tried to persuade him otherwise.

Each time the bishop found a parish in financial straits, he moved me there, and over the next ten years history repeated itself several times. Thanks to Seattle College and occasional advice from my dad, I had a knack for turning financially troubled parishes around. And, since I was well rehearsed at wielding the priest's secret weapon, authority, I never had to report an obstinate assistant. I instilled the kind of fear the bishop talked about on my own.

By the mid-1950s, my star had risen so fast in church circles that I heard my name being bandied about as a future prospect for bishop. My friend, Percy Knox, referred to me, most of the time derogatorily, as, *"God's little bean counter."* I was the bishop's favorite priest and mighty proud of it.

I was smug, satisfied, and content. Little points of doubt did surface from time to time, if I allowed myself to think about some of the teaching I rigidly enforced. Doubt was a major sin, though, and I quickly banished such thoughts. My old friend the Reverend Poppinjay is the only Protestant I associated with, believing he was harmless.

One afternoon that changed. Jay Jay had finally acquired a church building, and gave me a tour. It was a dilapidated storefront in a bad part of town. As we were leaving, he said, "We does de Lawd's supper on Wednesdays."

"What?" I said.

"De Lawd's supper, jus like dem early deeciples do it back in Jayrusaylum."

It finally dawned on me that he was talking about Holy Communion, but in the Protestant way of a communion service. I almost scoffed, but caught myself. Still, I let it slip, "And I suppose you use grape juice in those little paper cups instead of wine."

"Whatever we gots handy, Sonny boy," he replied seriously. "De Lawd doan mine if we uses grape juice or soadie pop."

Thankfully, Jay Jay didn't catch my grimace. "De Lawd always come to are suppers," he said, "an' bring he graces wid him. De Lawd bless dis place. He love us."

His face radiated sincerity, but the passion behind his words had rocked my peaceful boat. *"It's all a mockery of the blessed sacrament,"* I finally concluded. I put it out of my mind, I thought.

The incident with Jay Jay was just a tingle on a shock meter compared to the jolt that hit me next. History, unpleasant history, repeated itself.

Like a boomerang, an ancient fear circled back to haunt me one night when I was hearing confessions. I had never liked this part of my job. Having sat in a confessional for twelve-hour stretches, I can tell you from experience it is nothing to envy.

A confessional usually has enclosed stations on each side for the penitents. The priest sits in the middle and raises a window, exposing a screen to hear an individual confession. The screen blocks any view but allows conversation. Since it was a weeknight, I didn't expect many sinners to approach. A half-hour passed before I heard someone enter. I raised the window.

"Bless me, Father," I heard a young girl whisper.

I braced myself, because I detected great anxiety in her voice.

"For I have sinned." She started to cry.

"It's alright," I tried to comfort her. "Just tell me your sin."

"This can't be about sex," I thought, realizing the penitent was young – no doubt less than ten.

Finally, after several more sniffles, she confessed what was troubling her. "I-I-I," she stammered. "I ate a hot dog on Friday."

The screen between us rattled from her trembles as she explained how she had lived in mortal fear the past two days. "I even tried to make myself vomit," she said. "And I've been so scared."

A momentary glimpse of my past crossed my inner eye. I remembered the fear I felt watching Leezie riffle the pages of the Baltimore Catechism as we had sat in our secret hideaway. My heart began beating faster and a cold sweat wet my brow as I recalled his words.

"Sorry Mew. It's mortal, an' you has to go to confession for eatin' Blinky's summer sausage on Friday."

The similarity rattled me. The young girl cleared her throat and I snapped back to the present, thinking, *"God, what have I done to land in this predicament?"*

"Are you sorry for the way you have offended God?" I asked. My inner voice said, "*How can you be so callous?*" I shut it out.

She blew her nose and said, "Yes, Father."

A wave of compassion hit me. I stifled that too. Instead of letting my own bad experience temper my judgment, I treated her harshly. None too gently, I said, "For your penance say two decades of the rosary, the sorrowful mysteries."

"Oh thank you, Father," she said sweetly. "I feel better now."

I didn't, though, especially after I remembered I had demanded the same penance from her that Father Goldsworthy had given me.

I brooded over my action for days. Fear had driven the girl to the confessional. Yet Jesus constantly told his followers "Do not be afraid." *What kind of a heaven can heaven be if it's full of fearful people?* I wondered. I had never eaten meat on Friday again, but it hadn't made me better.

It didn't help that one of Leezie's sayings kept pestering me. "*A dog that's a-scared of you will mind, might even fetch if he's afeared enough, but he'll pee in your boot when you ain't lookin.'*"

I couldn't quite grasp what *peeing in the boot* might mean, but ignoring one of his stupid adages wasn't as easy this time.

It was this recollection of Leezie that started what, over the next few years, became my private obsession. I assumed he was still in prison, but I hadn't heard from him since I sent him my frosty letter in late 1943. I decided to find him.

I began with Leavenworth, but they wouldn't give me the time of day. Soon, the folder on my desk was filled with letters and negative replies from friends and family. I kept a log of the telephone calls with the same disappointing results. "*A strange reticence to talk about him*" appeared next to the notation of the day I'd called his mom and dad.

After a year of not one result, and a great amount of frustration, I asked a parishioner to lend a hand. Lieutenant O'Toole O'Sullivan, a detective with the Seattle Police Department, agreed to help. Frankly, I didn't see what he could do that I hadn't already done.

Thus, I was more than surprised when he showed up at my house a week later with his own folder, jammed with papers.

He waved off my invitation to sit in an easy chair and took a seat at the table and began spreading out papers, mumbling through a pencil stuck between his teeth.

"Since this ain't a case to go in front of a judge, I used a back channel to get these," he said.

"My lips are sealed," I said.

"Good," was all he said as he passed me one of the papers.

It looked official and he assured me the Leavenworth Penitentiary heading was genuine. It was signed by Leezie and listed his Home of Record address on a street in Kansas City, Kansas.

"How about this woman?" O'Sullivan asked, putting his finger next to the name *Mildred Parsons*.

"Never heard of her," I said.

"You sure?"

"Positive," I said.

"Damn," he muttered under his breath as if a promising clue had been shot down.

"The address is no good either," he said. "It became an office building some years back."

Another form appeared from O'Sullivan's stack.

"Then we got a problem here, Father, 'cause your story of a long prison sentence don't cut the mustard."

He assured me his words were a figure of speech, and I dropped my *"innocent until proven guilty"* look.

"This can't be," I said.

Boo, as his fellow officers called him, guaranteed me it was, pointing to the final paragraph. It was the disposition of Leezie's incarceration, and read:

"Private L. Eleazor Smith is hereby released from Leavenworth Prison, and returned to active duty in the U. S. Army, and restored to his previous rank of Sergeant. He is to be honorably discharged with full rights and benefits, on this date: 2 December, 1944."

I was thunderstruck!

"I'm just a cop, not a lawyer," O'Sullivan said. "But my gut tells me your Mr. Smith was exonerated."

My stupid look prompted him to go further.

"Does he have any rich buddies?"

"Leezie? No."

"How about friends in high places?"

"*Just the Windknocker*," I almost blurted, quickly convincing myself it was just a nonsensical thought and not a Freudian slip.

"I think there is more to this story than you've let on," he said. "Want to tell be about it?"

I hesitated.

"I'll take a stab in the dark then," he went on. "You and your buddy, Leezie, didn't exactly part as friends."

I slumped in my chair, numbed by the revelation that Leezie may not have been guilty after all. Vulnerability makes for a good confession, and mine was pure textbook. I told him the entire story, leaving out a few things, but not my rush to judgment.

I quoted verbatim most of the angry letter I had written to Leezie. My voice was so choked with emotion I doubt he understood most of what I said.

Boo studied me after I finished my ten-minute recital of friendship treason.

"*I know I'm a louse, just tell me*," ran through my mind.

Instead I heard him say, "You're beatin' up on yourself somethin' fierce, Father, and you shouldn't be."

I started to protest, but he ignored me. "I been a cop long enough to know when a man has actual fact regrets, Father. No one can ask for more than that. I don't care who they are. An' most of all not the man upstairs."

I was still too dumb at the time to know that something important had happened. My uneasiness about Leezie didn't go away; in fact, it would increase. But I no longer felt guilty. The window to my soul had just cracked open. It had been painted shut by years of devotion to dogmas and rituals designed to placate an unfeeling God. Admittedly, the chink was tiny – just enough to let in the first whiff of fresh air.

Chapter Twenty-Four

It was about this time that the bishop moved me to a new parish. It was smaller than I had grown used to, with an ethnic congregation. I should have felt right at home among a people so feverish in their loyalty to the Pope and radical about the Mass. They had all of the Latin responses committed to memory.

Latin was also used outside the church. Even young children greeted me, *"Deus vobiscum, Pater."* That meant *"God be with you, Father,"* and at first it stroked my ego. Soon, however, I realized the greeting was mechanical. It was hollow, with little feeling or genuineness to it.

Their piety and excessive devoutness make me feel uncomfortable, but I wasn't sure why. My friend, Percy Knox, called it my *"pious puzzle."*

I spent four-and-a-half years at Saint Simon of the East Church. It took a lot less time than that to untangle their financial problems, and my tenure might have been shorter but I locked horns with the bishop over an issue that soured his attitude about me. Maybe I just rebelled, but to this day I'm proud of what I did and the way I stood my ground in the presence of His Excellency.

It was the Sunday before Labor Day and I had responded to a hand-written invitation to dinner at the home of a prominent parishioner. *"Dinner will be at 2 p.m., and we have an important matter to lay before you afterwards,"* it read.

From experience I was pretty sure this meant they had already decided how to respond to a petty church matter and wanted me to ratify it. I was wrong about *"petty"* but right on the other.

After dinner, we gathered in an alcove off the dining room, which had been converted into a chapel. Present were the parents, Reuben and Julianne Mealman, and their daughter, Phyllis. I had a queasy feeling; I had previously counseled Phyllis about birth control.

Phyllis had delivered another child since that conversation, so you can guess the gist of my advice to her.

Reuben laid out his case, succinctly and confidently.

"Phyllis here," he said, jabbing a finger toward his daughter, "wants to be matron of honor at a weddin' in a Protestant church. It ain't Lutheran; something like that though."

He glanced at his wife, who mouthed the word for him.

"Episcopalian, that's the one, Father. Anyhow, we told her no."

I breathed a sigh of relief. Even though Reuben was unfeeling about it, at least it was a cut-and-dried issue; Catholics weren't permitted to associate with Protestants. You may think having parents dictate to their grown children on church matters – Phyllis was thirty-two and a mother of eight – was unusual. In that era it would have been considered odd if they hadn't. Ultimately, it made my job easier, since most cases were settled in the home and I was not called upon to decide.

That changed when Phyllis spoke up.

Reuben interrupted, saying, "We grant you that Philly here is adopted, but it still don't make no difference."

Now I was intrigued, and told Reuben, politely, to be quiet and let Phyllis have her say.

I listened to a horror story of being raised in a foster home until she was ten years old. You have heard tales of abuse, so I won't elaborate. The one bright spot in the narrative was her friend. The longer she talked the more I thought it sounded like a relationship enjoyed by identical twins. In any event, this bonding had allowed the two girls to survive a hostile environment.

"And this woman, your childhood friend, is the one about to be married?" I interrupted.

A smile lit her face. "Oh yes, Father, and she is so happy. Both of them are. She's met such a wonderful man."

I didn't often run into this kind of genuine affection. Obviously, their friendship was no mere childhood acquaintance, but something much deeper.

Phyllis spoke for another fifteen minutes, but nothing I heard convinced me to change Reuben's edict. She sensed that and pleaded, "Father, I have to do it. Lizbeth is more than just a friend, she's part of me."

"Wha-What did you say?" I stammered.

She repeated it, emphasizing "Lizbeth."

I don't know where I went, but a part of me left the room. Lizbeth was the pet name Hildred Smith had always called Betsy. I reverted in an instant to the little boy denied my right of friendship to attend Betsy's funeral.

Anger I didn't realize was there boiled to the surface, and I relived in a moment those terrible days. Two voices intruded. First was my mother's, trying to calm my sobbing protests. *"Now, Mew, you know we have to do what Father says."* Then Hildred, saying, *"It's okay, Mew, it's not your fault, you're just a wee boy."*

"But it's not okay," a long-dormant part of me shouted. Leezie had always teased me about biting my lip when I was annoyed, and I did so now. It's remarkable I didn't draw blood. I wanted to shout, *"But it's not okay! It wasn't okay then, and it's not okay now!"*

"Father?" I heard someone say, snapping me back to the present. Somehow, I calmed the turmoil inside me. I looked around the room, my eyes tracking the religious symbols and landing finally on a picture of Jesus calming the sea.

I settled back in my chair, and reached out for Phyllis' hand. I said to her, "You not only have the right to attend, but the obligation as a friend. You have my blessing. Go to Lizbeth's wedding."

She smiled and thanked me.

Reuben, of course, took exception, and gained an audience with the bishop. That resulted in the summons I told you about. The bishop gave me the option of reversing my decision or having him do it for me. "I'm disappointed in you, Moosington," he said when I told him I wouldn't back down.

Phyllis received an official letter prohibiting her participation; I'm happy to say she ignored it and served as Lizbeth's matron of honor anyway.

Reuben eventually mellowed, and confided in me one day that he had been wrong. "I'm sorry I got you in trouble with the bishop," he said. "You did what was right."

Ironically, Reuben was the impetus behind a renewed search for Leezie. It had been on a back burner for months. The last I'd heard from Lieutenant Boo was about an unsuccessful try to access his army service records.

"You need to hire a genealogist," Reuben told me.

Other than my ancient Hebrew grandfather, family history had never interested me. "Have your genealogist start their search in Kansas City," Reuben said. "They might be able to turn up that Mildred Parsons."

It was one of those, "*why didn't I think of that?*" ideas. A month later I received a manila envelope in the mail. Inside I found a marriage certificate. Leezie had married Mildred Parsons in December 1944. My heart beat a drummer's tattoo inside my chest. "At last, some evidence!" I exclaimed.

I spent almost two-hundred dollars paying a professional genealogist. All I had to show for it was another folder full of worthless letters and papers. Leezie's trail went cold again. The last letter I received from the genealogist concluded: "*Parsons is just too common a name. I have exhausted all the avenues I can think of to search further for your friend through his wife's family.*"

My forty-fifth birthday coincided with my next appointment, which was a wealthy parish south of the ferry landings on Puget Sound. It bolstered my confidence that if nothing else, the bishop still held my financial abilities in high regard.

With wealth comes extravagance, and what I discovered appalled me. I was surprised the bishop had waited so long to remedy the financial debacle in my new parish. Maybe his anger at me for not bending to his wishes over the wedding had caused the delay, I reasoned. It took me nearly a year to set things right. Even then, it needed the combined efforts of my dad and me, working together, to finally put the parish back on a sound footing.

"I think you can manage now, Mew. If not, you'd better call upon a higher power instead of me," Sam said, grinning.

I was feeling pretty good, and happy to be back in the good graces of the bishop.

One afternoon the telephone rang. My secretary had gone home for the day and I answered.

"Father, this is Lieutenant O'Sullivan," Boo's familiar voice echoed in my ear. "I have some possible news about your friend."

"Oh?" I said, hiding my elation.

"If it's true, it's not good," he said.

I listened as he told of sending out a routine missing persons report on Leezie. "I got a hit from Tallahassee, Florida," he said.

Then, he told me what I least wanted to hear. "They have a John Doe body in the morgue down there that matches your friend."

Dismay clutched my heart and I couldn't say anything. "You still there, Father?" he asked after several moments of silence.

"Yes," I answered. "But what do you mean, a John Doe body?"

"Well, it's not quite that," he said. "This body is filed under all they could find out about the deceased, and is marked with a tag, *E. Smith.*"

He said the police department in Florida would send some pictures for me to identify.

"It's going to take awhile, Father," O'Sullivan said, "probably a month or so. I'll call you when I get them."

He hung up. I sat for several minutes with the dead receiver in my hand.

Chapter Twenty-Five

The news devastated me. At first, I didn't know how I would survive waiting for the pictures to arrive from Florida. My experience with the zealots at Saint Simon of the East Parish came to my rescue. Their example offered me a way to cope with the news from Detective O'Sullivan.

"I had done something wrong, and displeased God," I thought. *"If I had,"* I reasoned, *"I could set that right."* So I embraced the Church's age-old piety, which said if I tried to be more devout, what I acted out would become fact. If you're not Catholic, or if you're a Catholic born after these events, my actions may confuse you, and possibly even seem incredulous.

I buried myself in prayer books and devotions to obscure saints. I set records for the number of rosaries prayed in a day, but placed most of my focus on church rituals. The Latin Mass was made-to-order for this, and my fervor knew no bounds. Since holiness can always use company, I dragged the congregation along on my quest.

I delivered a fiery sermon about reverence, pointing to my example. That was easy, since I had fine-tuned my gestures, like bowing, breast beating and genuflecting. The sonorous tone I used to enunciate the Latin phrases of the Mass was exemplary. When I pronounced a word like *"vobiscum"* it provoked an immediate picture of Jesus at the Last Supper.

I laced my talk with three words: *"propitiate," "expiate" and "appease,"* letting them roll off my tongue slowly, like cold syrup. I explained how reverence, demonstrated by gestures and a prayerful appearance, would expiate or appease God's wrath. It was good Catholic theology so I was on safe ground, which was no doubt the reason the people responded the way they did.

I noticed an immediate uptick in the number of people going to weekly confession. Sins of being inattentive, lazy kneeling – with one's butt resting against the pew – and not carrying a solemn face forward to the communion rail literally bombarded my ears. The clincher was the elderly man who confessed, "I talked out loud in church."

Silence in God's house was at the very root of reverence, and I gave him a stiff penance for the offense.

By the end of the month I felt rejuvenated and ready for anything. Lieutenant O'Sullivan's telephone call, saying, "I'm on my way over with the pictures," burst that bubble and brought me back to earth.

We exchanged pleasantries; both of us were more nervous than two cats on a water slide. My newfound piety abandoned me when Boo said, "I guess there ain't no sense waiting."

Reality of the inevitable clutched my throat, making me light-headed. "You okay, Father?" he asked.

I shook my head, which caused a wave of nausea.

O'Sullivan reached into an inside pocket and produced a flask. "You better have a jolt of this."

"God, what is that," I sputtered, as the alcohol set fire to my belly.

He chuckled, saying, "Ninety-nine proof Irish whiskey. If it don't blow the top of your head off then my name ain't Benjamin O'Toole O'Sullivan!"

"I suppose you use that on suspects all the time," I squeaked.

O'Sullivan smiled. "We ain't allowed to punish them. You knows that, Father."

Boo laid the first picture of the dead man, labeled, *E. Smith*, on the table. A grainy image tried to stare back at me, but it was too blurred to make any sense of. A second appeared; clear enough that I started shaking again.

"Anything?" Boo said.

I didn't answer, and he placed the third and last photo in front of me. This one was in sharp focus. I opened both eyes and peered closely, hoping against hope. Suddenly, I lost my composure, and great sobs shook me from head to toe. O'Sullivan tried to console me, but I pushed him away. Another spasm caused my heart to pound. I saw through my blurred vision that Boo was reaching for his flask again.

"It's not Leezie!" I shouted. "It's not Leezie!"

"Are you sure? He yelled back. "Are you sure?"

Another wave of relief swept over me. It infected Boo, and soon both of us were bent over, consumed with laughter.

A minute passed before we were able to speak.

The picture of the dead man in Florida did show a slight resemblance to Leezie, but the scar had decided it.

"See," I said. "The scar is on the wrong side and is vertical instead of the other way around."

The detective gave me an inquisitive look and I told him the story of how Leezie's teeth marks became permanently embedded below his lip.

Boo gathered up the pictures, saying, "I'll notify Tallahassee. I won't tell them how happy it made me that we couldn't solve their case." He smiled, and put an arm around my shoulder. "I didn't really know until today just how close you two were once upon a time."

His parting words haunted me. *"Once upon a time"* stuck in my head like lyrics to a song you can't get rid of. I was so lonesome for my old friend that for the next several months I walked around with a lump in my throat more often than not. I had never had these lost feelings about Leezie before. It was especially painful on November 8th. That was his birthday.

My religion saved me again. I rationalized that the path I'd taken toward becoming a more devout priest must have caused a miracle. It didn't occur to me at the time just how convoluted that reasoning was, since I had embarked on it after the fact. Originally, if it *had* been Leezie in that Florida morgue, then somehow God would have had to find a different body to substitute for his.

I intensified my reverence campaign. It wasn't long before my parish rivaled for devoutness the people at Saint Simon of the East. Percy Knox visited me in early December, on his way to another assignment. Known for his ultra orthodox expressions of Catholicism, Percy was impressed.

I commented on his latest transfer, saying, "You've hardly been at Saint Jude's for six months. Either you have some hidden talent that makes the bishop move you around or he's doing it out of spite."

Percy assured me that it was his ability to relate to young people that caused him to be in constant demand. It sounded plausible at the time, and I didn't think any more about it. Besides, he sidetracked me with an idea.

"You should plan a real example of your new devotion for Christmas Midnight Mass this year," he said.

It was just the stimulus I needed, and I started preparation for a celebration that would be the envy of Seattle. Midnight Mass was the perfect venue for the ultimate in pomp and circumstance.

Some minor opposition surfaced when I first broached what I had in mind. The parish did have some traditions of their own. These revolved around a caricature of Saint Nicholas (the parish was named in his honor) being carried in a procession to begin a solemn High Mass at Midnight.

I wanted something more somber, more reverent. First, I hired a first-rate organist, known for his ability to play the best that Bach had to offer. All of the hymns, I decided, would be in Latin, which caused the choir to practice endlessly to memorize their lines. Other, more elaborate innovations would be added later.

December 24th arrived and I was more excited than a rooster learning that chickens had just been placed on the endangered species list. Everything went according to plan. I had practiced my gestures and delivery, leaving nothing to chance. The first solemn chords of Bach set the tone, and I thought overall that the congregation liked it. All save one.

I first noticed him at the introduction when I faced the people. He was sitting in a back row, alone. He was the only person that night wearing a tuxedo. The next time I saw him was when I mounted the raised pulpit to read the gospel. Getting a better look, I could see his full attire and it disturbed me. He wore a tuxedo jacket, which I could see was studded with rhinestones and was quite shabby, with shiny spots from wear. Worse, he wore a scruffy pair of Levis.

Just as I was finishing my sermon, I happened to look again. I was incredulous. He sat licking a huge sucker. I didn't know they made suckers that big, but this one was red and had to be six inches across. Our eyes met. I blinked. He didn't – just kept licking.

"Where are my ushers, and why haven't they removed him?" I wondered. I was incensed that anyone would mock a sacred service by nonchalantly licking a sucker. *"Can't they see him?"* Then it crossed my mind that maybe I was the only one to take notice. Visions were beyond my comprehension, but the thought did keep me from making a fool of myself by demanding that he be ejected.

I nearly had apoplexy when I turned again, this time to distribute the sacred host to the congregation. He had moved over a few seats to the left, and now was positioned on the end of the pew. He was young, probably less than twenty. His face was handsome, but was creased with troubled lines. Our eyes met again, mine full of anger and his with a questioning calm. I was about to look away when he took several quick licks from his sucker. I could see red stains on his chin where the candy had rubbed off.

"What am I to do if he presents himself in line to receive communion?" That one had an easy answer and I looked to make sure the ushers were manning their stations.

My fears were unfounded. When I looked out after that part of the ritual was over, he was nowhere to be seen. No doubt several people wondered what I was doing as I stood on my tiptoes scanning every pew to see if he had moved. But he was gone.

To make sure I had not made it up, after the celebration I went to the pew where he had been sitting. I half expected to find his red sucker lying there, but no such calling card greeted me. *"You were probably just seeing things,"* I thought. You can imagine my shock then, when I rubbed my hand against the pew and felt the sticky residue of his red sucker.

Thanks to the accolades showered on me by the parishioners for arranging such a splendid Midnight Mass service, I went home and forgot about tuxedo jackets and red suckers. Two nights later I had a horrible dream.

I don't remember the details, only the final panorama. I'm sure I woke screaming, although that too may have been a figment of my imagination. The dream's final sequence was a crucifixion scene, very gory and excruciating. The alteration of the execution provided by the dream, however, was far worse. In it, Jesus hung on the cross wearing a tattered tuxedo jacket festooned with rhinestones.

My heart pounded as I fought my way back to consciousness. I scrambled out of bed, but try as I may, I couldn't put the dream out of my head. Desperate, I put on my long cassock, remembering at the last moment to add my biretta because it was cold outside. The door slammed behind me, and I set off running to the church.

Thankfully, no one saw their parish priest fleeing across the parking lot in the middle of the night. My eyes were filled with fright and I was clad only in a long cassock, with my bare legs sticking out the bottom.

Save for a few flickering candles the church was dark. I stood at the back, trying to catch my breath. I gazed toward the altar, taking in the different statues and the nativity scene. A sense of calm came over me, which is probably what allowed the next thought to penetrate my thick head.

"What if the boy licking the red sucker was Jesus, come in person to give commentary on what I thought was true worship?"

Chapter Twenty-Six

My life went into a tailspin. I began to understand what Leezie meant about a dog peeing in your boot. He was talking about rebellion.

A month after the holiday season, I met Lieutenant O'Sullivan at his favorite hangout for cops. "You need a lawyer if you expect to get access to your friend's army records," he said.

"I'll think about it," I told him. "In the meantime I'll contact some of his friends again. Maybe they've heard something."

O'Sullivan chuckled. "Not likely, but don't ask them to send any more pictures."

I agreed, glad that I too could laugh about the trauma the photos of the dead man had caused.

"So how was the Christmas service at old Saint Nick's this year?" Boo asked.

I started the long version, but hadn't said twenty words before telling him about the man in the tuxedo jacket and red sucker.

He chuckled again, and a smile crossed his eyes. "I think you had a visit from Barmy Ben."

I responded with a blank look.

"Did he have a little hook at the end of his nose, a high forehead and an almost double set of eyebrows?"

O'Sullivan's description fit the intruder at Midnight Mass perfectly.

"Yes!" I said.

"You said he wore a tuxedo jacket?"

I nodded.

"Figures."

Barmy Ben, I learned, belonged to a family from Boo's old neighborhood. Barmy's dad had been a part-time stand-up comic, the tuxedo being part of his routine.

"But his daddy died fifteen, sixteen months ago," Boo said. "Ben ain't got over it yet."

"How's the tuxedo fit in here?" I asked.

"The story is that Ben's daddy dressed up in it on Christmas Eve to pass out presents for the kiddos," O'Sullivan said.

"Does this Ben really have a screw loose?"

"Maybe a few cobwebs in his upper story," Boo smiled. "But Barmy's okay."

Barmy Ben might be okay, but I wasn't.

By the time I made it back to Saint Nick's, my stomach hurt. Thanks to the dream of Jesus crucified in a tuxedo, I didn't know what to think anymore. It didn't help knowing the cause of that nightmare was named Barmy Ben; in fact, it didn't go one whit's worth to relieve what was bedeviling me.

I couldn't get it out of my mind that the dream was meant to show me how God felt about what I considered to be true. That called into question everything I believed. Barmy Ben may be a real person – now – but I couldn't set aside the likelihood that Jesus used him as the messenger.

So you won't think I was some kind of a mental case at the time, this hadn't happened overnight. The dream was simply the final earthquake that brought down my house of cards.

My turmoil had been building a long time, caused by a lifetime of ignoring doubts and sidestepping the questions that bombarded me. The intensity had increased, starting on the day I had failed the young girl who confessed to eating a hot dog on Friday. In retrospect, not even that is correct. I could trace my present bewilderment all the way back to the day at Hooverville when I had shared a piece of dried-out gum with Floyd.

I had begun to see the unfairness of church doctrine and how it suffocated rather than set people free. For the past month I had been peeing in the church's boot. My rebellion upset me. After I got home I sat brooding. An hour passed before I reached for the telephone. I knew someone who might be able to help.

After the seventh ring I was ready to give up, when suddenly a voice came on the line.

"Freddie, is that you?" I asked. I breathed a sigh of relief to learn it was, and quickly said, "Is it okay if I stop over?"

"Over" meant a hasty trip to catch the next ferry heading across Puget Sound to Bremerton. I was on my way to see Alfred Timmerman, alias Freddie. Freddie, also a priest, was three years behind me at seminary, where we had become fast friends. He came from a poor family in Anaconda, Montana and what he lacked in worldly goods reminded me a lot, at the time, of Leezie. Freddie, however, was attracted to my generosity of sharing my abundances, like Old Gold cigarettes, whereas Leezie had never been impressed by my wealth.

Freddie greeted me, saying, "So you've finally started to wonder about all the bullshit on the menu of holy mother church?"

His crass remark gave me a shiver because I had only begun to think heresy. Freddie had been dealing with the same problem for years.

I unloaded the events of the past months on him.

"Barmy! Is that what he called him?" He said with a laugh. "Barmy Ben, now that's a good one."

I didn't think it was so funny.

We talked long into the night that first day, and examined the gamut of wrong-headed thinking in the Church. Limbo, Purgatory, Protestants, the Virgin Mary, saints, indulgences, extreme unction, transubstantiation, and even the elevated status of the Pope were part of the litany we covered.

I aired one of my pet peeves, saying, "I'm sick to death, Freddie, of playing nursemaid to a bunch of people who aren't allowed to think for themselves. 'What about this, Father,' and 'what about that, Father?' It's a holy wonder they don't ask me if it's okay to have sex on Sunday."

Freddie giggled, saying, "Don't worry, they'll get around to it. At least they did with Bud Clay." Bud was another priest friend.

"Oh?" I said. "What did Bud tell them?"

"As long as you don't enjoy it."

I slapped my forehead, remembering one of our classes on morals in the seminary.

"You're thinking of Rosy Cheeks, aren't you?" Freddie said.

Rosy Cheeks was the nickname we used for the priest who taught the class, and he'd given the same answer delivered by Bud Clay.

Freddie had had an affair with a woman the summer before he was ordained. I didn't learn of it until years afterward, but asked him at the time, rather hesitantly, "What was it like?"

"Delicious, my dear Barto. Mutually delicious."

He had always called me Barto, and had become my sounding board on all things female. He was much more sensitive toward women, and railed on the way they were treated by the male-dominated clergy.

I remember him spitting in disgust, as he walked me back to my car that first night.

"Why do you think we have altar rails?" He asked.

Altar rails were just that – for those who don't remember or wouldn't know in the first place – a railing in the church that divides the sanctuary from the people.

"It's to keep women from contaminating the holy of holies!" He said. "They're unclean! Don't you remember Rosy Cheeks explaining that?"

I did, as a matter of fact. "Don't forget their role as the tempters of men," I said.

"Frankly, my dear Barto, I often wonder why women in the church put up with it."

Our conversations didn't end there.

"We need each other, Barto," he said. "So we should get together more often."

We did, and these conversations continued for several years. I remember one more than the others. It took place on a night I was particularly depressed.

"You have to snap out of this funk you're in, Barto," Freddie said.

"Why?" I said. "You're not that much better off than me."

"There's still the Eucharist," he said softly.

Eucharist is the church's sacrament, sometimes called Holy Communion. The priest consecrates the bread and wine, turning them, as the church teaches, into the body and blood of Christ.

"I don't know why you bring that up," I said. "We both agree something is dreadfully missing, even in that."

Freddie pondered that a moment before I went on.

"Look at the people," I almost shouted. "Week after week they partake of Holy Communion, but does anything change in their lives – in our lives?"

"Ouch!" Freddie said. "What you're saying is it makes no difference what a person says they believe, because how they live tells the truth of the matter."

Neither of us said anything for a moment.

Finally, Freddie said, "Have you heard the rumors?"

"What rumors?"

"About Pope John and the fact he might call a council and try to right some of these wrongs in the church?"

That was a new one on me. "So what's he going to do, legislate new rules about how many venial sins it takes to make a mortal one?"

Freddie chuckled. "Ordinarily I would agree, if it weren't for Yves Congar."

"Who?"

"Congar is a French theologian, who got a bit too radical for the likes of the church," Freddie explained. "He got censored by the last Pope."

I raised an eyebrow.

"He stuffed a sock in Congar's mouth," Freddie added.

"So!" I said.

"Yves Congar is now one of Pope John's close confidants."

That got my attention.

"You sure about that, Freddie?" I asked.

He nodded his head.

"So why don't we tough it out a bit longer to see what happens?" he suggested. "Then if it all comes to naught we can say the hell with it."

I took his advice, but it became increasingly more difficult to put on an act. The wheels in Rome were turning but I didn't know if I could hold out until the results of the Vatican Council were made public. As the months went by, my depression worsened.

"*Something has to give*," I thought one night in early 1965. Due to a screw up in scheduling, my assistants were all unavailable to hear weekly confession.

I fumed my way through supper. I knew I would have to do it and had a good case of heartburn going by the time I entered the confessional at the rear of Saint Nick's.

"*Just one hour*," I consoled myself. "*Seven to eight o'clock and you'll still have time to catch the last half of GUNSMOKE.*"

Fortunately business was light and I scanned a paperback novel in between confessions. After a long interval, I heard a noise that indicated someone was approaching. I let out a long sigh and put down the book I'd been reading, a dog-eared copy of Leon Uris' BATTLE CRY.

I heard a grunt, then a clump. Someone had just hit the kneeler very hard. I raised the window and delivered the perfunctory Latin greeting for the new penitent. What I heard next jolted me completely out of my senses.

"Hey Mew, Mew, you old homo." It was a snarl I recognized. "I'll give you the dime I owes you if you tells ole Abner where he can find a little poontang."

I honestly don't know what kept me from having a heart attack. Abner Pong, a nightmarish nemesis from the past, had returned to taunt me, and add to my misery. Probably, if I hadn't then heard a slight snicker, I *might* have swooned. The snicker came again. Long-unused brain cells started communicating. The third snicker was less constrained.

"*It can't be!*" I thought.

By this time the snickering was nonstop, and much louder. The electrons in my head reached critical mass. They fired a lightning bolt, saying, "It's him!"

"Leezie!" I yelled. "Leezie!"

I leapt off my bench, hitting my head on the low ceiling, but managed to jerk open the door. I took one step and tripped, falling flat on my face. Undeterred, I jumped to my feet. My instincts hadn't deceived me, for not ten feet away stood Leezie.

"Leezie," I blurted, "where and the hell have you been?"

"Well, Mew," he said, taking a step toward me. "That's a pretty long story."

Chapter Twenty-Seven

It was a long story better told from the pages of Leezie's Big Chief Tablet. Leezie was hesitant to clear up the mystery, and what Mew did learn was frustrating because it was incomplete and vague.

You'll recall that Leezie started using the Big Chief Tablet in the summer of 1929, when he wrote the first letter. This composite from the tablet, edited slightly, answers the questions from what Leezie and Mew later called, *"the missing years."*

Dear Mew,
November 1, 1941
    I found Petey!!! I heard that a young feller had been hit by a train trying to hop a freight in Casper. The man was in the hospital in pretty bad shape.

    I didn't know if it was the Windknocker talking to me or what, but the story threw me for a loop and I couldn't get it out of my head. I knowed me a trucker who was taking a load of spuds to Boise over the mountains by way of Cabbage Hill. I hitched a ride and the trucker hooked me up with another headin' into Lander. I hitchhiked the rest of the way to Casper.

    It was Petey in the hospital alright. He reminded me of a scrawny, scared little chicken with half his feathers plucked out. The train had wrecked his leg, and they had to cut it off.

    I got me a job at a feed mill, and stayed there until Petey got out of the hospital. For the first couple of weeks it didn't look like he was gonna make it, but Petey is a fighter if he ain't nothing else. He was

155

real surprised when I told him about you being at the reunion. After that about all he wanted to talk about was you, and retellin' stories about growing up.

The feed mill found out what I was doing there, and they helped buy tickets for me and Petey to get home on the train. Petey is living with me. I guess I told him enough of my Windknocker stories, cause he quit the bottle and seems to have the reasons now to keep living. Thor Johnson made him a wooden leg so's at least he can get around.

Fort Riley Kansas
January, 1942

I don't suppose I has to tell you what happened on your birthday. Harry and Billy said they was going to join up and go fight the war. It didn't seem right I should keep out of it. Petey tried to talk me from it. "You got no business lettin' dem Germans use you for target practice," he told me. "Dem Nahzi's ain't fraidy cats you know."

Petey was still mad at me when I left on the train, but I was one jump ahead of him. I knowed I wouldn't be no good at shootin' Nazis or Nips. But Pop give me an idea, and I been working on that since I got to Fort Riley.

Yesterday I got transferred to the Quartermaster's Corps. I signed up for the Graves Registration Service. We's the ones who takes care of the dead soldiers. Course we has to find them first and git them off the battlefield. I got orders for New Jersey where they teaches you about this stuff.

Don't know what there is to learn about picking up a dead person, but I guess I'll be findin' out. We don't have to carry guns if we don't want to. Maybe I can keep safe and not have to worry about shootin' me or somebody else. Don't laugh, but my buddies here is already callin' me *Undertaker Smith*.

North Africa
April, 1943

I been in Africa and ain't seen me no pygmies yet. Remember when Betsy was talking about being a missionary? I was going to tag along and scare the pygmies away for her. Seems like a million years ago now.

The fighting has slacked off the last few days. I ain't never seen the likes of this Mew. That German Nazi General chewed up our boys pretty good. We is in the mountains, but they don't look like the ones back home. Every place there's a pass there's somebody guardin' it.

That's what happened to Harry. He was at Kasserine when ole Rommel's tanks mowed them down like a sickle in the cheat grass. I been thankin' the Windknocker ever since, cause one of the other squads found Harry's body. I saw him at the morgue, which aren't nothin' but a tent, and it's hotter than haydees here.

Harry didn't know what hit him. He just had a tiny hole in his head right above his eye where the bullet hit him. It made me really sad Mew, cause I didn't have much time to tell him goodbye. The Major runned me out of there too quick. About all's I could do was wash Harry's face. He couldn't never keep his face clean from the times he was little. I told him when I was leavin', "We'll get together one of these days, Harry, and sing some more songs." Harry never quit talkin' about that night at the park. Don't you be frettin' Mew. The Windknocker will be lookin' after him.

Right now I've got two skulls I'm working on. I went to school and they made me study identifications. I has to look inside the mouths, takin' a look at their teeth. If I can see where some dentist did something out of the usual, then maybe we can match them up with their records. This is all that was left of their bodies, just their heads.

Troopship
Somewhere off the coast at Salerno, Italy
September 9, 1943

I'm smack dab in the middle of the biggest fireworks shoot off you ever did see Mew. We're landing behind the 36th Division, and they must be getting pounded because about an hour ago all the big navy guns opened up, and there's airplanes buzzin' all up and down the beach. It's broad daylight but it's still dark out, and you can't believe the noise. We's close to a Limey cruiser, and when their big guns go off all you hear is Waa-BOOM! Waa-BOOM! Waa-BOOM!

The landing in Sicily wasn't this bad. I was more scared when we went ashore in North Africa, but that's on account of we didn't know what to expect. Sicily was a bloody mess, but I don't like the looks of this. They told us Salerno would be easy cause we was going to surprise the Nazis. Don't look that way to me.

I almost got captured on Sicily. There was a big fight at a place called Tronia. It lasted almost six days until the 18th Infantry finally got the high ground. The Germans retreated after that, and our work really started. I don't remember how many dead soldiers I hauled away. We was happy cause there was a little river there to wash in. Blood Mew, more blood and guts than you can think on. I was covered, an' when you sweats it runs in your eyes, and gags you when it gits in your mouth. The Major kept us at it till we was ready to drop. Major Calhoun Samples, that's his name. He's getting' wore to a frazzle, and takes it out the men.

Some of the men in my platoon went off their rockers in Sicily, but I'm holdin' up pretty good. Following the Windknocker around helps. At least in Sicily we didn't have to get the bodies out of so many burned out tanks. That is grewsome work Mew!! I won't never get that smell of fried bodies out of my nose. When a tank burns it gets mighty hot. Their arms and stuff just come off. I don't mean it funny like, but it's like pullin' a drumstick off a overdone chicken. We has to take those bodies out in pieces. Sometimes we have to scrape pieces off the metal. The first time I didn't think I would ever stop puking, but I did. They made me a sergeant on Sicily. Bet you never did thunk your buddy Leezie would be Sergeant Smith. Don't worry, you don't have to salute sergeants.

We just got the word Mew. We's goin' in. My heart is startin' to tick like a base drum doin' a fast march. Wish me luck.

Field Hospital somewhere in Italy
September 15, 1943

Hey Mew, guess what? I got shot. Took out a piece of the bone right above my knee, and blew a big hole right through the muscle. The doc patched me up and said I should be able to walk okay. The big trouble is I'm gettin' court marshaled on account of I wouldn't follow the Major's orders. Just couldn't do it Mew and if they throws the book at me I'll just let 'em.

Leavenworth Prison
Summer, 1944

My biggest worry was I had lost my Big Chief Tablet, but it showed up with my gear a month after I got to Leavenworth. They just operated on my leg again and put in a new skin graf. This is my third operation. Last time was right before I got your letter. I wanted to answer you, but just couldn't think of how to say it. I guess I'll wait until we see's each other.

Yesterday a lawyer came to see me. He is from the Judge Advocates office in Washington DC. His name is Frank Parsons. He's this skinny runt of a Second Louie, but he thinks he can get my court marshal overturned.

Leavenworth Prison
December 1, 1944

I'm gittin' out of here tomorrow, Mew, and they give me back my Sergeant's stripes. My leg is a lot better, but the doctor told me I been suffering from battle fatigue (along with "shell shock" a WWII term for PTSD) and the army has doctors on the outside that can help me. I guess it is caused by all the grewsome things we saw. Pickin' up dead soldiers ain't something I would want to do for a livin'. I hope I can get rid of them pictures in my head. I knows the Windknocker helped me make it through the war, so I don't think he's done with me yet. I tried my hardest, Mew. I don't think I let Harry and Billy down. I didn't shoot no one, an' I sure weren't no hero. Harry and Billy are the heroes. But I thinks I took care of the dead soldiers like their moms and pops would a liked.

Frank Parsons, he's a Captain now, has a sister in Kansas City. Her name is Mildred. She's the other reason I knows I can make it. We plans to get married next week.

Nova Scotia, Canada, not far from Sidney
June, 1950
We moved up here in early 1945 to take care of Mildred's mom. Tilly, that's her name, died a month ago. Mildred is going to have a baby, so we's movin' back to the States.

Burlington, Vermont
Late fall, 1957
I've had a pretty heavy heart, Mew, since a week ago when Mildred died. We knew from the start that our marriage might be short, because she had childhood diabetes. Mildred was the finest woman you could ever imagine, full of fun, smart, beautiful, and best of all she put up with my Windknocker stories. I have the sweetest little daughter you ever laid eyes on Mew. Her name is Gloria Elizabeth. I call her Glory.

I've been going to night school on the GI Bill. My records got fouled up or I would have started sooner. They had them filed under, *L. E. Smith*, instead of *Eleazor L.* Frank Parsons helped me to set it straight. We live on a farm just outside Burlington. This is some pretty country. Mildred's real dad, Pinky, still runs the farm. I'm studying mechanics and have been taking one class on writing. Since I learned to use a dictionary, my spelling is better, at least I thunk it is.

Burlington, Vermont
Winter, 1963
Some of my old army buddies have been looking for me. Larry Wilson came to see me last week. He is trying to talk me into moving, and going to work for him. Guess where? Seattle! We might have ourselves a reunion one of these days.

Chapter Twenty-Eight

The reunion that Leezie had alluded to in the Big Chief was a shock to both of them. It was several minutes before Mew realized how badly he'd been suckered.

"I should have known better," Mew thought. *"Leezie always was the master impersonator of Abner."* Then he started to take notice of other things, like the fact that Leezie walked with a pronounced limp.

"Leezie, what happened to your leg? You're limping."

He chuckled. "I thunk I told you I was in the hospital," he said. "I got shot. Matter of fact I got shot by the Major."

My eyes squinted almost shut, and my mouth must have dropped open.

"Don't worry, Mew, I'll tell you about it."

I saw an old pickup parked on the street in front of the parish house. It was aged but appeared shiny and new.

"She's a forty-one Chevy," Leezie said. "Purrs like a kitten, too."

Mrs. Brooks' eyebrow cocked at a ninety-degree angle when she apprised my guest. She had been my housekeeper at Saint Simon of the East too, and had an inbred sense that rowdiness in any form was to be discouraged. Leezie disarmed her, though, and it wasn't long before a plate of baloney sandwiches, tastefully arranged with pickles and potato salad, appeared.

"Would you like a beer with that, Mr. Smith?" she asked.

Leezie thought a moment, and deadpanned, "I'd better not Mrs. Brooks. "My parole officer might hear about it and lock me up again."

"Ah now, Mr. Smith," she said, tapping him playfully on the shoulder. "I won't be tellin' him."

I hadn't seen her smile the way she did since the bishop had complimented her on the ravioli she served him on Veterans Day.

"How about some root beer?" Leezie said. "I could do with a bottle of that."

"Comin' right up," she said.

A teetotaler, her look told me Leezie's stock had just risen a hundred points.

The clock kept ticking and almost two hours passed before I could ask a serious question.

"What did you mean when you said the Major shot you?"

"Major Samples, you mean?"

I nodded.

"Cause I wouldn't get out of his way so he could shoot the wounded German."

That sounded far-fetched. *"After all,"* I reasoned, *"Americans didn't go around shooting wounded people."* As the night went on I began making a mental list of answers to questions I'd like. In general, Leezie's account of what he did in the war left me in the dark.

"I thought you might want to see what she looked like," Leezie said as he reached inside his jacket and brought out a picture.

"That's Mildred the day we got married," he said, scooting over next to me on the couch. His finger rested next to an extremely pretty woman. "An' me," he chuckled, tapping a man I barely recognized, wearing an army uniform.

It was Leezie, there was no doubt about that, but I couldn't quite take in his haggard appearance. *"She's nothing but a bag of bones,"* was my Aunt Bertha's favorite expression. The description fit Leezie's photograph. Deep lines etched a gaunt face. Were it not for a glimmer of his smile I may not have known it was him.

"See, I told you I was a sergeant," he said.

"Harry was a Corporal," I said.

Leezie smiled. He seemed genuinely proud of being a sergeant.

What he didn't say about the war he made up for by talking about Mildred.

"She even put up with my Windknocker stories," he said.

I stiffened.

"Relax, Mew," he said. "I know that gives you the jitters."

It was a little after midnight when I first noticed my mood of recent months lifting. Leezie radiated something that got inside my head. I chalked it up to his laugh and ability to tell jokes about himself. He was infectious, and Mrs. Brooks must have taken note of it too. She came into the room about that time to tidy up for the night. I noticed her observing, and giving me a puzzled look.

"What?" I said.

"Oh nothing, Father. It's just good to see you not looking so mopey."

Leezie snickered.

"Mopey Mew! That's what we used to call him, Mrs. Brooks, when he got to wrasslin' and tryin' to figure out all the world's problems."

"Mew? That's a strange name. Did you really call him that?"

Leezie laughed again. "Blame me, Mrs. Brooks, but I can't help it if couldn't get my tongue around that big name of his."

I decided to intervene and told the story for Mrs. Brooks' benefit.

"Lands sakes, Father," she said. "I guess I just never thought of you being a feisty little boy."

Leezie snickered again.

"And what did you do in the war, Mr. Smith?" she asked.

He hesitated, then said, "Not much, but I met a lot of nice guys. Matter of fact I'm workin' for one of them right now."

Mrs. Brooks said goodnight, and I quickly followed up, asking, "What kind of work are you doing?"

"Bein' a mechanic for Larry Wilson," he answered. "Larry came all the way to Vermont to fetch me out here."

Wilson, I learned, owned a service station on a busy street near Lake Washington.

"I been working for him goin' on a year now."

"*That's ironic*," I thought, and wondered how Wilson had been able to find Leezie when one of Seattle's best detectives couldn't.

Around two that morning I was finally able to broach the delicate subject of the letter.

"I've regretted for over twenty years ever mailing that letter to you," I told him, hoping to God he wouldn't ask, "*what letter?*"

"Harry an' Billy dying," he said. "I knows was hard for you. So I didn't blame you."

"Is that why you stayed away?"

"I suppose maybe in the last few years, not knowing what to expect made it worse. But I got no hard feelings, Mew. It took me longer than I thought to think up a good way to break the ice." He snickered. "Then I remembered old Abner and the dime he owes you. Honest though, I didn't mean to scare your liver into conniptions."

"The confessional says to me your bag of tricks has gotten bigger," I said.

"It ain't a new idea. I used pull it on Father Goldsworthy all the time."

"You're kidding," I said, knowing he wasn't.

"I'd sneak into the confession box and make up funny sins like, *I melted my ice cream before eatin' it*," he said. "Another time," he said, before a laugh stopped him. "Another time," he said again, '*Bless me father cause I stole the lead out of Marcy Born's pencil.*' '*And?*' *Father Goldsworthy says to me.* '*I dunno*', *says I.* '*She writ me a letter but there weren't no writin' to read.*'"

"Didn't he ever catch on beforehand?"

"I would always send Petey in just ahead of me," Leezie said. "I'd tell him to play like he was going to throw one of his fits."

By this time we were both laughing so hard I was sure we'd rouse Mrs. Brooks from her deep slumber.

Then, quick as a wink he turned sober, saying, "We can't waste another twenty years, Mew."

I walked him to the door. He gave me one of his patented bear hugs, and said, "You're a beautiful sight for these tired old eyes."

I was too choked up to reply, but he echoed my thoughts.

"There were times I only had our memories to keep me goin,'" he said. Then he switched gears, asking, "You know what Mildred told me one time about us?"

"Will I believe it?"

Leezie laughed. "I think so. She said, 'You guys sound like two puppies joined together with the same collar.'"

Leezie honked three times when he pulled away from the curb, and the silhouette of his pickup reminded my of his old toy truck.

The scene was still there when I woke up in the morning, refreshed and feeling full of energy. I bustled through several Sunday masses, hoping afterward that I hadn't startled the participants with the cheerful gusto I displayed.

There were several things that perplexed me about Leezie's story, starting with Leavenworth Prison. I couldn't understand the government turning a prisoner loose quite that easily. It wasn't that I didn't believe him, but I thought, "What if he'd gotten off because of some tricky lawyer?"

Several days later I had the bright idea to visit him at work for some answers. I found Larry's Service Station easily enough, but not before two near misses of getting on the bridge, which would have taken me across the lake.

I pulled up to the pump and was met by a snappily dressed attendant. "Fill her up," I said.

"Ethel or regular?" He responded.

I checked the pump price and decided to splurge, figuring that only four cents more for Ethel wouldn't break my wallet. "I'll take the twenty-nine-cent-a-gallon one," I said. While the attendant – his name patch indicated his name was Eddie – went to work I said, "Eddie, is Leezie around?"

"Who?"

"Leezie," I repeated. "A fairly tall guy, walks with a limp."

Eddie hesitated, and then stuck his head inside the station's door. "Larry!" He yelled. "There's a customer out here asking after Sarge!"

"It's just not many call him that," Larry Wilson informed me after I explained myself. "Have a seat," he said. "I'm just taking a break for lunch."

Wilson fit my image of what a drill sergeant is supposed to look like – close-cropped hair, stoic features and a deep voice. A voice, I must add, that knew more cuss words than Abner Pong ever dreamt of. I was traveling incognito, having changed out of my priestly garb, and I got an earful.

"I suppose Sarge told you our job in the damn army meant we just went around mowing grass in the cemetery," Larry responded to my question. "Just what was it you guys did in the war?"

"Something like that," I smiled.

"Graves registration meant we was the ones that picked up the dead bodies," he said.

I gave him a disinterested look.

"Stinkin', mangled, even headless bodies," he said. "Try fried bodies stuck in a burned-out tank that you have to scrape out in pieces."

That made my stomach turn flip-flops.

"Sarge had the shitty job of indentifying those," he went on. "It was one of things he was trained for."

"We made three landings together," Larry said. "Salerno was the worst. That's when that son of a bitchin' Major Samples stuck it to Sarge."

"That's when he got court marshaled?"

"Sarge was a goddamned son of a bitchin' gold plated hero! Should a got a medal, maybe even the Silver Star, but that bastard Samples..."

Larry continued on for ten minutes, backtracking to North Africa where it all began. Major Samples, a despot to start with, slowly deteriorated from the rigors of running a graves registration platoon.

"Sarge was the only one the Major respected," Larry said. "And Sarge kept him off our backs right up to the end."

"What happened?" I asked in a barely audible voice.

"Sarge found a wounded German officer at Salerno. The Kraut was under a pile of our own dead," he explained. "The Germans had overrun a company of the 143rd Infantry and wiped out a hundred Americans. Sarge hoisted the wounded German over a shoulder and was set to carry him to the aid station when that son of a bitchin' dick lickin' Samples pulls up in a jeep."

Major Samples, I learned, ordered Leezie to put the German down, which he did, under protest. "He's hurt bad, Major. Got himself a bayonet wound in the belly."

"You think I give a crap in the dark, Sergeant? These bastards just butchered over a hundred of our men. And ain't you or anybody else going to give aid and comfort to the enemy. Step back, Sergeant," he said, unbuttoning the flap on his holster. "Back up, I said! That's an order!"

"Wha-what are you doing, Major?" Leezie asked, taking a couple of hesitant steps.

The Major pulled his forty-five. "I'm about to blast that Kraut bastard into kingdom come. That's what I'm fixin' to do!"

"The men were too shocked to move," Larry went on. "Mind you, I wasn't there but my buddies were. Anyhow, right after Samples cocked his pistol Sarge dove in front of the German and took the bullet. It near tore his damned leg off."

"And he got court marshaled for that?" I said, incredulous.

"You bet your sweet ass he did," Larry said. "A field court found him guilty of disobeying an order under battle conditions. Not guilty of giving aid and comfort to the enemy. Humph! Some enemy. The Kraut would-a probably died anyway."

"Leezie would have felt responsible," I mused more to myself than to him.

Suddenly, a queer expression came over Larry's face. "Shit!" He said halfway under his breath. He said it again, louder, followed by, "Damn! Now I gone and stuck my pecker in the peanut butter for sure." Looking at me he said, "You're him aren't you?"

"Huh?"

"You're the priest back home that Sarge talked about all the time?"

I must have nodded, making him think I said yes.

"We all thought you were God the way Sarge rattled on about you. I remember one time on Sicily when the Jerry snipers had us pinned down for three hours."

Wilson got a far off look in his eyes that gave me the shivers. Then he composed himself, and taking a deep breath, went on, his voice quavering. "Sarge just kept tellin' us not to worry because Father Mew was back home prayin' for us. I don't know if you were, but we believed Sarge. If it weren't for that and those Windknocker stories I'm not sure any of us would have made it back."

I must have smirked at the mention of the *Windknocker,* for Larry said, "Don't laugh, those stories got us over some mighty big humps, and out of some pretty nasty scrapes."

I had learned more than I had wanted to know, and it ended when Eddie leaned in, saying, "Your car's all ready."

"Sorry you missed Sarge," Larry said, helping me ease into the front seat. Sticking his head in the window he said, "I can't help you with how Sarge got out of prison. Go talk to his brother-in-law."

Since I obviously didn't know what he meant, Larry said, "Frank Parsons, the lawyer. He lives down in Olympia."

Chapter Twenty-Nine

Frank Parsons wasn't that hard to find, but getting past the sentinels who guarded the inner sanctum of his law office was.

I finally reached the desk of the matronly woman standing sentry over my last obstacle. She interrogated me, "What's this about, Father Moosington?"

"I just need to talk to Frank, briefly. About his brother-in-law."

"Why?" she snapped. "Has he done something?"

"Oh, no!" I said quickly. "This is not legal business, just personal."

She tapped my card several times on her desk, I guess to get the wheels spinning in her head. Abruptly, she got up and disappeared into the inner sanctum.

Two minutes passed before I heard a voice say, "So this is one of my lucky days. I finally get to meet the famous Father Mew."

Short and chunky best described Frank Parsons. That's more charitable than short and chubby. Good looking, he spoke with the trace of a New England accent. I moved through the preliminaries hastily in case he had to leave suddenly. My worries were unfounded.

"You're in luck, Father," he said when I got to the purpose of my visit. "It wasn't until last month that Leezie's case was declassified."

"Classified!" I sputtered. "You mean like in secret?"

"Absolutely," Frank answered. "And not hard to understand if you're familiar with the way the army works. I blinked and he explained, "It's called, *cover your ass*."

Frank laid out a story that could have been used as the plot in a horror novel.

"My first job was to review cases where men were sentenced to Leavenworth," he said. "And when Leezie's crossed my desk something just didn't seem right about it."

I wished he would hurry up and get to the crux, but Frank wasn't in a hurry.

"He had a lot of commendations and had been a model soldier from the beginning," he said. "Going from private to buck sergeant in North Africa also caught my eye."

"I thought he made sergeant in Sicily," I said.

"He got promoted to staff sergeant there," Frank corrected me. "Which also didn't add up."

Parsons sped up his explanation a little. "I found witnesses," he said, "and got signed depositions that supported Leezie's testimony."

But, I learned, when he took those affidavits back to Washington, no one wanted to listen.

"The brass studied them and decided not to pursue it," he said.

I sucked in my breath, impatient to learn more.

"Part of the good ol' boy network," he said. "Officers stick together. Anyhow, I pitched the file in the completed basket and forgot about it. But a month later the shit hit the fan. The Chief Judge Advocate marched into my office one morning more upset than a giraffe with whiplash. We made a hasty trip to the War Department and got our asses reamed by a Major General."

"What?" I said.

"It was the German," Frank said. "Obermeister Fritz Knukel, or something like that."

"He was still alive?" I asked in one explosive breath.

"Alive and crowing like a naked rooster on a frosty morn in Montana," he said.

Frank told of his trip to the German POW camp in the South. Fritz Knukel, indignant, arrogant and full of outrage, had threatened to take any steps necessary to see the major punished and the soldier who saved his life rewarded.

"How'd he expect to do that from a POW camp?" I asked.

"Friends in high places," Frank answered.

"What?" I asked again.

"Influence, Father! Who you know works the same the world over. Knukel was from an aristocratic and wealthy family in Germany. How it happened in this instance I could never nail down for sure. The way I figure it, someone in the Knukel family got to someone who knew someone in Washington."

I was shaking my head by this time, but his reasoning made perfect sense.

"It could have been something else," Frank said. "But I don't think so."

He paused to light a cigar, and went on. "The War Department was having a hissy fit. That I know for a fact. The same Major General had them cut me emergency orders and I flew out that night to Italy. Someone important had to be twisting the War Department's tail to get that kind of action. In Italy I confronted Major Samples with the evidence I'd gathered. By then he was just a shell of a man."

"What did he tell you?"

"He 'fessed up to everything I already knew or had guessed," Parsons said. "How he intimidated the witnesses and then arranged quick transfers for them to England. He had some power, Samples did. Just bulldozing the top brass to convene a field court marshal tells you that. And all just to get back at Leezie." He spit a piece of tobacco into a wastebasket.

"Why?" I said. "Did you ask him?"

"He wouldn't say, but he intimated that Leezie got under his skin. I gathered from hearing him talk that Samples had been raised with a lot of hellfire and brimstone religion. Leezie no doubt reacted to that, and told him it was so much baloney. I figure it needled Samples, and he was afraid to admit that maybe he'd been fed a pack of religious lies."

"Did they punish Samples?"

"Didn't have to. He bought it later that month."

"Huh?"

"Sniper got him. Right here," he said, tapping his right temple.

"There's one thing I don't quite get, Frank," I said. "From what I've heard it makes it sound like shooting prisoners was an everyday occurrence. Samples was an exception, right?"

"Fat chance," he spat. "It happened a lot more often than you or I or anyone else wants to admit."

I must have looked naïve, because he followed with, "Geez, Father, where do you think the expression *'War is hell'* came from?"

Chastised, I said, "Is that the end of story?"

"Not quite," Frank said. "The Army tried to diddle the ewe on the river bank, so to speak."

I don't think Frank caught my blink, because he kept right on going.

"They decided to reduce his sentence to time served and give him a general instead of an honorable discharge."

"That's outrageous!" I fumed.

"My boss thought so too. In fact, he was so mad at the injustice that he got me appointed as Leezie's personal representative."

He tapped a long ash off the end of his cigar before adding, "That's how Mildred got involved. She was my courier, delivering papers for Leezie to sign. Leavenworth didn't like it, so we elevated her to a status that demanded anytime access. It was signed by the big man himself, General Marshall."

Frank went on. "Anyhow, before long, Mildred started using any flimsy pretext to visit Leavenworth."

"And they weren't just reading law books together," I chuckled.

He laughed too, and said, "They were made for each other, Father. I've never seen the likes of it, then or since."

Frank got a wistful look in his eye. "I wish you could have met Mildred. She was a real peach."

Then as an afterthought, he added, "He has a child. Did you know that?"

I was too shocked to answer.

"She's being raised by our aunt in Vermont," he went on. "Probably the sweetest woman next to Mildred that I know."

"How old is this child?"

"Just turned eleven this year," Frank said. "Her name's Gloria Elizabeth, but everyone calls her Glory."

Frank stubbed his cigar in an ashtray. "We finally convinced the army that nothing less than complete exoneration would do" – he underlined with a slap on his desk – "and a letter of apology in his records."

He took a deep breath. "I didn't want some idiot coming along later thinking he'd beaten the rap because some tricky lawyer hoodwinked the review board. He was innocent, dammit! Makes me mad all over again to talk about it!"

Frank smiled and relaxed. "The only concession we made was to bury the records. After that, they caved in and Leezie was a free man. But not before Fritz Knukel signed off on the deal."

My own ears were still smoking from the rebuke he didn't know applied to me. "Really?" I said.

Frank laughed again. "Oh yes, but Fritzy boy still insisted on rubbing their noses in it. He demanded to meet the soldier who had saved his life. That's how Leezie and Mildred got to spend their honeymoon down south. They had the time of their lives, and all on the army's dime."

I made a motion to leave. "Hold up a minute, there's one more thing."

I settled back in my chair to hear Parsons say, "Leezie was traumatized by the experience. He had enough trouble just dealing with the battle fatigue that the war caused." Frank paused a moment before saying, "Did you ever try to find him?"

"Yes!" I exclaimed, and told him about Lieutenant O'Sullivan.

Frank chuckled. "Well, I know that Leezie made a secret trip back to that home town of yours."

"When?"

"January 1945," Frank said. "He made sure his parents wouldn't say a word. As far as I know, they haven't to this day."

"I can testify to that," I said.

I sat for several moments. "Did he have reason to be that paranoid?"

"I'll take the fifth on that one, Father."

When I didn't say anything he said, "Just remember it, because he still tends to be secretive. It should help when he finds out his file has been declassified."

Chapter Thirty

The coming years would pass in a blur. Leezie and I were determined not to repeat the mistake of the *missing years,* and more resolute not to waste a single day. I had the space over the garage made into a cozy apartment, and he moved in.

The bond, forged at age two, we learned was still strong.

"It's not exactly like old times a-cause we're not kids no more, but I think I still knows you," he said more than once.

Most of the adjusting had to be made by me. We weren't equals and never had been, thanks to the superiority instilled in me by Uncle Horace. That was still stored in my subconscious, but thankfully my dad knew it too.

I didn't take too kindly to his insight when he first enlightened me.

"Mew, your trouble is that you lack the one thing Leezie has plenty of," he said.

"Oh?" I replied. "And what's that?"

"Horse sense," he said. "You might be bright, but you'll never be smart without horse sense."

I frowned but knew enough to listen when Sam said something.

"It's time you let Leezie teach *you* a few things."

It boiled down to respect, and I started paying attention. The first thing I noticed was that Leezie read a lot. In fact, he read anything he could get his hands on. I subscribed to practically every magazine there was in the religious spectrum, and that became part of his new diet.

"Mew," he said to me one morning. "That Pope Johnny of yours is settin' to turn the Windknocker loose and open some windows in your church."

"You've been reading about the Vatican Council again?" I said.

"Yup, and I hope you're ready for what's comin'".

I thought I was, but nothing could have prepared me for what happened at the end of 1965 when the council completed its work. Just like the birth of Christ had divided history into before and after his coming, we would use *"pre-Vatican II"* to describe the old church.

It took some time for everything to filter down to our level, but when it did "flabbergasted" didn't describe it. I got a telephone call from Freddie one morning. He was brief, saying, "I'm on my way over. Can you make it?"

We decided to meet at a picnic ground next to a small amusement park. I brought a lunch that Frannie fixed, and stopped on the way to buy a large bag of salted in the shell peanuts.

Freddie was already there when I arrived. I watched him for a minute, pacing rapidly back and forth, obviously deep in thought. He spied me, finally, and his face lit up. He tripped over an untied shoelace, smiled for nearly taking a nosedive, and then rushed to greet me. Clapping me on the back, he exclaimed, "My God, Barto, I can't believe what's going on!"

We sat down after I covered the grime and graffiti on the tabletop with a cloth. I handed him the one bottle of beer in Frannie's basket. He'd sip on that, making it last most of the afternoon. Next, I handed him the conversation starter. "Hot damn," he said. "You remembered the peanuts." I could tell he was really excited about something.

Freddie was addicted to peanuts and ate several as part of his start-up routine to a conversation guaranteed to be lively. He took a short sip from his beer and brought out a book. It was his copy of the Vatican II documents, already dog-eared and studded with paper clips to mark pages he found interesting.

"Look at this," he said, sliding the book under my nose.

I read an explanation of why the onerous edict banning the eating of meat on Friday had been done away with.

Leezie had already pointed it out to me one morning when he said, "Hey Mew, remember that time you ate Blinky's summer sausage on Friday?"

I nodded.

"Pope Johnny says it ain't gonna be a sin no more."

Leezie used *Pope Johnny* as a figure of speech, more as a synonym for anything to do with Vatican II.

"By comparison it's a small thing," Freddie said, taking his book back. "But I know eating meat on Friday isn't small to you."

I smiled, thinking of the grief it had caused me.

Freddie patted his book and said, "Barto, everything we've ever complained about has been changed, or is in the process. Can you believe it?"

Then I witnessed something extraordinary. Freddie started to cry. He wasn't an emotional guy, in general. Thinking he was too cynical to display that kind of feeling, his tears of joy really touched me. A big lump choked my throat. I reached across the table and put a hand on his shoulder.

"They almost robbed us of our faith, Freddie," I whispered. "But Vatican II has tossed us a life preserver." He looked at me. "And I have you to thank for making me wait," I added.

"I think I only did it to buy *myself* time," Freddie said. "But I appreciate the sentiment. God damn son-of-a-bitch! Can you believe a grown man like me, blubberin' that way?"

He wiped his eyes and blew his nose. "Holy suffering cat shit!" he exclaimed. "I can still hardly believe it. Vatican II is almost too good to be true. Thank God for Giuseppe Angelo Roncolli!"

I offered an *"amen"* and like him, gave the credit to, Roncolli, better known as Pope John XXIII, for having the courage to make it happen.

"What are we going to do now?" I asked, jokingly. "We're no longer heretics."

He laughed. "I don't know about that. All I know is I have *life* in me that I didn't have before. Barto, this has to be the biggest thing to rock the church since Christ rose from the dead!"

The metaphors I had used to describe it, like earthquake and a volcanic eruption were puny compared to Freddie's. His was so apt that I never found a better one.

I often thought the Vatican II reformers must have had some kind of a telepathic access to our thoughts. Freddie was right. Everything that had ever bedeviled me about that church had been changed. The weeks that followed were heady days.

Several Sundays later, Saint Nick's church experienced the most visible change. For the first time in centuries the people heard the Mass prayed in their own language. As I looked out on the sea of faces that morning I saw expectation, apprehension and some obstinacy. I was tense. The new liturgy, as it was now called instead of the Mass, demanded participation. My flock was used to being entertained by a magnificent choir and occupying themselves with other devotions while the priest mumbled his way through the Latin prayers.

The first attempts at singing were feeble and the sounds reminded me of the frog pond on the edge of the church's property. But my sermon was pretty good that day. I based it on a theme of the early disciples also being hesitant to embrace strange new things. It wasn't until just before communion was distributed that the congregation relaxed.

It was supposed to be called the Kiss of Peace, but I fudged and simply said, "Now is the time to turn to your neighbor and offer them a handshake or a kind word." No one seemed to grasp what they were supposed to do until I did the unthinkable – I left the altar and went amongst the congregation. I shook hands and offered a greeting to all I could get to. The people warmed up and began reaching out to those around them. The farther I went toward the rear of the church, the more the thought kept going through my mind, "*This is so right; this is so right.*"

When I returned to the altar and turned toward my parishioners, I witnessed a sight I had not seen in my quarter-century as a priest. I was greeted by a mass of smiling faces.

That afternoon I went fishing with Leezie. We had a favorite place on Puget Sound, sheltered from the wind by a rock jetty but where we could still watch the big ships coming in.

"Not a bad sermon this morning," Leezie said.

"You were at St. Nick's for that? I don't believe it."

"Sure," Leezie laughed. "I was hidin' in the confessional."

I snorted only to be interrupted by the squeal of his fishing reel.

"Fish on!" he shouted.

He landed a big cod, and it took another ten minutes before I could ask him what he thought of the morning's events. He knew I was excited and took the moment to tease me.

"If they wasn't such good eatin', I would throw them ugly critters back."

"I wasn't talking about the cod," I said, biting my lip.

He eyed me seriously. "Well, nobody there can think Pope Johnny ain't serious. Most like it, some is scared, and a few has got their backs bowed."

"Backs bowed? How do you mean?"

"Pope Johnny took their rules away," Leezie said. "Give people fifty rules to follow and they's happy. But tell them you can't get the Windknocker to like you by followin' rules – well that's sure to upset some folks."

I thought I understood but wasn't sure.

"Pope Johnny made it personal," he said. "Just like your new service this morning."

"You mean because it was in English?"

"No, a-cause the people saw that instead of all that bowing and scraping, when they shake their neighbor's hand they's shaking hands with the Windknocker too. Some of them even felt that this mornin', and more is sure to."

I wasn't entirely sure of his meaning but it did put a smile on my face.

"What you grinnin' about?" he asked me.

"*Horse sense*" had crossed my mind, but I answered, "Nothing really, I just remembered something Sam said."

"Some of them people will be wantin' their rules back, Mew," he said.

I thought of Percy Knox, who had been in a state of hysteria since the changes went into effect.

"Vatican II is church doctrine now," I said.

Leezie started to laugh, and I thought he was scoffing at my remark.

"No – No," he said. "I wasn't makin' little of what you said."

"What then?"

"I was just thinking," he replied. "Pope Johnny propped open the door, and afore long you're going to see some Catholics get borned again."

I had adjusted to "*Windknocker*," but Leezie's born-again mantra still needled me. I wanted to say, "*Whaddayamean, borned again?*"

Two months later he repeated this, and more, to Percy Knox. I didn't warn Leezie in advance of Ox's panic about Vatican II. Percy's life was about the power being a priest gave him, and he wasn't about to let that go.

Percy, as he usually did, tried to dominate the conversation, but he seemed flummoxed by Leezie. I expected Ox to be breathing fire and spitting lightning bolts after three minutes. He didn't react until Leezie repeated, "You're going to see some Catholics get borned again."

Ox scoffed and made a derogatory remark about Protestants. Then he quickly apologized.

"*This is not like Percy*," I thought. Later, he asked Leezie to walk him out to his car. I watched from the window, observing an animated discussion on the sidewalk. It ended in a handshake, and Percy drove away.

"Whew," Leezie said. "Your friend doesn't think much of Pope Johnny."

Percy's visit was quickly forgotten, and we went to work planning a hiking trip through Olympic National Park. Leezie was gone a lot, so we picked a time at the end of the summer.

"Let's plan our little stroll for late August," he said. "I should be back by then."

I didn't like to pry, but he intended to be gone longer than usual this time.

"Where are you going?" I asked.

"Vermont for sure, to see Glory," he said. "Then maybe Saskatoon. If I have time on the way back I'll stop in North Dakota and at our old stompin' grounds to look in on Petey."

I wondered how his boss, Larry Wilson, reacted to these absences. Often, Leezie seemed to just take a notion and disappear for a week, or sometimes a month, with no more explanation than, "I got me some business that needs tendin' to."

Wilson had just laughed when I asked him about it. "I don't worry about Sarge," he said. "When he runs out of Windknocker stories, he'll be back."

That night, just before turning in, Leezie asked me, "Does your friend Percy like little boys?"

"Of course," I answered. "He's always worked with young people. You might say it's the one specialty he has."

Leezie gave me a strange look.

"What is it?" I asked. "What's wrong?"

He shrugged, saying, "Nuttin' probably. He just reminds me of a guy I met in the army."

His odd look stayed with me. I vowed to mention it to Freddie.

Chapter Thirty-One

That promise remained stuck in limbo for better than two years. To be honest, I forgot about it.

One weekend Percy and I worked a retreat for teenagers together. I did most of the work while Percy hung out with the younger boys. There was something odd about his demeanor that upset me. Leezie's strange look when he had asked, "Does your friend like little boys," came back to me. The alarm bells that went off in my head prompted a long telephone conversation with Freddie. Since Freddie had a free afternoon coming up, he agreed to come over to talk about Percy.

Leezie had yet to meet Freddie, so I decided to take him along. "Since he's coming across from Bremerton anyway, why don't we just get together at the Wheel House?" Leezie suggested. He explained it was a tavern near the waterfront. I bit my lip like I always did when he proposed something different from what I had in mind. "Don't worry, Mew," he said, "you'll like it. But we better take your car. It would be a little crowded in my pickup."

I agreed. Freddie was a little too broad in the butt to make it a threesome. I still had my blue and white 1955 Oldsmobile. Leezie had recently overhauled the engine, installed new seat covers, and put in seat belts.

"What do I need those for?" I'd asked him.

"Get with the times, Mew," he replied. "Before long you won't be able to buy a car without seat belts."

We picked Freddie up at the ferry landing on the eighth of June 1968. I mention the date because it has significance. Bobby Kennedy had been killed the night before. The nation was in shock, coming as it did on the heels of Martin Luther King, Jr.'s assassination in April. I had thought about postponing, but Freddie vetoed the idea.

Freddie was ecstatic when he heard Leezie's suggestion for our get-together. "Holy son-of-a-bitch! A tavern!" he said, pumping Leezie's hand like a plumber working a plunger on a stubborn toilet. "I think I'm going to like you, Mr. Smith."

The Wheel House Tavern was located on Harbor Avenue, perched on a knoll overlooking Puget Sound. As you might have guessed, the theme was nautical. Dominating the large room, decorated to resemble the deck of a ship, was a great spoke wheel from an early sailing vessel. Leezie led us to an alcove near a side window. On the wall a sign read, *"Captain's Cabin."*

"Hot damn! This is perfect," Freddie said, parking himself on one of the sea chests that served as seats around a table. It was a unique piece of furniture, and I guessed a ship's captain might have used such for plotting his course. "In fact, Barto, I'm thinking we should make this our new office. It beats the hell out of that amusement park."

"This is Jack," Leezie said when a tall muscular man in a white apron appeared. "He owns the place."

Sticking out of Jack's mouth, precariously dangling at a downward angle, was a lit Pall Mall cigarette. "So you're both men of the cloth," Jack said.

"Would you have known" Freddie asked, pointing to Leezie, "If he "hadn't told you?"

"Not much gets past Jack," Leezie volunteered. "He would have figured it out."

"Don't let it bother you, Fathers," Jack said. "Sarge here brings all kinds of weirdoes to my place." He grinned, and somehow the cigarette managed to stay attached to his lip.

You could have heard Freddie's booming laugh across the street. "Weirdoes! Did you hear that, Barto?" he said. "Damned appropriate when you consider what we're here for."

"The Wheel House is famous for clam chowder," Leezie interrupted. That got our attention, and we each ordered a large bowl.

"Shit on a biscuit! But I do like this place," Freddie said. "Is it always quiet this time of day?"

"It gets lively after the fishing boats come in," Leezie smiled. "But that won't be until later."

As if primed to make a liar out of him, a big parrot in a cage by the front door sounded off. A large black man entered, banging the door behind him. "Ahoy, ahoy, ahoy," the colorful bird squawked. The man ambled toward the bar and I watched as Jack drew him a mug of beer. After a whispered conversation and a headshake, the black man turned and headed in our direction.

"Oh-Oh," Leezie said. "Here comes Leonard."

Leonard stopped at the entrance to the alcove and peered in. "Hiya, Sarge," he said, grinning. His face registered a relieved look, like he'd just found his lost billfold.

"Step inside, Leonard and pull up a seat," Leezie replied. "We're just having some chowder. Want some?"

"Naw, Sarge, you knows I don't like nothin' that reminds me of gook food."

"It's pretty god-damned good," Freddie spoke up. "Are you sure?" Leonard smiled but didn't answer. "How about a burger then? We can get Jack to fry one up for you."

"Sure, I'll have me a burger," Leonard said.

"Jack!" Freddie bellowed. "Would you bring a burger for our friend Leonard?"

"With fries or onion rings?" Jack shouted back.

Leonard looked indecisive so Freddie shouted, "Both! And put it on my tab."

Leezie introduced us, emphasizing, *Father* Mew and *Father* Freddie."

"Naw shit," Leonard said, shaking Freddie's hand. "You're a priest?"

"Naw shit," Freddie answered. "But this is my day off. Welcome to weirdoes anonymous by the way."

Freddie's humor went over his head, and Leonard shook my hand, saying, "Sarge already tole me bouts you." He said it with a broad smile so I reasoned Leezie had exaggerated my reputation. I remembered to squeeze Leonard's hand. Leezie had coached me out of my tendency toward an anemic handshake.

"Shaking hands with most priests feels like pattin' a plate of cold noodles," he had said. He made me practice until it became second nature to offer a firm grasp in return.

Leonard's burger arrived and he attacked it, coming up for air once to say to Leezie, "Can you spare me a minute after I eats, Sarge?"

"No time like the right now," Leezie said, watching the rest of the mouthwatering hamburger disappear into his mouth. "Bring your fries and rings. We can sit over by the life boat."

"What do you suppose that's about?" I said.

"Don't know," Freddie replied, dabbing the last of his second bowl of chowder with a piece of bread. "Leonard don't look too prosperous so my guess is he needs a loan."

We got down to the business of Percy Knox.

"I always did assume he was homosexual," Freddie said. "But I never held that against him."

"How much do you know about pedophilia?" I asked.

"Jesus Christ, Barto!" Freddie exploded. "Is that what you're thinking?"

He was genuinely upset. At first I thought he was having a flashback to our days at Saint Edwards. For two years running Freddie had roommates he swore were homosexual. "No, they weren't open about it," he had told me. "And we were still friends."

His present uneasiness was different, as I discovered when he confided, "I had a younger cousin that got groped by a pedophile." "Pedophile," was enunciated and came out like a gunshot.

"What happened?"

Freddie smiled. "A bunch of us older boys jumped him one night when he staggered out of a bar," he said.

"Older?" I said. "I'll bet it wasn't by much."

"Bein' eleven in Anaconda is not the same as where you grew up," he laughed. "We suggested he get out of town, and he did."

Few of Freddie's rough edges from growing up in a tough town remained. I did chide him about his crude vocabulary, but in church circles he didn't have that reputation. He was most popular in Bremerton, but his star was rising, especially after the bishop asked him to write a weekly column in the diocesan newspaper. His parish was on the cutting edge of the Vatican II reforms and if you ever wanted an example of a "beloved pastor," he was it.

I spread a paper on the table, and he did the same. Each of us had prepared a list of all the parishes that Ox had served in. "Son-of-a-bitch," Freddie said. "This is pretty damned impressive by itself." Counting them up, after erasing the duplications, our list contained thirty-nine different parishes.

We divided up the names of the present pastors, based on how well we knew them. I ended up with twenty-two names. Our plan was to ask enough people until we got some answers about Percy.

"Eventually," Freddie said, "one of them will let something slip."

Freddie's mood had changed. He was somber. We talked some more, going over strategy of how to approach people so they wouldn't know what we were after. He finally tired of that and said, "You know what really bothers me about this?" He didn't give me the chance to answer. "If our suspicions are true, then someone high up had to know about it."

"Not necessarily," I countered. "Percy can talk his way out of just about anything."

"Bullshit! I don't believe that for an instant." He eyed me for a long minute, rubbing his temples. "We have to agree, Barto, right now, that if we get confirmation the news has to go straight to the top."

That was more sobering than you might think. "There's a real possibility the bishop will shoot the messenger," I said.

"Bye bye career," he said, tossing a kiss toward the window.

"Blow the man down," the parrot squawked as Leonard stood up and walked toward the door.

"His name is Conrad," Leezie said in response to our question about the parrot, the guardian of the door.

Freddie got up and we watched as he had an animated conversation with Jack at the bar.

"What's he up to?" Leezie asked, emptying his bottle of root beer.

Freddie couldn't talk without some pretty wild gestures, and I thought for sure that he'd knock the cigarette off Jack's lip. "I don't know," I said, "but I hope he's not giving Jack a lecture about the evils of smoking."

"Ha!" Leezie quipped. "He won't be the first to try that."

Five minutes passed before Freddie and Jack shook hands. It was obvious some kind of agreement had been reached.

"Guess what?" Freddie announced when he came back and eased his bulk onto the sea chest.

"You told him to quit smoking," I said.

"Well hell yes I did," he said. "But in a kindly sort of way." Freddie was beaming. "Nope, you guessed wrong, Barto. Nope! It's a lot better than that. We got ourselves a new office."

Freddie had been lobbying for a year to find a better meeting place in Seattle. Thinking he simply meant the tavern, he corrected me. "No, this," he said. "The captain's cabin. All we have to do is call ahead and Jack will reserve it."

Leezie snickered. "You could rename it," he said. "Let's see," and he paused a second, then grinned. "You could call it *the monk's nest*."

"Boo!" I said.

"Well," he said, "since there's no doubtin' you'll be doing a lot of eatin' here, why not name it, *Mew's Mess*?"

"Ho! That's a good one," Freddie said. "But I vote for, *'the keel over.'*"

"That's terrible, Freddie!" I shouted. Leezie's snickers were growing. He was no doubt proud of himself for drawing us into one of his dumb word games. But I played along and said, "We should just call it, *B. S. before the mast*."

"Ah, Mew," Leezie laughed. "You knows they already have a name for that. It's called *the poop deck*."

Freddie's face was red, and he was shaking with laughter. Conrad the parrot came to our rescue, finally, putting an end to the rename game. His loud squawks heralded the entrance of two men. They bypassed the bar and headed straight for our table.

"Howdy Sarge," the first one said. "We just heard you were here."

"And stopped in to see if we could buy you a root beer and basket of peanuts," the second man said. I quickly labeled them Mutt and Jeff, and it did turn out they were brothers.

"This is Sam and Jeff," Leezie announced. I thought guessing right on one out of two was pretty good but hid my sly smile. They were more our vintage in age and I presumed rightly that they were army friends of Leezie's.

They only stayed a few minutes and departed in an obvious hurry, but not before leaving an order for root beer and peanuts at the bar. "They work at Boeing," Leezie informed us. "Headed in for the afternoon shift."

Freddie gobbled most of the peanuts and Jack brought a refill. "It's good to see somebody likes them besides Sarge," he said.

"Sarge?" Freddie said. "I take it you were in the war."

Leezie offered a slight nod.

"So what do you think of this bullshit LBJ has been feedin' us about Viet Nam?"

"You'd have to ask that question to someone that's been there," he answered. "Somebody like Leonard."

"Leonard! Our hamburger-eating champ was in Viet Nam?"

"He was at Khe Sahn," Leezie said.

Freddie and I looked at each other. A fierce battle had raged at Khe Sahn from January until April. Surrounded and outnumbered, the embattled Marines had been under constant attack and bombardment for seventy-seven days. The nightly television news had brought their struggles into every American living room.

"Damn! Son-of-a-bitch! Khe Sahn!" Freddie blurted. "I wouldn't have guessed that just meeting Leonard."

"He has one of them purple hearts to prove it," Leezie said.

Neither of us knew how to respond to that. Finally Freddie said, "Now I get it. His reference to *"gook food"* was about his dislike of anything Viet Nam."

That earned him another nod from Leezie.

I figured Freddie was about to probe Leezie about his counseling session with Leonard, but he looked at his watch and said, "Shit on a biscuit, if we don't get a move on, I'll miss the four o'clock ferry."

Conrad squawked one more time when we left the Wheel House. "How does Jack shut that crazy bird up?" Freddie chuckled.

"He has an old piece of sail he tosses over the cage," Leezie answered.

"Maybe you could teach him a few of your cuss words, Freddie," I offered, as we walked up the street toward our parking place.

Leezie snickered, saying, "A guy already tried that."

"A-a-a-nd?" Freddie questioned.

"Conrad went mute for a month and wouldn't say a word. Jack threatened to sue the guy."

"See, Freddie, you need to clean up your language," I joked. "Imagine what the bishop will say if Jack sues the diocese over a dumb parrot."

Leezie snickered again, and Freddie harrumphed. It was a fitting end to our introduction to the Wheel House. The association for Freddie would last until he left the diocese five years later. For me, well, practically forever.

Fortunately, it didn't take an eternity to unravel the thorny problem that Percy Knox presented, although it seemed like it. That would take a sinister turn two years later and end up costing me – dearly.

Chapter Thirty-Two

That happened on November 21, 1971, four days before Thanksgiving. Although it has nothing to do with what happened, and just points out why I remember the time so well, a man named D. B. Cooper hijacked an airliner the same day. Cooper's exploit caught the imagination of the nation, as he bailed out of the aircraft south of Seattle, taking with him $200,000 in ransom money.

I had returned home very late the night of the 21st. For some reason the security light didn't go on. Then, I found the door unlocked, which didn't particularly bother me until I noticed partially dried footprints in the entryway. I started to back out the way I'd come, but stopped when I saw an envelope lying on the floor.

Curiosity overcame my fright. I bent down and picked it up. My name, misspelled with a double 's' instead of two 'o's', was scribbled on the outside. In bolder letters it was marked: *PERSONAL!*

A shiver went up my weak backbone when I read what was inside:

"If you really want to know about Father Knox go and visit prisoner #279223 at McNeil Island Prison."

Our search for the truth about Percy had been met with a stone wall of silence for two years. Now it appeared Freddie's prediction that someone would eventually let something slip had happened.

"Damn!" I thought. *"It couldn't have come at a worse time!"* Leezie was in Vermont, and Freddie was at a Vatican II confab in Rome. *"You're stuck, Moosington,"* I thought. *"Like it or not, you have to do something on your own."*

The next morning I called the chaplain at McNeil Island, only to be told, "I'm sorry, but I can't help you." I turned to Frank Parsons to see what he could do.

Two weeks later I traveled to Tacoma and took a boat to an island in Puget Sound to the west. There, I came face-to-face with prisoner #279223. Knowing that McNeil Island Federal Penitentiary housed a host of very bad people, I was surprised to meet a studious looking man in his early thirties. Some of my old feelings of being short on bravery surfaced, as I pondered what my first question should be. I decided to go for something bland, and asked, "What are you in for?"

To this day, if I think about it, his answer unnerves me. "For screwing little boys!" he said.

"The prisoner won't know who you are any more than you know who he is," Frank had counseled me. His advice helped settle my nerves, and I decided to go for the jackpot question, saying, "Do you remember a priest named Father Knox?"

I won't repeat the bulk of our conversation, which lasted over twenty minutes. What he told me is too depraved and sickening. The gist is, he said, "Yes, I was one of Father Percy's altar boys." A giggle followed, and then he elaborated. "I was nine, and I thought he was God. At least being a priest and all, as close to God as I'd ever see on this earth. He started out just touching my privates."

"Were there any others?" I interrupted.

"Sure."

I waited, not wanting to prompt him more than I had to. Then, like a dam breaking, he poured out the whole sordid story of molestation.

"We called ourselves, me and the others, Percy's Fondlers."

He gave me the names of three men from that illustrious group. Later that week, two of them corroborated his story, and one refused to see me. Frank Parsons tried to talk me out of it, but by this time I was seething with anger, and took what I'd learned to the bishop.

I arrived at his office unannounced and stonewalled my way past his secretary.

"I assume, Moosington, you've got a good reason for barging in like this," he said, trying by his steely look to put the fear of Jesus into me.

"Would the fact that you've been harboring a criminal be reason enough?" I asked.

"Perhaps you'd better explain that!" he shot back.

I did, and before I finished I thought he would die of apoplexy. He ranted and told me it was none of my business. Angry, I stood my ground. Sensing that I was still losing the fight, I tried to mellow my tone, and said, "I have a friend, Your Excellency. He's a policeman by the name of Detective O'Toole O'Sullivan. If you won't listen maybe I should go talk to him."

That set off a volcanic eruption that raised his chair several inches off the floor. Finally, he regained his senses and attempted to pacify me with a promise to look into the matter. I took him at his word.

After that my name was mud. If the bishop wanted to talk to me he did so through an intermediary. In a sense, I had the last laugh, though, because I never revealed Freddie's involvement. That's how Freddie got to be a bishop and I didn't.

Freddie's appointment as bishop of a diocese several hundred miles east of Seattle happened in 1973, two years after the stormy meeting I just described. Freddie called me, saying, "Barto, let's have one last hurrah. Meet me at the office."

The Wheel House Tavern was empty that afternoon and quiet as a church on Monday. "God, I'm going to miss this place," he said as we settled ourselves around the table in the captain's cabin.

I would miss our times together too, especially the camaraderie and what I'd learned there. Freddie had used it as a platform to preach about what the Vatican II renewal meant. That was often condensed to, "*Get your ass out of the Dark Ages and into the modern world.*" His audience was small, usually just me.

"I'm going to miss this place," he said again.

"Congratulations," I said.

"Thanks, Barto. Coming from you I consider that a real compliment. But I want you to know I didn't campaign for the appointment." After licking the foam off his small mug of beer, he added, "I don't even know if I want it."

"I agree you might not like it, but if you manage to clean up your language a bit, you should be okay," I said.

"Ho-ho, Barto, ain't you the smart ass today?"

"Try smart aleck instead of ass," I advised.

"Okay Mr. smart aleck," he chuckled. "But it still should be you instead of me putting on the bishop's hat."

I knew he was sincere. He had come back from Rome three weeks after the blowup with the bishop over Percy Knox. I had to almost physically restrain him from marching in to confront the bishop, not just about Percy, but the way I'd been treated.

"Relax, Freddie," I said. "We both knew the bishop would probably shoot the messenger."

"It doesn't make it a damned bit easier, and it still pisses me off to high heaven." He took another taste of his beer and chuckled. "You sure as hell stirred up a hornets nest. And you know damned good and well that the bishop knew what Percy was up to. I said that all along too, if you remember."

"If he did," I replied, "he didn't let on that day."

"Shit fire, Barto, it's a fact, just admit it. It wasn't two days after you confronted him that Percy got suspended and sent off to that monastery."

"It's water over the dam Freddie. By the way, do you know where Percy is now?"

"Out of our hair, that's for sure," he answered. "He got reinstated a couple of months ago and has some kind of paper-pushing job at a diocese in Massachusetts."

"Someone should make sure they know Percy's history," I said. We talked it over and both of us agreed to write letters to the diocese in Massachusetts.

"Satisfied?" he asked. I nodded, and he said, "Good," followed by, "have you heard the rumors?"

It was Freddie's way of changing the subject.

There was no doubt his favorite person of the twentieth century was Giuseppe Angelo Roncalli. He may have become Pope John XXIII, but Freddie never called him anything but Roncalli. I expected to hear more accolades about him, but Freddie had something else on his mind.

"I've been to Rome twice in the last five years," he said. "If I learned one thing it's that the old guard is not happy with what Roncalli did. In fact, they are downright pissed at the changes in the church."

"So what," I said. "Vatican II is a done deal."

"Barto, you haven't been there and listened to some of those old men. They can still derail what Roncalli started. Don't forget, the Council left a lot of things up in the air."

I disagreed, and deliberately pushed his Cardinal Spellman button. Usually, just the mention of the name would cause Freddie to rant for five minutes. "Spellman already tried to throw the train off the track. And he failed."

"It's little pissants like him I'm talking about," he said, making me think he'd taken the bait. "There's plenty just like him running around the Vatican in their long silk dresses."

Cardinal Spellman of New York once made a famous statement. I think it was in 1964, when the Vatican Council was underway in Rome. "Don't worry," he said. "None of those changes will ever get past the Statue of Liberty." Freddie loved the quote, and had used it to start innumerable conversations.

"Nice try, Barto," he said. I grinned, knowing he'd tasted it, but then spit out the hook. "I just hope I'm wrong, but there might come a day when the reforms of Vatican II are nothing more than a memory."

"Okay, suppose you're right. Then what?" I asked.

He leaned back on his sea chest, and took a deep breath. "The Gar communities, Barto. That's our bottom line."

Gar communities went back several years, and were an experiment we had started in our parishes. "You don't think the name sounds too corny?" Freddie had asked at the time. *Gar*, represented the initials of Pope John's given name.

It was our effort to solve the first dilemma thrown at us by the renewal Vatican II created. "If we just leave the people waking up spiritually in the big church," Freddie believed, "they'll get the life sucked right back out of them."

We formed them into little communities. Imagine a platoon in the army, and you'll get the idea. The platoon, still part of the big picture, has a common purpose, and all of their energy is directed toward a mutual interest, in their case, staying alive.

"*Community*," was one of the lynch pins of Vatican II thought. We made up the model as we went along, using the description of the first small communities in the New Testament as a guide. The jury is still out on the success of our experiment, but we were enthused about it.

"Hell," Freddie said, "I don't know what's going to happen. I just hope I'm wrong about the naysayers in Rome getting control again."

"I do think you're a little paranoid about it," I said. "The renewal is rolling along quite well at the moment."

He let out another long sigh, and then held up three fingers in a mock Boy Scout salute. "Be prepared, that's all I'm saying. And," he added, beating a tattoo with his hand on the table, "shoot your mouth off if it happens."

"Ha! That's not likely. I don't exactly have a pulpit or soapbox anymore."

"Don't worry, Barto. By hook or crook I'll make sure you do."

I wanted to explore that intriguing statement, but we were interrupted.

Jack appeared, followed by an entourage. His perpetual Pall Mall glued to his lip, Jack motioned toward the rear of the assembly. One of his popular waitresses, dressed in a baker's uniform, stepped forward bearing a large cake.

She set it on the table. Freddie, as I've said before, is not an emotional guy, but it brought tears to his eyes. The cake, baked in the shape of a bishop's hat, had the inscription: *Bon Voyage, Father Freddie. We love you!*

As if by a prearranged signal, Conrad squawked, and a host of well-wishers flooded the Wheel House. It turned out to be a gala event that lasted most of the afternoon.

Leonard, the Viet Nam vet, was there too. I hadn't seen Leonard since his departure for the police academy over a year ago. He looked stunning in his uniform.

"He's one of the Windknocker's success stories," Leezie said. "But believe me, Mew, none of them are easy."

Leonard's part in this story illustrates the great need, and how Leezie tried to help them. The Viet Nam war had brought a steady stream of Leonards knocking on my door, all asking the same anxious question: "Is this where Sarge lives?"

Finally, stuffed full of cake and good wishes, Freddie said, "Sorry, Barto, but it's time to go." He crooned at Conrad, as he always did, as he went out the door.

His car was parked in front and mine across the street. I stepped off the curb but he stopped me. "Hold up a second, Barto, I've got something to give you." He reached into his shirt pocket and brought out what looked like a business card.

"The Gar community idea has to live, Barto, even if everything else dies. And if you forget it I'll kick your ass all the way to Mount Rainier."

"All the way to Mount Rainier?" I grinned.

He smiled too and showed me the business card. It read: *"The World's best Summer Sausage,"* with a company name and address.

"This will help you remember, Barto," he said, tearing the card in two. He handed me half. Summer sausage is a pretty good analogy of all that was wrong with the pre-Vatican II church," he said before sputtering to a stop.

"Good god," he started up again. "I can hardly believe we had prohibitions like not eating meat on Friday. Anyhow, keep that as a reminder that Gar can't ever die. And, that we're never going back to the old ways! And if you do –"

"I know, I know, if I do you'll march off of that bishop's throne of yours and kick my butt all the way to the big mountain."

He reached out and we touched cards.

"Agreed?" he said.

"You're double damned tootin'," I answered.

"Shit, Barto, that's really corny."

I sat in my car, watching him drive away. The thought hit me for the first time that he wasn't just leaving, but entering an entirely different realm of the church, one that I was not privy to. "Goodbye, Freddie," I said, "I hope we do, but I doubt we'll see each other again."

Fortunately, Leezie returned three days later, or I may have moped longer than I did. As it were, it would take a bizarre turn of events to shock me out of the doldrums.

One morning, two weeks after Freddie left, my phone rang. I answered, and thought at first he had dialed the wrong number. It was the bishop.

"Moosington, how are you?" His voice was cordial. "Can you come and see me tomorrow? I have a proposal for you, and it's time for us to bury the hatchet." I was too flabbergasted to say much in return.

Our meeting lasted eight minutes the next day, and the bishop's demeanor was a repeat of his telephone call. We buried the hatchet, or at least he did, as I really didn't have one to bury. I was getting ready to leave when the thunderbolt came.

"Moosington," the bishop said, "before he left, Father, 'er, Bishop Timmerman recommended *you* to take over his weekly column in the Diocesan newspaper.

I sat straight up in my chair. The job had a certain amount of prestige, but I'd also be following Freddie. He had used the column like a bugle to lead the charge for reform. I would have the liberty to do the same, and more.

"I suppose you'll want to keep up his discourse about Vatican II," he continued. "Will you do it?"

I just sat there, stunned.

"Well?" the bishop prodded.

"I'll do my best," I answered.

I don't know how Freddie had pulled it off, but knowing him I suspect there was more of the crook than a hook to it. In any event, I sure didn't ask the bishop what had happened between them. All I knew is I had my soapbox. I left his office thinking, *"now all I need is something to write about."*

Unexpectedly, my first column landed in my lap from out of the blue. Sadly, it was the last thing I wanted.

The Reverend Popinjay died.

Chapter Thirty-Three

Jay Jay was seventy-nine.

His funeral was held in a ramshackle building not far from where Hooverville had once stood. His son preached a powerful eulogy. One piece I remember in particular, "The Reverend Mr. Jay Jay is sittin' up there right now havin' supper with all the blind and the lames he helped. Only today they is waitin' on him."

I looked over at my dad, sitting beside me. His face wore a satisfied smile. "*Ah,*" I thought, "*Sam Moosington, one of the great enigmas in my life.*" He had been, for almost forty years, Jay Jay's partner. They were two men cut from the same bolt, not impressed by dogma. Their only doctrine was "*To live for the Lawd God a-mighty, an' dem that gots nuthin'.*" It was from them that I learned the real world was different than the cozy little cocoons the affluent spin.

At times their belief system clashed with some of the things I took great security in. I remembered my dad saying one day, "You and your mother may take Holy Communion on Sunday, but I have the *bread of life* seven days a week." That had confused my young mind. He had never participated in the "sacrament" of Holy Communion, yet his life showed all the signs that should result from doing so. "*How can that be?*" I wondered.

I looked at my dad again. I smiled, knowing some of the worry lines etched there had been my doing. They were barely noticeable, though, overshadowed by the look of peace that his face radiated.

After my mother died, ten years earlier, Sam began giving away his fortune, pouring much of it into the hands of the Reverend

Popinjay. He now rented a one-room apartment over a hardware store. Jay Jay had remarked on it one of the last times I'd seen him. "He's happier doin' de Lawd's work den a kitty in a cream bucket."

I had thrown off the shackles of a religion based on a dictatorial God. I was happier now that Leezie had returned, but I had never experienced cream-bucket happiness. As Jay Jay's funeral concluded, I suspected I had missed something.

My first column in the Diocesan Newspaper followed a week later. It began: "*It was a rainy November day in 1935 that the Reverend Popinjay took me to Hooverville.*" My prose didn't really impress my church readers. However, it did attract the attention of a religion reporter at The Seattle Post Intelligencer, commonly shortened by Seattleites to "The *P-I.*"

I answered the phone the following Friday to hear a voice say, "Father Moosington, this is Wilbur Lester at the Seattle P-I. We're doing an anniversary story about Hooverville and I'd like to interview you."

I guess I imagined the *Seattle P-I's* religion writer would be a plump little man with a neat Vandyke beard, a pocket protector and wire-rim glasses. Instead, Wilbur Lester was a six-foot-seven African American, built skinny as a pen refill.

The interview resulted in a two-installment article about Hooverville. My contribution was small but a picture that my dad found was worth a thousand words. The relic from 1936 showed Jay Jay, Sam and me standing beside the old bakery van. Wilbur's caption under it read: "*The Reverend Popinjay and his helpers.*"

Wilbur and I didn't get off on the right foot at first. He was a Protestant and attended a Pentecostal Church. To him even the new Catholic liturgy was too sedate.

His knowledge of religion, however, was vast, insightful and objective. He knew more about the workings, politics and intrigue in my own church than I could ever hope to, far surpassing even someone like Freddie.

"I honestly didn't think Catholics were even Christians in the old days," he said that first day. "But after Vatican II I started seeing Catholics come alive with a new faith, and a different idea of God."

His remark hit a little too close to home.

I got up from where I was sitting; tired of watching Leezie read the last installment. Finally, he folded the newspaper several times and pointing to the photo I mentioned, said, "Holy cow, Mew! I hardly remembers you ever looking so young."

"Well, what do you expect?" I said. "We're both pushing sixty."

"Which reminds me," he said. "Are we still going to that opera thing to celebrate our birthdays?"

After Leezie had returned we started observing our birthdays again. We rotated each year, when one of us would choose what to do. I found a concert in Ashland, Oregon, and bought the tickets.

"Opera!" I snorted. "The 101 Strings Orchestra is hardly opera."

Leezie tried to look chastised, which he could never do, and instead reminded me of a pesky imp.

"It might be a moot point anyway," I said after taking a deep breath. "What about that big bump on your head?"

Much to his chagrin, a midget wielding a quart can of motor oil had attacked Leezie. It would have been comical had it not landed him in the hospital overnight.

Larry Wilson told me, "Sarge was working, changing spark plugs on a Dodge pickup, when Runt Malone climbed up on the bumper and thumped him with the oil can."

"Malone?" I questioned.

Leezie described him, saying, "He stands four-foot-nine and weighs ninety-five pounds soakin' wet."

"He's just like all the others," Wilson elaborated. "Always pestering Sarge with their problems."

"Doesn't the Army have doctors to treat them?"

Leezie laughed. "Sure, but that means taking pills."

"So?" I said.

"I think Sarge means it ain't as simple as it sounds," Larry said.

"Runt was a tunnel rat in Viet Nam," Leezie explained. "He could squirm into the tiniest hole in the ground and worm his way through them burrows the Viets dug. One day Runt tossed a grenade and got buried by a cave-in. For two days he was trapped, a-lying under the corpses of the Congs he killed. Mixed him up pretty good."

"It still sounds like you're making excuses for him," I said.

Leezie laughed. "The runt needs all the excuses he can git. He's more screwed up than a fiddle with one string."

The episode gave me a better insight into my friend. The thought hit me: "He *goes a step beyond Jay Jay and my dad.*" The blind and the lame to Leezie *might* stand for physical, but more likely he took it to mean spiritually crippled.

"So, what's the answer for Runt Malone?" I'd asked. "I heard you bailed him out of jail the next morning."

"All the Runt needs is to get borned again," he said. "But he's stubborn and just wants some easy fix to make his bad dreams go away."

I kept quiet, because I wanted to avoid our age-old argument.

"That's what made the Runt mad enough to conk me on the head."

"How do you mean?"

"He figures the Windknocker is the cause of his misery, not the solution."

The swelling on the back of Leezie's head went down over the next few days.

"You're sure you can go?" I asked. "Ashland is over four-hundred miles."

The concert in Ashland commemorated our fifty-seventh birthdays, and was a great success.

"I lost track tryin' to count and see if there really were 101 stings in that opera band," Leezie said. "But they sure can play a tune."

Three years later it was his turn to choose, and starting in May he was in a dither. "It's our sixtieth birthday coming up," he kept saying. "And I has to think of something big."

One night in August he was late coming home from work. It was after nine, when he barged in the door waving a paper in his hand. "A-ha!" he said. "You'll never guess what I've got here."

I took the two slips he handed me. "North to Alaska," he shouted gleefully, "that's where we're going!"

It wasn't quite that, but we did have tickets on the Alaskan Ferry. We were going as far as Prince Rupert, Canada, about halfway between Seattle and Anchorage.

"Larry Wilson bought a car up there," Leezie explained. "He wants me to go pick it up in Rupert. Wilson paid for these here tickets. All we have to do is buy our gas coming home."

His enthusiasm got to me, and five minutes later we were huddled over a map, tracing the route from Prince Rupert to Seattle. "Looks to be around 1,200 miles," Leezie said. "Three or four days."

Frannie Burke, my housekeeper, came in about that time and Leezie reminded her, "Frannie, we'll be needin' our birthday cake on September second."

Frannie's eyes lit up. "So you figured out where you're going?"

He nodded.

"I'll have your cake ready. Should I put sixty candles on it or just leave it to your imaginations?"

She baked a small cake for us each year, but this was the first time we were traveling under such conditions. I laughed, and said, "Without the candles if you please, Frannie."

She smiled.

"By the way," I said. "Do you have something we can carry it in?"

She assured me she had just the thing.

"*Just the thing*" turned out to be a round plastic tub with a snap-on lid and a carrying handle. I was a little self-conscious that Thursday morning when we boarded the huge ocean-going ferry. Both of us carried a bedroll, a pup tent and big backpacks. Plus, Leezie had the toolbox he never went anywhere without. To help balance my load, I carried the cake. The round box seemed to grow more conspicuous each time it got in the way as we threaded our way though the maze of fellow passengers. I didn't have the luxury of stashing it in a cabin. Thanks to Leezie's experience on a troopship during the war, we had elected to sleep on deck.

"I don't think anybody even noticed the cake box, Mew," Leezie said. "Well, maybe a little when you turned too quick and knocked the crutch from under that crippled fellow." He grinned.

We were sitting on the poop deck at the time, called so by Leezie because the sea gulls had left a mess there. "Don't matter," he said, "besides, the view is good. In fact, it's purty close to perfect."

It was mid-afternoon and the ferry was cruising north through Puget Sound. I watched the breeze wave strands of Leezie's long white hair. The sun highlighted the silky threads against the blue sky. Lazy fat clouds bounced like giant cotton balls across the heavens, rising and falling on command from a divine choreographer.

"Look at that!" Leezie exclaimed, pointing. One of the cotton balls rode a downdraft and we thought for a moment it would crash into the well of green thrown up by the San Juan Islands that speckled the surface. "Perfect ain't the right word," he said.

"Try idyllic," I said.

Before dark we found a sheltered place near the stern to bed down for the night. "Right here looks good. We can sneak in there if it rains," Leezie said, pointing to an alley between some big crates. Several wooden pallets butted against each other, creating a cubbyhole.

The stars were out by the time I popped the lid off the cake box. We examined the contents by the dim light from a porthole above.

"I was afraid we'd have chocolate upside-down cake by now," Leezie quipped. "But it looks okay."

There were two big pieces for each of us, and he finished his first one before I took my third bite. He sang "Happy Birthday" while I caught up. His voice choked a little, like it always did, but ended on a loud note, which caught the attention of a deckhand on an inspection tour.

"We might be in for a blow," the man said, and ambled off into the darkness. Neither of us paid him any attention, intent as we were on devouring the cake.

"That Frannie bakes a mean cake," Leezie said, licking his fingers.

I wasn't sure just what kind of relationship Leezie and Frannie had. It teetered, I knew, between friendship and romance. Mildred, however, still occupied a big place in Leezie's heart and I wasn't sure if Frannie could ever replace her.

"You never did learn to eat cake," I chided. "Is that a Smith family tradition to inhale it?"

"Are you going to eat the rest of yours or just play with it?" he asked, reaching out as if to snatch it.

We went to sleep, finally, with refreshed memories of our good times together. Sometime in the night, I guessed it to be about two in the morning, we hit a big storm barreling down the Straits of Juan de Fuca. It woke me up as it rocked the big ferry. I tried to go back to sleep but the rain followed the wind within an hour. Five minutes later we were soaked and scrambling for the niche between the crates.

It was pitch dark out, but we managed to haul everything under the tarpaulins stretched across the opening.

"Did you bring Frannie's cake box?" Leezie shouted.

I hadn't, and went on a frantic search for it. After I bumped my head against a stanchion and skinned a knee when I tripped over a tie down, I found the box and hauled it back to our lair.

We didn't get much sleep the rest of the night, but it seemed nothing could put a damper on our spirits. We were like two school children on their first field trip.

The wind quieted by noon the next day, but the downpour continued. We stood watch on the poop deck by day and sought the shelter of the cubbyhole at night. By the time the ferry docked in Prince Rupert at dusk on the third day, we looked like two bedraggled roosters that had missed the launching of Noah's Ark.

"Wow!" Leezie exclaimed. "I'm glad to get off that floating bath house."

"Speaking of houses, where are we going to put up for the night?" I asked.

"I vote for the Sea Dog," he said of a hotel recommended by one of our shipmates.

The cake box slipped off my finger and landed in a puddle. "Look, it floats," Leezie chortled. I rescued it from the water and we walked up the street from the ferry landing, giggling as we went.

I expected the clerk at the Sea Dog to be taken aback by two scruffy men seeking a room, but he wasn't. Leezie's toolbox rattled when he set it on the floor to sign the register. I propped the cake box on top of my gear and turned to do the same. It fell off the pile. Helplessly, I watched it roll across the lobby. A woman sitting next to a totem pole that decorated a far corner caught it. She turned the container over, inspecting the bottom.

"CakeTender," she said cheerily. "I haven't seen one of these in years."

Smiling, I stopped it with my foot when she rolled it back. "He's a baker," Leezie said.

"Oh," she said. "Then you must know my cousin. He used to bake buns for the Aleutian Bakery in Juneau."

I mumbled my regrets for not having made his acquaintance, only to have Leezie chime in, "He only bakes cakes and shoo-fly pie."

By this time my sense of humor was stretched a little thin and I hastily signed my name to the register. The hotel clerk whispered in my ear when he took the money for our room. "Honestly, what's the cake box for?"

"We're going to rob the bank here in Rupert and stash the loot in it," I said.

A humorless sort, he gave me a serious look. "And then we're going back to the States and buy a bakery."

"We tried starting one from scratch," Leezie cut in, "but a bakery needs lots of dough."

By this time, the clerk was catching on. "What if I call the Mounties and tell them about your little caper?"

"The yeast you can do is keep your mouth shut," I said.

"Yeah," Leezie said. "We're just two old fruitcakes looking for something to loaf at."

"You Yanks!" the hotel clerk grinned. He handed me our key, saying, "Third floor. The bathroom's down the hall."

Chapter Thirty-Four

The next morning I waited at the lobby door, while Leezie went for the car. I had the cake box buried under our gear. An hour passed before a, beep, beep-beep, beep, attracted my attention. My mouth dropped open, and then I knew why Leezie had evaded my questions about what kind of car Larry Wilson had sent us to fetch.

Leezie got out, smiling as usual. No, he actually unfolded himself from the driver's seat in increments. "Your chariot awaits," he said, taking our backpacks from my hand.

"How old is this relic," I snipped, "and why didn't you tell me it was a Volkswagen Beetle?"

"It's a 1959 VW," he said, "and like I told you it gets good gas mileage."

I was more aghast when we tried to stuff everything inside. "We could tie it here," he said, addressing my biggest concern. He tapped the passenger side mirror with the cake box. That melted my frosty mood, and after one further mishap, we left Prince Rupert behind.

Seven days later we reached Seattle. My housekeeper, Frannie Brooke, met us at the door. "Lands sake, Father," she said, "you look like a flag pole bent over in the wind!"

"That's what a week's riding in that," I said, pointing to the tiny car, "will do to you, Frannie."

"Honestly," she said, looking to Leezie, "that's what you went to Prince Rupert for, to get a VW Beetle?"

"Not just any old Beetle," Leezie said, "but a classy model, one of the best the Krauts ever built."

Classy? I didn't quite remember it that way, but do admit it ran better than I'd ever expected it to, albeit slow. As far as class, the Beetle's was limited to a bright orange ball affixed to the antenna, and a faded NIXON/LODGE sticker from the 1960 election, on the rear bumper. Legroom was sorely lacking, and the dashboard, I'm afraid, had worn permanent divots into my kneecaps.

Fortunately, Leezie had been able to fix the passenger side door. The first day out of Prince Rupert I had to work my way, stomach first, in the driver's side. On the initial attempt the gearshift had pinned my private parts to the rear of my pants. I didn't tell Frannie about that, or the expletives that went with the experience. Instead, I handed her the cake box, saying, "Thanks for the use of this."

"You didn't!" she exclaimed.

"Didn't what?" Leezie said.

"I bought this at a garage sale for a dime," she said. "I just assumed you would throw it away. I can't believe you lugged a big box half way to Alaska and back."

The scene of the cake box rolling across the lobby of the Sea Dog Hotel came back to me, but I didn't say anything. Nor did I dare look in Leezie's direction; for fear that Frannie wouldn't understand why two grown men would suddenly break into hysterical laughter.

Make no mistake. I cherished the memories of the trip to Prince Rupert. I think I have recorded those events accurately enough for you to see why.

One thing nagged me, though, and after another twenty minutes of telling about our adventures, I broke away. The desk in my office was cluttered with notes and papers needing attention. I ignored them, dialing the telephone instead.

A former parishioner from Saint Simon of the East answered his private number. "Afternoon Doc," I said, and after exchanging pleasantries, I described a *little spell* that Leezie had on the way home. We had camped one night, and smoke from a nearby forest fire hung heavily in the air. It didn't bother me, save for being annoying, but Leezie labored to breathe, and spent most of the night coughing. The next day, after we left the haze behind, save for some minor wheezing, he was fine. "What do you make of that, Doc?" I asked.

He gave me the usual, "Hmmm," and then offered, "probably an allergy, or possibly an asthmatic condition." He must have detected my relief, and added, "Regardless, he should have a checkup." I was afraid of that, knowing Leezie's aversion to white gowns, and the sound that hands make being inserted into latex gloves.

I explained, ending with, "I'll see what I can do."

"I'm harmless, tell him that," he said. "In any event don't hesitate to call me if it happens again."

I put the phone down, deciding to wait and see if it reoccurred. I watched him closely in the coming months, but didn't detect anything that aroused my suspicions. After another year passed I forgot about it. He did come back from Vermont in the spring of 1978 looking haggard, but I chalked that up to his strenuous itinerary.

"It's no wonder you look pooped, Leezie," I said, after tracing his travels. "That's almost 8,000 miles." His main mode of transport was the bus, resorting at times to thumbing rides. His journey overlaid on the map reminded me of a hopscotch game. He stopped first in McFall, Missouri, went to Vermont, Saskatoon, back to Vermont, on to Pennsylvania, north into New York, and ended in Golva, North Dakota. How many places in between he visited is anyone's guess.

"Golva?" I questioned. "That's the second time you've mentioned North Dakota.

"Golva is just a dot on the prairie," he answered, "not much bigger than a two-cow dairy."

That was no revelation, as he spent a lot of time in such places.

"Got a Windknocker buddy that lives there," he said.

Since Leezie was in the buddy making business, that was no surprise either.

We were sitting in my office, where I had been working to finish my weekly column for the newspaper. I wanted him to say more about Golva, but instead he talked about his daughter. About all I knew is she had a degree in botany, and worked somewhere in Montpellier.

"Not anymore," Leezie said, "she bought a newspaper."

"I hadn't heard the New York Times had changed hands," I said.

Leezie laughed, saying, "It's not that big." I learned it was located in Essex Junction, Vermont, a small town not far from Burlington.

"Her paper is called *The Junction Journal*," Leezie went on. "It comes out twice a week, on Tuesday and Friday." There was more than a hint of pride in his voice. "Here, look at these," he said, laying several pictures on my desk.

Luckily, Leezie hadn't chosen photography as his life's work.

"That's Glory at her desk," he said, pointing to a woman talking on the telephone.

He was an expert in fuzzy images. I had yet to see a photo of her that revealed what she really looked like.

"It's a good picture of your thumb," I said. "The FBI could use that to lift your fingerprint."

He snickered and offered another. "Me and Glory having a game of darts at the Empty Mug Tavern," he said.

Taken from the backside of the dart throwers, it didn't reveal anything except the inside of a rather quaint looking inn.

Another photo caught my eye, and I picked it up. "Who is this?" I asked.

"That's Satch," he said. "He's the guy from Golva I told you about."

"The one with the dairy?"

"No," Leezie protested, "Satch is a school principal. The dairy was just a simile to show how tiny Golva is."

I grinned and he punched my shoulder, letting me know he'd seen through my poor humor. Still, I marveled at his use of the word *simile*. He still went to night school and could, when he took a notion, write or talk like a well-educated man.

I didn't learn anything further about his friend, Satch, and wondered why he was reluctant to talk more about Golva.

Mew's perception was on the money, and the Big Chief Tablet from the time offers a partial explanation. Leezie wrote:

Satch was the first Catholic at Saint Mary's to get born again. It happened when he went to one of those Catholic charismatic meetings up the road in Dickinson. That's where I met him. Satch went home and told some of his friends. Now there's a little group of them I've been helping out, eight or ten. They are a close-knit bunch. Come to think about it, they remind me of what Mew is tryin' to do with them Pope Johnny groups of his.

It's a funny thing about Catholics like the ones in Golva. They want to be Catholics and wish Saint Mary's would catch up to them. Frustration might make them quit going to church but they won't go somewhere else. They need a church person who doesn't wear a religious straight jacket to lead them. Hmmm. I knows another group where Mew could do that!

It wasn't until later that the idea of a treasure hunt to lure me away from Seattle entered Leezie's thoughts. Still, it took a long time to germinate, and was nearly foiled in the end by the unexpected. *"It's the only way I can think of to get him there,"* is how Leezie wrote it down. How he carried it off is another story.

I only had a passing interest in Golva, and quickly forgot about it. Leezie left, saying, "Me and Frannie's going to the Wheel House; want to come?"

I begged off and spent the next three hours fine-tuning my weekly contribution to the diocesan paper. It was titled, *Unfinished Business of Vatican II.*

I remarked on the work involved a day later at a chance meeting with Wilbur Lester, religion writer for the *Seattle P-I.* "I don't know how you do it, Wilbur," I said. "I can barely get my column done, and you write one every day."

We had bumped into each other at McDonald's.

"But it's all I do," Wilber said. "That's a big difference."

He arranged two Big Macs in front of him, and then tried to get his long legs under the table. "Besides," he said, giving me a solemn look, "you're an important cog. Vatican II needs defending."

His comment threw me. I considered myself a mouthpiece or teacher on the subject.

"Defending?" I asked.

"If you aren't now, you will be," Wilbur said.

Before I had the chance to interject, he asked, "How much do you know about Cardinal Ratzinger?"

I had to think a minute. "He was one of the reformers at Vatican II," I answered. "He got appointed Cardinal last year."

"My sources tell me he's done an about-face and has been preaching that Vatican II went too far," he said.

I must have grimaced, because he added, "Ratzinger is a real rising star in Rome."

I remembered my favorite Ratzinger quote that I recited for him.

"Yes," Wilbur said. "And he even went farther. I can't recall it exactly, but he advocated that ordinary church laymen follow their consciences, and disobey if their bishops get out of line."

For a non-Catholic journalist, Wilbur's knowledge was vast.

"It appears he had a bad experience during the German student riots in the late 1960's," Wilbur said. "Rather than being comfortable to just let the unrest run its course, he blamed Vatican II as the cause."

"So what's he saying today that makes you think he's switched sides?"

"You talk a lot about the *Spirit of Vatican II*, right?" he asked me.

I nodded. It was a fundamental belief of the original reformers that their intent, although not specifically spelled out, would be what steered the renewal of the Church.

"Ratzinger says there is no such thing, and a literal reading of the Vatican II documents will be the guiding force in the future," Wilbur said. "Properly interpreted, I might add."

I was flummoxed. For one thing, the point of my most recent article was the exact opposite. Ratzinger's mindset could derail the renewal faster than anything I could think of. Derail brought to mind my last conversation with Freddie.

"You don't look so good," Wilbur said.

I admitted it gave me a sick feeling.

"Don't quote me on what I said because I've pieced this together from several sources," he said.

I didn't say anything for a long while, and instead watched Wilbur finish the last of his triple order of fries.

He eyed me seriously, and said, "Have you ever thought what it would be like to stand in front of your congregation some morning and have to say, 'I'm sorry dear fellow Catholics, but the new life you've experienced from Vatican II was all based on a wrong interpretation? And, we're going back to the old ways?'" Wilbur wiped his mouth with a napkin.

Again, I was speechless.

"Worse than that, on your own personal gut level how would it make you feel?" Wilbur glanced at his watch, and got up abruptly, saying, "Sorry to rush off. I'll do some more checking and get back to you."

By the time I watched the golden arches disappear in my rear view mirror, my mind was going a thousand miles an hour. Fortunately, I'd been on the southeast side of Seattle, and the long ride home gave me time to think it through. *"Time will tell,"* I finally told myself. *"But in the meantime no one is going to shut me up."*

Cardinal Ratzinger's name appeared in the news infrequently over the next two years. I couldn't detect that his star was rising or that he had reversed his thinking about Vatican II. It seemed that Wilbur's prediction was wrong. As the years passed the renewal continued to flourish, and I concluded that the rebirth was too strong to be stopped. If the Vatican did try to reverse course it would be counterproductive.

Besides, other things occupied my mind. To be more specific, I was concerned about Leezie's health. In the summer of 1979 he had another one of the "little spells" he had that year on the way home from Prince Rupert. He labored to breathe and for several days coughed and wheezed, but he wouldn't hear of going to a doctor. In August his symptoms disappeared almost overnight, and I started to rest easier.

He went to Vermont for Christmas that year, and when he came home I was alarmed. He looked terrible, and at times had to bend over to get his breath.

"It's just a cold, Mew," he said. "Don't worry, I'll be okay."

Two days later he was worse, but insistent he didn't need a doctor. He went to bed early that night and I decided I'd had enough. I called his brother-in-law, Frank Parsons.

Leezie put up a feeble protest the next morning when Frank appeared.

"Stuff it, Sarge," Frank told him. "You're going to the Vet's Hospital. I've already made the arrangements."

Leezie didn't have much fight in him and he went peaceably. But as they backed out of the driveway he rolled down the window and gave another perfect impersonation of Abner Pong.

"An' I ain't paying you that dime I owes you," he snarled at me. "You big tattletale."

Frannie was worried, and pestered me all day wanting to know, "Hasn't Frank called yet?" I suggested she go visit her sister, but she declined, saying, "No, I'll just wait here until we hear something."

It was after five before Frank called. He was matter of fact and didn't waste words. "Sarge has emphysema," he said. "He also has a bad bronchial infection, a low white count, possible thickening of the heart muscle, and arthritis in his bad leg."

He paused, taking a deep breath. "Other than that, he's fine."

Fine, I learned, was relative. When I next saw Leezie at the end of the week the transformation was remarkable. Leonard, the Viet Nam veteran that Leezie had helped get his life straight, brought him home. We didn't get a quiet moment until later in the day, and I could finally ask him, "How do you feel?"

"I feel good," he said, "but I wish if I had to get something it coulda been something I could spell."

Chapter Thirty-Five

It was Frannie who came up with the idea.

I was at a new parish, affectionately called, Saint Ruthie's, by people of Bulgarian extraction who comprised most of the congregation. Leezie lived in the parish house at Saint Ruthie's, with a big room of his own that had a good view of Mount Rainier.

Once his bronchial infection had cleared up you had to watch closely to know anything was wrong with him. I knew that emphysema wasn't curable, and life expectancy depended on several factors. One side of his heart had also thickened. That was a secondary problem caused by the heart having to labor pumping blood through constricted lung vessels. That condition concerned me more than anything.

His limp had gotten worse, and he worked less frequently for Larry Wilson. He still traveled but did most of it closer to home, and with the exception of Vermont, didn't venture much farther than the old hometown. At least that I knew about.

"Will you ever quit your frettin' about me," he said often. "I still got seven out of eight cylinders working."

Frannie broached what turned out to be their mutual idea in late September. She was in the middle of vacuuming when I'd walked in after a long telephone conversation with Wilbur Lester.

"Have you heard the news?" Wilbur had begun.

"What news?"

"About Cardinal Ratzinger."

Ratzinger had just been appointed as head of "*The Congregation for the Doctrine of the Faith.*"

"Ugh!" I said.

That office was the most powerful in the Vatican. Up until 1908 it had been known by the more infamous title, "*Sacred Congregation of the Roman and Universal Inquisition.*"

"Word has it that his charge is to censure theologians who don't agree with Rome," Wilbur said. "It looks like Charles Curran will be the first."

I had left my office stunned. "*So much for my theory that Ratzinger didn't have any power,*" I thought. I had a lot of respect for Charles Curran.

Frannie got my attention when she suddenly shut off the vacuum.

"No need to do that," I said.

"Why don't we have a special birthday party this year," she blurted, "and invite lots of people?"

After our escapade to Prince Rupert five years ago, we had toned down our celebrations. Since Frannie was the same age, we had decided to make our yearly observance a threesome.

I must have given her my usual blank look, and she added, "We'll all be sixty-five – me in October, Leezie in November and you in December." She smiled. "You're the youngest, so you could choose, but I suggest the first of December."

"Why do I suspect Leezie put you up to this?"

She smiled again, saying, "He said you would mention that."

The big event is six months in the past now. Well-attended is an understatement; even the bishop came.

Leezie captured center stage that night.

"You want me to give the speech?" Leezie wailed. "And what am I supposed to talk about?"

"Don't you have a good story to tell?" Frannie asked.

He thought a moment, then said, with a sly grin, "I might know of one."

"*Yes,*" I thought, "*and it will be about the Windknocker.*"

Leezie, it might surprise you to hear, was an eloquent speaker. He could spellbind an audience as he mixed his homespun wisdom, alternating between dead seriousness and humor that put his listeners in stitches. The story he told on our sixty-fifth birthday, however, was new, and for good reason.

As with all of his Windknocker stories, he rambled, leading the listener like hungry cattle after a hay wagon. For our birthday he reverted to the speech pattern of bygone years. He exceeded what I thought was possible.

"I remembers a winter back in Vermont," is how he began.

"That woulda been the winter of 1957. My wife, Mildred, had died earlier that fall. I was helpin' Pinky Parsons on the farm. Pinky was Mildred's daddy. Pinky was still pretty mad at the Windknocker about losin' his only daughter.

"Pinky asked me one morning what he should do about his birthday comin' up in a week. He was turnin' sixty-five that year too. I suggested we go to the Empty Mug Tavern and play a game of darts. Since Pinky was a good dart thrower and could always beat me, he thought it was a good idea. Vermont people will tell you that they invented the game, and maybe it's true, I don't know. They don't like nobody who beats them, I can tell you that. Since I didn't have to worry about winnin', they thought I was okay even if I did come from a state they couldn't spell.

"I used to take Mildred to The Empty Mug in the Christmas time for eggnogs and cinnamon crackers. Pinky always tagged along, so I hoped he wouldn't go misty-eyed on me this time, thinking about her. They had the Mug – you has to remember them Vermonters never said a word they didn't have to, so that's what they called it – sometimes it just came out, 'Been to Mug lately?' Anyhow the Mug was all decorated up for the Windknocker's birthday when we got there. It was dark out, but still early.

"There were lots of folks there already, 'cause it was one of them Vermont holidays. They have, I swear, just about one for every day of the year. Pinky's coincided with Chief Moo-boo-moo Day, at least it sounded like that. I wasn't in no hurry for Pinky to give me another shellackin' at the dart board, so I let him roam around and shake a few hands and pat a few backs, whilst I nibbled me some crackers. All of a sudden I felt a little pitter-pat-pat in my chest. I thunk (Leezie winked in my direction) 'oh, oh, I wonder what's up.' That used to happen to me, when my ticker would go bonk-bonk-bonk or pitter-pat-pat. But it hadn't done it much since the war. Back then when it happened, I had good reason to think the Windknocker was wantin' my attention. So I started takin' notice.

"All at once a strange idea popped into my head. I looked around and smiled, thinkin', '*Ain't that just like the Windknocker?*' Pinky was just startin' in on his arguin' session with Sammy Sloan about the right way to put a shoe on a workhorse. It give me plenty of time and I slipped out the door.

"Down the street was a bakery. Mildred got Pinky's birthday cake there last year after gettin' off work. Mildred had brung home one of them tailor-made cakes, all gussied up with decorations. I didn't have time for that and just figured since the bakery made cakes, I'd still have me a chance of findin' one.

"I was in luck, 'cause they had some ready-mades. I took awhile to have me a look. About that time Mr. Morgan come out of the back room with a great big cake in a sheet pan. That one had Pinky written all over it 'cause it had a chocolate frosting about four inches thick. Frostin' was Pinky's favorite part of a cake. I talked the baker into squirtin' on some writin' under the greetin' to say 'Pinky.' All he had was some orange-colored stuff, and it didn't match the purple happy birthday sentiments too good. The baker spelled Pinky's name with an 'ie' instead of 'y', but I didn't figure Pinky would mind. I had surprise on my mind, and Pinky kind of lost his marbles in them situations.

"For instances – if you could catch Pinky when he wasn't lookin' and shout, 'boo!' he would jump out of his shoes and take off runnin'. Only he didn't go nowhere, but just stood there runnin' in one spot. He reminded me of a tap dancer on a stool when he did it.

"Then the baker fished in one of them file boxes. You know the kind I'm talking about? His was a shoebox, and he had it spaced off with them alphabet dividers. I didn't guess what the baker was doing until he held up Mildred's account sheet. He rattled it some, set her down, and after a lick or two on his pencil, he wrote down the kind of cake I had just bought. He was slower than a snail in a turtle race, and only had to ask me how to spell chocolate twice. Finally, he got her done, and went to stuff the paper back in the file, but it stuck on something.

"Mr. Morgan gawked up at me with a crooked look on his face. His hand came out of the file, and a-twixt his fingers was an onvelup. He waved it in front of my nose like he was makin' to swat a fly. It was one of those little bitty onvelups that folks use to put a card in. Then they clips the card to a holder that you are supposed to stick in the cake. I had already figured that out, but the baker explained it to me anyway.

"He handed it over, and I opened the onvelup up to have a look. He asked me what was so funny, cause I cracked a pretty big smile.

"I was thinkin', 'If this don't beat all! If it don't beat all, then I ain't never heard the Windknocker sing a tune!'

"I told him happy Chief Moo-boo-moo Day and headed back to the Mug. I sneaked in by the back door and caught the barkeep's eye and told him all about it being Pinky's sixty-fifth birthday. He caught on right away and quicker than a magpie can steal an egg, got a table cleared to put the cake on.

"The barkeep took the Chief Moo-boo-moo feather out of his hat and walked over and whispered in his fiddle player's ear. The fiddler changed chords and did a little crescendo to get the crowd's attention.

"Then the barkeep hollered for Pinky to get up in front next to him. He announced for everyone to hear, includin' half the town that weren't there, that it was Pinky's sixty-fifth birthday. The fiddler didn't give Pinky no chance to beg out of it and swung right into the Happy Birthday song. Them Vermonters have got more than one verse, and I believe we sung all five of 'em.

"Right after, the barkeep, his name was Solly Jasper, invited everybody to help Pinky eat his birthday cake. Pinky was pretty surprised and I didn't let on that I had anything to do with it.

"Pinky, a-course, wanted to know what the holder gizmo was stuck in his cake. It had kind of leaned over by this time, but he reached out and plucked the onvelup with the card in it, before the whole contraption fell in the frosting.

"He opened her up. He was really, really surprised this time, and had to sit down to read it again.

"Want to know what it said?" Leezie asked the rapt audience. Two hundred heads bobbed in unison.

Leezie reached in his shirt pocket and brought out an envelope. He removed a small card, saying, "I still have it, and this is what the writin' on the card said:

'Papa, Happy sixtieth-fifth birthday! I love you 65 times over – Mildred!'"

Leezie let that sink in, then went on.

"But Mildred had made a big old mistake, 'cause at the bottom she had to do some explainin'."

Leezie's voice cracked just a little as he read: "*Papa, I'm sorry. I honestly did think today was your sixty-fifth, but then I remembered it's really your sixty-fourth. I'll just have them file this and give it to you next year.*"

Leezie stared at the floor as he carefully slid the card back in the envelope and returned it to his shirt pocket. The room was deathly quiet.

"There weren't no mistaking it was Mildred's writing," Leezie said, looking out at the audience again, a wry smile on his face. "Her penmanship was very distinctive. That's why it was such a shock for Pinky."

"Later, after I told Pinky how it all come about, he told me that if the Almighty could go to that kind of trouble over him, the least he could do was let Mildred go and stop blamin' the Windknocker. Pinky didn't call him that, a-course. I just included it to let you know that I been lookin' forward to my sixty-fifth birthday so I could finally tell this story."

And that was that. End of story. Leezie stepped away from the microphone and moved toward his seat. The applause grew with each step he took. I couldn't resist adding to the noise. Frank Parsons, Jr., was there with his dad, and I watched him worm his way through the tables. He was in his Marine Corps uniform, a troubled young man after serving two tours in Viet Nam. He caught up to Leezie and they hugged each other. I was close enough to catch Gunnery Sergeant Parsons' words.

"Uncle Leezie, if he can help Granpa Pinky like that, then maybe there's hope for me," he said.

They hugged again, and this time I noticed the younger Parsons had a few tears rolling down his cheek.

The next morning, the three of us had a cup of coffee together.

"So Frannie, what did you think of our big party?" I asked.

Leezie snickered so I knew they had already talked about it.

Frannie responded, "Well, Father, it was all a bit emotional for me. I think we'd better wait another ten years before we do it again."

The bishop called me that afternoon, saying, "I want to thank you for the invite. That was quite a party. By the way, who is that friend of yours that told the story?"

I gave him a brief history, wondering what he was leading to.

"His talk was inspirational," he said. "It had realism to it that we either don't experience, or are afraid to express as Catholics."

I tried to hide my surprise.

"But there's something I want to ask," he added.

"Oh?" I said.

"Yes, Moosington," he went on. "Just what the hell is a Wind-knocker?"

I told Leezie about the bishop's question that night. We were fishing down near our favorite jetty.

"What did you tell him?" he said.

"Nothing," I said. "We got interrupted when he got a call from Rome."

"Too bad it weren't Pope Johnny calling," Leezie said.

About that time the sun sank behind the Olympic Mountains to the west. The sky turned into a giant rainbow, and the waters of Puget Sound shimmered from red to gold, depending on how the rays hit it.

"Do you remember when we were kids?" Leezie asked. "And how we used to sit on Meadowlark Ridge to watch the sunset?"

I mumbled an answer that stood for "yes."

"Think there's anybody there, right now, doin' the same thing?"

He was leading somewhere, and I kept quiet.

"I think we're lookin' at the Windknocker's spirit," he said.

The tint in the sky had intensified to the spellbinding stage.

"His spirit is dressed up in them colors, so we can see it and let it seep inside," he said.

"*God, that's a novel concept,*" I thought, for once having a clue what he was talking about.

"Let yourself go real quiet for a minute, Mew, and tell me what thoughts pop into your head."

"Well?" he said after a few moments.

"I was thinking how hard Blinky had it trying to keep that meat market open."

"Anything else?"

"Well, maybe Abner Pong." I ventured. "It was pretty rough for him growing up."

"Think you could ever give him the forgiveness for being such a little bastard?"

He chuckled. I didn't smile, though, because it was the actual thought my mind had latched onto. Abner had suffered unmercifully as a young boy, being a bastard in an era of intolerance for out-of-wedlock children.

"I suppose if he asked, I could."

"Suppose there weren't no more sunsets until you made up your mind?" Leezie asked.

That one did go over my head, and it would be years before the meaning hit me.

Instead of answering, I asked my own question. "So what did *you* think about?"

"Ah," he said. "I was wondering if Frannie has any cake left over from the party."

Chapter Thirty-Six

Leezie tried to have his cake and eat it too. For the next two years, he carried on as if things were normal, ignoring the emphysema. Even traveling closer to home worked against him. More people learned about the man who lived at Saint Ruthie's, who was always ready to pass on a blessing. His mail arrived in bundles, often outnumbering the parish's ten-to-one. On occasion he would read different letters to me. Two examples stick in my mind.

A dentist wrote to him, saying: "*I met you in Yakima last year. You spoke at my wife's little Bible study group. All of my life I have been an agnostic. If there was a God, I sure didn't want anything to do with the God manufactured by religion.*

"*You told me, 'Well, invent a new one then – but make sure it's the kind of god worth believing in.' I took up your challenge. Nothing happened until remembered your last advice – 'Just make sure you pick a god too good to be true.' Thanks.*"

The other letter came from a mother: "*Can you come to Tumwater? I just want to hug you for helping my son. Ralph was always a handful, and got worse after he grew up. He said he met you at that gas station where you work, right after his second divorce. I was afraid for Ralph, because he was soooo depressed. I knew Ralph could hide his hurt from most people, but you saw through that within five minutes. Ralph told me, 'When he did, mom, I scrammed the hell out of there.'*

"*Ralph was bowled over when you showed up at his apartment two days later and invited him to some tavern you like. I don't know anything about this "windknocker" that Ralph talks about now, but I think I would.*"

Leezie called what he did *"puttin' a wet finger to the wind."* In religious speak it means finding what direction the wind of the Spirit is blowing. Leezie claimed, and I don't dispute him, that *"puttin' a wet finger to the wind"* led him to people in need of a blessing, or to be less archaic, to spread happiness.

In later years, if you wanted to answer the question about his whereabouts, all you needed to do was lick a finger and hold it in the air.

In the summer of 1984, he went to Vermont. I learned, after the fact, that he had a mild heart attack and spent almost a week in the hospital. He protested about his medicine, saying, "I feel like a walking drug store."

Frannie was the first to notice his emphysema was acting up too. That did it for me. I went to the bishop and told him about Leezie. "It could be months, or it could be years," I said, "but I'll need lots of time off to spend with him."

"The only assistant I have available is from the new conservative school," the bishop said. "You'll have to keep a close eye on him or he'll be reinstalling altar rails at Saint Ruthie's."

I assured him I could handle that. The bishop surprised me when he said, "Just keep me in the loop, and wish your friend well from me."

Leezie regained some of his old vigor, but right after Thanksgiving he was in the hospital again. His blood pressure had gone off the charts.

"Look at these," he said, showing me another pill bottle. "Pretty soon I won't have enough pockets to hold 'em."

That Christmas I disguised Leezie's present in a corn flakes box. Frannie had placed it behind the tree so it was sure to come up last.

"What's this, Mew?" he said, shaking it so the contents rattled mysteriously. He tore off the wrapping, and said, "corn flakes?"

"Open it, you silly man," Frannie said.

I'd never seen his eyes light up the way they did when he saw what the envelope inside contained.

"I've always wondered what the indoors part of the King Dome looks like," he said after recovering from the shock.

One of Leezie's few passions in life was baseball. The two season tickets for the Seattle Mariners games I'd given him generated just about more excitement than he could take.

We were at the King Dome on opening day in 1985, when the Mariners played Oakland. Our seats were right behind the first-base dugout, and Leezie was transfixed. He watched the raucous crowd, numbering somewhere over 37,000, in amazement. He grunted when Seattle's power hitter, Stormin' Gorman, struck out.

"Did you see that curve ball, Mew? Wow! This is better than pineapple upside-down cake with real whip cream."

In the meantime, I raided Uncle Horace's trust fund and bought a pickup and matching camper. The truck was a 1975 Chevy with less than twenty thousand miles. The idea to take Leezie camping had come to me one night when I couldn't sleep. On days the Mariners were out of town, Leezie and I left for whatever remote part of the Northwest that suited our fancy.

We didn't venture far from home to begin with, although Leezie suggested, "Hey, we should drive up to Prince Rupert." I think our second outing was to see the tulips in bloom at Puyallup. "Did you remember to bring the hot dogs?" he asked twice before we got there.

That night we roasted them over charcoal. "Remember that County Fair in 1930 when Sam bought us hot dogs?" he said.

"Indeed I do," I answered.

Neither of us said anything for a long while, although the silence didn't prevent Leezie from eyeballing the last wiener sizzling over the coals.

"What were you meditatin' about just now?" he asked.

"I just recalled it was one of the best times we ever had."

He pondered that for a long moment, and I asked, "So, what were you thinking about?"

"I was just wondering if those Mariners can beat them Yankees next week," he said.

That series was played in late May, and Leezie was in a state of ecstasy to actually witness the successors of Babe Ruth take the field. He never went without his mitt, and in the first game he narrowly missed catching a foul ball off the bat of the great Yankee slugger, Dave Winfield. The Yankees' Rickey Henderson hit a three-run homer and we cheered.

"Holy cow!" Leezie said after the game. "We got skunked eleven to one, but that was the most fun I've had since we put that chili pepper in Gravedigger Bill's chewin' tobacco."

The language of baseball even found its way into my column. The reforms of Vatican II by this time were under murderous assault. I likened it to the Mariners playing in the bottom of the ninth.

"Behind by a run, the Mariners eked out a walk and a double, putting runners on second and third," I wrote. "Will the batter knock them in, or will he let the opposition win the day?"

It was supposed to be a rallying cry for the majority in the church to raise their voices and drown out the minority, who were intent on destroying the renewal.

The article brought the naysayers out of the woodwork and my hate mail ran about eighty–twenty. Leezie liked it, though, and told me so from his hospital bed. He was at the Vets Hospital being treated for an irregular heartbeat.

We had our same seats for opening day in 1986 against the California Angels. The Mariners won eight to four in front of almost 50,000. By now, in order to get Leezie in and out of the King Dome and accommodate his oxygen bottle, I resorted to a wheel chair.

Larry Wilson welded a rack on the back of the camper to hold the wheel chair. We spent more time in the woods that summer and missed some games, but neither of us cared.

"Mew, the Windknocker's big outdoor cathedral is the best place to iron out our differences," Leezie said.

Although those were few now, what remained were the same as had divided us for over fifty years.

"Whaddayamean, borned again?" I repeated one night in late September. We were camped at Cape Lookout in Oregon. It was one of the few times we built a campfire, and we did it on the beach. Leezie was sitting on the downwind side, out of the smoke. The tide was coming in and the moon was high in the sky, lighting the crest of the breakers.

"How many times have I told you, Mew, that I can't explain it? You act like I'm supposed to hand over an owner's manual with *'borned again'* printed in big letters on the front."

"Well, it might help," I said.

"Just stop thinkin' about it and let it happen," he said. "That's all I can tell you."

I did stop thinking about it and concentrated on enjoying the time we had left together. He made life tedious at times, and we had a more contentious row that fall. It happened when he announced one morning that he was going to ride the bus, "And take me a little trip to Vermont for Christmas."

"That's a harebrained idea if I ever heard one," I said.

"What you got against riding the bus?" he shot back.

"Smoke, Leezie," I explained. "People smoke on buses, and your lungs won't take that."

His army buddies chipped in for a plane ticket. He came back in the early spring, too late for the start of baseball season but in decent health, for him.

That could change, and quickly, as happened late one afternoon at the Wheel House Tavern.

Leezie called the outing, "Mewing at the movies." Each Wednesday we'd take in two of the best movies the matinees had to offer.

He was wheezing before he finished his first bottle of root beer. Jack, the bartender, tried tapping his oxygen tank with a bottle opener.

"That help any, Sarge?" he asked.

Taking a closer look Jack decided he didn't like the look of Leezie's blue lips.

"Zeke," he hollered to a flabby man sitting at a table close to the parrot's cage. (Conrad, by this time, had been replaced by an understudy named Popeye.) "Get your lard butt over here and tend to Sarge."

Zeke, who I learned was an ex-army medic, waddled quickly across the room. He performed a cursory examination. I breathed a sigh of relief, for Zeke seemed to know what he was doing.

"Call an ambulance, Jack," he said as he leaned over and began massaging Leezie's heaving chest.

That was one among many of the scares the advance of his disease caused. He recovered, and as you might expect, blamed it on the root beer.

"It was that fizzy kind I don't like, Mew, and some of the bubbles got up my nose."

Leezie knew he wasn't fooling me or his friends, but his cheerful attitude helped prolong the inevitable.

He had a bout of pneumonia in early summer. After the incident at the Wheel House I learned there was an abundance of ex-army medics like Zeke. Since there was a spare room at the parish house, I enlisted their help to care for him.

It was two weeks, I think, after he recovered from pneumonia that he hatched another of his off-the-wall plans.

"You're going to do what?" I said, exasperated by the idea.

"I'm going to take me another trip," he repeated. "Back to our old home town."

We were fishing from the jetty on Puget Sound at the time, and he had already needled me about being ahead in the fish count five to one.

"I'm going," he said a third time. "Leonard offered to drive me in his Mustang."

I complained again, but there was no talking him out of it. I didn't detect at the time that the plan was another of his schemes. My suspicions that he was indeed up to something were aroused, though, when he returned two weeks later. His health didn't appear to have suffered, but he had a strange smile on his face for days. *"See if you can top this,"* it seemed to say.

He had written the final chapter in his life's book. I didn't realize it at first, but as the weeks went on I watched him run down like a wind-up toy. I spent most of every day with him, and we talked for hours.

Late one night, when I was at a priest's retreat in Tacoma, I was called to the desk to take an urgent telephone call. I picked up the receiver and heard Larry Wilson say, "Father. I'm at the vet's hospital." He hesitated for a moment. "It looks like Sarge is about to make his final landing. You'd better come."

It was another heart attack, a bad one. Traffic was light until I reached the outskirts of Seattle. There, I got delayed by a shift change at Boeing and then found the elevator at the hospital out of order. By the time I reached the Intensive Care Unit, my breathing sounded like an out-of-shape marathon runner.

The doctor met me at the door and watched me anxiously for a moment. After he decided I wasn't his next candidate for an angiogram, he said, "You'd better go right in, Father. He doesn't have much time."

I found Leezie hooked to all kinds of the tubes and gadgets. Thankfully, he was conscious.

His eyes brightened when he saw me. When his lips moved, I bent down to listen.

"Glad you could make it," he said.

The twinkle in his eye told me he was joking.

"I never did tell you what Father Martin really said to me that day," he said.

At first, I thought he was hallucinating. But he wasn't, and after a minute I realized he was back in our childhood.

"That's right," he said. "The day you tried to make me into an altar boy."

"That was your idea," I protested.

He ignored me, saying, "Old hot foot Martin told me I should think about becoming a priest."

"What?"

"Honest Injun," he said. "I'm just glad you went an' did it instead of me."

Father Martin had talked to him for a long time that day, and I had always thought there was more to the story.

"It's a hard job bein' a priest," he went on, starting to slur some of his words. "And it's going to get harder for you, Mew, but I think you'll get some help now."

"What's he talking about?" I wondered.

He didn't say anything for several minutes, and then I heard, "Thanks." He reached feebly for my hand, and said, "Next to ole Bub, you is the best friend I ever had."

I wasn't in the mood for his jokes but didn't have time to ponder it.

"One last thing," he said.

"What?" I said.

"A promise," he whispered. "Promise you'll take my will serious when you reads it."

Since I didn't have a choice, I said, "Okay."

He started to snicker, like my *"okay"* would give him the last laugh.

He licked his finger and held it feebly in the air. His last words were, "Got me some business to tend to." Then he looked up at me and grinned, not a huge one, but still the one I'd known since age two.

He died a few moments later, leaving this world as few do, with a smile on his lips.

Chapter Thirty-Seven

My housekeeper, Frannie Burke, had been in love with Leezie practically from first sight. His death hit her hard. To help console her, we went to the Wheel House that afternoon for clam chowder. I had received a surprise condolence call early that morning. Along with it the bishop had offered the gymnasium facilities of large Catholic High School for Leezie's funeral.

"I don't know what plans you have, but if you need the extra room, it's yours," he had said. "I still remember that story he told at your birthday party."

His sincerity surprised me. I couldn't imagine a large crowd turning out for Leezie's service, but left the offer open, and ended the phone call.

More well-wishers greeted us at the Wheel House.

"We used to come here often," Frannie told me. "Just to be among friends helps a lot."

The next morning I was giving Father Armstrong his marching orders for the day when I noticed Frank Parsons' car pull into the driveway. Armstrong was the priest the bishop had sent to handle my absences. He was a severe-mannered thirty-five-year-old, and ultra-conservative. No doubt he would have thought liberals had corrupted the church of my youth.

"*That's strange*," I thought as I watched Frank escort a younger woman to the door. I answered the bell and invited them in. After a good look, my mouth dropped open and I stood flat-footed, staring. The resemblance was unnerving.

"Well," the woman spoke. "You sure don't look like a devil to me."

I mumbled something, too shocked to really speak.

"That's what my Burlington grandmother used to say," she said, her face breaking into a smile. "I don't think I ever believed it, but she thought all priests were devils."

Her voice carried the same melodious lilt, albeit with a New England accent.

"I hope my daddy warned you that I tease when I should be serious."

"Same smile too, only broader," I thought.

"No! He forgot to mention that," I said. "Neither did he tell me you were practically a spitting image of his sister, Betsy."

"I guess I don't have to introduce you," Frank spoke up. "But just in case, this is my niece, Glory, Sarge's daughter."

She hugged me, kissing me sweetly on the cheek.

"I don't think I could have come unless I knew I'd finally get to meet you," she whispered.

"We don't have much time," Frank interrupted.

"Is this about the funeral?" I asked.

"I guess you could say that," Frank answered. "But it kind of depends on how you react to what Sarge wanted."

My eyebrows shot up and I seated them around the table. Frank relaxed and we shared a time of sweet memories. Finally, he took a paper from his briefcase, saying, "This is the portion of Sarge's will that gets to the question." He laid it in front of me. "Read the highlighted section."

It read: *I don't really want a funeral. But the Windknocker might have other plans. If my friend, Mew, agrees to conduct a service, then whatever Frank and Glory decide where and how is okay with me. No Mew, no funeral though. Mew should have some things to say about us that might help others. It might help him too.*

It gave me a queasy feeling. Generally, it was a bad idea for people close to the deceased to play a pivotal role in the service. I sat back, thinking for a moment, and decided I could maintain my stoicism long enough to do what Leezie wanted. He only made me promise to take the will seriously, and I knew the final choice was mine.

"Okay," I said.

Frank breathed a sigh of relief and Glory smiled.

"Where and when?" I asked.

"We don't know," Frank said. "But it might have to be bigger than we originally thought."

I told him about the bishop's offer and they exchanged relieved smiles. I noticed Glory's eyes had the same trait as Betsy's – they didn't just sparkle, they danced.

"Can you give me the bishop's private phone number?" Frank asked.

By the middle of the afternoon I had the order of the funeral service down on paper and faxed it off to Frank Parsons. He must have had a printer standing by because shortly after supper my own fax machine delivered the finished program.

My finger followed the order of events and stopped for a moment. Frank had moved my sermon to the end, and after thinking about it, I decided it fit well there. The funeral would be on Saturday afternoon at St. Peter's High School gymnasium.

"*Good*," I thought. It was Thursday evening, plenty of time to compose my sermon. I decided I could wait and tackle that in the morning, since the job should be easy.

Twenty-four hours later, I had a wastepaper basket full of wadded pages from a legal pad but no sermon. I was exhausted, frustrated and humiliated. By midnight I was a raging maniac. I tried every trick I knew to relax and make my mind focus. I took time out to pray, trying to be convincing and sincere. Next, I fixed a bologna sandwich smothered in green olives. All that did was give me heartburn.

I hadn't taken a walk in the middle of the night since the days I worked for Tyrannical Tommy, but I did now. I shuffled along at first and then sped up, thinking that if I got the blood flowing it might sweep the cobwebs out of my brain. I was panting by the time I reached the little park where I had often pushed Leezie in his wheelchair.

It was deserted at two o'clock in the morning. I sat down in a familiar spot, forcing myself to be still. *"Maybe it's the place,"* I thought, *"but I feel calmer now."* Calmer didn't, however, come with any new insights.

"Look what you've gotten me into, Leezie," I said. "Your funeral is twelve hours away and I've got no speech to give."

"Can't you just tell one of your stories?" I looked around, surprised that the words came from inside my head and not the nearby rhododendron bush. *"That's what Frannie had said to Leezie before the birthday bash,"* I remembered.

I did have stories, plenty of them. Several popped into my mind all at once. I quickly rejected the one about the big event of Leezie's life – the revival tent incident. I rejected a few others and soon, the stories became muddled and ended up in fragments I couldn't remember. Finally, I quit in disgust. I stood, and after leaving a few uncomplimentary remarks for Leezie, walked home, where I fell asleep on the couch in my office.

The telephone on my desk jolted me from a dreamless sleep. Groggily, I tried to get off the uncomfortable couch. The caller gave up and I had barely closed my eyes again when the wall clock chimed. I counted them. *"Nine! How can it be that late in the morning?"*

I cut myself shaving, but only once – a miracle considering I was trying to compose a sermon and listen to other thoughts at the same time. I laughed, nicking my chin again, when Leezie's oft-repeated proverb surfaced. *"Nine o'clock in the morning? It's the best time of day! That's the hour the Windknocker blowed out the windows in that upper room."*

His allusion to the day of Pentecost, however, didn't provide an ounce of inspiration. My head was pounding by the time I had to give up on my sermon and leave for the service. I jotted a few quick notes and raced out the door, the paper stuffed in my shirt pocket.

I had only been to St. Peter's once before, at night. I got lost twice on the way. Then I noticed the gas gauge on my six-year-old Ford

Taurus was riding on empty. Somehow I made it and steered into the parking space reserved for me with five minutes to spare. *"I'm sure the crowd will be modest,"* I consoled myself, knowing I had never been this ill-prepared. *"I'll just have to bluff my way through."*

Frank Parsons met me at the door.

"You all ready for the big show, Father?" he said cheerily. "Everyone's excited to hear what you'll have to say."

I gulped. I was not good at bluffing and wished I could be anywhere but there at that moment.

He didn't seem to notice anything wrong and said, "Shall we go? It's time."

St. Peter's was a large building, and Frank led me down several corridors before I saw the doors of the gymnasium. He took my arm and helped squeeze me past a few late arrivals.

"It holds about fifteen hundred," the bishop had told me when he offered the facility.

I walked up a short ramp into a blaze of lights, and was confronted by my worst fear. The gym was full.

"You okay, Father?" Frank said. "You look like you swallowed a hotdog sideways."

"Who are all these people?" I stammered.

Frank gave me a *"that's a dumbass question"* look. "Sarge had a lot of friends," he said.

My legs were wobbly and I was short of breath by the time I reached the podium. I hoped Frank didn't sense my anxiety during our whispered conference to make sure I was straight on everything.

"A violin and a fiddle?" I questioned. "I thought they were the same thing."

"One fiddles and the other does violin music," Frank answered, adding, "in this case, AMAZING GRACE."

Glory is the only person singing, when she does HOW GREAT THOU ART at the end. I looked at the program to see that Stradivari and Hecklefiddle led off after my introduction.

"That's just great, Leezie!" I thought. *"Why didn't you just have Runt Malone or somebody play AMAZING GRACE on a car horn?"*

I managed to get through the opening. I sat down, hoping the look I got from Frank wasn't a critique on how stiff and formal I sounded.

The acoustics of the gym were amazing, but not nearly as awesome as the rendition of AMAZING GRACE I heard that day. The unlikely duo alternated parts and combined them, spontaneously. What they produced was a perfect blending of sad and toe tapping. Frank had to clear his throat to get my attention to introduce the testimony part of the program.

That lasted fifty minutes. A tiny man led off, approaching the microphone timidly, and Frank, Jr. had to prompt him to take it.

"I'm John Malone," he squeaked. "Some call me Runt, but Sarge taught me they don't mean no harm in it. If it weren't for Sarge I wouldn't be alive to say that. And that's all I got to say."

Soon, an unrehearsed theme surfaced. I had feared it would either turn into a chest-pounding, back-patting way to get attention, or build Leezie up into something he wasn't. There were several interjections of words I was familiar with, like *"born again"* and *"Windknocker."* It was the strangest funeral crowd I'd ever encountered. They were patient, polite and most of all, attentive.

Many who spoke had traveled great distances – from Missouri, Wyoming, Wisconsin and points in between. The last man who reached the raised platform in the middle of the gym announced, "I'm from Saskatoon, Canada."

That got my undivided attention. Leezie had always mentioned Saskatoon, but I'd never asked him about it.

"I never fought in a war, like Sarge and a lot of you, 'eh? So my story isn't aboot bombs, napalm, or seein' your buddy get his head blown off."

I wondered what it *was* about.

"My daddy was cold and mean, and he shoved religion down my throat," he continued. "So I grew up thinking God was the same way, ornery and bitter. I gave God and daddy the boot and left home when I was seventeen."

He told an uplifting story of building a successful career and how he conquered alcohol because, "It made me like my daddy."

Rapid fire, he listed why he'd come. "It's aboot something different. I was just a plain vanilla Marvin kind of guy; no big troubles, good wife, happy enough, not looking for anything, especially religion with that monster god they foisted on me. I thought life was good until I met the hunger man. Up home we call him that."

Leezie, we found out, was waiting to change trains one day in Saskatoon and stopped in a market to buy a root beer.

"My wife's car had stalled, and he got it running," the man said. "That was twenty years ago."

I had to agree after listening to more of Marvin's examples why he labeled God a "*monster.*"

"It was finally the goodness in that man's heart," he said, gesturing toward the coffin, "that changed my mind. It was almost an otherworldly kind of goodness. I finally decided that sort had to come from outside a man.

"And if it did," he added, waving an arm so it clunked the microphone. "It could only come from one place. It had to come from God, but not any God I knew aboot."

I was starting to fear he was *going to be a tough act to follow.*

"Leezie nurtured a hunger in me," he said. "And before long I was aboot starved to death to find the source of that goodness. See why we call him the hunger man?"

His story so far had covered a span of ten years.

"Finally, I said to him one day, how can God be that good? Do you know what he spoke back to me?" He paused a moment, eyes examining the bleachers. "We were out in my grage one afternoon. I remember it like last week. 'Marvin,' he said, grinning that big smile, 'he ain't.'"

"I still remember my dismayed feeling. But he followed that with, 'He's better than good. He don't knock the bad out of a person. Instead, he blows goodness into 'em. On the wind comes the goodness; let him do it, and then you'll know.'"

That brought a ripple of clapping, and Marvin concluded quickly, saying, "Long story short, I got born again, and haven't been the same since. And that's what it's all aboot, 'eh?"

My insides were trembling when I stepped to the microphone to deliver the sermon I didn't have.

Chapter Thirty-Eight

The paper stuck in my pocket when I tried to take it out. I coughed nervously and looked out upon the crowd. They reminded me of a packed house at the boxing arena I had taken Leezie to one night, all of them anticipating the main event.

I cleared my throat and happened to look down at Leezie's coffin fifteen feet in front of me. It was plain, which suited him.

My eyes were drawn to two items of memorabilia I hadn't noticed before. His Seattle Mariner's cap and baseball mitt were the only decorations, and the nostalgia overwhelmed me. A huge lump plugged my throat, followed by a bigger sob that heaved my shoulders. At first I was embarrassed, standing in front of fifteen hundred people and crying like a baby. But I couldn't control it. My soul was numbed with the grief that hadn't been released, and it poured out in great bursts of anguish.

The grief and desperation I felt made me open to help from the outside. In a real sense, I stood in front of the crowd, vulnerable – stripped of my pride and logic. I remember pleading with God for help. Soon, the well-worn phrase, "Be careful what you ask God for," would take on real meaning.

What I received in answer to my plea was a closeness to God I had never believed possible. Time stood still for a short moment. All of my thoughts and runaway emotions seemed to be cast aside, only to be replaced by an entirely new idea. I remember saying, "I feel like a new person."

I doubt it was audible, but I don't know. I took an immense breath, savoring the air as it was driven deep into my senses like the fragrance of an apple tree in full bloom. No lights flashed and no thunder boomed, but I knew in that instant I'd just experienced what Leezie had always talked about. It was also plain how he'd latched onto his Windknocker acronym!

"I've been born again!" echoed in my mind.

Thankfully, I didn't try to analyze it. But later, with a healthy dose of retrospect, I'll provide you some answers.

My tears subsided and I wiped them dry. My thoughts were racing, but slowed so I could grasp what they were saying. "I guess it's time for me to speak now," I thought. And although I still had no good idea what to say, I knew all I had to do was open my mouth.

My lips broke into a huge smile first, and I noticed my audience was still there, waiting patiently. I have no idea how long this hiatus lasted; five to ten minutes is my guess.

"We're here today," I said, amazed at the strength of my voice, "to honor a man who just might be one of the greatest men of this century!"

I followed with, "The best story teller I've ever known was my dad, Sam Moosington, and second was Leezie Smith. Be assured, I'm not in their league. Thankfully, I don't have to be, because all it takes is one who was there and remembers it like yesterday."

The images of our life together were coming almost too fast to grasp, and it caused me to laugh. I decided I might as well start where I was supposed to.

"Leezie and I were fourteen at the time it all began," I said. "He talked me into going to one of those old fashioned tent revival meetings. Actually, there were three of us, because his big dog Beelzebub went with us."

That brought smiles to several of the faces I could see. I could feel a great energy building inside me, and I sensed the dam holding back our memories was about to burst.

"Come to think of it, today is very close to the fifty-seventh anniversary of that event." The story poured out as I described Leezie lurching to his feet to answer the preacher's altar call. "He was gone a long time," I said. "But finally he returned, he and Beelzebub. I noticed he had a strange look on his face – Leezie, not the dog."

A lady in the front row tittered. "*Go easy on your dumb jokes, Moosington,*" I admonished. "I asked him: '*What was that all about?*' 'The preacher said I just got borned again,' he answered."

I told the rest of that story and what took place the following day at the County Fair. "But it all started that night in the revival tent. It was from that sense of having the wind of Pentecost knocked into him that Leezie coined the word, Windknocker."

I remember little of what I said after that. I simply told Leezie's life story that had never been heard before. Later, I was astounded to learn I spoke for fifty-two minutes.

I finished, returning to the beginning.

"I admit I'm biased, but he was a great man." My voice cracked for the first time, when I mentioned his smile and how it could light up the darkest room.

The timber returned to my vocal cords.

"He didn't want to be holy." I waited a moment for that to sink in. "Oh! I see that you've heard him say that," I said, seeing several nodding heads.

"Even the rituals in my own church bothered him because he thought they over emphasize acting holy. 'Too much pleadin' and bleatin' for me, Mew,' he'd say."

I heard a ripple of soft laughter. After it quieted I said, "Leezie had a poem he liked, and read it to me often. It's a poem that pretty much sums up what he thought about holiness. *And,* it pretty much describes Leezie." (The writer's name, Earl King, popped into my mind at that moment, but I didn't reveal it.) "I don't remember the entire poem," I said, "just this part."

"I don't believe in the saints,
I cannot know their God
If there are saints then who am I
Who were my mother and father
Who was their God?

I believe in sinners
I know their God and am not afraid
For I am one of them."

I paused for several seconds, and decided this was a good place to end. I said, "Do you remember the question I asked Leezie that day at the County Fair?" I heard a couple of people say, 'whaddayamean, borned again?'"

I let my eyes roam the crowd, not trying to hide my growing smile. "I'll wager that plenty of you have asked it too." Wagging heads told me it was true.

"Well, don't feel left out," I said. "I've asked that question for well over fifty years." My smile was getting bigger. "And I can almost hear Leezie's snickers rattling the pearly gates right now. No doubt he's saying, 'and the answer has been a long time coming, ain't it?'"

I had preached at more funerals than I could count, but this was the first time the audience had ever applauded. I sat down, basking not in the limelight but in a growing awareness that God had touched me this day.

Glory sang her own farewell. I doubt St. Peter's gymnasium had ever experienced the emotion it aroused. Everyone joined her for the last refrain: "Then sings my soul, my Savior God to thee; How great thou art! How great thou art." My own ears and senses were more finely tuned than the violin that began it all, and truly my soul did sing.

The rest of the day was a blur of activity. Glory's flight back to Vermont left at nine that night. She was escorting Leezie's casket to its final resting place beside his beloved.

The Wheel House Tavern was nearby and we went there, just the two of us. I assured her the clam chowder was good and we ordered that.

We were both famished, and most of the fishing boats were still out, giving us peace and quiet. After I wiped the juice from my second bowl, she said, "I'm sorry we put you through that. You were so grief stricken."

"Don't apologize," I said. "I had to do it. Besides, I had a little help."

She got up and put her arms around me, holding me tight for several moments. "Thanks," she said. "Daddy always said when you put your mind to it, you were the best speaker there is."

"I would downgrade that to fair in most cases."

"If today was any example, you're much too modest," she said. "Only a man who knew him the way you did could have done it. The story you shared about his sister really touched me. It's the first time I've heard it."

That surprised me and I told how Betsy had the idea to tutor me so I could go to first grade with Leezie.

Her face took on a meditative look. A minute passed before she spoke again. "I wonder if you would write some of this down," she said.

I gave her an amused expression.

"No, I'm serious," she said. "I know so little about some things. Daddy told me most of it, of course, like how he cut his lip and how he botched the alarm when you tried to tip over the sheriff's outhouse."

She pondered another moment and said, "I think others, like Betsy, hide some of the things that made him tick."

"I've never thought about it," I said.

"Would you consider it?"

"You're not intending to serialize this in your newspaper, I hope."

She laughed, tossing her long black curls to and fro. "I hadn't thought of that. Maybe I should."

Glory let the subject drop. The day passed, and before I knew it the Wheel House was filling up with the evening crowd. A quick glance at my watch alarmed me. We had talked much too long, and if we didn't get a move on, Glory would miss her plane.

Frank and Frank, Jr. were at the airport, anxiously waiting for us. Six of Leezie's army friends were waiting too, chosen by lot for the honor to escort the coffin to the waiting plane. Runt Malone was the first to spot me, and all of them rushed to greet us. They were dressed in full uniform. How they found a proper fit for the medic, Zeke, is beyond my imagination, but he looked striking. Runt didn't say anything but his grip as he shook my hand was fierce. Leonard had also made the distinguished group, and talked my leg off.

It was the most somber moment of the day, watching my friend leave on his final trip. His honor guard carried the casket with pomp and precision across the tarmac. As the coffin began its slow trip up the conveyor, I raised a hand, feebly it seemed to me, and waved goodbye.

Chapter Thirty-Nine

Runt Malone was the first, followed by a multitude that transferred Leezie's mantle to me. Like it or not, I was in the *blind and the lames* business. Malone, a man of few words, became my friend, assuming, in the process, he should also be my protector.

The first time I noticed was one night after I left the Wheel House and found a man loitering near my car. The tavern was in an upgraded area of the city, but being close to the waterfront still collected an assortment of unsavory characters.

My aging Ford Taurus didn't exactly shout, "*steal me*," and the person who appeared from the shadows was not a poster boy for *mug your neighbor week*.

"Evening, Padre," he said. "You forgot to lock your car again. Malone axed me to keep a eye out."

Over the next three years I became a job finder, encourager, marriage-grief-and-drug counselor, matchmaker, money advisor, and the hearer of sins and countless bad jokes. When Runt was ready, I got *him* a job interview with K-Mart, where he quickly rose to foreman at their shipping and receiving warehouse.

Successes like Malone didn't come easy, and my life was further complicated by the growing conservatism in the Church.

"You had what?" my friend, Lieutenant O'Sullivan, said one Monday morning. I'd just told him about the demonstrators Saint Ruthie's had the day before. "Well, I guess it's not that surprising," he said. "Your parish *is* one of the dwindling outposts of Vatican II."

That was true. People had been leaving the Church in droves. Some became Protestants; others just quit. The remainder became members of parishes like mine.

"What can I do about it?" I asked. "I draw the line at protestors disrupting Sunday worship."

Lieutenant Boo outlined a plan.

The following Sunday was worse than the week before. There were six intruders distributed among the congregation. I began, and so did they, some chanting prayers in Latin and others saying the rosary, all in very loud voices.

These were called Tridentines, the most radical of the Catholic fundamentalists taking over the church. The Tridentines believed the Vatican II liturgy was an abomination and that the present Pope was an imposter, and were demanding a reinstitution of the Latin Mass.

Taking O'Sullivan's advice, I nodded to an usher, who called 911. Soon, the sound of wailing sirens could be heard. I took a deep breath and tried to start over. The activists only cranked up the volume, and they never realized the sirens shut off when they reached the parking lot in front of the church. Lieutenant Boo met the police at the rear of Saint Ruthie's. He issued quiet instructions and four policemen removed the stunned protesters, who went quietly, and the liturgy resumed.

The bishop was aghast and the local media had a field day when the word leaked out.

"Moosington, what kind of an example of Christian charity was that supposed to be?" the bishop asked me on the telephone.

"They're unruly children," I offered in defense. "And you know what happens when disruptive kids aren't called to task."

"Ba-but," he sputtered in response. "Couldn't you have found a little less visible way to do it?" Before I could answer, he went on, "My God, twenty police cars and three ambulances, that's a bit excessive!"

I ignored the deliberate overstatement and patiently asked, "What would you suggest? They'll no doubt show up at the Cathedral next."

He let out a deep sigh. "You could be right," he said. Exasperated, he hung up.

Saint Ruthie's weathered the storm and we were never bothered again. I was proud of the people. They displayed no rancor; in fact old Mrs. Wendsea, a Vatican II stalwart, had hugged one of the perpetrators before the police led him away. Tuesday's edition of the *Seattle P-I* carried a headline on their local news page, quoting one of my parishioners. "*Things are never dull at Saint Ruthie's,*" it read.

My own column that week urged a proactive approach and a call for the American Bishops to confront those who would destroy the reform. For once, what I wrote created a groundswell of support. Regrettably, the writers took their ire out on Seattle's bishop for not demanding that Rome stop the piece-by-piece dismantling of Vatican II.

The bishop took it personally and came within an inch of firing me. Luckily, he had arrived back in town after Wilbur Lester's op-ed piece appeared in the *Seattle P-I*. Wilbur had interviewed the editor of the diocesan newspaper and concluded his column with: "*The amount of positive mail generated by Father Moosington's column is not only astonishing, it's sending a message. The message here is an emphatic 'Listen to us!'*"

Unfortunately, no one listened, and as Leezie predicted, my job got harder. Irony was also abundant because when I attempted to talk about being born again, I was met with the same kind of skepticism I had shown whenever Leezie brought it up.

I used the *term "born again"* sparingly, but didn't hesitate to if I wanted to get a person's attention. On the day of the funeral, my relationship with God changed from the remote to the *real*. It was a life-changing minute for me.

Is there a defining moment when an individual's connection to the creator changes dramatically? Leezie would say, "If you have to ask, that should be your first clue." My general response was, "probably."

I allowed room for exceptions, but if someone reacted, asking, "*Whaddayamean, born again?*" I too relied on Leezie's experience. If they questioned, I told them the story of what happened to me at the funeral.

Leezie also said it other ways. One of his favorites was, "You need to get kissed by the Windknocker." He particularly liked that because he could then explain, "Borned again is the Windknocker reachin' out to you, and it ain't because you're good. You gets good by lettin' the Windknocker be good to you."

Often, I marveled at his wisdom, most of which I'd previously ignored. For instance, I had tried all of my life to be good, and give my life to God. What I learned when I became vulnerable in my moment of grief was that I had finally let God give himself to me! Being born again, I can testify is not a reward for being good. It's a tangible demonstration of God's love. My thoughts about it would evolve some, as you shall see.

Gradually, I recovered from Leezie's death and adapted to my new role of helping the *blind and the lames*. I wasn't prepared, however, for the next great distress that was about to confront me.

Wilbur Lester, the *Seattle P-I's* religion writer, had lost his taste for Big Macs. Three months after the protest incident at Saint Ruthie's, he invited me to a late lunch at Red Lobster.

The switch to gourmet food had done wonders for Wilbur's waistline.

"It just proves that Darwin was right," he joked, patting his stomach. "I've evolved into a middle-aged-man with a paunch."

I hadn't seen him for six weeks. He had just returned from South Africa and Rome.

"I stopped to see Glory in Vermont like you asked," he said. "It was no trouble since I flew into Montreal and was driving to Boston anyway."

My face, I'm sure, had a coaxing look. He ignored it as the waiter set plates on the table: beer-battered shrimp and chips for him and an oven-broiled flounder for me.

"She thinks you should turn your story into a book," he said.

Wilbur was talking about the short story I'd had him deliver to Glory.

"Fat chance!" I said. "I had enough trouble writing that much."

"I told her you'd probably respond that way. She appreciates the effort, though," he went on, alternating between shrimp and chips. "But about all you did was whet her appetite."

"Me write a book? That's a laugh." It was beyond my skill level. "Besides," I thought, *"all I have to rely on is my poor memory. Leezie didn't exactly leave behind volumes of source material."* However, delivering the story I'd compiled wasn't the only reason for having Wilbur stop in Vermont.

After he finished a large piece of key lime pie, he set three photographs in front of me.

"I think these are what you wanted," he said.

They were pictures of Leezie's grave.

"That's from the foot of the grave looking west," Wilbur pointed out.

"Is that Lake Champlain in the distance?"

"Pretty, isn't it?" he answered.

The finality was striking too, completing the last part of the healing process that had eluded me. I had watched the coffin disappear into the airplane, and this stark reminder of grave and tombstone told me how it ended.

"You've had some hard knocks the past few years," Wilbur spoke up. "First Jay Jay, and then your dad dying a year ago, and this. You holding up okay?"

"Yes," I said. "And as you know I haven't exactly had the time to mope."

He eyed me pensively a moment and said, "You seem a lot calmer, and your sense of humor has gotten better."

"Only because you feed me so well," I ventured.

He chuckled. "Your newspaper columns have been darned good recently. And judging by that I don't know what gives you the idea you couldn't write a book."

I didn't say anything because usually when he buttered me up in this fashion, it meant he had something to reveal that he didn't want to.

"Here's an example of what I mean," Wilbur said, showing me a highlighted section from the column that had drawn the outpouring of mail.

"*Instead of telling yourself how bad you are, tell the bad in you how good God is.*"

"That could be a quote from someone," I said, "but I've never been able to find the source. Leezie said he made it up, and I stole it from him."

"I know," Wilbur said. "But not the next one."

"*You can act like the most reverent person on the planet. You can chant Latin prayers, beat your breast forty times daily, genuflect perfectly, and even kneel, insisting the priest put the communion host on your tongue instead of in your hand. But if you don't love the one sitting in the pew next to you, or the obnoxious neighbor across the street, your actions have no more worth than a foul ball off the bat of Ken Griffey, Jr.*"

I smiled, because I liked it too.

"You should rethink Glory's suggestion," he said.

I frowned.

"If it helps any, Glory wasn't put off by the Catholic under-pinnings of the story you wrote."

Wilbur's remark got my attention. One reason I had balked at even writing a short story about Leezie and me was that I would have to write it from a Catholic viewpoint. I reasoned, "*If it doesn't bore a non-religious person to death, it's sure to offend one who isn't a Catholic.*"

"Will you at least think about it?" Wilbur said.

"Sure, I'll consider it," I answered. "At least until I get to the parking lot."

That shut him up, and he reached into a folder, bringing out a paper stamped "*CONFIDENTIAL*" on the top.

"Do you agree not to breathe a word of this?" he asked, his voice changing to one of professional seriousness.

I had caught a glimpse of the paper's subject: "*Grand Jury Investigation in the Case of the State of Massachusetts vs. the Diocese of Boston.*"

"Is this something I want to know?" I asked.

"Definitely not," Wilbur answered. "But this story is going to break next week and I thought you deserved a heads up."

"Okay, I promise to keep my mouth shut." He pushed the transcript across the table.

Five minutes later I was still in a state of shock. The grand jury was going to indict my old friend, Percy Knox, on multiple counts of sexual abuse against altar boys. Further, the same body was considering bringing the bishop of Boston, Cardinal Law, into court on charges of covering up Percy's activities.

Finally, I recovered enough to be minimally coherent. I said, "Good God, Wilbur! Cardinal Law is the most powerful man in the American church."

"There are already rumors of giving the Cardinal a cushy job in Rome so he can't be called to testify," Wilbur said.

"What?" I exploded.

"I'm afraid these grand jury findings are only the tip of the iceberg," he said.

It dawned on me that Wilbur didn't know that Percy had once served in the Seattle Diocese. I decided not to enlighten him. Both Freddie and I did write our letters to Boston, exposing the history we'd uncovered about Percy. I still had in my files, somewhere, the stilted but polite response I had received from one of the Cardinal's lackeys in Massachusetts.

As Wilbur predicted, the story broke the following week. It surprised me that it didn't create many waves outside of New England. I could only hope Wilbur's prediction of worse things to come was exaggerated.

Chapter Forty

Spring was a long time coming the next year, capping months of a dark winter for the church. Wilbur had been right; Boston was just the beginning. Soon, the scandal spread nationwide, bringing to light all the sordid details. Priests had been sexually abusing children for years, and the bishops had been covering it up.

I advocated a *"take no prisoners"* stance in my column, drawing fire from both my own bishop and those in the church who still refused to believe the news.

For the first time in three years I felt restless. I had a strong sense I was spinning my wheels and should be doing something else.

Appropriately, confirmation of that sense arrived on April fool's Day. I was working in my office late that night when the doorbell rang. Expecting my substitute housekeeper to get it, I was surprised to hear a familiar voice at my office door.

"I thought I'd just let myself in," Larry Wilson said.

I had only seen Leezie's former boss twice since the funeral. He had aged, and his sixty-seven years belied the toll several surgeries and chemotherapy had taken. He limped into my office with the aid of a cane and sat down.

"You look like a man on a mission," I said.

He sighed, saying, "You always were good at reading a man's face, Father. Aye, regrettably it's so."

Supposing he was about to tell me a tale of woe so I would take on the burdens of another of the blind or lame, I waited.

"I don't like to place blame, you know that, Father Mew, but that little prune-faced son of mine has really gone and stuck his you-know-what in the jam jar this time."

Larry had several sons, so again I waited.

"You remember my boy Herbie, don't you?"

I nodded.

"I found this letter in the jockey box of his car this afternoon," he said, dropping an envelope on my desk.

I flinched. It was a letter from Leezie, properly stamped and addressed to me.

"The sniveling little mutt," Larry said. "He owned up to what he did after I threatened to thump him with my cane." He banged it for emphasis several times on the floor.

I was in the dark and said so.

"Herbie promised Sarge he would mail that letter for him."

"When?"

"I just hope it's not something important," Larry said. "Sarge gave it to Herbie the same night he had his heart attack!"

Larry stood up to leave five minutes later, and I hardly remember him saying good night.

Snapping off the desk lamp, I sat in the darkness. My mind spun, churning out different scenarios of what a letter from the grave might mean. A door slammed, signaling the departure of the housekeeper. I turned on the light and picked up the envelope, slitting it open.

My hands shook. Inside was a single piece of paper. Written in pencil with a shaky hand, it read:

"In case I don't get the chance to tell you. Remember how you joked about me not sitting still and having to always be on the move, like a snowball salesman in Arizona? You never could figure out what I did on them trips, and why they were important.

"Well, if you're up to a little treasure hunt in your old age, follow what I say to find out."

"Darn you, Leezie Smith," I said aloud. "You're the one enthralled with treasure hunts, not me."

"Father Goldsworthy holds the key," his letter continued. *"If you visit him in the middle of the afternoon, chances are good someone will show up to explain what you find. You get just one little hint. Look under Beelzebub's favorite place. The best times for you are right around the corner, I hopes anyhow."*

I wadded the paper and then smoothed it out again. He knew I was a sucker for treasure hunts, and the idea would get my attention. I smiled, thinking back to some of the previous intricately devised mind teasers he'd talked me into.

"It means a trip to my old home town," I thought. *"That's where Father Goldsworthy is buried."*

Patience wasn't my strong suit and it took almost a month to make arrangements. I had bought a new camper after Leezie died, but quickly found spending time in the woods alone depressed me.

Herbie Wilson, anxious to atone for his misdeed with the letter, got the pickup camper out of storage to make it road worthy. He drove by the parish house to pick up my list of things that needed fixing.

"I didn't know you had one of them new Alaskan camper units," he said. "Nice rig."

In appearance the Alaskan resembled a sheepherder's wagon, because it had a rounded top that collapsed for travel, barely protruding over the top of the truck cab. Unlike mail delivery, Herbie was meticulous about anything mechanical, and he delivered it two days before I was set to leave.

The three-day trip took me four because of a freak spring snowstorm in eastern Washington. I found refuge in a small town just outside of Spokane and got a late start the next morning. I would turn seventy-five this year, and although my health was superb, the scary roads had tired me out.

It was almost dark when the Chevy pickup finally topped the rise just north of my birthplace. Lights flickered in the distance and dark humps marked where the familiar hills would have been. I half expected to find the town just a notation in a history book. It wasn't thriving, I could see that, but the park was still there. I let the pickup coast to a parking spot at the end of an oval surrounding a gazebo. Too weary for anything but sleep, I settled in for the night.

A long-forgotten sound woke me from a deep, dreamless slumber. Killdeer! The birds were in the field just outside my window. A glance at my watch surprised me. It was almost nine in the morning, "*Windknocker time,*" as Leezie would have said.

My stomach growled, reminding me I hadn't eaten since the same time yesterday. I'd seen a sign advertising a café the night before and set out on foot, deciding to forego a health nut's idea of breakfast for something substantial.

The building was dimly familiar but clearly the restaurant was recent. I sat at the counter and ordered the number one special off the menu board on the wall.

"Two eggs or three?" The waitress asked.

"Three, scrambled," I answered. "And the short stack of pancakes."

No doubt half the town already knew about the strange camper that had spent the night at the park. The information highway was nothing new to tiny hamlets, but the café crowd mainly ignored me. On a notice board I did see two names that were possible descendents of people I had once known. The drawing for a free milkshake was still a week away, so I didn't register.

It felt strange sitting in this spot. A half-century had passed since the class reunion in 1941.

"What you doin' in these parts?" the cook asked while delivering my breakfast.

"I'm on a treasure hunt," I answered.

"Ha, ha, that's a good one, buddy," he said. "The last treasure found around here was bull semen."

"Really!" I said.

"Yup, a group of farmers thought there was money to be made testing bulls for virility."

That didn't seem to be a problem with any bull I'd ever encountered, but fortunately the waitress distracted the cook with another order, and I dug into my food.

I discovered on my after-breakfast stroll that Saint Bart's Church was still standing. Several of the windows were boarded up and it sadly needed paint. I had no doubt the building hadn't been used for years. I looked across the street, pained as I noticed our old house was gone, replaced by a manufactured home. I walked past the school on my way back to the park and stopped to watch a group of boys engrossed in a game of baseball. "*Some things never change*," I thought.

I frittered away the rest of the morning, whittling sticks, cleaning my windows and watching the killdeer. I fell asleep once, which I attributed more to the satisfying breakfast than old age. Finally I got tired of waiting and decided one o'clock was close enough to the mid-afternoon specified in Leezie's letter.

I assumed people were still being buried in the cemetery at the base of Meadowlark Ridge, and found it so. The parking lot was paved now, and the same asphalt marked the walkways meandering through the grounds. Father Goldsworthy's tombstone was more prominent than I expected, and I found it easily.

"*Now what?*" I thought, taking out Leezie's letter to refresh my memory. "*Father Goldsworthy holds the key*," I read again. My plan was just to observe, sure that I'd receive some inspiration, but nothing came to me. "*What if he means a real key?*" I went back to the pickup and rummaged in the toolbox until I found a large screwdriver.

Looking around to make sure I was alone, I probed under the left side of the stone, thinking, "This *might be hard to explain if I get caught*." Soon, I had a big hole that revealed nothing. I tried the middle with no success. My knees cracked like two eggs dropped on a counter when I got up. Stepping away, I studied the gruff old priest's tombstone again. Suddenly, I grinned, noticing at the bottom, precisely positioned over a gallon-sized flowerpot, was a small cross. It fit the way Leezie's mind worked, so I hastily removed the pot and dug in the soft ground underneath.

Just under the surface my screwdriver scraped against something metallic. Gingerly, working like a world-class archeologist, I excavated deeper, slowly revealing the shape of a can. My fingers did the rest of the work, prying loose what became the remains of a Prince

Albert tobacco tin. I shook it and heard the clink of metal against metal.

I upended the contents in my palm and stood staring at a brass key, one not unfamiliar to me. It was the old Union Pacific railroad key that had once fit the padlock on our treasure box.

The brass key went into my pocket. I returned the screwdriver and prepared to leave, but decided on another look around. A gravel path leading toward the town overlook forked from the pavement, so I took it.

Betsy's grave sat by itself in the shade of an ancient locust tree, which was in full bloom. The sweet scent tickled my nose. I nibbled some of the blossoms, savoring their taste. I patted her tombstone, but didn't linger.

It was pleasantly warm, and I found a bench to rest on. Lazy clouds played peek-a-boo with the sun, casting random shadows over town, giving the appearance a puppet master was bouncing them about.

"I've been lured here, for what reason I don't know," I thought. *"It could be just another of Leezie's pranks."*

The scene before me said no as I began picking out familiar landmarks. St. Bart's Church was hidden by the big trees. My mind drifted; word pictures with sounds of the past replaced thoughts.

An hour passed before a footstep scrunching in the gravel, startled me.

"Sorry," the man said. "I didn't mean to scare you."

"It's okay," I said, turning to meet a stranger. "I was just admiring the view."

"That must be your camper truck in the parking lot," he said.

His speech was halting and raspy, reminding me of a file being stroked against a piece of metal much too hard for it. He had wrinkled features, similar to the treasure hunt note in my shirt pocket. One walking shoe, well worn with a Velcro fastener, nervously toed the grass.

Saw your Washington plate," he said. "What part?"

"Seattle," I replied.

"Do tell," he said. "Always wanted to go there myself."

We passed a few minutes in pleasant chitchat. I was thankful he didn't pry.

"Well, I'd better scat afore the wife sends the grandson out looking," he said.

"Do you come here often?" I asked.

"Oh sure," he answered. "Every day at this time, except yesterday. We had company. But I usually make it. Doctor's orders you know."

I stole a glance at my watch, which read five minutes to three, the middle of the afternoon.

"Perhaps you can help me with something," I said, fishing in my pocket and bringing out the key. "Would you know anything about this?"

An eyebrow shot up, pushing against several deep furrows that reshaped his brow.

"Where'd you get it?" he snapped.

"Under the flower pot on Father Goldsworthy's grave."

Inexplicitly, something struck him funny, shaking his whole body with laughter. I began to wonder if he was ever going to quit. Finally, he thumped his chest twice, and sucked in a deep breath.

"Which is it?" I smiled. "A collapsed lung or did your prostate tickle your funny bone?"

"Probably both," he grinned, taking another gulp of air.

I waited, while he studied my face. I started to get uncomfortable.

"Well, are you going to tell me what you find so amusing?"

Instead of an answer he stuck out his hand.

"I can't believe it's been over sixty years," he said. "I'm glad to see you again."

My grip was anemic, unrecognizing.

"Your name *is* Mew, ain't it?"

I think I nodded.

"I'm Abner Pong," he said.

Chapter Forty-One

You could have knocked me over with a snowflake!

Abner brought a worn coin purse from his pocket, stirring the contents with his finger.

"Here," he said, handing me a dime. "I owe you this. Hope you don't charge interest."

I almost bit it with my teeth before pronouncing it genuine, but refrained.

"Where have you been?" he asked. "Leezie buried that key more than three years ago."

I was slow to answer.

"I was supposed to watch for you, but I gave that up a long time ago," he went on. "Wow, you really threw me for a loop. I was expecting some potbellied priest dressed up in a penguin suit. You still a priest, ain't you?"

I assured him I was, and tried to pry some information from him about the treasure hunt.

"All I know, Mew, is it has something to do with St. Bart's. You know how crazy Leezie would get when someone mentioned a treasure hunt. All he did was laugh about how you would spend most of the time biting your lip and cussing him."

We sat talking on the bench for a long time. Finally I said, "I came to a school reunion in 1941. Where were you?"

"Sucking a wine bottle on skid row," he answered. "Does that surprise you? If it weren't for Leezie Smith, I'd probably still be dead drunk, or just plain dead."

His early life, I learned, had been wasted.

"I couldn't even join the gol-damned army to fight in the war," he sputtered, tapping his chest. "They said I had a bad ticker. After he got out of prison Leezie came back here for a few days and found me. Did you know he spent time in Leavenworth?"

I nodded. "And he made you believe in yourself again, right?"

"Yes!" he shot back, and I could see for myself the inner strength in his eyes. "Then I met Matty, that's my wife, and the years have been good to us."

I directed his attention back to St. Bart's.

"The place ain't been used for twenty years or so," he said. "Folks here have to travel sixty miles nowadays to find one of your Papist churches."

I frowned. *"Papist"* was a word often used to demean Catholics. "Oops! Sorry Mew," he said, "I didn't mean the papist thing. I just slide into old ways sometimes."

"Is there any way we can get in there?"

"St. Bart's, you mean?"

"Yes."

Abner thought a moment. "Jimmy Benton might let us in."

Jimmy Benton turned out to be a man in his early fifties, and he met us twenty minutes later at the sagging front steps of St. Bart's. He seemed astonished when he discovered who the visitor was that Abner had alluded to over the phone.

"Mew Moosington," Benton said, shaking my hand. "I can't hardly believe it's you. You're close to famous to some of us around here."

"You must be hard up for entertainment."

He clapped me on the back. "No, I mean it. Your outspokenness taking on the church establishment is downright admirable."

Strange words coming from a voice in small-town America, I thought.

The door to St. Bart's opened easily on well-oiled hinges.

"The outside looks bad," Jimmy said. "But we keep up the inside."

I moved into the entryway but wasn't prepared for the step back in time. Nothing had changed, save for the lack of adornment.

"The Bishop took it all," Jimmy said as I followed his finger around the room.

He was right; everything had been striped except the altar and the statue of Saint Bartholomew with its broken thumb. A wave of anger came from out of the blue and knotted my stomach.

"Where do we start looking?" Abner interrupted.

We split up and began searching any nook or cranny that might conceal a wooden box. I soon learned that Jimmy had understated how they cared for the place. It was clean and in excellent repair. Recent varnish covered the confessional and several windows had new putty. I discovered the ancient pump organ, glowing under a coating of wax. Jimmy told me later that it was privately owned.

The rope to the belfry dangled just above my head. I reached up and gave it a tug, only to have it come spiraling out of its recess and land in a dead heap on the floor.

"Someone made sure they took the heart out of the building," I thought. *"Any hope the community could be restored would have died when the pillagers removed the bell."*

Our search was fruitless.

"Maybe he put it outside somewhere," Abner suggested.

We were standing at the rear of the church and I barely heard him. Fast-forwarded film clips were flashing across my inner eye. Suddenly, one stopped and I saw Beelzebub, Leezie's big black dog.

"Look under Beelzebub's favorite place," I recited from his note.

"There!" I shouted, causing Jimmy Benton to jump. "It's there, under the altar."

"What makes you think so?" Abner posed. He was leaning his skinny frame against the corner of the altar.

"It has to be the reason the Diocese didn't take this," I grunted back, stymied by its weight. Jimmy Benton didn't know what I was talking about either, and I explained that the altar sat over a gaping hole in the floor.

"Liability," Jimmy snorted. "The Bishop wouldn't risk that."

"It's budging," Abner said. "Put your weight into it."

"If I do, my hard arteries are going to pop out my ears," I protested.

Slowly, we moved it, revealing as I predicted, a chasm underneath.

"There's something down there!" Abner shouted. "Looks like a wood box." He leaned over the edge. "Hold my feet so I can reach it."

Exploring the contents had to wait. For the moment I made sure the key worked the ancient padlock. I owed Jimmy Benton a more detailed explanation, and gave him one. Finished, I said, "You don't seem to be a bit surprised or skeptical."

He smiled. "There was a day I would have been," he said. "But not after I met Leezie."

I took Abner up on his offer to park the camper in his back yard. "First you have to come inside and meet Matty," he said.

The house, originally log with several additions, sat in a grove of weeping willows. He directed me to ease the camper in amongst them where it would receive the most shade.

"Matty, I'm home," Abner announced, sticking his head in the door.

A white-haired woman in a wheelchair appeared, clutching a TV remote. She abruptly terminated the evening news and a smile lit her face when Abner said, "I brought company." He whispered in her ear what I assumed were my credentials, for she looked up surprised.

"Welcome!" she said. "Abner hasn't sounded this excited since our daughter gave us our first grandchild." I found out soon enough that was the first of four – all boys.

"By chance are any of those kids good runners?"

"How did you know?" Matty asked, puzzled. Smiling, Abner assured her it was too long of a story for the moment, because we had business to tend to.

The camper was self-contained. The setup mainly amounted to stringing a power cord and connecting a water hose. Finished, Abner said, "I expect you're anxious to explore the contents of that box, so I'll leave you to it."

My heart skipped a beat as I took our battered treasure box off the shelf and set it on the table. The padlock released its hold with a sharp click. Holding my breath, I raised the lid.

"I don't believe it," I said aloud when I discovered six of Leezie's Big Chief Tablets. I knew of their existence, of course, and had wondered what had become of them.

I took them out, reverently almost, and cursorily paged through them. I was astounded to learn the first entry was dated 1929. The last writing occurred on the day Leezie had told me he was taking a ride in Leonard's Mustang to this place.

I emptied the box, which contained little more. An envelope fluttered to the floor and I picked it up. It contained three pictures. The first was of me, Leezie's half of the snapshot taken at the County Fair in 1930. I remembered his remark about it like yesterday: "That's you, Mew," he had said. "There ain't no guess to it."

The next subject wasn't grinning, but it made me smile. Bub stared back at me. Beelzebub wasn't really the miracle dog we made him out to be, but he came close.

Then, I turned over the last photo. It startled me. I remembered the picture being taken. It was at an end-of-the-year school picnic, but I had never seen it. A tear trickled down my cheek as the long-ago memory became fresh. I was standing with my arm around Betsy. I had just finished first grade, and she would die seven months later.

The photographs went back in the envelope and I picked up two tattered books. It was no mystery why I found those included, as Leezie's favorite author, George MacDonald, wrote them. *"I'll look at them later,"* I thought, and put everything back in the box.

"Something's amiss here," I thought. I was nearly overwhelmed to learn the box truly contained a treasure. *"But why didn't Leezie simply give them to me in person?"* I wondered. *"Obviously, there must be another reason he lured me here."*

The first clue arrived a few moments later, when I heard a soft tapping on my door.

Chapter Forty-Two

My first thought was that Abner's curiosity had gotten the better of him, and he'd come back to ask about the box. I didn't bother to button my shirt.

The Alaskan camper has a Dutch door – split in two, top and bottom. I opened the upper half and found myself looking into the eyes of a stranger. An attractive woman stood gazing up at me. She didn't give me time to apologize for the lack of hair on my chest, and instead came right to the point.

"I'm Jimmy Benton's wife, Father, and I have to talk to you."

I invited her in and managed to clear a place for her to sit. "Just call me, Mew," I said. "*Father* only works in Seattle."

"I'm just Gail," she said. "Named after my grandmother."

She sat, composing her thoughts, I guessed. A flash of anger wrinkled her brow, throwing me off guard.

"What troubles you?" I asked. "I hope it's not because of my coming here."

"It has everything to do with that!" she exclaimed, and started to cry.

Experience had taught me to wait, which I did. She looked up finally, wiping her tears.

"Damn it!" she said. "Jimmy would shoot me in the foot if he knew I blew it like this." She wiped a last tear, and said, "Anyhow, Jimmy said you're leaving tomorrow, is that right?"

I nodded.

"We wondered if you would stay an extra day."

"Is it important?"

"For us, I suppose," and hesitated. "We just thought it would be nice to have you wait and say Mass in the old church."

"That might be difficult," which is a stall tactic any good priest uses when we aren't sure how to respond.

"You're a bit of a hero in these parts, Mew. I doubt you know that, but it's true."

I gave her my best scoffing look, which didn't deter her in the least.

"The bishops keep destroying our parishes and taking us back to the Dark Ages," she said. "And you're the only one that's raised a protest."

"*Destroying* might be too harsh," I said.

"I can't help it, but that's the way I feel."

I gave her a well-practiced "*harrumph*," and asked, "This is a long way from Seattle. How is it you know so much about me?"

"Leezie!" she said. "He brought us all the articles you wrote and ones from that other man about you in the *Seattle P-I*."

"Wilbur Lester," I said.

"Yes, he's the one," she said. "But after Leezie died both Jimmy and I noticed something changed. You no longer wrote the same."

"I got a new computer; that could be it," I said.

She giggled, and said, "No it wasn't that because before, you were a wee bit on the academic side."

"I know where you're going," I interrupted. "And to save you the time, something did happen."

"Well, don't keep me in suspense," she said when I didn't elaborate. "What was it?"

"To quote another famous person, I got the wind knocked into me."

"Hot damn!" she exclaimed. "I won our bet!"

"Dinner at Red Lobster," I said after she told me about the wager between her and Jimmy. "Be sure to try the key lime pie."

She also cajoled out of me the how and when of the moment that changed my life.

"That's hilarious," she cackled when I finished. "I can just see Leezie dying of laughter."

We looked at each other.

"Well I know he was already dead," she said sheepishly. "But I can just picture him saying to Jesus, 'Would you look at that; Mew finally figured it out!'"

I decided to turn the aside back to her request, and said, "If I agreed to stay an extra day how many people would show up?"

"This is not the city, Mew," she said. "Our group is small, maybe a dozen. Leezie always called us '*the last gaspers*.'"

I started to ask the reason behind the name but she interrupted and went on to describe them. The more I listened the more it sounded to me like what I had tried to do with Gar Communities the past twenty-five years.

"*If nothing else,*" I thought, "*Gail's group resembles a tight knit family.*"

"Leezie taught us how to get along and settle our disputes when we didn't," she concluded.

Tucking the Gar Community resemblance away in my memory, I changed the subject.

"Parishes are being closed everywhere," I said. "So why can't you just find a new church to attend?"

"I'm sure we could," she said. "But it's like sleeping in a motel instead of your own bed."

"What?"

"I didn't mean we go to church to take a nap," she smiled.

I put on my devil's advocate mask. "The Church is about sacraments. Surely that's worth driving, what, sixty miles?"

"You make it sound like going to the service station," she said. "Only in this case we tank up on bread and wine. And, you should know, it's closer to seventy miles."

"Even if it does appear like a service station, what's wrong with that?"

Her eyes flashed. "Mew, in case you hadn't noticed, the only thing that gets shared at a service station these days are the nozzles, or in the case of a church, the pews. We want more than that."

I hoped she would elaborate but she went backward in time instead.

"We were in our thirties when the bishop closed St. Bart's," she said. "It ripped something out of our parents, but we didn't feel that way at first." She swiped at a new tear, and said, "Then some of the people moved away, and others became Protestants. Soon, the tiny sense of community built around the church was gone too. We got hungry for what we'd lost."

Abner's big German shepherd barked outside the window, and took off chasing a cat. Gail ignored the commotion, saying, "I finally met God personally, and was born again. It happened to me in the ladies restroom of a country school." Her smile softened the lines and added luster to her big brown eyes. "Or, like you, I got the wind knocked into me."

We had a good laugh together.

"Count yourself lucky on the country school," I chuckled. "At least you didn't get humbled like I did in front of 1,500 people."

I had wondered when it happened, and she read my mind. "It was right after we met Leezie for the first time."

I was trying to do the math in my head, but she saved me the trouble. "That was 1974."

The time frame was right, as Leezie was absent a lot from Seattle in those years.

"He rounded up all the Catholics he could find and had us sit down together," she said. "We've stayed together since." A sad look marred her pretty face. "We're struggling, though, without Leezie."

All of a sudden, a siren split the quiet night! Not just any siren, mind you. I had to cover my ears, shouting, "What is that?"

Gail was laughing. She fumbled in her purse and brought out a pager. The siren quieted only to begin again.

"The fire station is just a block up the street," she said.

I had to strain to hear. I caught other sounds, first one, and then two pickups, speeding by on the street. The volunteers were racing to answer the alarm.

"It's a grass fire," she said, reading from her pager, "about six miles from town."

Mercifully, someone shut off the infernal screech of the big siren atop the fire hall.

"Want to watch?" she asked, getting up and holding the door open for me.

Flashing lights and the wail of a smaller siren seemed to blast open the doors of the fire hall. A gleaming red fire engine emerged.

Glancing at her watch, Gail said, "Under five minutes. Not a bad response for firemen who don't get paid a dime for their efforts."

A second fire truck appeared and took the same left turn on Main Street. The driver missed a gear in his haste to catch up with the leader, and killed the engine. Several bystanders on the sidewalk hooted, then clapped when the motor roared back to life.

"That's Gear Jammin' Billy," Gail laughed. "He's part of the last gaspers."

It was a warm night and we settled in chairs Abner had positioned on a concrete patio. The lights and sirens faded into the dark, and I said, "I've forgotten what small towns do for excitement."

Gail abruptly changed the subject.

"If you would say Mass in the old church, just maybe we can recapture a tiny bit of our identity," she said. "For Pete's sake, we're Catholics too!"

The look in her eyes was beseeching, causing me a feeling of regret for hesitating in the first place. That increased when she said, "Honestly, Mew, we could really use a shot of hope. Can you help us?"

The risk of stepping on territorial toes was my only reason for reticence, but it was slight. At worst, the local bishop might vent some ire at me for saying Mass in his diocese without permission.

"Okay," I said. "I'll do it."

"Honest? You mean it?"

Gail's purse emitted a vibrating tone and I didn't get a chance to answer. She reached inside and brought out her pager. "Whoops," she said. "Looks like I have to run. They're calling for the ambulance."

I started to say, "You have an ambulance too?" but caught myself. Instead, I hurried to remind her, "We can't exclude the other Catholics in the neighborhood. How will you get word about Mass at St. Bart's out to them in time?"

"Mew!" she said, digging in her purse for the keys to her pickup. "We're it; we're all that's left. That's why Leezie called us *the last gaspers.*"

In her haste to find the keys, a county map fell out. I picked it up but she was on the run.

"Keep it," she shouted back at me. "The fire is in the river breaks area."

I tried, after another episode of flashing lights and sirens, to get some sleep. That failed, so I unfolded the map. Finding the river breaks was easy with the topographical markings provided. *"They'll be out half the night fighting fire in that mess of canyons,"* I thought.

My eyes roamed over other long-forgotten place names and landmarks. Tiny towns, most of them on the long gone rail line, speckled the map. Each time I closed my eyes the map would appear, dotted with tiny flashing lights. I knew what the pinpricks represented. They were people – people like Gail, Jimmy and Gear Jammin' Billy.

"Abandoned" appeared several times on the county map. *"Suppose it means abandoned people,"* I thought. Some of Leezie's words came back to me: *"If you want to see what's coming in your church, go to where it's already happened."*

Insomnia defeated me at that point. I went looking for a book to read and remembered those in the treasure box. Surprised, I noted they were novels, not dry religious tomes. I did know a little about the author. George MacDonald didn't write ordinary books. His genius, as I soon learned, was an ability to incorporate spiritual truths into a fictional story.

Still the title of what I chose, THE ELECT LADY, threw me off, but I hadn't gone far before I began rubbing the print to see if it was dry. First printed in the 1800s, the words and wisdom could have been written this very night. It made me wonder if the author had been a mouse in the corner during Gail's visit. I sat straight up in bed, conking my head against the ceiling light, when MacDonald blew my devil's advocate arguments out of the water.

I went back and read his sobering words again, and jerked open a drawer to find a paper and pencil. I wrote down the quotation, along with another. I fell asleep before the fire trucks returned.

Chapter Forty-Three

Saint Bartholomew's Church had come to life when I arrived that night. We'd decided on nine o'clock so everyone would have a chance to get there.

There was no electricity. A faint glow of candlelight seeped out the boarded-up windows, and the soft murmur of voices signaled, for tonight at least, it was no longer a tomb. I stepped through the door at the same time someone's fingers coaxed a chord from the ancient organ.

I found a diverse group had gathered. A smattering of young people mixed easily with their elders. Jimmy Benton latched onto me and pumped my arm like a frenzied farmer trying to draw water from a dry well. "You don't know what this means to us, Mew," he said.

I massaged my elbow, saying cheerfully, "Is everybody here?"

"Just about," Jimmy answered. The door opened at the same moment, and we both looked in that direction. "There's the last of them now," he said.

On old man, stooped and fragile looking, struggled to get his cane in sync with his wobbly legs. Slowly, he made his way across the floor toward me. As he drew near I could see he epitomized the saying *"rode hard and put away wet."* A young woman who appeared to be of Mexican descent, either his nurse or a granddaughter, aided him.

A lopsided pair of wire-rimmed glasses with thick lenses framed his gaunt features. The magnification caused his pupils to appear as lumps of coal. His clothes smelled of wood and grass smoke. I learned later that he lived deep in the river breaks where the fire had finally been extinguished around four in the morning. The old man blinked, but he just stood in front of me, teetering on his cane. Everything about him said, "*remember me?*"

Finally, he spoke. His voice squeaked at first, reminding me of a clarinet being coaxed to play a note. "I hope that you is better at sayin' the Mass than you is at shootin' dem damned marbles."

Petey Gorman!

"Didn't know who I was, did you?" he said.

"Well, it has been over sixty years," I said.

Petey's lip quivered and he dropped his cane. His eyeballs rolled backward in his head, and he started to shake. Panic gripped my insides, but I had the presence of mind to grab his arm before he fell.

No one seemed to take notice of his fit. In fact, Jimmy Benton's grandson was laughing. Then I heard Petey's laugh, which had always sounded like the hoot from a constipated owl. Between peals, he managed to say, "But you remembers dem fits I used to have." His free arm went around my shoulder and he hugged me like I'd just rescued him from a sinking ship.

Unlike most gatherings I was used to, I soon found Petey and I were in the middle of a huddle. The rest had joined us to share the reunion. At last, Petey came up for air, saying, "Where did my dad-blasted cane go?"

"I want to see you afterward!" I said.

Just as I was ready to begin, a bump against the door announced unexpected guests. Our numbers swelled to fourteen when Abner entered, pushing Matty's wheel chair. She smiled at me. Abner's grin was lopsided, nervous. I wasn't sure if he'd been at a real church service before. When everyone was ready I signaled the organist.

To this day, I don't have the words to describe what happened when the strains of the melody from a song called "ABBA FATHER" shook the building. It's not a bombastic tune, mind you, but it nearly suffocated me. The music seemed to replace the oxygen, not sucking the breath out of me, but pumping life into me.

No one sang. We were too stunned. I presumed at the moment it had more to do with the resurrection of St. Bart's, but that was only part of it. Jimmy Benton caught my eye and smiled. A tear trickled down his face.

A deep calm settled on us when the song ended. Like me, I assumed the others were still singing the words in their heads. Haunting words, expressive words, like, *"Abba Father ... you are the potter ... we are the clay ... mold us ... fashion us ... into the image ... of your son."*

I had experienced the presence of God in the past three years, but this was more like Jesus had walked in to join us.

Jimmy's young grandson sensed it too, and he whispered in my ear, "Like wow, man, our group just growed by one."

We resembled happy children, awed by the mood, the atmosphere – call it what you like but no better word describes it than presence. In spite of all our imperfections, God used this night to bless us with his company.

Abruptly, one of the quotations from the book I read the night before surfaced. I had it committed to memory. *"If a man has the company of the Lord, he will care little whether someone else does or does not believe that he has."*

Remembering it when I did made the decision that came later much easier.

I didn't have a sermon to give and decided if one did materialize, I'd deliver it at the end. That wasn't orthodox, but did fit the tone, considering what inspired me later.

St. Bart's was resplendent in her simplicity. The flickering candles bounced light in all directions, lighting nooks and crannies in random order. I caught Petey's eye and knew his mind was working overtime to take it all in.

He said as much to me when the liturgy reached the time to offer each other friendly greetings. This is another of the *"reform of the reforms"* that Rome was demanding, arguing that, placed where Vatican II did, the Kiss of Peace interrupted the solemnity and dignity of the Mass.

I had witnessed a brief tiff earlier between a pair I assumed were married. I learned later they were brother and sister. They used this, "the Kiss of Peace," to do just that. They kissed and made up. Far from undignified or distracting, it was the exact opposite.

Earlier, during the time allotted for shared prayer, Matty Pong revealed the depression that afflicted her. Coming as it did during the Prayer of the Faithful allowed the rest of us to gather around and pray briefly and specifically for her. In most parishes this opportunity had been squandered, as they have resorted to canned prayers, and either discourage or flat out disallow extemporaneous petitions from the people. Matty was moved by the caring and I noticed Abner was taken aback by the gesture.

Abner presented me with one huge dilemma a few minutes later. I started to distribute the bread and wine. The little assembly approached as if they'd just been called for a long-awaited holiday dinner – joyful, but with a sense that they knew and had deep respect for the host. *"If Rome really wants to know what reverence is all about,"* I thought, *"they should first know that it has to be a free expression of a mutual friendship."*

Suddenly, Abner Pong stood in front of me. He had pushed Matty's wheelchair and I never dreamed he would expect to receive communion himself.

Had I known his personal struggle to arrive at this point, my attitude might have been different. Instead, all I could think about was the grief he had caused me growing up. It made me mad all over again, and I wanted to lash out, perhaps even shouting, "You big bunghole!"

A great heaviness hit me and words thundered in my ear. Leezie had said them one night as we watched the sun go down over Puget Sound. "Think you could ever give him the forgiveness for being such a little bastard?"

"I suppose if he asked, I could."

"Suppose there weren't no more sunsets until you made up your mind?"

For Leezie, the Holy Spirit was present in that sunset, and his meaning hit me. If I ever expected the Spirit of Jesus to be fully active in my life, it involved the kind of forgiveness I was facing now. Not, however, a twisted idea of forgiveness that demands others go first.

I reached out and laid a hand on Abner's shoulder, hoping he didn't detect the quaver in my voice. "I'm sorry, Abner, for all those years when I did and said such stupid things."

Not knowing what to expect I was surprised to hear him say, "I've prayed this day would come, Mew, when I could get that monkey off my back and get you to forgive me, too."

I placed the bread in Abner's hand, only to see that Petey was next.

"Abner's a good man," he said. His hand shook, but steadied. He took the bread, saying, "Thank you Jesus." Then looking up, he added, "and you too Mew."

During a silent moment after communion, I thought about the decision mentioned previously. The last gaspers were unique, much more mature than any Gar Community I'd nurtured. *"But they are so small,"* the thought kept coming back to me. *"How can I, a person used to great numbers, huge churches, and multi-million-dollar budgets, reconcile that?"*

The second of George MacDonald's sayings I'd read last night drifted on the fringe of my consciousness. At first I couldn't pull it out of the memory slot where it was stored. Then I looked around the table, and suddenly, the words came back to me: *"If I find I get more help and strength with a certain few, why should I go to a gathering of a multitude to get less?"*

The next part of what he'd written was more compelling:

"Why should it be more sacred to worship with five hundred or five thousand than with three? If he is in the midst of them, they cannot be wrongly gathered."

I made up my mind. The idea was fraught with risk, not to mention embarrassment. I was going to retire and somehow talk the bishop of this diocese into reopening St. Bart's. Given that opportunity,

I was going to try to take this small group to the limits of what Vatican II intended.

Thinking it was time to finish the liturgy, I started to get up, only to be distracted by a noise. No one else seemed to hear it; they weren't even paying attention to me.

I looked around the old church again. My eyes roamed familiar places, each one containing a memory, some several. The rustling noise I'd heard came once more, turning my gaze toward a recess in the wall. The statue of my namesake stood there, but he wasn't alone.

I shook my head to clear it. My heart fluttered, and I swiped at the perspiration I was sure had wetted my forehead. I was certain someone was about to ask, "Mew! Are you okay?" I looked up again. He was still there. Standing by Saint Bartholomew's statue was Barmy Ben.

I rubbed my eyes and almost blurted out the obvious, "What are you doing here?"

Barmy wore the same shabby tuxedo I had seen him in on a Christmas Eve many years ago. The candlelight shimmered when it struck the jacket's rhinestone buttons. Barmy Ben hadn't aged and there was no mistaking who he was.

Our eyes met, and he showed me his hand, as if to say, "See, no sucker tonight." He smiled, hesitant at first, and then broke into a full grin, much different than our previous encounter. He didn't say anything but his message was clear, "Do you see better? Do you get it now?" Then, in a poof, he was gone.

I tried to act nonchalant, wondering how I had dreamt up such a scene. *"Imagined or not, it was real,"* I thought. After my blood pressure dropped fifty points I chuckled. At least Barmy Ben had given me my sermon.

The Gospel message that night was difficult to base a lesson around. It was a story about a blind man, but different than most miracle stories, it took Jesus two tries before the man could see clearly.

"I know a man like the story talks about," I started my sermon. "And you're looking at him." That led me into telling them the story of Barmy Ben, and how I'd first met him years ago during Midnight Mass.

"I didn't see clearly that first night either," I finished. "But the second time around I do."

I told no one of my decision. That could wait.

Chapter Forty-Four

In addition to Leezie's treasure box, I also found my baseball bat, Old Cobber, on that trip, and have it with me now. My dog is also here, at the moment stalking a squirrel about to scurry up a lodge pole pine. *Now* is early fall, and the Alaskan camper is parked on the shores of a pristine lake in the high mountains of Montana.

That mouthful contains two mysteries, the bat and the dog. The lake is simply the jumping off point, or the beginning of my next adventure. Taking them in order, the bat doesn't have a good explanation.

I left just after sunrise the morning after the liturgy at St. Bart's. I blame part of what happened on the café being closed, where I had intended to get my morning's fix of coffee. Not far north of town the highway curves west, then enters a long straight stretch.

About halfway across this piece of road I noticed a boy step out of the ditch. Seeing a farmhouse nearby, and other than the fact it was early, I didn't think much about it.

As I got closer, I could see he was dressed in overalls and was carrying a baseball bat over his shoulder. I decided he wasn't going to cross, but moved into the other lane anyway. We met at mile marker twenty-two, and he turned at that moment, raising a hand in greeting, and then smiled.

"My God!" I exclaimed, and slammed on the brakes. Even with the weight of the camper, the pickup fishtailed, leaving a path of black skid marks that were sure to arouse the curiosity of other travelers. Finally, the Chevy came to a jerking halt. I jammed it into reverse.

I couldn't see the boy in my mirrors, but quickly found the mile maker and headed for it. I overshot and came to a stop right next to a convenient place to park.

Stepping out of the pickup, I tried to quiet my hammering heart. The boy was nowhere in sight. It was flat ground, covered by short grass. *"He can't be hiding,"* I thought. I reached the mile marker and let my eyes search in full circle. Seeing nothing, I crossed the pavement and did the same thing.

My breathing had returned to normal as I stood, leaning against the post.

"Hello," I shouted, listening to my voice echo in the cool air. "Are you there?" I yelled louder.

That was answered by a solitary meadowlark.

"This is stupid," I said, and turning, marched back toward the pickup.

A stick in the grass caught my toe and I tripped, stumbled, and fell heavily to the ground. Now, my temper was starting to flare. I licked the scrape on my hand, and examined a bigger one on my knee through the rip in my pants.

Getting up none too nimbly, I dusted myself off, and then saw what caused my fall. Reaching down, I jerked my hand back before I fell victim to another imagined embarrassment. I nudged it with my toe instead. It was real.

Long story short, what I'd discovered in the grass was Old Cobber, the prized Louisville Slugger that I hadn't laid eyes on for sixty-one years. It had been well cared for, although the scars and dents of innumerable games were evident. You can imagine my gasp of incomprehension that morning when I ran my finger over the burnt-in inscription at the base of the knob.

"*Mew*," it read. Leezie had put it there one day at the blacksmith's shop.

I walked for several minutes with the bat over my shoulder, searching intently for the boy. I started toward the farmhouse, but stopped when I discovered a muddy piece of bare ground that ran parallel to the highway for two hundred yards. There were no tracks.

No doubt you don't understand this any better than I do, and other than being happy to have Old Cobber in my hands again, it remains a mystery. I have to admit, though, that I still believe I saw a young Leezie alongside the road that day.

In contrast, the dog is easy to explain. A month before my retirement became official I was called to the home of Andrei Blum.

Andrei, who I'd met through Wilbur Lester, greeted me at the door, saying, "I just heard you're leaving us," which I acknowledged with a nod.

"Follow me," he said. "I've got something to show you."

He led me through the kitchen to a rear door that opened to a small back yard.

Andrei whistled. A great black dog cocked her ears and came at a lope across the lawn.

"It's my boy's," he explained.

"Hank?" I asked, wondering what had become of him.

"That's the one," Andrei answered. "He's the reason I ended up with this big goof-off of a mutt."

He reached down, fishing for the dog's collar.

"Hank's National Guard unit is still in Kuwait. Down girl!" he admonished when the dog put her paws against my chest.

"What kind of a dog is this?" I asked, stroking the hair around her neck. The fur was soft and irresistible. She was similar in size to Abner's German shepherd. Her black coat was perfectly marked with brown patches above her eyes and on the muzzle. Beautiful brown fringes decorated the backs of her legs, but the ears distinguished her. They were big and floppy, reminding me of what you would see on an overgrown cocker spaniel.

"She's a Gordon setter," Andrei said. "And this critter that just got your shirt dirty needs a new home. I thought you might be interested."

"That's all I need right now," I thought. But I was distracted by the dog's antics and didn't answer. I watched her cavort around the yard. A heavy-boned creature, I expected her to be slow and clumsy. But

the opposite was true, as she went chasing a butterfly only to change direction like a pirouetting ballet dancer. It made me laugh.

"Betsy! That's enough!" Andrei shouted. "Give it a rest." To me, he said, "Butterflies don't have the sense to fly away, and she don't know when to quit."

"What did you call her?" I said.

"Betsy. That's her name," he said. "You could change it if you don't like it."

"No, no, Betsy's just fine," I said. I'd never been known for being impetuous, but I made an instant decision, which explains how I got the dog.

I looked out the window of the Alaskan just to make sure the squirrel had retreated safely up the tree. Betsy was lying with her head between her paws, waiting no doubt for the morning's next entertainment.

My appointment with the bishop was in two days, and I hadn't begun to fret about it until I got up this morning. My task was a formidable one – unheard of in fact. Bishops didn't reopen closed churches for reasons like I had in mind, especially this bishop.

Being made bishop had gone to his head, so I had heard. Some even reported he'd had a severe case of scarlet fever, a church analogy for a man lusting after the red hat of a cardinal. On the positive side I had one thing in my favor. The same reports stated the man had mellowed in recent years.

Betsy needed a lot of exercise, which she didn't get being chained to the bumper of the pickup. That meant long walks. Betsy had sled dog potential; I'd learned the first day she pulled me to the small park near St. Ruthie's. Three weeks of training by a professional had helped, and Betsy was great on the hikes we took as long as a bird didn't interfere with her concentration. Did I mention that Gordon setters are bird dogs?

My shoulder hurt when we returned at dusk from a stroll along the lakeshore, and I noticed her perpetual jerking on the nylon rope had worn a blister on my hand.

"You're a no-good mutt," I said when I slipped into bed that night. Betsy growled, which I learned was a characteristic of the breed. They used it to communicate. Different growls meant different things, and I had yet to learn them all.

Betsy put her front paws on the bed and nudged my arm. I gave her a pat and she licked my hand. That was "*good night*," and she curled up in a ball on the floor, soon falling fast asleep.

"*I wish I could go to sleep that easy*," I thought. Instead, I played my twenty scenarios game of what could happen at the bishop's office. One of Leezie's oft-repeated remarks helped calm and lull me to sleep. "*Nincompoops are the Windknocker's bread and butter*," he would say. "*He spreads the butter and they get toasted.*"

We left the lake a day early, and the morning after found us trying to negotiate the traffic of the city. Betsy was a good traveler but didn't like crowded streets. She barked when a late-for-work man in an old Cadillac convertible jumped a green light and made a left turn in front of us. Her annoyed bark startled me, causing the camper to lurch when my foot hit the gas pedal.

I finally found what I was looking for, two blocks past the bishop's office building. The camper coasted to a stop on a street shaded by giant elm trees. I cracked the windows and admonished Betsy about barking at strangers for no good reason. "Forget about cats too," I said, patting her head. She nudged my hand, and gave me a sassy look of, "*do you plan to be gone long?*"

No one manned the information desk at the bishop's officialdom, although several of his minions stood around watching a copy machine spew out papers. Others were having a gabfest at a pop machine down a corridor. None greeted me. I consulted the directory, locating the bishop's office on the second floor.

I turned, only to have his life-sized picture stare back at me. It dominated the entire wall across from the elevator. I walked over, noticing the overly ornate frame, and studied his face. A brass plaque at the bottom read: "*His Excellency, Alfred Timmerman.*"

"Freddie," I said. "You've gained weight."

Chapter Forty-Five

Stepping out of the restroom, where I'd gone to muster my courage, I thought, "*Good God, I haven't been this nervous since the fourth grade spelling bee.*"

Leezie's repertoire of wisdom came to my rescue once again. "*When the Windknocker starts to play his fiddle, don't toot your own horn.*"

I stepped confidently into the lion's lair.

"I just hope Freddie is good at hearing fiddle music," I whispered.

He let me cool my heels in an ornate chair for a terribly uncomfortable twenty minutes. His prim secretary kept eyeing me. I supposed she disapproved of me choosing civilian garb, complimented by cowboy boots, instead of the black and somber priest's clothing.

She must have been doubly irked when Freddie's voice boomed from his office door, "Barto! Get your ass over here and let me look at you."

Whether she was triply miffed by the enthusiastic hug that Freedie gave me, I didn't notice.

"Holy Jesus Christ," he said, after finally releasing his grip. "How long's it been, Barto?"

Rather than cleaning up his language, Freddie had been polishing his ability for the profane.

"I had clam chowder at the Wheel House in Seattle a few nights ago," I answered. "But the last we were there together was eighteen years ago."

"I guess you're right," he said, ushering me to a chair. "So how are things at the Wheel House? Jack's still running the place, I hope?"

"He died in eighty-nine," I said. "Lung cancer."

"I always told the son-of-a-bitch he smoked too much," Freddie said. "But I'm sorry to hear it."

We exchanged a few more pleasantries. Soon, my nervous stomach returned, warning me to the get the conversation on track.

"Tell me, Barto," he said. "What brings you to this side of the mountains?" He had opened the door, and I stepped through it.

I told him about my camping trip to the Montana lake. "Down close to your old stomping grounds," I said.

He took off his glasses, and rubbed his eyes. "Lucky cuss," he said. "It's not that far, but I haven't been back there since St. Timothy's was dedicated."

"When was that?"

"Nineteen-sixty-five, I think."

St. Timothy's was a rock chapel, built high on a mountainside overlooking the lake where Betsy had salivated over the squirrel.

Freddie rubbed his eyes again, stuck for the moment in nostalgia. Looking up, he shook a finger, saying, "Those clothes become you. Does it mean you're serious about retirement?"

I fidgeted, rubbing one hand nervously on my pants leg.

"Hmmm," he said. "It appears this is more than a social call. What's on your mind, Barto?"

"I want you to reopen a church."

"Not likely," he responded. "But what exactly are you talking about?"

I told him a little, holding back what I hoped were my trump cards.

"Same answer, Barto," he said when I finished. "I can't do it."

"Sure you can, Freddie," I said. "You're a bishop and they can do anything."

"Ha!" He retorted. "Don't I wish"?

Undeterred, I said, "It's Saint Bartholomew's. Your predecessor closed it twenty-some years ago."

That had no effect. He just changed the subject, saying, "What do you think about the deal with Percy Knox?"

I shrugged. Freddie already knew my take on that. Fortunately for him, his predecessor was dead, taking any secrets of covering up for pedophiles to the grave with him. Freddie had attacked the problem aggressively, earning him respect in the media.

"You know my take-no-prisoners attitude about perverts, Freddie."

He eyed me, then looked away.

"*Easy, Moosington,*" I said to myself. "*Don't toot your own horn.*"

"Saint Bartholomew's," he said, letting the words roll off his tongue in a slow drawl. "I don't think it's even on our list of properties."

"I'm not surprised," I said. "Since you don't own the land, and the building was never demolished."

Gail had revealed that fact. The deed to the land had been screwed up many years ago, and a parishioner ended up with it. Before dying, he had willed it to the town, and the city fathers wouldn't issue a permit for the demolition.

"What?" he said, and picked up the phone, connecting with Miss Prim in the outer office. I listened to a one-sided conversation that ended, "Well then get someone down to the basement and have those records brought to me."

A pause of three seconds elicited, "No, not now, RIGHT now!"

Freddie could learn some lessons in diplomacy, and I started to say so. But he interrupted.

"Look," he said. "In spite of the pain in the ass you might turn out to be, I'd probably give you a small parish, but..." his voice trailed off.

"I want Saint Bartholomew's," I said.

"Even if what you say is true, Barto, you know it's a moot point. Reopening a tiny parish for no better reason than what you offer is not something I can do."

"Not even for a Gar Community?" I said, laying one of my cards on the table.

That sat him straight up in his chair. The door opened with a thud at the same moment and an old man staggered in carrying a heavy box.

"The records you asked for," he said, wheezing to a stop at the edge of the desk.

Freddie scrambled to clear a space.

"Set it right there, Oscar," he said. "You sure that's everything?"

"Aye," Oscar answered, "savin' for that dang blasted bell I stumbled over. Stubbed my toe, yer ellancy"

"What kind of a bell?" Freddie asked.

"Church bell," the old man said. "It has the same file number as the box. Do you want me to fetch it too?"

Oscar was relieved when told it wouldn't be necessary, and limped toward the door.

"You didn't say anything about a Gar Community before," Freddie snapped at me. "So for friendship's sake I'll hear you out, providing you don't hold back on me this time."

I gave him a fifteen-minute synopsis of what I'd learned about the last gaspers.

Finished, I watched him settle back in his chair. "The last gaspers? That's some moniker."

"Well," I said, "what do you think now?"

He let out a long sigh. "I wish I could help you, but I can't."

I unsnapped my shirt pocket and took out my hole card. Tossing it on his desk I said, "Do you still have your half of that?"

He picked up my part of the business card, originally advertising, *The World's Best Summer Sausage.* "Yes," he growled, "I have it somewhere."

"Do you need to make sure, or do I have to kick *your* ass all the way to Mount Rainier?"

"That's enough, Barto! You're pushing the limits of our friendship."

"*God, he still has a temper,*" I thought. Then he seemed to settle down, wiggling his big butt deeper into the chair.

"When did you get to be such a rabble rouser?" he asked.

"If you'll remember, I had a good teacher."

His stern look wavered a moment, and I knew he had to fight to hold back a smile. Abruptly, however, he flicked his wrist, dismissing me. I jumped up, not wanting to push my luck.

The doorknob turned in my hand, and I heard him say, "Come back in the morning, Barto. I want to see what's in this box."

The waiting room was full and I beat a hasty retreat past them, stopping at Miss Prim's desk.

"What's that your radio is tuned to?" I asked.

Evidently, my stature had risen in her eyes, and she was very sweet, saying, "It's NPR, and it's the county fiddling championship."

My smile lasted for the time it took me to walk the two blocks to my camper. Betsy was there, patiently waiting behind the wheel. She growled a long refrain when I opened the door, letting me know what she thought of my extended interview.

"It couldn't be helped," I assured her, and headed out of the city, looking for the Wal-Mart we'd passed on the way in.

Freddie had neglected to tell me what time to *come back in the morning*. I found a good secluded spot to park in the Wal-Mart lot and took Betsy for a long walk. By nightfall I had decided that early risers rarely changed their habits. Freddie had always boasted he could have a day's work done by the time most people got to work. Banking that hadn't changed; I set my alarm for five, intending to visit Freddie at six.

Luckily, at that hour of the morning the coveted parking places in front of the building were vacant and I took the one right in front of the door. The door, however, was locked. I tapped loudly on the glass with my key, standing at the same time on Betsy's leash, just in case an early bird happened to fly by. It took three more tries of staccato rapping before I got someone's attention. A figure approached and I breathed a sigh of relief to see it was Oscar.

"Bout time you got here, Mr. Father," he said. "His ellancy's been espectin' you."

Betsy was apprehensive and wouldn't cross the threshold into the elevator. We took the stairs instead.

"What's this? What's this?" Freddie said when Betsy bolted through his office door ahead of me.

Betsy sat down and stuck out her paw. Freddie laughed and gave it a good shake.

"Where did you ever get a Gordon setter?" he asked.

I told him the story. "She's a female, I see," Freddie said. "In my opinion they make the best bird hunter."

"I just took your advice," I said.

Freddie cocked his head at a funny angle, and I explained. "You always told me I should get better acquainted with the female sex."

Laughing, he said, "sit down, sit down." I did, and watched Betsy worm her way between his legs and lay down under his desk. "*So far, so good,*" I thought.

Freddie had a strange gleam in his eye that made me wary.

"Look at this," he said, taking a black and white framed picture out of the box of St. Bart's records. The ancient photograph was of a group of young people at a church gathering. "Who do you reckon this young lad is?" he asked, tapping my sober face, captured after I was confirmed.

"It's me," I said. "But how did you know?"

"Bishops have special deductive powers," he said. "Or had you forgotten that?"

He flipped the photograph over. "See, it has your name listed on the back."

It was my turn to laugh.

"You neglected to remind me that you grew up there," he said.

"I didn't think it was important."

"Well," he said, the same gleam returning to his face. "It does lend a mite of validity to your request."

I wanted to say something, but no words came.

"Tell me more, Barto. How you would shape this Gar Community, these last gaspers?"

I gave him the plan that had matured over the past five months.

"In a nutshell," I said at the end, "I intend to take them to the spiritual limits that Vatican II intended a community to go, maybe even beyond."

He looked at me for a long time. Betsy raised her head to see what had caused the silence.

At last he said, "Suppose I consented to this cockamamie idea; what would you be willing to give back in return?"

"*Oh-Oh!*" I thought.

I couldn't believe what he said next.

"How much do you know about the Priest's Retirement Fund?"

Freddie handed me the fund's financial statement. One look told me there wasn't enough money to meet obligations.

"Would your magic work on that?" Freddie asked.

After two hours of negotiating, he came away with a Priest's Retirement Fund manager and I won several concessions. The community, the last gaspers, would have a semi-autonomous parish council. In other words, they would govern the parish, a concept unheard-of since the earliest days of Vatican II.

"When you sign the constitution they write, will it be binding on the next bishop?" I asked.

"No," he answered. "But precedence tends to do the same thing."

He thought a second, and went on. "Shit on a lamppost, Barto, a bishop can hardly fart without checking to see if it's been done before. And, if it has, he has to make sure it's done exactly the same way. Bishops are locked into precedence, too much so in my opinion."

At that point, I decided to go for broke.

"Suppose the parish council's constitution says the people have to approve any new priest sent to them," I said.

"What? What the hell are you saying, Barto? You know damned good and well people don't get to vote on who they want for a priest. Besides, it's against Canon Law."

I told him about an idea I'd gotten from a canon lawyer in Seattle. "If it's worded right, we might get around the law."

"You sneaky son-of-a-bitch!" Freddie chuckled.

His laughter finally disturbed Betsy, who came out from under his desk. He patted her head, saying, "Dog, you better watch your step. Your master might end up smarter than you."

Freddie stopped laughing finally and said to me, "I'll give you six months. If the retirement fund is at least solvent by then, I'll sign the last gasper's constitution with that idea in it. Deal?"

"You're double damned tootin' it's a deal."

"You might be smart, but you're still corny," Freddie laughed.

We shook hands, after which he said, "Anything else?"

"Yes. I want the bell."

"Okay," he said, easing his bulk out of the chair. "Let's go find Oscar and get it."

Chapter Forty-Six

They told me it was a mild stroke. I took the doctor at his word, and reluctantly swallowed his annoying pills. The longing began about this time, which was my sixth year at St. Bart's. Something in my life was yet undone. What it was I had no idea, but the ache was constant. Oddly, I had just finished giving away the money in Uncle Horace's trust fund. Another task was almost complete, but neither task was the source of the longing.

Uncle Horace's trust fund was considerable, and I went from a wealthy man to a pauper in the span of two years. I can only imagine my Uncle's reaction, since most of his riches had been squandered on the social strata he most disdained.

The last gaspers were more than I'd thought, and it didn't take me long to see the difference between them and Gar Communities. The people at St. Bart's had been malnourished by the church for years and were spiritually hungry. They also had few of the distractions or options found in the city, like another church close by. Leezie had laid a solid foundation. The last gaspers believed little in a "me" form of Christianity and everything in being a blessing to others.

I still laugh when I think back to the day I first proposed my great idea: "*You should be able to vote yes or no on any new priest sent to you.*" Instead, they offered their own plan, one that was so brilliant it left me with my mouth hanging open.

Gear Jammin' Billy; known officially as Bill Stanislaus, suggested, "We could have more priests than we know what to do with if we'd just get them to retire here."

A green light wasn't needed, but I gave them one anyway. They built a small duplex, with funds they had saved over the years. After it was finished, we screened, from more applicants than you can imagine, two retired priests, who moved into the duplex. There was no rent or other expenses, and in return the priests provided limited services that go with a priest's job. Those were minimal because they were retirees.

The vetting process did what my lofty theory *might* have done. The priests selected had to match the ideologies and goals of the last gaspers. So in essence, the priests voted, not the parishioners.

Freddie had retired and died a year later. The new bishop fought our idea but there was little he could do. He was upset because ordinary Catholics could make decisions like that.

We called it the *Stanislaus Security and Social Plan*. Its real aim was more than just a place for priests to retire. Billy believed priests were maladjusted.

"It's about time they got in the real world and let somebody love them," he said.

Translated, it meant the retirees got absorbed into the community, voluntarily or with a little arm-twisting.

Sickness was one of the negatives about Billy's idea, but the last gaspers nursed them when it happened. It taxed their resources at times, especially when it required 'round-the-clock duty. The community had close ties, however, to many Protestant friends they could call upon in an emergency.

What they wouldn't do was pamper them.

Father Mike Tidbit complained at first. "I haven't had to make my own bed for forty-seven years."

"Get used to it," Gail told him.

Then she hugged him, saying, "I hate making beds too."

Going out the door she hollered, "And don't forget the fireworks party tomorrow. Jimmy barbeques a mean burger."

Mike laughed about it a week later, saying, "How does that woman know all my weak spots?"

Mike would never be an extrovert, but he learned things about relationships that they never taught in seminary.

Not long before he died, Freddie visited St. Bart's. Gar Communities had always been his dream. He left misty-eyed, saying, "The last gaspers will still be here long after we're gone. It's Roncalli's vision come to life, Barto."

Two weeks before I left, the last gaspers started construction to add a third apartment to the duplex. They were reaching out too, and had two satellite communities nearby.

My departure came the day after my eighty-second birthday. If you wonder about my sanity, leaving on a long trip in the winter, I did too. I'm not sure if Betsy had similar thoughts, but I reminded her anyway, "Sometimes old girl, you just have to bend in the wind and go where your heart leads you."

I had never been east of the Mississippi before, but we crossed the great river at Red Wing, Minnesota a few days later. From Red Wing we turned northeast toward Canada.

On a Sunday morning, just south of the Canadian border, I stopped in a fair-sized town and decided to go to church. At first, I had the impression I'd mistaken the place for the senior citizen's center. The priest was young, however, and I was able to adjust, with some difficulty, to his exaggerated efforts to appear reverent. I was quite proud of myself actually, and we didn't part company until his sermon.

It was a cross between a harangue and a lecture to second graders, but it did have a theme, two of them in fact. The first was a scolding about church music and how it had to be faithful to the quality of worship Almighty God deserved. He rattled off a list of songs, which included my favorite, ABBA FATHER, as his examples of those that God didn't like.

He based his other point on the reading of the day. Using the boat (the tempest on The Sea of Galilee when Jesus walked on the water) he told how right-thinking Catholics should believe.

"The boat represents the Catholic Church," he said. "And if you're not in that boat, you're not in the church that Christ founded."

He didn't mention Protestants by name, but left little doubt they were a misguided and troublesome lot. I eased out of my perch in a rear pew when he finished and didn't let the door hit me in the butt on my way out.

Betsy and I crossed the border into a foreign country. I felt less like an outsider than I had in that church.

That night, after a side trip delayed our progress north, I called my old friend, Wilbur Lester. Wilbur had just been promoted to religion editor at the *Seattle P-I.* "What are you hearing out of the Vatican these days?" I asked.

"Do you mean Operation Backwards?" That's how he described the dismantling of Vatican II. He brought me up to date.

Wilbur spent a lot of time in Rome. His interest was partly personal. As a Protestant, he had been amazed at the positive impact Vatican II had on the lives of ordinary Catholics. Now, *the reform of the reforms,* which he called, operation backwards, was news.

"How can they just repudiate a sacred council of the church like that?" I asked.

"The Pope doesn't see it that way," he said.

"What's your best guess how far back they'll go?"

"No guessing. Back to the church you grew up with."

I hung up twenty minutes later. On a piece of paper I made two columns that I labeled, *Goldsworthy and Moosington.* Goldsworthy represented the pre-Vatican II church, and I its successor. I listed the differences. Juxtaposing the old and new brought things into focus and presented me with a real dilemma. I couldn't go back, and I couldn't think of a way to bridge the huge gap that separated me from the modern version of Father Goldsworthy I'd experienced in church this morning.

The sacrament of Eucharist was meant to bridge that great divide. However, in the old and new church, the concept of God that Eucharist evokes in the mind of the faithful is vastly different. I feared the disparity was becoming an obstacle rather than a unifying force.

I recalled one of my pet sayings. *"Don't worry about it. WE, the people in the pews, and not Rome, are the real church."* That worked at a time when people still had a say in the direction the church took. I looked at Betsy, saying, "But it's not going to work in the future." The weather postponed the solution to what would work.

It changed abruptly, and the next morning I battled a snowstorm for seven hours. I had to spend the next two days in Sudbury, Ontario. Betsy took advantage of the reprieve by exploring every bush and snowdrift in our nearly deserted campground. I finally gave in to her pestering and took her for a walk. She managed to wrap her leash around my leg and then take off in chase of a raven. Thankfully, the spill I took wasn't witnessed by anyone. To compensate for my chagrin and a bruise on the knee, I received a big slurp on the nose.

In the end, it was providential, as it confined me to the camper. I got to thinking about Freddie. He had confessed to me the negative impact becoming a bishop had on him. "You can't believe the power it gives you, Barto," he'd said. "It's intoxicating. I forgot about the powerless."

The last time we saw each other, I think it was a month before he died, he said, "The son-of-a-bitch that really figured things out was Saint Paul. Granted, he had a pussy-wimpy attitude about women, but not when it came to the church. Read about it sometime."

I chuckled, saying to Betsy, "I guess I'll see what old pussy-wimpy has to say." I didn't delve into the letters that Paul wrote, and spent my time reading about his missionary journeys. I hadn't gone far before I realized, *"he's describing a church situation not that much different than the present."* The Apostle Paul would arrive in a new place, and the first thing he'd do was head off to the church, the local Jewish Synagogue. Shortly, I realized that the church he described was much the same as the Goldsworthy wing of my own – conservative, one demanding total allegiance to those in charge, one steeped in tradition, and very fundamentalist.

An eye-opener hit me – Paul couldn't co-exist with his church either. Very soon after his arrival at the synagogue, he'd run into a communications impasse. When that happened he couldn't stay.

Much like my recent Sunday experience, Paul didn't let the door hit him in the butt on the way out.

Instead, Paul took his message to those who were more receptive. He planted the seeds that grew into a multitude of tiny home churches. Paul, I discovered, also knew about Leezie's method of *pointing a wet finger to the wind*. He could tell where the winds of Pentecost were blowing, or not. A question of Paul's leapt off the page at me: "Didn't you receive the Holy Spirit when you believed?"

"If that doesn't remind me of Leezie, I don't know what does!" I said. Paul got a negative reply to his question. He could have just as easily used Leezie's approach in that situation, and said, "Sit down then, while I tell you one of my Windknocker stories." I could also hear someone among Paul's listeners saying, "*whaddayamean?*" if he posed the question about being born again.

The images stayed with me, and I woke up the next morning thinking about it. I concluded that Paul wasn't that much different than me, if, of course, you discount my inability to be saintly. He couldn't stay in a church that insisted on stamping out renewal either. Instead, he kept Jesus' vision alive by planting the message elsewhere.

I chuckled, as bits of a sermon popped into my head. I delivered the gist of it to Betsy.

"*Cardinal Ratzinger,*" I began with my pulpit voice, "*once said that the best way to prevent the church becoming a dictatorship was for individuals to follow their conscience, and dissent when necessary.*"

"*The result? Millions of Catholics have walked away. They are often seen, as no doubt I will be too, as church wreckers. Some even question whether they are, or ever were, Christians. At best the derogatory term, Lone Rangers, is applied to them.*"

Betsy raised a sleepy eyelid, which quickly fluttered shut again. "I can see you're impressed," I said.

"*But the ground has to be fertile,*" I went on, "*to plant Roncalli's vision in. It still burns in the hearts of a few, who have remained in the church, but one day they will die, and then what?*"

"*I'm going to do what Paul did, and take the message to those who will listen. If Roncalli's dream stays alive, then the church will rise someday from the ashes.*"

That, at least, earned me a tail thump from the dog.

"*For me it's the catholic thing to do. The church is out there. It's probably not in a building, or wrapped in vestments and dogmas. I just hope I can find it in the time I've got left.*"

I left Sudbury the next morning in sunshine and melting snow. Heading south, I skirted Toronto and turned east. Three days later I reentered the United States. Finally, on the 16th of December, bleary-eyed and with Betsy raising growls of protest, I reached the small town of Essex Junction, Vermont.

Chapter Forty-Seven
The Last Chapter

Leezie's daughter, Glory, had a cozy bungalow built adjacent to her massive stone house. Her home wasn't massive, just the rock it was hewn from.

"It came from a quarry not far from here," she said as she settled me into my new quarters. "That was just before the Revolutionary War."

I whistled, causing Betsy to look up from her perch, which overlooked a pond full of ducks.

"I've never seen anything built in the 1700s," I said. "You're sure about that?"

She smiled and hugged me again. "Oh yes, I'm sure. It was right after the Boston Tea Party."

"Glory seems excited to see us," I said to Betsy as we walked later from the bungalow to the house for supper.

Glory reinforced the feeling, and talked constantly during the meal. She had fixed partridge with wild rice stuffing.

"I was so surprised to get your phone call last month," she said. "And then I started worrying about you driving. I even thought about sending you a plane ticket."

"I just hope I'm not imposing," I said.

"Imposing?" she almost shouted. "Imposing indeed! I'm so happy to see you I can barely contain myself."

I ate too much and by the end of supper my eyelids were drooping like limp flags at half-mast.

She said, "Are you sure you don't want me to go with you in the morning?"

I assured her I could find my way, and she reminded me, "Then don't forget to meet me at the newspaper office at four. I have a little surprise for you."

The streets were quiet the next morning, and I found the cemetery with only two wrong turns.

"There it is, Betsy," I said, pointing to the sign over the entrance, *Lakeview Cemetery*. "It's what I brought you all this way to see."

I didn't know what to expect, but I found Leezie's grave, thankful that someone, probably Glory, had put a bench there. I sat down and the longing I'd felt for the past year disappeared.

"Well, Leezie," I said. "We're here, which probably doesn't surprise you."

Talking to a tombstone is not really rational. After all, the deceased, as all good church teaching tells us, is no longer there. I knew that wasn't entirely true. Something of Leezie's spirit remained, and had drawn me here. "Leezie," I said, "why do I have a strange feeling about this?"

I stayed most of the morning and came back in the afternoon.

Since I had already scouted out the location of *The Junction Journal*, I drove back to the bungalow and decided to walk. On the way I passed a small white Catholic church. Two people were working on the outside. Young in appearance, I guessed them to be in their late twenties. I shook hands with Bob and Rita Turner.

"What's the name of the church?" I asked.

"Saint Isaac's," Bob answered. "That's the short version anyhow."

"Saint Isaac Jogues is the real name," Rita said. "But you probably don't know who that is."

"On the contrary I do," I said, remembering the Jesuit killed by the Indians from stories my mother had read to me.

After we got past the questions of where I was from, where did I get my strange accent, what was I doing in Vermont and what kind of dog is that, I learned that Saint Isaac's had joined the ranks of the abandoned two years ago.

"But we keep it up," Bob said.

"And we keep hoping," Rita said.

"We seem to be running out of hope," Bob said. "But I don't suppose you know what we're talking about."

"Are there any others like you?" I asked.

"Four, maybe five," Rita answered.

"Do you know what it means to be born again?" I asked.

"Whaddayamean, born again?" Bob said.

I laughed, thinking, *"Boy you've come full circle, Moosington."*

"It's what will keep your hope alive," I said. I told them where I was staying. "Come by tomorrow night, and I'll tell you more." I'd seen their hungry look in enough eyes to know they would.

Rita confirmed it. "Can we bring our friends?"

I smiled. "Sure," I said. "But no dogs. Betsy is territorial."

Glory was waiting for me at the Journal office. She said, "We're going to the place daddy used to take me all the time." As soon as the words left her lips, I knew where it that was, but didn't spoil her surprise.

The Empty Mug Tavern was everything Leezie had advertised it to be. The combination of eggnog and cinnamon crackers was hard to describe. Glory challenged me to a game of darts, which I lost, although the Vermont state sport felt like something I could master.

"You're sure you've never played before?" Glory said on the way home.

My nervous stomach was acting up when we settled into comfortable chairs after supper. I had yet to get to the second point of my trip here.

Then Glory threw me off guard, saying, "Mew, I have something I want you to think about."

"Okay, what is it?"

"Why don't you stay?"

"Well, I intended to stay for a few days," I said.

"No, I don't mean that," she said. "Permanently."

I don't think I gasped, but I may have.

"I built that bungalow for dad, you know. I hoped he would settle here, especially after he got sick. But he couldn't. That would have meant being separated from you."

"You're saying that since we're together again I shouldn't leave?" It was the same thought that had struck me at the cemetery. I was an only child, with no kin left, and few friends. Everything I owned was in the camper.

"Does it sound silly?" she asked. I started to answer, but then noticed a tear trickle down her pretty face. She brushed it aside, saying, "You could do worse, and I adore your dog."

Her offer just about overwhelmed me. "Can I have until morning to think it over?"

"Not a moment longer," she smiled.

I got up and found the shopping bag I had brought with me.

"I think I'll leave you for the night and let you ponder something else," I said.

I took out of the bag the bulky manuscript I had completed six months ago. "At least you'll have something to lull you to sleep," I laughed, handing it to her.

When she figured out what I'd given her, she jumped to her feet. Her squeal caused Betsy to give several excited barks.

"You did it, Mew!" she exclaimed. "You actually wrote the book!"

"I'm afraid it ended up more about me than your dad," I said. "But I think you'll find enough in it to satisfy your curiosity."

I didn't tell her about finding Leezie's Big Chief Tablets, which enabled me to write it, but I intended for her to have those.

She hugged me, dancing a jig at the same time, and then kissed me sweetly on the cheek. "Oh, Mew, she said. "I'm so proud of you."

There was a winter's chill to the wind as I walked back to the bungalow. For the fifteenth time since my arrival in Vermont, I didn't know what to think as I pulled the covers back and slipped into bed. Betsy put her front paws on the quilt and nudged my arm.

"What do you think, Betsy?" I said, patting her head. "Should we camp out here for awhile?"

Betsy gave a longer-than-usual growl and jumped up on the bed. She lay down, putting her nose between her paws, and stared at me. Her tail thumped several times. I gave her another pat and said, "You like it here, don't you?"

As Mew drifted off to sleep, it began to snow. Glory looked out the window after she finished several articles for the paper, noticing she couldn't see the bungalow through the swirling mist. She smiled, saying, "Please, God." Turning, she threw some more logs on the fire and sat down in her favorite rocking chair.

She picked up the manuscript. Tucked inside the first page she found a legal document signing over ownership and all rights of the book to her. Representing the law firm, the affidavit was signed by her cousin, Frank Parsons, Jr.

Glory turned to page one and began to read: *I was raised in a small town. It was the kind of place where they roll up the streets at night; at least that's how my mother described it.*

Author's Postscript

WINDKNOCKER is fiction. Since I couldn't expand the era it covers beyond 1998, certain events had to be moved backwards a number of years to fit the time frame of the novel. Notable examples of this are the sexual abuse scandal in the church and the systematic dismantling of Vatican II.

Several years ago I wrote a short story, which I titled, "A Dog Named Beelzebub." I gave a copy to my friend, Jeff Spackman. I don't know exactly what struck him about the narrative, but he liked it. I remember thanking him and saying that I was writing a book. That was not WINDKNOCKER, but a western novel.

For the next two years Jeff pestered me, wanting to know if the western was finished yet. It took me awhile to grasp that he was more enthused about it than me. And it took me longer to understand that he believed more in my abilities than I did.

I visited him on the day he died of brain cancer, and I'm sure if he hadn't been in a coma, he would have chided me again, saying something like, "When do I get to read that book?"

In many ways you can say that Jeff was the inspiration behind WINDKNOCKER. The short story, "A Dog Named Beelzebub," became the working outline for what you've read.

Recall for a moment the scene at the end of the book when Mew visits Leezie's grave in Vermont, and says, "*Something of Leezie's spirit remained, and had drawn me here.*" In a similar way, something of Jeff's spirit remained. It inspired and, at times, even cajoled me to turn the original short story into this book. I also learned from Jeff about friendship, and it's those lessons you find brought to life in WINDKNOCKER. Thanks Jeff, and rest in peace.

Like any book, I encountered several stumbling blocks. Finding the right idea for Leezie's army service is one. I did consider making him a pacifist, but the image of *"draft dodger"* didn't fit his character. Late one night I typed, *"care of dead soldiers"* into my Internet browser. That led to the Graves Registration Service and the accounts you have read from Leezie's Big Chief Tablet.

Caring for the dead is one of the untold stories of warfare, and Leezie's experiences are not exaggerated. Those who served in that element of the Quartermaster's Corps deserve much more recognition. The incidence of battle fatigue, or what we now call Post Traumatic Stress Disorder, was much greater for the men of WWII who served in the Graves Registration Service. In the accounts I read, the word *"gruesomeness"* is mentioned again and again.

Finally, The Wheel House Tavern, like everything else in the book, is a figment of my imagination. So is Mew's hometown, which could be located in any state in the Northwest. And Big Chief tablets, which accompanied children on the first day of school for nearly eighty years, are no more. If you were thinking of buying one, they are no longer available.

CPSIA information can be obtained at www.ICGtesting.com
Printed in the USA
BVOW041649081011

273129BV00006B/4/P